S0-BMY-598

THE OFFICIAL MOVIE NOVEL

FIVE NIGHTS
AT FREDDY'S

THE OFFICIAL MOVIE NOVEL

FIVE NIGHTS
AT FREDDY'S

ADAPTED BY
ANDREA WAGGENER

BASED ON THE VIDEO GAME SERIES "FIVE NIGHTS AT FREDDY'S" BY
SCOTT CAWTHON

SCREEN STORY BY SCOTT CAWTHON AND CHRIS LEE HILL & TYLER MACINTYRE
SCREENPLAY BY SCOTT CAWTHON AND SETH CUDDEBACK & EMMA TAMMI
DIRECTED BY EMMA TAMMI

Scholastic Inc.

If you purchased this book without a cover, you should be aware that this book is stolen property. It was reported as "unsold and destroyed" to the publisher, and neither the author nor the publisher has received any payment for this "stripped book."

Copyright © 2024 by Scott Cawthon. All rights reserved.

All rights reserved. Published by Scholastic Inc., *Publishers since 1920*. SCHOLASTIC and associated logos are trademarks and/or registered trademarks of Scholastic Inc.

The publisher does not have any control over and does not assume any responsibility for author or third-party websites or their content.

No part of this publication may be reproduced, stored in a retrieval system, or transmitted in any form or by any means, electronic, mechanical, photocopying, recording, or otherwise, without written permission of the publisher. For information regarding permission, write to Scholastic Inc., Attention: Permissions Department, 557 Broadway, New York, NY 10012.

This book is a work of fiction. Names, characters, places, and incidents are either the product of the author's imagination or are used fictitiously, and any resemblance to actual persons, living or dead, business establishments, events, or locales is entirely coincidental.

Library of Congress Cataloging-in-Publication Data available

ISBN 978-1-339-04759-1

10 9 8 7 6 5 4 3   24 25 26 27 28

Printed in the U.S.A.   131

First printing 2024

Book design by Jeff Shake

THE OFFICIAL MOVIE NOVEL

FIVE NIGHTS
AT FREDDY'S

PROLOGUE

The screw's sharp metal threads bit at Bob's fingertips, scoring deeply into the pads. Blood smeared the screw head and dripped onto the rusty, gray metal vent cover Bob was laboring to remove from the wall.

Bob had already freed two of the vent's screws. He'd tried to bend the cover back away from the wall, but the metal was too strong. He had to get a third screw out so he could swing the cover out of the way. The vent was large, big enough, Bob thought, for him to get through. It had to be. If it wasn't . . . well, he couldn't think about that.

"C'mon, c'mon," he muttered. The words came out in staccato gasps because Bob's heart was pounding so violently it felt like it was beating the air out of his lungs.

A heavy bang sounded behind Bob . . . a *loud* bang that vibrated the table Bob was crouched under. Involuntarily, Bob raised his head, whacking it on the table as he turned to look over his shoulder. The throbbing that erupted in his skull added syncopation to his rapid-fire breathing. Bob stared at the barrier he'd built up in front of the office's metal door. Was it going to hold?

Another bang. This one reverberated through the office; Bob felt the vibration course through all the bones of his body. The vibration turned into a panicked convulsion as one of the filing cabinets he'd piled on top of the desk teetered. The desk was wedged against the door, but if the cabinets fell, would the desk stay in place?

The wobbling filing cabinet bumped into the desk chair that topped the pile of office furniture Bob had cobbled into a blockade. The chair toppled over and crashed onto the office's linoleum floor. The desk twitched, but it stayed in place.

Ignoring the prickles between his shoulder blades as he rotated away from the door, Bob returned his concentration to the screw. The blood-slicked screw stubbornly refused to turn for a couple more seconds.

Bob gritted his teeth and put all his focus on the screw head. And finally, the screw came loose. He dropped it as the vent cover swiveled on its remaining screw and swung away from the opening in the wall.

Bob peered into the black shaft extending in front of him. Stuffy air wafted from the opening. Dust billowed upward. He suppressed a sneeze.

Behind Bob, a fingernails-on-a-blackboard screech preceded a deafening clang. Bob's head swiveled. The filing cabinet was no longer on top of the desk. It lay on the floor. And behind it, the desk began to move away from the doorknob.

Bob sucked in his breath and looked around wildly for his flashlight. He'd set down the club-style light when he'd begun working on the screws. Where was it?

Bob spotted the flashlight a few feet to his right. He lunged for it as another deafening metallic thud came from the office door. The overhead speakers hissed, and then they emitted a tinny shriek.

Time to go, Bob thought.

Flipping on his flashlight, Bob crawled into the narrow darkness. More thuds and thumps chased him away from the office. He scrabbled as fast as he could.

In his thirties, Bob had come to terms with his nerdish looks and receding hairline, but he'd never been thrilled with his slight body. For once, though, he was grateful for his narrow shoulders. And even so, he still had to squirm and wriggle his way through the tightened enclosure of the vent shaft. In spite of the close quarters, he made quick progress. The continued caterwaul coming from the speakers and the echoing bangs and thumps that sounded like they were pursuing Bob through the inkiness impelled him through the shaft at lightning speed.

In what felt like both seconds and centuries, Bob reached the end of the vent shaft that led away from the office. The passage split. Bob aimed his flashlight beam left, then right. The light revealed the same thing in both directions: darkness and more darkness.

Sweat stung Bob's eyes and dripped off his nose. The stench of his perspiration was fetid in the confined space.

Bob set down his flashlight so he could wipe his face. Another scourging howl came from the building's speakers. Bob snatched up his flashlight. Without thinking anymore, he headed down the left passageway.

Losing himself again in frantic crawling that defied his ability to quantify seconds or minutes, Bob clambered forward until he found himself looking at a vent cover like the one that he'd removed in the office. Bob groaned. Was he trapped? If this vent cover was screwed on as securely as the one in the office . . .

The cacophony coming from the speakers crescendoed. The vent shaft shook as the entire building quaked.

Bob hefted his flashlight and used the end of it to pound on the vent cover. To his shock . . . and relief . . . the vent cover came loose. It flipped away from the shaft and slapped the wall with a crash that made Bob cringe. Even above the din that filled the building, the sound carried, which meant it easily gave away Bob's location.

Bob quickly pulled himself out of the vent shaft. Every nerve ending in his body on alert, Bob stood and whirled in a circle, shining his light around him.

When the flashlight beam revealed stacks of boxes, restaurant supplies, and a closed, frosted-glass door, Bob let out a pent-up breath. He was in one of the pizzeria's storage rooms. And he was alone. For the moment.

Bob took a step toward the door. Reaching for the knob, he hesitated.

What was on the other side of the door?

Although Bob could see no looming shadows beyond the murky glass, his heart rate ratcheted up a couple more notches. His chest felt contracted, like metal bands were constricting around him. Bob really, really did not want to open the door that stood between his current . . . temporary . . . safety and what was roaming loose beyond the door. But he couldn't stay here forever. Locking himself in the office hadn't worked. Hiding in here wouldn't, either. He had to get out of the building.

Bob turned the knob and threw open the door. Willing himself not to think, Bob stepped out of the storage room. Checking left and right and seeing nothing but the dimly lit hallway, Bob took off at a sprint.

His rubber-soled athletic shoes slapping at the black-and-white-checked floor, Bob reached the hallway corner in seconds. He rounded it, and his gaze locked on the glowing red EXIT sign above the door just thirty feet away. Pumped up by hope, Bob shot toward the door.

Bob hit the door's metal crash bar at top speed. Fully expecting to catapult through the door into the sweet freedom of the night outside, Bob was shocked when his body bounced backward off the bar.

He windmilled his arms and kept his balance, barely. For a few seconds, he hung on to his hope, too. He threw himself at the door. Even though Bob knew he had no bulk, he wasn't a small guy. At five foot eleven, he had a little heft. Surely, he could bash the door open.

But no. The door remained closed, like it was nailed shut.

Bob tried again. And again.

Finally, panting heavily, he leaned against the door. And that's when he heard it.

"*Diddly dum dum diddly da . . .*"

The singsong voice echoed through the building as it came toward Bob. Its playful tone was like a spider crawling up Bob's spine.

Goose bumps erupting on his bare arms, Bob turned and looked down the long hallway behind him. As soon as he did, the corridor's lights went out. What little illumination there'd been turned to utter blackness.

"*Dum da dum dum . . .*" The mocking tones came closer.

Bob lost it. Turning, he pounded on the exit door.

"*Help! Someone! Help me!*" Bob screamed so loudly that the words abraded his throat like a metal file scouring at his vocal cords.

In spite of his cries, though, Bob easily heard the pounding footsteps that rushed up behind him. Going rigid, his whole body immobilized by his brain's inability to accept what was happening, Bob waited for the inevitable attack that would—

* * *

Clinging to a tenuous thread of awareness, Bob's brain attempted to process all the stimuli that were bombarding his senses. His eyes registered fluorescent lights, at once scathingly bright and then terrifyingly dark. His feet relayed burning pressure, vice-like clamping across the arches. His spine communicated jarring and bumping, cracking into a seemingly endless rock-hard expanse. His forehead felt warm with thick moisture; it ran into his ears. Bob blinked as his brain worked to make sense of all these bodily reports. He attempted to move.

As soon as Bob tried to get his body to follow his command, his brain reached a conclusion about his situation. Bob lifted his head and looked down the length of his prone body. He was being dragged down the hallway by his feet.

Looking into the on-and-off shadows, Bob couldn't see what had hold of him. But he didn't need to see it. He knew what it was.

Corkscrewing his spine in an attempt to get away, Bob's head slammed against the floor beneath him. He felt his hip knock against something sharp and realized he was being dragged around a corner. Stiffening, his stomach flip-flopped with the realization of where he was.

The grayscale of intermittent light was abruptly replaced by a swirling kaleidoscope of color. Red and yellow and purple and blue floodlights streamed swaths of radiance across Bob's field of vision. As his fingers flexed, in his attempt to grab at something—anything—to stop his progress toward wherever he was being dragged, Bob recognized the detritus of long-forgotten fun. His hand grazed over a party hat. His thigh rubbed up against a table leg.

Bob was tugged hard, and his body twisted. As it did, Bob's gaze landed on a wall covered with children's drawings. The yellowed, curling paper covered in crayon-rendered stick figures ruffled in an air current as Bob was heaved past the wall.

Bob had looked at that wall long and hard just a few hours earlier, well before he'd realized the danger that he was in. The wall had given him the creeps, serious creeps. One drawing in particular, one that was noticeably larger than the others, had captured his attention. This drawing, hung as if it was the central masterpiece of an exhibit, depicted a large yellow rabbit standing hand in hand with five happy children. In spite of the gaiety suggested by the cheerful scene, the image had troubled Bob.

As Bob caught a glimpse of the rabbit drawing now, he felt bile rise in the back of his throat. He tried to scissor his legs to free himself from his captor. The motion did nothing but amp up the pressure around his feet.

Bob was yanked hard. His head smacked against the wall as he went around yet another corner. For a few seconds, he thought he heard the undulating, distant sound of laughing children. Then the hint of cognizance that had surfaced to make him aware of his surroundings once again sank beneath a layer of cobwebbed dullness.

Bob, coward that he felt he was, welcomed the muffled understanding. Unwilling to face the truth of what was happening . . . and what was about to happen, he slipped into a dreamlike state that eased the hard edges of his predicament. He let himself float in and out of reality until, suddenly, his body was whipped from the floor and thrown.

When Bob's back smacked into cold metal, his mind was jarred into full alertness. His gaze immediately scanned his surroundings as he took in the pinching, pressing steel wrapping itself around his back, buttocks, and thighs.

Bob cried out and attempted to leap from the metal chair he knew he was in. Before his muscles could lift him upward, a green luminosity shone from a button on the side of the chair, and metal restraints snapped into place around his wrists. A thick leather strap snugged tightly around his chest. Bob writhed, but he knew he was wasting his energy,

The Parts and Service room, Bob thought.

Of all the eerie rooms in the pizzeria that he'd been hired to "guard," this was the room that had freaked him out the most when he'd first seen it. Its walls were lined with metal shelving that surrounded multiple stainless steel worktables and industrial-looking metal "recliners" that in no way conjured feelings of relaxation; the Parts and Service room was stuffed full of tools, wires, fasteners, and various disembodied robotic endoskeletons. Metal feet and arms and hands and legs and elbows and shoulders were tangled on the shelves and strewn across the worktables. When Bob had first seen the room, he'd felt like he was standing in a robotic torture chamber. He had quickly backed out and slammed the door closed.

Once again, Bob thrashed in the chair. Using all of the strength he could muster, he tried to free himself. The chair held on to him, and then it snapped backward, stretching him flat.

As soon as Bob was supine, a massive, furry brown bear mask loomed over his face. Bob screamed.

As Bob's pointless bawling filled the room, the bear mask opened up. The two halves of the bear face peeled back like the wings of a beetle, expanding outward. As the fur parted, spinning robotic mechanisms filled Bob's vision.

Razor-sharp and in constant motion, the inside of the bear

mask was a blur of clicking, clanking knifelike protrusions and pincers. Every edge of exposed metal was a small lethal weapon that would easily pierce human skin. Bob began fighting like an animal caught in a metal-toothed trap. He whipped his head from side to side. He bucked his torso. He kicked his legs.

At first, Bob felt like his efforts were futile, but then he felt one of the armrests begin to wiggle. Straining to crane his neck, Bob looked at his wrist. He couldn't see what was loosening, but something was. Maybe a bolt was coming free.

The despair that had been clutching at Bob since he'd hit the metal chair relaxed its grip . . . just a little. Bob let himself start to think he might be able to escape.

The mask's first cutting assault slashed into Bob's jaw.

Overcome by the stabs and slices that ripped at his forehead and cheeks and jabbed into his eyes and mouth, Bob realized escape was impossible. So was survival.

CHAPTER 1

Mike squinted in annoyance as the sun's insistent rays speared through the glass of the vaulted ceiling in the mall's food court and jabbed him in the eye. Scooting his yellow plastic chair a couple inches to the left, Mike ducked when a foam dart shot toward his head. He managed to avoid the spongy projectile as he wished he was anywhere but where he was. Rubbing his face, Mike blinked dry, scratchy eyes. His head felt so heavy that he wasn't sure his neck and shoulders had the strength to hold it up. Man, he was tired. He was so tired.

What I need is a vacation, Mike thought as he idly built a little tent on the table in front of him, using his napkins and paper cup. The notion of an actual vacation elicited an audible snort from Mike, and he brought down a fist on his napkin-cup construction. As if. Vacations were for people with lives. People with money. Mike had neither. If not a vacation, Mike would have settled for a little peace and quiet, but he wasn't going to get that, either. Certainly not here.

Mall security guards were only given twenty minutes for their lunch break, so Mike and his coworkers had only two choices for where they spent their compressed rest time. They could either hole up in the guards' dingy break room, which stank of pickles and bleach—not a good combination—or they could come to the food court. Usually the food court was preferable, but today, Mike wasn't so sure it had been the best choice. A kid was having a birthday party, and screaming munchkins were running amok. Some moron had given the birthday boy foam-dart guns as a gift, and the food court had turned into a chaotic battle zone of inept and giggling assaults.

In and around the pint-sized revelers, mall shoppers plowed through a variety of fast food. The aromas that surrounded Mike were another battle—an international one. Italian sauces warred with Mexican salsas, which sparred with the smells of fried egg rolls and sizzling burgers. Mike's nostrils were inundated with a jangling mix of curry and ginger and oregano and cayenne and dill.

Mike balled up the paper wrapper from the refried bean burrito he'd just eaten without tasting. Now that it was in his stomach, he belatedly realized the hot sauce on the burrito had been a little too hot. An inferno began to burn in his solar plexus.

Mike shot the balled-up burrito wrapper into a nearby trash can. Dozens of the large steel-mesh receptacles were interspersed among the rows of small square tables dotting the expanse of the mall's food court dining area. Mike's paper ball hit the back rim of the can and then dropped in with the rest of the food wrappers, napkins, and paper cups.

Score, Mike thought inanely.

Too bad he wasn't tall. For a few seconds, Mike blocked out the screaming children and imagined being someone much different than who he was.

At twenty-five years old, Mike was okay with his age. He was cool with his looks, too. He was five foot six and in pretty good shape, even though he didn't have time to work out too much. He didn't think his dark brown hair, hazel eyes, and regular features were particularly handsome, but they weren't ugly, either. On one of the rare dates that he'd had in high school, a girl had told him his eyes were "intense," because of his pronounced brow ridge. She'd also said he had a "chiseled" jaw. He thought she read too many romance novels. For sure, she'd expected a lot more "chivalry" from him than he'd been capable of. She hadn't wanted a second date. Now he couldn't even remember the girl's name.

No, it wasn't Mike's appearance that was the problem. It was his circumstances. Or maybe it was him.

Most of the time, Mike told himself that his life sucked because tragedy had robbed him of a normal childhood . . . and was robbing him of adulthood. But the truth was that the tragedy wasn't the real problem. The problem had come before the tragedy. *Mike* was the problem. If only he'd been someone different back then.

What would life be like if Mike had been the kind of guy that girls wanted to date in high school? What would he be doing now if he'd gotten to go to college? He wasn't tall, but he was quick. Maybe he could have played basketball. Or baseball. Or maybe he could have taken woodshop and stayed after school to work on projects; he'd always liked building stuff. He could have done a lot of things . . . if he hadn't had to stay home and . . .

"Listen to this."

Mike blinked and looked across the table. He frowned. He'd forgotten Jeremiah was there. And that took some doing. Jeremiah wasn't a fade-into-the-background kind of guy. He was an African-American, linebacker-sized man with a heft that testified to his love of burgers and copious consumption of sodas. Whereas Mike's dark blue, mall-guard polyester shirt and matching pants hung loosely on his lanky body, Jeremiah's huge shoulders and large belly stretched the seams of his uniform. Jeremiah was an okay guy. He didn't get on Mike's nerves the way most of the other guards—and people in general—did.

Jeremiah took a loud slurp of cola from the massive paper cup sitting on the blue plastic table in front of him. He waved the paperback book that he held.

Jeremiah cleared his throat and read aloud. "'And though the dreamer remains asleep, he walks through memory as if experiencing it for the first time, anew. No longer a passenger, but an ACTIVE PARTICIPANT.'" Jeremiah frowned. "Why is ACTIVE PARTICIPANT in all caps? Is it like a title or something? Like achieving the level of GRAND LORD in a video game?"

Mike figured Jeremiah's question was rhetorical so he didn't answer it. Jeremiah closed the book and looked at its light blue cover. Over the abstract image of a closed eye, the book's title, *Dream Theory*, stretched diagonally, in a wavering font as if the words themselves were falling asleep.

Jeremiah waved the book again. "Is this stuff for real?" he asked, raising an eyebrow at Mike.

Mike shrugged. "Some people think so. Guess it depends on what you believe."

Jeremiah nodded. He dropped his lids to half-mast over his round brown eyes as he gazed past Mike's shoulder. Mike could tell Jeremiah wasn't watching the foam-dart gun fight. Jeremiah was lost in his thoughts.

After a few seconds, Jeremiah sighed. "Summer of '82, I traded a mint-condition Cal Ripken Jr. rookie card for a used copy of *Missile Command*. That card's probably worth eight hundred bucks now. I'd like to participate in that memory. Actively kick myself in the ass for such a stupid decision." He let out a bark of laughter. Then he settled down and tapped the book. "Can I keep this?"

Mike reached out and snatched the book from Jeremiah's hand. "No."

Jeremiah's lips drooped. For a second, he looked like a down-trodden, oversized puppy.

"Sorry," Mike said. "I'm not done with it."

Jeremiah's usual happy-go-lucky smile returned. "No problem."

Feeling bad for snapping at Jeremiah, Mike said, "I think we have time for a shake. Want one? My treat."

Jeremiah lit up. "Really? Yeah. Thanks, dude."

"Sure." Mike stood and made his way over to the chrome and bright red laminate counter of the food court's Dairy Freeze. A woman who was wearing too much flowery perfume was at the counter, and as soon as Mike heard what she was saying, he started regretting his offer to buy Jeremiah a shake.

"I want a three-scoop sundae," the woman said in a strange accent that was half Southern drawl and half uppercrust British, "but instead of three full scoops of three flavors, I want half scoops of six flavors. I want rum raisin, banana nut, pecan fudge, straw-berry cheesecake, lemon sherbet, and licorice. On top of the rum raisin, I want strawberry syrup. On the peanut butter chocolate, I want marshmallow topping. On the . . ."

Mike shifted his feet. He took a long, deep breath and turned away, attempting to shut out the sound of the woman's intermi-nable order. She'd moved on from toppings and was describing how she wanted the ice cream arranged in the bowl.

Although the birthday party had ended, kids were still play-ing among the tables in the food court. Some of the kids, a group of five, were pretending to be cops and robbers at the edge of the tables, near the food court's central feature, a decorative fountain shaped like a big drink cup with a straw sticking up from the middle. Water spewed from the straw and was caught in multicolored lights that sprayed out from the rim of the cup. The fountain was a little cheesy, but Mike kind of liked it.

"Hands up!" one of the little kids near the fountain shouted. The sound came from a purple-haired girl. She had her hands fisted around a pretend gun. A black-haired boy was caught in her sights. He threw his arms up.

"Book 'em," the girl ordered another boy, a freckled kid with spikey hair. He marched over to the black-haired boy and pretended to put handcuffs on him.

Mike smiled. The things kids got from watching TV.

The freckled kid started leading the "handcuffed" kid away, taking him to . . .

Mike's smile abruptly disappeared.

Just beyond the pretend cop and the pretend criminal, a small boy, maybe six years old, was pressed up against the half-wall at the edge of the food court. The top of the half-wall was filled with plants, some of which drooped over the wall. The boy, his blond curly hair a tangle that flopped into his eyes, huddled under the fronds of some kind of fern. His brows bunched, his mouth compressed, his gaze darting left and right, his frail arms wrapped tightly around a plush penguin, the boy was a picture of fear.

Mike frowned. Why did the boy look so scared? Was he in trouble?

"Chocolate peanut butter twist?" a lively female voice asked.

Mike registered the voice but kept his attention on the little boy . . . until someone gently poked his shoulder. Mike turned toward the poke. A smiling gray-haired woman pointed at the Dairy Freeze counter. "I believe you're next," she said. Her voice was warm and kind, and it briefly brought back a memory of . . .

"You want your usual, right?"

This time, Mike turned toward the voice. "Hey, Cindy," he said. "Sorry."

Cindy flashed her wide smile at Mike. A pretty college student who worked at the Dairy Freeze to pay for classes, majoring in economics (so she'd told Mike even though he'd expressed no interest in her personal life), Cindy was friendly with everyone. According to Jeremiah, however, Cindy paid particular attention to Mike. Mike hadn't noticed.

Mike frowned, his thoughts on the scared little boy. Was the kid lost? Why was he alone?

"Your usual?" Cindy repeated.

"Huh?" Mike focused on Cindy. Her long brown hair was in braids today.

Cindy hovered her ice-cream scoop over a tub of chocolate peanut butter twist.

"Yeah," Mike said. "Sure." He might as well get himself something now that he was here. "And a chocolate shake for Jeremiah."

"Got it."

Mike turned away from Cindy and looked past the little girls, whose dance had degenerated into a giggle-fest. He took a step to his right so he could see the area by the half-wall's planter. He spotted the fern, but the boy . . .

. . . was gone.

Mike quickly scanned the area. Aware that his breath was quickening, Mike could feel a rushing sound in his ears. He recognized that sound . . . it was the sound of panic.

"So, when are you going to bring Abby by?" Cindy asked.

Mike heard Cindy but he didn't acknowledge her. He was still desperately trying to spy the little boy.

"We got a new flavor," Cindy continued. "Rainbow explosion. I bet she'll go bonkers for it."

Mike stepped away from the Dairy Freeze counter. Dodging a couple of roughhousing preteen boys, Mike strode past a row of tables.

"Mike?" Cindy's callout chased Mike as he broke into a half-trot, heading toward where he'd last seen the boy.

Mike's gaze was a laser probe of fixation. It ignored everything Mike saw except for . . .

There!

Mike spotted the boy. He was about forty feet away. No longer by the half-wall planter, the boy was heading toward the fountain. The boy mostly had his back to Mike now but Mike recognized the floppy blond curls, and he saw a penguin flipper sticking out from under the boy's bony elbow.

The boy was stumbling awkwardly through the food court, heading toward the mall's main concourse. And he was no longer alone.

As Mike jogged closer to the boy, he saw that a tall, dirty-blond man had his hand clamped around one of the boy's wrists. The man was pulling the boy along, wrenching him into a pace that was obviously far too fast for such a little kid.

"Hey!" Mike yelled.

Mike broke into a run.

Shoving through a young couple holding hands, Mike kicked chairs aside and pushed past anyone who got in his way. Only peripherally aware of heads turning toward him and a few annoyed grunts and angry protests, Mike sprinted through the food court.

Because the man was hindered by the awkwardly floundering little boy, Mike quickly closed the gap between him and the man. "Hey you!" Mike shouted. "Stop!"

Like most of the people around Mike, the man started to turn toward Mike. Mike briefly registered the man's raised eyebrows before launching himself through the last three feet of space between him and the jerk who was trying to take the kid. As Mike shot toward the man, Mike pulled back his arm, clenching his fist. He aimed a swift jab at the man's nose.

Mike heard a cracking *pop* as he felt cartilage give way beneath his knuckles. At the same time, Mike's momentum resulted in a tumbling collision with the man. Together, they spilled into the base of the water fountain.

When Mike hit the water, he lost his ability to logically process what he was doing. Something primitive in him took over, something that turned his arms into churning pistons that kept driving toward the man's face.

When the man fought back, landing a glancing blow along Mike's jaw and angling a knee into Mike's belly, Mike's rage revved into overdrive. He threw himself onto the man, flinging both of them down into the water. Whether a result of the man's retaliation or Mike's out-of-control fury, Mike bit his lip. He tasted blood. Mike felt blood on his knuckles, too—the warmth was a contrast to the fountain's ice-cold water.

Out of the corner of his eye, Mike saw red filaments swirling in the clear fountain water. The red triggered a memory, and the memory turned Mike's thoughts dark; so dark that it felt like he was falling into a black void.

CHAPTER 2

hrill beeping pierced through drifting, filmy clouds . . .

Mike opened his eyes and groaned. For a couple seconds, he managed to cling to the sensation of buoyancy left over from his sleep. But the beeping continued, piercing and insistent.

Mike flung out his left hand and slapped it toward what he thought was the top of the cheap plastic digital alarm clock that sat next to the battered metal desk lamp on his rickety nightstand. Instead of hitting the alarm, Mike's hand landed on the cassette player near the lamp. He felt his fingers brush against a paperback book, and then he heard the book swish off the nightstand and hit the thin carpet on his hardwood floor with a soft thud.

Mike pulled his hand back. His fingers, in full-on, early-morning klutz mode, once again bumped something. This time it was the plastic bottle of Mike's pills. Mike heard the bottle *tippity-tap* down the side of the nightstand and land on the carpet with a shushing sound. He cringed, hoping he'd remembered to put the cap on tight.

Mike started to sit up, but the motion sent what felt like a jagged shard of glass through his temporal lobe. Mike clutched at his head. The glass shard started moving around in his skull. The alarm's continued screechy beep seemed to drive the shard even deeper into his brain.

Mike squinted toward his nightstand and once again attempted to turn off the alarm. This time, his palm hit its target. The infernal noise stopped.

Mike groaned again and rubbed his temples. Sighing, he swung his legs out of bed and reached for the glass next to the cassette player. At least he'd managed not to knock that over. The glass was still half-full of water. Mike guzzled it and set the glass back down.

Mike's bare feet shifted, and his right one encountered his prescription pill bottle. Wincing as he bent over—because the motion intensified his headache—Mike picked up the dark amber plastic container. Thankfully, he had put the cap on the bottle. The little white prescribed pills—a couple dozen of them—were still safely inside.

Mike stuffed the pill bottle under his mattress, just a few inches from the edge. Then he leaned over again, gritting his teeth against the increased jabbing in his head. He picked up his *Dream Theory* paperback. Setting the book next to the cassette player, Mike hit the REWIND button on the machine.

Once the cassette tape started its whispery whir of motion, Mike managed to calmly inhale. Finally, his morning routine was starting to fall into place.

Usually, Mike's first motions after waking up were rote. Hit the alarm. Hide the pills. Rewind the tape. This morning, the unusually high pain level of his headache had turned Mike's routine into a one-stooge show. The tape's smooth rewind settled him back into a sense of normalcy.

"Okay," Mike said. He stroked his hands through his hair.

Standing, Mike took a couple steps away from his bed and planted his feet at the edge of his threadbare pale blue–and–gray rag rug. He stretched his arms overhead and willed himself to ignore his headache. Mike dropped to the floor and began doing push-ups. Not counting, Mike lowered and lifted himself over and over and over.

Beneath Mike's palms, the carpet felt scratchy and dirty. Vaguely, he tried to remember when he'd last vacuumed his room.

Lifting his head as he pumped his body up and down, Mike took in the familiar sparsity of his space. The nearly empty room—it held only his narrow bed and the small nightstand—was nothing but a bare cell, a cell that kept Mike separate from the world. Even his one window, which might have reminded him that a reality existed beyond his own suffering, was covered by heavy blackout curtains. Dropping his head again, Mike continued to pound out his push-ups. The routine, though painful, comforted him, as did his prison-like surroundings. A few more minutes of this punishment, and he might be able to face his day.

* * *

Abby bent over her drawing pad and concentrated on getting the image just right. Tucking her tongue between her teeth, she dragged her pencil across the page in a long, curved line. Pulling back, she frowned. *Did that look all right?* Not sure, Abby lifted her gaze. She looked out through the opening in the hidey-tent that surrounded her.

Constructed from blankets held into place by her white-painted nightstand, her matching small desk, and one edge of her squat bureau (also white, but not matching), Abby's tent snugged up to her bed, a bed she didn't like nearly as much as she liked the cozy confines of the hidey-tent.

With two fluffy pillows on its floor and another blanket scrunched up around the pillows, the inside of Abby's hidey-tent was like a little nest that made Abby feel like a safe and cared-for baby bird. The pillows and the blankets smelled like the detergent they were washed in. Abby had seen the detergent box; it was labeled RAIN SCENTED. Abby didn't think the detergent smelled like rain, but it didn't smell bad. It was kind of sweet and fruity. That meant that the inside of Abby's tent was sweet and fruity, too.

Abby liked it in her hidey-tent. She could handle almost anything when she was tucked inside of it. Take, for instance, the grunting coming from her brother's room. Mike was doing push-ups again, and Abby wished she didn't have to listen to him. He clearly didn't like doing them. Abby could tell that from all the moans and groans. When Mike did the push-ups, Abby felt bad, as if something hard was poking her in the belly. She didn't like feeling like that.

Although inside Abby's hidey-tent it was cool and dim, a fat ray of sun was sweeping past the tent's opening. The sun ray landed on the wall opposite the tent. Many of Abby's completed drawings covered that wall. Abby used the drawings as nudges to help her draw better. Although most of the things in the drawings were stick figures, some of them were more real-looking. Abby was getting better at drawing. That made her feel good.

Not a lot made Abby feel good. Forever and ever, Abby had felt like she didn't really know how to be. No one seemed to want her around much. Not her brother. Not her babysitter, Max. Not the kids at school or the ones at the Development Center. Well, "no one" wasn't quite right. Dr. Lillian seemed to like having Abby around. Dr. Lillian was the one who got Abby all the cool, colored drawing pencils she used now. Dr. Lillian said Abby was talented *beyond ten years old.* That meant Abby drew better than other kids her age. Drawing made Abby feel special. So did the things she drew. Drawing was Abby's way into a world that she liked being in. It was a world where she was wanted.

A sharp knock sounded on Abby's flimsy wood door. Abby put aside her drawing pad and pulled closed the two sections of blanket that formed the opening of her tent. She picked up Dolph, her plush dolphin. Through the narrow crack between the blankets, she looked toward the scarred pale brown surface of her door. She wished her door was big and thick and had latches on it, kind of like a castle door.

"Abby!" Mike called out from the other side of Abby's not-castle-door.

Abby didn't answer her brother.

"Are you ready, Abs?"

"My name's not Abs," Abby whispered. "My name's Abby, and I'm not here."

Abby's not-thick and not-locked door opened. Mike stuck his head into Abby's private space. He looked toward Abby's bed, then shifted his gaze to the crack in the blankets that Abby peered through. Abby clearly heard her brother's loud sigh.

Abby stared at Mike's feet as they headed toward her hidey-tent. Her brother wore a pair of black dress socks. They were faded and stretched out so they kind of crumpled around his ankles, and both socks were full of holes His left big toe stuck out through the largest of the ragged openings.

The sock-covered feet stopped really close to the front of

Abby's hidey-tent. The feet, or maybe it was Mike himself, smelled sweaty; Abby wrinkled her nose and put her face into Dolph's soft fur. Dolph wasn't as clean as the blankets in Abby's hidey-tent so he didn't smell sweet and fruity. But he didn't smell bad. He smelled kind of like Abby, and Abby smelled like lemons because her shampoo smelled like lemons.

"Abby," Mike said. "I know you're awake."

Abby squeezed her eyes shut. She heard whispery movement, and she felt the blanket flaps of her hidey-tent separate. Mike let out another long, loud sigh.

"Abby!"

As Abby kept her eyes closed, Dolph pressed against her face. She didn't move.

A scrape. A fluttering sound. Abby felt air whisk over her bare arms. She opened her eyes. Mike was shaking one of the chairs that held part of her hidey-tent in place.

"Okay, okay, okay!" Abby yelled.

Mike's head poked through the hidey-tent's flaps. His hair stuck up all weird. She thought it looked stupid that way, but he might have done it on purpose. Some of the boys at school had their hair like that.

Abby thought about her own hair. It probably looked stupid at the moment, too. Her hair always went all over the place when she slept, and it was thick and fine like her brother's so it tangled easily. Abby glared at Mike.

"You're being a jerk," Abby said.

Mike rolled his eyes.

When Mike rolled his eyes, Abby sometimes felt like she was looking at her own eyes in someone else's head. Abby's and Mike's eyes were a lot alike, even though his were a lighter brown than hers—they called his hazel. Their eyes sloped down at the outside edge, like they were a little sad all the time. That made sense, actually.

Besides their eyes and the black, thick, slightly wavy hair they both had, Abby didn't think she and Mike looked much alike. Mike's face was kind of hard, like his skin was stretched over metal or wood. Abby's face was softer and rounder.

Mike jostled the hidey-tent again. "Come on, Abby. I have somewhere to be. You know that."

Abby mimicked Mike's sigh. "It's not my fault you lost your job at the mall."

Abby sighed a second time. She knew that getting ice cream from the Dairy Freeze was not something that was going to happen much anymore, if ever. Mike had gotten a discount from the food court when he'd worked there. No more discount. No more ice cream.

"You're right about that," Mike said.

Abby knew he was talking about the job, not the ice cream she was thinking of.

"But if I'm late, that *will* be your fault." Mike lightly kicked the side of the blanket tent. "Five minutes. I want you dressed."

Abby stuck her tongue out at Mike. He copied her. She thought their tongues might have looked a little alike, but his was bigger.

Mike turned to leave the room. Abby looked at Dolph and raised an eyebrow at him. The dolphin seemed to go along with her idea, so she threw him through the opening of the hidey-tent.

Dolph arced through the air and plowed his blunt nose into the middle of Mike's back. As Dolph dropped to the yellow-and-green braided rug that covered Abby's wood floor, Mike turned around.

Abby looked at Mike's feet. "Nice socks," she said.

"You're one to talk," Mike said. He turned and left her room.

Abby crawled out of her tent and scooted forward to rescue Dolph. She scrambled upright and looked down at her own feet. She wore one red-and-white-striped sock and one yellow polka-dotted sock. Abby shrugged and hugged Dolph close. He didn't seem to care about her mismatched socks.

*   *   *

Mike glanced up at the gray clouds that hung so low it felt like they were pressing him down into the cracked concrete walkway that led up to the sad, rectangular brick building he didn't want to go into. The building, whose simple, downtrodden architecture shouted "Underfunded Government Office," looked like it could barely hold its own under the overbearing stratus clouds.

Mike hated stratus clouds. They were always iron-like and depressing, and they were spineless . . . all show and no substance. Stratus clouds made the sky dark and threatening, but they actually held very little precipitation. Mike had learned that in science class and, for some reason, he remembered it. Maybe that was because he felt a little like a stratus cloud himself.

Mike hesitated at the base of the shallow steps leading into the building in front of him. How many times had he been in this miserable place? He'd lost count.

Mike kicked loose a piece of crumbling concrete from one of the steps. He found the crunching sound satisfying. Squaring his shoulders, Mike slogged up the steps and went into the building.

The interior of the building that housed the city's social services offices was even uglier than the exterior. With dirty cream walls and industrial-grade, faded brown carpet, the lobby and main hall weren't much more attractive than a sewer. Not that Mike had ever been in a sewer . . . this place was close enough.

Shuffling forward, Mike plucked a number from a scarred, black number-dispenser near the counter at the far side of the lobby. He looked at the little piece of paper in his hand. Number twenty-seven. He looked up at the dimly lit number display on the wall. The number eleven flickered anemically under the fluorescent lights that cast a harsh glare over everything.

"Great," Mike muttered.

Mike dragged his feet across the nubby carpet as he headed toward a line of molded-plastic chairs along the left wall of the lobby. The other twenty-six people who held paper numbers, along with their spouses or children or friends (Mike had none of the above), crowded the relatively small area. However, an end chair was open. Mike headed toward it and took a seat. As soon as he sat, he used his butt to scooch the chair away from its neighbor. The middle-aged woman who sat on the adjacent chair was large, and her sweatpants-encased thighs encroached into Mike's space.

Mike felt the woman's gaze on him as he repositioned the chair. He heard her huff but he didn't glance up. Looking into the eyes of the other people waiting to see a social worker was never a good idea. You could get swallowed by a mire of life-sucking depression if you made eye contact with the other people in this building. Everyone here was in one crummy situation or another. Dealing with his own baggage was hard enough; Mike didn't need to get a glimpse of anyone else's.

Even though Mike didn't *see* the others in the room, he could sense them. Their presence felt like the bars of a cell.

Mike could smell and hear the people around him, too. The waiting area was filled with sounds—nervously shuffling feet, sniffles, coughs, throat-clearing, a couple weak sobs—and murmuring voices. Even though Mike didn't want to hear about other people's problems, some snippets of conversation got past his intention to mind his own business.

"So I say to him," one whining female voice related, "I say, 'You can't just do that to another person. Where're we supposed to go when you throw us out?'"

A deep male voice on the other side of the room boomed, loudly enough to be heard outside the building, "Man can't put food on the table with the peanuts they try to pay."

Mike mentally plugged his ears and stared at his feet. Tuning out his surroundings, Mike disappeared into his favorite game: "What would I be doing if I was . . . ?"

Mike liked to play out all sorts of imaginary scenarios when he indulged in this game. Sometimes he was a reporter or a travel photographer. Sometimes he was a scientist or a doctor or a judge. Most often, Mike was a contractor, the head honcho in charge of building big houses or interesting office buildings (*not* buildings like this one). Never, ever was Mike a security guard or a janitor or a mail clerk or an unemployed loser looking for whatever work he could find.

Mike knew that playing this kind of make-believe game was something he should have outgrown years ago, but letting himself imagine a life different than the one he lived was what allowed him to get up in the morning and put one foot in front of the other. When Mike dropped into being pretend-Mike instead of real-Mike, he could work with a clean slate. He could stow all the baggage, all the disappointment . . . all the guilt. And if he couldn't put that away from time to time, the weight of it probably would have driven him up the wall by now. Or killed him. Mike wasn't sure which would have been worse.

"Number twenty-seven?"

Mike looked up. Already?

A forty-something woman with a tight perm and eyes that looked like they'd seen little more than an hour or two of sleep per night for years looked around the room. Mike lifted a hand and got her attention.

The woman tugged on the hem of her wrinkled orange blouse. The blouse clashed, Mike thought, with the woman's rust-colored skirt. The skirt hung crooked on the woman's skinny hips; the skirt was two inches above the woman's right knee and an inch below the left. "Number twenty-seven?" the woman called out to Mike.

Mike nodded.

"Follow me," the woman said.

Mike stood.

CHAPTER 3

The tall, slender man who leaned back casually in a cracked, black-vinyl office chair had the manner of someone presiding over an executive boardroom. In fact, the man presided over nothing but a cheap wood-veneer-topped desk in a closet-sized, windowless office. An even cheaper acrylic nameplate at the front of the desk announced that the man's name was Steve Raglan. Under STEVE RAGLAN, the nameplate revealed that the man was a CAREER COUNSELOR. Given Raglan's smug expression that clearly telegraphed his inflated self-opinion, Mike was sure the guy thought he was the best career counselor on the planet. Or maybe just the best person on the planet. Mike really, really wanted to punch the guy.

Fiftyish with graying dark hair, Raglan studied Mike with narrowed eyes magnified and contorted by thick, round, black-rimmed glasses. The eyewear dominated a thinnish face topped by a high forehead.

Raglan flashed Mike a grin. The grin was toothy and looked more like a grimace than a smile.

"So, Mr. Schmidt," Raglan said, "what's your deal?"

Raglan's gaze ran up and down the length of Mike as if Raglan was sizing up a cow before its trip to the slaughter house. Raglan continued to recline in his chair. One of his large feet was propped against the ugly, scarred desk. The foot waggled as if Raglan was keeping time with a tune that only he could hear.

"Well, Mike?" Raglan asked. "Mind if I call you Mike?"

Mike shrugged. He didn't care what this guy called him. He didn't care what the guy had to say, either. Anything Raglan said would be annoying. The man had a grating voice—alternately raspy and nasally then smooth and singsong. It was as if Raglan couldn't figure out who he was or what he wanted to sound like.

But whatever. Mike didn't care about why Raglan sounded the way he did. All Mike wanted to do was get this meeting over with.

"So, what are you, Mike?" Raglan asked. "Some kind of head case?" Raglan used his waggling foot to push off the desk. He straightened his chair and leaned forward, propping his elbows on the beige felt blotter that held a single manilla file folder and red coffee mug, which appeared to be empty. The folder was the only one on Raglan's desk. Other than an old landline phone and an empty metal-mesh inbox, the desk looked like it was never needed for any actual work.

"Dr. Jekyll and Mr. I-Like-To-Beat-Up-Dads," Raglan said. "Is that who you are?"

Mike stared at Raglan. Not only was the man saying nothing he had expected to hear, there was something off about him. Mike's nose twitched. Maybe it was the guy's odor. Mike couldn't place it. It wasn't sweat or anything like that. It wasn't cologne or food. It was something . . . musky . . . something that made Mike think of the damp basement in his childhood home. He'd never liked going down into that basement. He didn't like Raglan, either.

Raglan didn't seem to care that Mike remained mute. "You attack a man in broad daylight . . . ," Raglan said.

Mike's inner eye replayed the fight in the food court fountain. He felt the cold water, tasted the coppery blood. Mike licked his lips and stayed silent.

". . . in front of his own child," Raglan went on.

Mike's memory took him back to the fountain again. He remembered the pressure of Jeremiah's arm around his shoulders. *"Mike!"* Jeremiah had shouted in Mike's ear. *"Come on, Mike!"* Mike had fought against Jeremiah as his gaze had searched for the little boy he'd just rescued. Then Mike had heard the boy scream, *"Daddy!"* Still holding his penguin, the boy had scrambled into the fountain to reach the man Mike was attacking. That's when Mike had finally let Jeremiah pull him away.

"One has to wonder," Raglan said, tearing Mike from the shameful memory, "what would possess a person to act the way you did?"

Mike looked down at his hands, which were twisted together against his churning stomach. "It was a misunderstanding," Mike said softly. "I thought that—"

"Yes," Raglan interrupted as he opened the folder in front of him. "There's a note here." He tapped the top page in the file. "Given your . . . unique . . . history, I understand how you could've made that mistake. But that's not the whole story of Mike Schmidt, is it?"

Raglan flipped through a few pages of Mike's file. He paused and cleared his throat. Tapping a page, he read, "'Tire Zone. Sales associate. Two months. Employment terminated for cause. Insubordination. Media World. Custodial staff. One week. Fired because of a . . . ,'" Raglan leaned over the page and read even more slowly, "'. . . generally unpleasant disposition.'" Raglan looked up. "Coffee?"

"What?" Mike asked. The non sequitur caught him off-guard.

"Would you like some coffee?" Raglan asked.

Mike couldn't process the request. How had they gone from a walk down the memory lane of his failures to a friendly offer of coffee? All Mike could do was stare at Raglan.

Raglan shrugged and pushed out of his chair. He grabbed the red mug and took two steps to a coffeemaker that sat on top of the gray filing cabinet in the corner of the office. Mike hadn't noticed the coffeemaker. He hadn't noticed the aroma of coffee, either. He'd been too distracted by that acrid odor that seemed to emanate from Raglan.

Mike shifted in his chair to look at Raglan's shoes. Had the man stepped in something that was causing the stench? Mike couldn't tell. Raglan wore scuffed brown loafers. They didn't appear to be stained.

Raglan poured his coffee, and Mike finally caught the nutty scent of the brew. Raglan tore open a packet of sugar and added that to the mug. He didn't bother to stir it. Instead, he turned and looked at Mike.

"I'll be honest with you, Mike," Raglan said. "Given your track record, your options are extremely limited."

Mike made a face. Time to grovel.

"I'll take anything," Mike said. "Any job you have."

"Even so," Raglan said. He lifted his mug and took a sip of his coffee. He smiled and closed his eyes briefly, as if savoring the flavor.

Mike resisted the urge to squirm with impatience. He watched Raglan amble back to his desk chair.

"Let's say I put you up for . . . oh, I don't know . . . let's say a

26

dishwashing job," Raglan said. "Next thing, I'm getting a phone call telling me that you tried to drown the fry cook in the sink with all the dirty dishes."

Raglan set down his mug and tapped it with his index finger. The dull clunking sound made Mike realize that it was oddly quiet in Raglan's office. Even though the adjacent offices were occupied by other social workers and the people who needed help, the nearby conversations sounded like little more than a swishy sort of roar, like the distant crash of ocean waves.

Raglan leaned forward and nailed Mike with a look so severe that Mike was tempted to lean away. Raglan's superior, jovial air seemed to morph into something else, something almost . . . threatening.

"That would be very bad for me, Mike," Raglan said. "Very bad. Not to mention the poor fry cook." Raglan leaned back, and the corner of his mouth twitched slightly. Joviality returned.

He's screwing with me, Mike thought. But what could Mike do about it? Nothing. All he could do was return to groveling.

"I'm not a violent person," Mike said.

"I'm sure you're not," Raglan said. The words were dripping in sarcasm. Raglan's mouth quirked.

Mike clenched his fists. He was seconds away from proving his last statement to be a lie. This man seriously needed to have the pompous expression beaten off his face.

"I can tell this is hard for you, Mike," Raglan said.

Mike saw the twinkle in Raglan's eyes. The guy was seriously enjoying baiting Mike.

"Being here," Raglan continued. "You don't like it, do you?"

Mike didn't bother to respond.

"You strike me," Raglan went on, "as someone who'd rather . . .

I don't know . . . dig their own eye out with a spoon than ask for help."

Mike stood up. "You know what? Forget this." Mike started to turn away from Raglan's desk.

"I think I have something for you," Raglan said.

Mike rotated his head back toward Raglan. But he remained standing.

"Come on," Raglan said. "I like to make jokes. A little levity lightens the mood. Why don't you sit down?"

Mike crossed his arms and looked down at the idiot behind the tacky desk. "You think you have something?" Mike asked.

Raglan tilted back in his chair. "It's a security gig," he said. "Full disclosure. It's not great. 'High turnover' is what we in the business call it. But you'd get to be your own boss, sort of. And you'd really only have to worry about one thing."

Mike waited. He suspected Raglan was still toying with him.

"All you'd have to do is keep the place tidy," Raglan finally said. "And keep people out."

"That's two things," Mike said.

A muscle twitched at the corner of Raglan's eye. The right side of his jaw bulged briefly.

That's what it feels like to be messed with, Mike thought. *Deal with it.*

"Are you interested?" Raglan asked.

Mike shifted his feet. He tentatively allowed himself to feel a little anticipation. "How's the pay?"

Raglan snorted. "What do you think? Not good. And the hours are worse."

Mike's anticipation dissolved into disappointment. Bad hours meant nights.

"I can't do nights," Mike said.

Raglan cocked his head. "I'm sorry?"

"I can't do nights," Mike repeated.

Raglan picked up his mug and took a long, noisy slurp of coffee. Mike inhaled the smell of the coffee beans but wrinkled his nose when he once again caught the strange stench that wafted from Raglan himself.

"Why can't you do nights?" Raglan asked.

Mike wasn't about to try to explain his situation to Raglan. It wasn't the man's business. It was personal. So, Mike said nothing.

Silence grew into such a commanding presence that it felt like a third person had stepped into the office. Raglan attempted to stare down Mike. Mike held the man's gaze and didn't move a muscle.

Raglan finally gave in. "Shame," he said.

Raglan reached out and pulled open the desk drawer in front of his lean stomach. He rummaged in the drawer. Mike heard a clatter, a rustle, and a metallic thunk. Finally, Raglan plucked out a business card. He held it out over his desk. "In case you have a change of heart," he said.

Mike didn't want to take the card. All he wanted to do was get out of there. But he wasn't in a position to burn bridges. He took the card. Then he stomped out of Raglan's office.

* * *

After Mike had left Raglan's office, he'd gone on his own job hunt. Who needed Raglan? Mike could find his own job . . . or maybe not.

By the time Mike gave up and headed toward home, the oppressive gray clouds were being consumed by a night that seemed to be in a big hurry to take over. Even though the day still held on to some light, the sun was nowhere to be seen. Just as well. Mike wasn't in the mood for sun.

As Mike turned the corner onto his street, his old sedan back-fired. The car lurched, and Mike had to stomp on the gas to keep the car from stalling out. Man, he hated this car. An amalgamation of old parts from the junkyard, Mike's car might have been the ugliest vehicle on the road. If he hadn't been so grateful to have something . . . anything . . . with wheels and an engine, he'd have been embarrassed to be seen in the thing. But then again, Mike wasn't really that easily embarrassed. When you carried around the kind of regret that he hauled everywhere he went, the usual things that embarrassed people didn't make a dent.

Take the neighborhood Mike lived in, for instance. The bedraggled street of little more than shacks was considered to be "*that* part of town." Originally built as makeshift housing for the dirt-poor immigrants brought in to work in the town's factories, the petite houses hadn't been much when they'd been put up. Now they were even less.

All the houses on the street were essentially identical—give or take the variety of faded colors and the various old cars, lawn equipment, toys, and other junk piled around them. Mike and Abby's house was yellow, or at least it used to be. It was more tan than yellow now because it was so dirty. The shallow roof, originally black, was fuzzy with green moss. Like many of the houses on the street, Mike's place had no front lawn. All it had was a collection of weeds and the ever-widening oil stain that Mike's car added to every day.

Mike turned into his so-called driveway—a dirt and gravel expanse that held said oil stain. He turned off his car, and the engine coughed several times before expiring for the night. As soon as the engine went silent, Mike pulled the key from the ignition. But he didn't move.

Sometimes Mike got stuck in the moment. He couldn't convince himself that moving onto the next thing was worth his trouble.

It wasn't that Mike was suicidal or anything. He wasn't ready to meet his maker . . . he wasn't even remotely ready for *that* accounting. But Mike often wished life came with time-outs. Or maybe freeze-frames. It would've been helpful to have a remote so he could stop time and catch his breath.

Nearby, an engine revved. The sound kick-started Mike again. He opened his car door, got out, and loped up to his front porch . . . if you could call it that. Only a three-foot-square rise of concrete under a miniscule overhang led to a door with peeling, dirty, white paint. A red sheet of paper was taped to the door.

Mike grabbed the rusting doorknob with his right hand. With his left hand, he tore the paper off the door. He knew he didn't need to look at it, but he did anyway. It was like goggling at a car wreck. Sometimes it was impossible to turn away from foulness.

The paper said exactly what Mike expected it to say: NOTICE OF DELINQUENCY.

"Tell me something I don't know," Mike muttered as he stuffed the paper in the pocket of his wrinkled black slacks and opened his front door.

* * *

Maxine had heard Mike's car pull up in front of the house. How could she not? The beater needed a new muffler, among a hundred other things. When the engine's thunderous sputter had gone silent, Maxine had waited to hear the car door slam. When it didn't, she knew that Mike's day hadn't gone well. If only Maxine could comfort him.

Maxine snorted and turned up the sound on Mike's TV. The TV was an old analog set, one with truly crap reception. Continuous wiggles of static wormed across the screen, no matter what channel you were on.

Maxine currently was watching QVC. She liked QVC.

When Mike had teased Maxine about her addiction to the shopping channel, she'd pretended that his words hadn't bothered her at all. Maxine was good at pretending. Nonchalance was her go-to defense mechanism. When you wore a bored expression, moved languidly, and kept your words few and as apathetic as possible, no one knew what you were actually thinking or feeling. It made for good armor. Maxine could never be hurt because she pretended that she was hurt-proof. Or at least that's what she told herself.

Maxine finally heard Mike's car door slam as her favorite hostess introduced the next product, a silver ring with an emerald-cut cubic zirconia stone. The ring was one in a line of "affordable" jewelry designed by the other woman on the screen, an ex-actress who probably now made more money selling rings and bracelets and necklaces than she'd ever earned from her B-movie roles. Both the hostess and the ex-actress had big hair and fake tans, but Maxine didn't mind that. The superficial fakery was part of QVC's appeal for Maxine. She enjoyed watching others put on the same kind of don't-look-at-me show that she did.

"Not every guy can afford a real diamond," the hostess said, "so it's awesome that you've created this line of cubic zirconia engagement rings."

"Isn't it?" the ex-actress responded ever-so-humbly. "This particular ring is one of my favorites."

Even though Maxine watched QVC obsessively, she didn't like all that much of what the channel hawked. The ring on the screen, for instance, was gaudy in the extreme, and its price tag was laughably high.

"At only $79.99," the hostess said, "this ring is a bargain."

"It's worth less than a wad of tinfoil," Maxine told the hostess on the screen.

Mike came through the front door, and Maxine quickly affected a bored, I-don't-give-a-crap-about-anything posture. Already reclining, she let her lids fall half-closed, and she made sure her feet were drooping over the edge of the sofa's sagging mustard-yellow cushions. She quickly arranged the black shirt she wore with faded jeans so it revealed just the right amount of cleavage.

In her mind's eye, Maxine assessed the picture she made. A slender five foot five, Maxine was petite enough to look a lot more feminine and helpless than she was. Sometimes that annoyed her, but sometimes she liked to make it work for her. With large, wide-spaced eyes and high cheekbones, Maxine knew she was attractive enough. She had long dark hair that was thick and shiny. Guys went for that. Or at least most guys did.

The one guy that Maxine cared about stepped into the shabby, stamp-sized living room. Maxine gave him a limp wave. *Not a care in the world. Doesn't matter at all that you don't see me.*

Maxine had given a lot of thought to why Mike was immune to her charms. Ha! Charms. But hey, Maxine wasn't ugly, and she was only a few years younger than Mike. She wasn't dumb or obnoxious or anything. In fact, she was smarter than Mike. She was taking social sciences classes at the community college, and sometimes she even read a book for fun in between marathon sessions of QVC-watching.

"Hey, Max," Mike said.

Maxine tried to ignore the way her shoulders tightened when Mike used her nickname. She'd been trying to wean people off that name for years. She didn't want to be Max. She wanted to be Maxine. Not tomboy trailer trash. Sophisticated woman. But "Maxine" wasn't catching on. To everyone but herself, Maxine was Max.

"There's Stouffer's," Maxine told Mike. "Should still be warm if you're hungry."

Mike dropped onto the red vinyl seat of one of the chrome chairs next to the small tan-Formica-covered kitchen table. He looked toward the small gas stove tucked between an old squat fridge and the inadequate bit of counter that surrounded a dingy, white-porcelain sink. Maxine had left half of the microwave lasagna in a plastic pan on top of the stove.

"Did Abby eat?" Mike asked.

Maxine swung her legs off the sofa and raised an eyebrow at Mike. "What do you think?"

Mike gave Maxine a half-grin. Something about the grin got past Maxine's normal defenses. Her gaze landed on the ugly ring on the TV, and she sighed. Before she could think about what she was saying, she blurted, "I wish someone would buy me a ring."

Mike said nothing.

Immediately mortified at her slip, Maxine stood up, switched off the TV, and picked up her jacket and old black leather backpack from the end of the sofa. Keeping her face turned away from Mike, Maxine said, "Abby's been in her room all evening. She's yakking away with those friends of hers."

Maxine glanced at Mike in time to see him frown. She hurriedly went on. "She's getting really good, by the way. At drawing?"

Mike grunted as he pulled a crumpled piece of red paper from his pocket. Maxine knew what that was. She was surprised he was reading it.

Maxine crossed the few feet from the sofa to the kitchen table. She paused behind Mike and looked down at him. She liked being this close to him. He smelled really good, not sweet like cologne or anything. He smelled like a man. Just clean and simple.

"Y'all should get a dog," Maxine said. "A big mean one. Chain him outside."

Mike looked up; the skin crumpled between his brows. "Huh?"

Maxine pointed at the delinquency notice. "We used to get those, too," she said. "Then we got Bonesy. Poof. No more notices."

The furrows between Mike's brows deepened, but otherwise his expression didn't change. "I'll keep that in mind," he said.

Maxine shrugged. Miss Who-Cares. She headed toward the front door. Just before she reached for the doorknob, she stopped and spun back to look at Mike. "I almost forgot," she said. "Your aunt called."

Mike made a snorting sound.

"Something about lawyers and you'd be there tomorrow or else?" Maxine went on.

Mike dropped his head into his hands. Maxine stared at his long fingers and the thick hair between them. Her hand twitched, wanting so much to reach out and . . .

Maxine got a grip on herself. She turned back toward the door. "Well, see ya," she said as she opened it and stepped outside. She tried not to let it bother her that Mike didn't say good-bye.

CHAPTER 4

Mike waited for the door to close. He listened to Max's footsteps tap across the concrete "porch." As soon as he was sure she was gone, he clenched his fists and squeezed his eyes closed so hard that his entire body trembled.

Mike clamped his mouth closed, too. If he hadn't, he was sure he'd have screamed. A wail of despair and frustration and fury was churning in his chest, and it took everything he had not to let it come roaring out, leaping up his throat like a lion finally freed from a cage.

Gazing at the delinquency notice, Mike thought about his aunt's message. *Or else.* Mike knew what that meant. Damn his Aunt Jane. When was she going to back off?

Mike shook his head. "Never," he said aloud.

Taking a deep breath, he shoved aside thoughts of his aunt. Smelling the lasagna's sauce and cheese, he thought about eating, but that idea immediately brought a wave of nausea.

Mike stood up and looked at the half-eaten pan of lasagna. It was cold, and the cheese was starting to congeal. He was tempted to dump it in the trash, but maybe if he warmed it up, he could get Abby to eat.

Not holding his breath but figuring he should try to feed his sister, Mike put the lasagna in the little microwave next to the stove. He pressed a couple buttons and turned to head toward Abby's room.

As Mike rotated, he saw the delinquency notice. His rage and frustration combusting, he grabbed it, balled it up, and flung it into the plastic bin under the kitchen sink. Then he kicked the bin, slammed the cabinet door, and looked up at the dirty white ceiling.

Three feet above Mike's head, a spider was scurrying up a long strand of webbing. The webbing was attached to a half-completed web that stretched from a grungy glass ceiling light to the corner of the room.

"Go," Mike said to the spider. He hoped the thing had better luck at getting his home in order than Mike was having.

*   *   *

Abby loved her hidey-tent, but she also loved her desk. Too bad she couldn't fit her desk inside her hidey-tent. Drawing was much easier at her desk.

Toying with the shoulder strap of her favorite red overalls, Abby looked at the array of colored pencils splayed out next to her drawing pad. Which green would be better for the big tree? Deciding, Abby picked up the darkest green pencil and began carefully sketching in the fluffy edges of a tall pine tree's branches.

The squat, orange metal lamp that sat on her desk shone down on the tree like sunshine, making the yellow sun Abby had already drawn above the tree even brighter-looking. The golden warmth of the desk lamp made Abby's animally friends and the black-haired man and black-haired little girl under the tree look even happier than Abby wanted them to look. Even as Abby bent over the task of creating dozens of little green pine needles on the tree, she glanced at the creatures she'd drawn, and at the man and girl. She'd meant for it to look like they were all playing ring-around-the-rosy, and she wasn't sure she'd pulled that off, but the big curved smiles she'd put on their faces made it clear they were playing and having a good time.

For a second, Abby's pencil stopped moving as her feelings pushed past her concentration on the drawing. If only the drawing would come true. Abby wished Mike would play with her sometimes. He used to, but lately . . .

Behind Abby, her bedroom door squeaked. She glanced over her shoulder as Mike stepped into her room.

Mike lifted a hand in greeting, and Abby returned the gesture. Then she swiveled back around and bent closer to her drawing. She went back to sketching in green pine needles.

"What're you drawing?" Mike asked as his shuffling steps crossed her carpet.

"Trees," Abby said simply. She looked up when Mike stopped beside her white desk chair. The desk chair was what they called a ladderback chair—Mike had told her that. She didn't like it as much as the desk. It was hard and made her back hurt if she sat in it for too long. That was why sometimes she drew in her tent, even though the drawings she did there were never as good.

Mike's arm slipped past Abby's shoulder. He tapped the man in her drawing.

"This good-looking dude I recognize," Mike said. He moved his fingers to one of Abby's friends. "Who are these punks?"

Abby kept working on the tree. "My friends," she said. "It's not done yet."

Mike sighed loudly in Abby's ear. She ignored his unspoken criticism. She knew how he felt about her friends.

The floor creaked as Mike took a step back away from Abby's chair. "You can finish later," he said. The words sounded sad. "It's time to eat."

Abby set down the green pencil and picked up a yellow one to add a little more detail to one of her friends. "Not hungry," she said.

Mike let out another sigh. Abby didn't feel this one, but it was louder. "Don't care," Mike said. "You need to eat. Let's go."

The floor creaked again, and Mike's hand closed around Abby's upper arm. He attempted to pull her from her chair.

"No!" Abby shrieked as she dropped her pencil and whirled to face her brother. The word came out like a siren from her mouth, the one small sound raising and lowering in pitch and volume. Abby twisted her arm to shake off Mike's hand.

As soon as Abby pulled away from Mike, he let go of her. Abby rubbed her arm. It didn't really hurt. Mike had held her firmly, but he hadn't been rough. He was never rough.

Sighing for the third time, Mike backed away from Abby and sat down on the edge of her bed. She stayed in her chair and watched him. The thin mattress sank under his weight and the box springs let out a squeak.

Mike rubbed his palms over his face. Then he looked at Abby as if he was about to beg her for a favor. "Abs," he said, his voice really soft, "the day I'm having . . ." Mike swallowed and shook his head. "Just please come and eat some food. Please."

Abby looked at her brother. She thought he looked pale, and

the little lines at the outside corners of his eyes were bunched up tighter than usual. She shifted her gaze to the mattress.

"You're sitting on my friend," Abby said.

Mike snorted and stood. "You know what? Do whatever the hell you want. I don't care."

Mike started stomping toward the door, but then he stopped. He spoke again, with his back to Abby. "But you should know what happens to little kids who don't eat their dinners."

Mike rotated toward Abby in super-slow-motion. He squinted at Abby and scrunched his face into what Abby thought was supposed to be a mean look, like he was trying to be one of the bad guys in a cartoon.

Abby didn't feel like playing along with Mike's stupid game, so she stayed silent. She looked at him, careful to keep her face totally blank.

"When kids don't eat," Mike said, leaning forward, "their bodies stay the same size forever."

Abby shrugged and rolled her eyes.

Mike waggled a finger at her. "And that means that they die without ever getting to ride the adult rides at the amusement park."

Abby almost smiled at that. But Mike didn't deserve a smile.

Abby looked away from Mike, back to the now-empty bed. She studied the spot where Mike had sat.

"My friend says you're an idiot," Abby told Mike, glancing toward him again.

Mike's face went rigid. A vein at the edge of his forehead got bigger and looked like it was hopping up and down under his skin. Abby thought she could hear his teeth grinding as he turned around and headed toward her door.

Just shy of the door, Mike stopped. He looked back at Abby. "At least I'm real," he said. His voice was hard and unfriendly.

Mike strode out of the room and slammed the door behind him. The *kablam* took a couple seconds to fade out. The yucky feeling Mike left behind lingered for longer than that.

Abby looked over at the bed. "He doesn't mean it," she said quietly. "He has stress."

From beyond the door, Mike's bellow was muffled and distant. "No, I don't!" he shouted.

* * *

Mike dropped onto the edge of his turned-down bed. He sat down so hard that the bed's wood-slatted headboard knocked against the wall.

As if in response to the thud, a dog barked in the distance. The *chirr-crackle* of tires on the street and the purr of an engine reached in through Mike's closed window.

Mike looked at his pillow. All he wanted to do was flop down and put his face in it, make like a human ostrich, and block out the day. But he couldn't sleep yet.

Raising his butt off his bed, half-standing, Mike reached under his mattress and grabbed his pill bottle. Wrapping his fingers around the hard, smooth plastic, he closed his eyes, savoring the momentary relief he always felt when he started his nighttime routine.

Mike opened the bottle's childproof cap and pulled out one of the small white pills. Immediately popping the pill in his mouth, Mike reached for the glass of water he'd put on his nightstand. He took a few sips of water, washing down the pill.

Finally. Mike could put this day behind him.

Leaning forward, Mike pushed PLAY on the cassette player. Immediately, his bedroom was filled with peaceful forest sounds. Mike closed his eyes and focused on the sprightly chirps of birds, the cracks and snaps of branches being rustled by the wind. He took a deep breath and let it out slowly. Then he lay down flat on his bed.

Opening his eyes, Mike looked straight up above his bed. Seeing past the images of the day that flicked through his mind like a herky-jerky slide show, Mike focused on the poster taped to his ceiling.

PINING FOR FUN? the poster's heading read, VISIT NEBRASKA.

The words, popping from the paper in a bright yellow block-letter font, paraded across the tops of a shaggy cluster of pine trees. As Mike gazed at the trees, the slide show in his head continued. He saw the ugly, brick government building, the social worker's uneven skirt, and the paper number twenty-seven. He saw Raglan's smug face. He saw a series of HELP WANTED signs and a matching series of head shakes as he was told he wasn't right for the jobs. He saw Max's big eyes and Abby's dark ones. He saw the red delinquency notice and the lasagna he'd ended up throwing away because he'd microwaved it too long and because Abby had never come out of her room to eat.

"Breathe," he told himself, zeroing in on the sounds of the bab-bling brook that were coming from his cassette player. He squinted at the pine trees, putting all his attention on his ritual so he could let the rest of the day fade away.

Briefly, Mike remembered the first night he'd put up the poster. It had seemed like such a stupid idea, but he was desperate. That night, it had taken forever for the cassette's sounds and the poster's image to work their magic. Now, though, the effect was more immediate.

In a matter of seconds, Mike's mind let go of the day's

impressions. His consciousness slipped into the pine tree scene, and the forest sounds grew clearer, more and more realistic.

Mike's gaze was full-on committed now. He was homed in. The forest was no longer a picture on a poster; the trees weren't frozen in a photograph—they were moving. The sounds didn't come from a cassette; they came from a real forest. The wind that Mike could hear was swaying the trees in a gentle back-and-forth rhythm.

Mike's eyelids began to flutter. Then he felt them droop. Lower and lower. Closed.

But the trees didn't disappear.

A gentle breeze caresses the heavy branches of a cluster of pine trees. The branches shimmy back and forth in what almost looks like a choreo-graphed dance.

In front of the trees, a beam of sunshine slants downward onto bright green wild grass. The light catches moisture at the tips of the grass blades, making them sparkle. Above the grass, caught in the sun's brilliant illumi-nation, an orange toy plane arcs through the air.

A little boy's hand grips the body of the plane. The little boy looks to be about four years old. The boy has tousled black hair and bow-like lips.

"Garret," a woman's voice calls out. "Stay close."

Garret and his airplane whip past a picnic table and disappear from view just as a red spray of ketchup splats over a burger on a paper plate lying on the table. A smiling dark-haired man, who looks like an adult version of little Garret, walks past the picnic table. The man, carrying a couple sleeping bags, laughs and calls out, "How about some burger with that ketchup, hon?"

Mike, twelve years old and all about having fun, grins at his mom. She looks at the ketchup bottle in her hand and winks at Mike.

"Everything's better swimming in ketchup. Right, Mike?"

"Right!" Mike reaches for his soda and accidentally knocks over the bottle with a thunk.

The soda's fizzing escape from the bottle sprays across the table. The frothy brownish liquid sounds like it's sizzling as it pools on the wood.

"Oops!" Mike's mom says. She turns away from the table. "I'm going to go grab a towel. Keep an eye on your brother."

Mike starts to turn toward Garret, but as he does the edge of a Frisbee nearly grazes Mike's cheek as it whizzes past. Mike instinctively jumps up and jogs away from the picnic table to retrieve the bright blue disc, which has landed at the edge of his family's campsite.

Mike reaches the Frisbee in seconds, and he bends over to pick it up. As his hand closes over the plastic rim of the disc, Mike hears the sound of a car engine revving.

Mike straightens and looks around. He doesn't see the car, but there's something else even more important that he doesn't see.

"Garret?" Mike calls.

Garret is nowhere in sight. Frisbee dangling from his hand, Mike starts walking toward the far side of the campsite. His pace is casual at first. Then his brother's continued absence fills him with urgency. Mike starts trotting toward the trees that line the little road that leads to the site.

"Garret!" Mike calls again.

Mike hears the crackling, pinging sound of tires churning over gravel. Through the trees, he sees the hulking shape of a black car as it peels away from the campground.

Mike breaks into a full-out run.

"Garret!" Mike's shout is shrill and piercing.

Mike is in the trees now. The long pine needles poke at his face. The branches slap at him; it feels like they're trying to grab him. Fallen twigs and pinecones crackle under Mike's feet. His nostrils are filled with the sharp smell of pine resin and the moist scent of the ground's soft soil.

Mike bursts out of the trees just in time to see the black car pick up speed. The car is at least fifty feet past Mike. It's zooming away.

Mike, panting hard, looks toward the back of the car. His heart feels like it's being twisted in his chest as he looks at car's rear window.

"Garret!" Mike gasps.

Garret's pale, wide-eyed face looks back at Mike through the window. Clutching his orange airplane, Garret puts a hand to the glass. Garret's eyes are filled with tears. His mouth is wide open, calling out.

Mike opens his mouth, too. He starts to let out a scream . . .

The *beep, beep, beep* of Mike's alarm felt like a lasso that cinched up around him and yanked him out of sleep. Pulling a face, Mike reached for his alarm.

Today, his palm managed to find the top of the alarm. As soon as the beeping stopped, Mike smoothly went through his morning routine: Cassette player off. Rewind. Pills under the mattress. Push-ups.

Mike's head didn't hurt as much this morning, but that didn't mean he felt any better. He wouldn't feel better until he could . . . fix things. And after thirteen years of trying, he was starting to think that would never happen.

CHAPTER 5

atching a trio of little boys roll down a grassy hill, their high-pitched whoops tumbling together with their laughter, Mike let himself bask . . . for a few seconds . . . in the kids' glee. The boys were a blur of motion—curly hair, a red tennis shoe, skinny white arms, plump-faced grins, a triumphant fist. The boys appeared to be racing, but their race devolved into a wrestling/ tumbling match. When they reached the bottom of the hill, they shot to their feet and raised triumphant fists; they all seemed to think they won.

What would it be like to be so carefree? Mike asked himself. Thinking about his dream, he reminded himself that he had a micro-taste of that kind of devil-may-care fun every night. He almost wished he didn't, though. When that feeling was stolen from him, over and over and over again, as his dream repeated night after night, the loss was made more profound by that memory of what fun felt like.

The boys ran back up the hill, and Mike watched them start another tumbling round. Then he broadened his gaze to take in the Child Development Center at the top of the hill.

In contrast to the government building Mike had been in the

day before, the Development Center was a sleek, modern, white flow of long, glass-filled walls under a gleaming metal roof. Surrounded by nature—the expanses of grass, as well as expertly landscaped displays of flowering bushes and tall trees—the center was not even in the same universe as the ugly brick building that housed Social Services.

Even the sky was prettier here. Or so it seemed. Yesterday's suffocative gray sky was gone. Today's sky was cyan blue, and it was filled with playful white clouds—all puffy and soft-edged and rolling through the sky, not unlike the boys rolling down the hill. The sun was playing peek-a-boo with the clouds; its brilliance nipped in and out as it peeked from behind the white sky-suds and then dipped back behind them again.

The little boys weren't the only kids having fun on the grassy hills outside the center and on the playground equipment in a sandy circular area near the edge of the grass. Twenty-plus kids were running around or pumping themselves higher and higher on the swings or climbing on the monkey bars or teeter-tottering with a friend. The kids ranged in age from about six to fifteen. The older kids weren't playing. They were either sitting in the grass or on one of the wrought-iron benches placed throughout the area. They either chatted with each other or spoke to white-coated adults. The adults were the doctors—MDs and PhDs—who oversaw the kids who came to the center.

The center's doctors had a wide array of expertise, Mike had found out. They were trained to help all sorts of kids with all sorts of developmental problems.

Leaning against the chain-link fence at the outer edge of the center's sprawling property, Mike vaguely wondered how his life might have turned out differently if he'd had a place like this to come to when he was twelve. Grief was a developmental problem, wasn't it? Loss and guilt could stunt growth every bit as much as the kind of psychological problems they treated here.

Turning away from the more active children, Mike forced himself to look toward his sister. He'd spotted her, of course, as soon as he'd gotten out of his car. Abby sat on one of the benches not far from the center's portico-covered entrance. Bent over her drawing pad with her colored pencils, Abby was well away from all the other kids. Even so, she was talking.

Mike was far enough away from Abby that he couldn't hear what she was saying, but he could see her lips moving. He could also see her turn to look beside her or look out in front of the bench, as if she was speaking to invisible companions.

The sun burst from behind the clouds again, and the light blinded Mike. Closing his eyes, he wiped his face with his palms. Man, he was exhausted. No matter how much time he spent in bed, he never got enough rest. No mystery there. Sleep wasn't sleep for Mike. It was a project.

Mike felt a cool hand on his forearm, and he inhaled the scent of orange blossoms. He opened his eyes and did his best to smile at the slender white-haired woman who stood in front of him.

Dr. Lillian, Abby's psychologist, was a nice lady. With large eyes that might have been dark blue or green or brown (Mike hadn't been able to figure it out because the color seemed to change depending on lighting, or maybe depending on the doctor's mood), Dr. Lillian had a friendly face with a wide, full-lipped smile. Tall and graceful, Dr. Lillian wore her hair in a shaggy, chin-length cut, and her clothes were as casual as her hair; she usually had on loose, light-colored yoga pants and pastel-colored tunic shirts. She didn't wear a lab coat.

"They're here," Dr. Lillian said. "Are you ready?"

Mike's weak smile disappeared entirely. "Not really," he said.

Dr. Lillian patted his arm but she didn't speak. Mike was sure she wanted to help, but there were some things she couldn't do.

"Let's get this over with," Mike said.

*   *   *

Usually, Mike was pretty comfortable in Dr. Lillian's office. A nice large room with thick blue carpet and furnished sparsely but comfortably with a small white desk, a row of matching shelves stuffed with books and a few nature-themed photos, a high-backed, pale blue office chair, three matching plush thick-armed guest chairs, and a long, blue-and-cream-striped sofa, the office was obviously designed to be calming. Most days, it was. But not today.

It wasn't possible for a room to be calming when Aunt Jane was in it. Her presence was calm's kryptonite.

At just five foot four, Jane Schmidt wasn't an imposing woman. Her petite appearance was helped along by the pastel pantsuits she nearly always wore. Today's suit was a very pale green.

When Jane stood still . . . and if you didn't know her . . . she could look insubstantial, even inconsequential. With short, dirty-blonde hair that Mike was pretty sure she dyed now—she was, after all, in her fifties—Jane had a pale, freckled complexion, ordinary brown eyes, and a narrow face shaped like an upside-down egg. In the abstract, she might have been pretty . . . if not for her personality.

"Just look at him!" Mike's aunt angrily shouted. She waved her arms wildly. Combined with her exaggerated facial expressions, the flapping arms made her look unhinged. And she thought *he* had problems.

Well, he did have problems. But that wasn't the point.

Dr. Lillian's guest chairs were arranged in front of her desk, spaced about two feet apart. Two feet wasn't nearly enough space. Mike, sitting to Aunt Jane's left, had to lean back when she threw her arms out.

On the other side of Aunt Jane, her lawyer cowered in the other guest chair. He was sitting so he was canted back and away from his client. Clearly, he didn't want to be close to her any more than Mike did.

Dr. Lillian, safely behind her desk, was the only person sitting straight. She was also the only person in the room who seemed to be benefitting from her calm décor.

"What is it? Ten o'clock in the morning?" Jane continued with her tirade. "And he can barely keep his eyes open."

Mike, who was aware his eyes were half-closed, resisted the urge to shut them entirely. As tired as he was, his eyes weren't drooping because of that. He had them partially shut to try to dampen the impact of his aunt's tantrum. This was a trick he'd learned many years before.

Aunt Jane was wound up for a very specific reason today. She had an agenda. But it wouldn't have mattered if she didn't have one. She was just a high-strung woman. Petty, loud, and judgmental, Jane was the reason Mike had learned the word *narcissistic* when he was a boy. It was the word his mother had always used to describe her sister-in-law.

Jane whipped her arms through the air again. Mike pulled back like a turtle shrinking into its shell. If only he had a shell to shrink into.

"This *degenerate*," Jane continued, "is being entrusted with the well-being of a mentally ill child?"

Mike involuntarily brought a hand up to cover his right ear. Jane's high pitch, which would have done an operatic soprano proud, was literally hurting his eardrums.

Cocking his head, Mike looked behind Jane to see if the lawyer—*"Just call me Doug; I'm not much on formalities"*—was having the same problem, but he couldn't tell. Doug, a large man whose body was freakishly similar in shape to a melting ice-cream cone, gave no indication that he was hearing or seeing anything. The only reason Mike could tell Doug was alive was that Doug's chest heaved visibly with the effort to breathe, and he made a faint whistling sound each time he exhaled.

Studying Doug, Mike had a hard time understanding how the man had become a lawyer, or how he kept a practice going. He looked like he was on the verge of going into a coma. Jane might have been making a big deal about Mike's droopy eyes, but what about her lawyer's slack lids? Heck, his whole face was slack. Round and jowly, Doug's cheeks pressed up against a fleshy nose and squeezed a too-small mouth. His tiny eyes were gray and dull-looking. They matched his suit, which was the color of the previous day's clouds. The suit was baggy and wrinkled.

Mike shifted his attention away from Doug and returned it to his aunt, who was still ranting. He tuned back in, just for kicks. ". . . who care for the mentally ill should have at least a hint of maturity." Jane pointed at Mike's jeans and T-shirt. "Do you see maturity in him?" Jane put her fists on her hips and glared at Dr. Lillian.

Dr. Lillian ignored the question. "As I've made clear many times," Dr. Lillian said, "Abby is not mentally ill."

Aunt Jane made a sound that was half-snort and half-raspberry.

"Oh, right," she said. "Of course not. Because it's perfectly normal to sit around by yourself drawing pictures and talking to magical creatures who don't exist." Jane wound herself up even tighter. "That child is a trainwreck," she shouted. "She's light-years behind where she should be at this age, and it's only going to get worse." By the time Jane got to the end of the sentence, her face was bright red, and her voice was cracking.

"How about we all take a slow breath," Dr. Lillian said, "so we can calm down."

The "we" wasn't a "we" at all. Dr. Lillian was calm. Doug was so calm he was practically unconscious. Mike was tense, but he was calm enough. Jane was the one who . . .

"Don't you dare tell me to calm down!" Jane shrilled. She pointed a finger at Dr. Lillian. "You're *her* doctor. But you're trying to make me feel like *I'm* the cuckoo one here."

There was no trying, Mike thought. Jane was the cuckoo one in the room.

"And what he did to that poor man," Jane said. The volume of her words dropped startlingly, and her tone changed to what Mike thought was supposed to be sympathetic.

Mike watched Jane's lower lip quiver. He suppressed a smile when he saw Jane squinch up her eyes like she was trying to squeeze out a tear.

Jane waved a hand like a Southern belle attempting to stave off an attack of the vapors. "I'm sorry," she said breathily. "I just . . ."

Jane dug a tissue out of a large cream-colored purse. She blew her nose loudly.

Mike glanced over at Dr. Lillian. She met his gaze and gave him a sympathetic look. Real sympathy. Not the fake crap that Jane was attempting to sell to the room.

Jane blew her nose again. Mike, Dr. Lillian, and Doug sat silently. This was a one-woman play. All they could do was wait for her to get to her next line.

Jane finished nose-blowing. She dropped her dirty tissue on the floor. Mike looked at it, and he felt his lip curl. He really hated his aunt.

"Now, look," Jane said.

Mike wasn't sure who she was talking to. Him? Dr. Lillian? Obviously not Doug.

"I tried to play nice," Jane went on. "I really did." She clasped her hands together and pasted a nicey-nice smile on her face.

Mike managed not to puke.

"But I have to think of Abby now," Jane said. She arranged her features into an expression that Mike thought was supposed to be regret. It looked more like constipation. "Enough is enough," Jane said.

Finally, something Mike could agree with. He'd had more than enough of this meeting.

No one said anything. Jane looked at Mike. Then she turned toward Doug.

Doug still looked like he needed a ventilator. Mike wasn't sure Doug had heard a word Jane had said.

"Doug?" Jane said.

Doug didn't move.

Jane leaned over and poked Doug in the ribs, hard. "Doug!" she shouted.

Doug jerked, coughed, and blinked several times. He looked around as if to remind himself of where he was. Once oriented, he cleared his throat and picked up the briefcase that sat next to his small feet. The feet were tucked into expensive black shoes; Mike thought they were called oxfords.

Jane tapped her long, manicured fingernails (covered in pale pink polish that in no way matched her personality) on the slick leather of her bag. She pulled her lips together into a disapproving purse.

Doug was oblivious of his client's scrutiny. He concentrated on opening his briefcase. When he finally pulled out a sheaf of papers, Jane snatched them and turned to shove them at Mike. He had no choice but to take them.

Glancing down, Mike's stomach shriveled. They were custody papers.

"In your heart," Jane said, "you know this is the right thing to do."

Mike didn't know that at all. In his heart or any other part of his body.

"I hope you'll sign," Jane said.

Mike lifted his head. "And if I don't?"

Jane waved a hand toward Doug. "Then my lawyer and I will take you to court, where any judge with an ounce of sanity will make sure you never see your sister again."

Dr. Lillian cleared her throat and began, "That's—"

Jane shot up from her chair and held the flat of her palm toward Dr. Lillian like a traffic cop. "That's it," Jane said. "We're done here."

Jane took a step toward Doug and whacked him on the shoulder. Like an obedient, if abused, dog, he closed his briefcase and stood.

Dr. Lillian stood, too. "What about Abby?" she asked Jane. "Have you considered what she may want?"

Jane slowly turned toward Dr. Lillian. Pulling in her chin and drawing her eyebrows together, Jane tipped her head to one side as if she was studying something in a circus freakshow. "Abby," Jane said, ". . . is . . . ten . . . years . . . old."

*   *   *

In contrast to the serene oasis of Dr. Lillian's office, the Development Center's hallways were a chaos of color and light. The walls were papered in red, purple, and orange stripes, and the hall floor was covered in carpet squares of nearly every color imaginable. When Mike and Abby first met with Dr. Lillian, she had explained that a lot of kids at the center needed an abundance of stimulation.

That might have been the case, but the "visual stimulation" got on Mike's nerves. Especially now.

After Jane and Doug had left Dr. Lillian's office, she'd asked Mike if he needed a minute. He'd shaken his head and stood up. He was really rattled. And furious. And . . . actually, he didn't know exactly what he felt. He couldn't put a word to it. All he knew was that his stomach was in at least fifty separate knots—his colon felt so tangled, he wouldn't have been surprised if food never got through it again. His head didn't feel so good, either. His ears were hot, and he was sure an invisible hand was clamped onto his skull, trying to press him down through the floor.

Mike didn't want to feel this way in front of Dr. Lillian. He needed to get out of there.

That was why they were in the hall. When Mike said he had to go, Dr. Lillian had insisted on walking him out.

Other than all the color, the hall was empty. Surprising himself because he'd planned on just getting away without saying a word, Mike blurted, "She doesn't want Abby. She wants the trust fund."

Dr. Lillian glanced at Mike and gave him a gentle smile of understanding. Dr. Lillian was good at understanding. Maybe that was why Mike kept talking.

"The trust was set up for *Abby*. Not for anyone else. Not me, either. I can't even use it to pay the rent, and that's fine. I'm glad it's there for her."

Dr. Lillian gave Mike another smile. This one seemed to be one of approval.

"But Jane and that lawyer are going to find a way to get into the trust if she gets custody of Abby," Mike went on. "I just know it. That's what her long-term plan is."

Dr. Lillian didn't disagree.

"And in the short term, she'll get the checks from the state," Mike said. "It's not about Abby. It's about Jane. It's always about Jane."

Dr. Lillian opened her mouth but then closed it. Another sympathetic smile told Mike that, once again, she didn't disagree with him.

Together, they turned a corner, heading toward the center's Activity Room. A couple boys about Abby's age went racing past. The smells of dirty socks and chocolate went with them. So did the pounding of their feet.

"She makes some good points, though," Mike said. "Aunt Jane. I hate to admit that. but she's right that I'm not really fit to be raising a kid."

Dr. Lillian finally spoke. "I know a little girl who would strongly disagree."

Mike threw up his hands. "Come on, Doc. You can't be serious. Abby talks to the air more than she talks to me. I could drop dead and she'd be too busy drawing pictures to even notice."

They'd reached the double doors that led into the Activity Room, but Dr. Lillian kept walking. She motioned for Mike to follow her. He did.

Just past the doors, a long, wide window looked into the room with thick, bright blue rubberized flooring and multiple play areas.

Some of the areas were nothing more than a collection of colorful pillows and cushy play cubes that kids stacked into forts or lay on to draw or play games. Some were climbing towers. Some were elaborate cave-like areas similar to Abby's "hidey-tent" but more sophisticated. The play areas were placed wide apart so there was plenty of open space for the kids to run around. Mike did a quick count; nine kids were either chasing one another or playing games.

There were also several little tables dotting the room. The only one currently occupied was the one on the far side of the room. That was where Abby sat. By herself.

Mike gestured toward his sister. "See what I mean?"

Dr. Lillian watched Abby as she spoke. "You know, pictures hold tremendous power for children." Dr. Lillian shifted to face Mike. "You've heard the expression 'Seeing is believing'?"

Mike frowned and shrugged. "Sure."

What was the doctor getting at?

Dr. Lillian crossed her arms and leaned back against the glass. "Before we learn to speak, images are the most important tool we have for understanding the world around us. What's real, what matters to us most, these are things children learn to communicate about almost exclusively through pictures."

Dr. Lillian paused, and Mike nodded. "Okay," he said. He still didn't see her point.

Dr. Lillian cocked her head and thought for a second. Then she tried again. "See, kids aren't all that good at consciously accessing what they feel. Their artwork is sort of like their subconscious."

"So, you're saying Abby's drawings actually mean something?" Mike asked when the lightbulb finally came on.

Dr. Lillian nodded several times. "Without question."

Mike chewed on that for a second.

Dr. Lillian put a hand on his shoulder. "So let me ask you this. Who's featured, prominently, in nine out of ten of Abby's drawings?"

Mike didn't speak, but he knew the answer to Dr. Lillian's question. Mike was in most of Abby's drawings.

Dr. Lillian squeezed Mike's shoulder. "I can see you get it." She laughed. "Like it or not, you're her world." Dr. Lillian chuckled. "You might not believe you're the man for the job, but your sister certainly does."

Mike stared at Dr. Lillian for a few seconds. Then he shifted his attention back to Abby. Could it be true? Was he really the best thing for Abby?

For a second, Mike felt his shoulders lift. His stomach started to unknot. But then the inner snarls kinked up again. His shoulders slumped.

Even if he was good for Abby, how could he take care of her if he couldn't earn enough to support them? And how could he give her what she needed when he couldn't even give himself what he needed? And then there was Aunt Jane. How could he stop her from getting custody? These and a dozen other questions swirled through Mike's mind.

"What if it's not up to me?" Mike asked, voicing one of the questions aloud. "My aunt's an idiot, but she's right. No judge in the world is going to take my side."

Dr. Lillian shook her head. "Don't be so quick to throw in the towel," she said. "You're Abby's primary caregiver. Have been for some time. And you're her immediate family. Demonstrate even a modicum of stability, and a judge might surprise you."

Is that true? Mike wondered. Did he have a chance?

Dr. Lillian tilted her head. "Have you found a job yet?" she asked.

Mike didn't answer the question, but his face must have done it for him. Even a second of thinking about his job-hunting failures probably made him look like he'd just sucked a lemon.

Dr. Lillian patted Mike on the back. "That would be a good place to start," she said.

CHAPTER 6

Mike sat at his kitchen table. In one hand, he held his cell phone. The other hand was turning a soda can around and around on the scratched Formica surface. The ever-circling can was next to Steve Raglan's business card. The card was crumpled.

Sweat beaded the outside of the soda can, and Mike's fingers were wet and getting wetter. Still, he kept turning the can. He couldn't bring himself to do what he knew he needed to do.

Mike glanced over at Abby, who sat on the sofa watching a noisy cartoon. Mike wasn't sure what she was watching, but there was howling coming from the set, and a lot of raucous laughter. It was getting on Mike's nerves.

Well, no, the sounds from the TV weren't really what was getting on his nerves. It was Abby herself who was bugging him.

As Abby watched the TV, she frequently pointed at it and then looked to her left as if sharing a moment with someone Mike couldn't see. Another invisible friend. What was Mike going to do about Abby's imaginary friends?

Looking away from Abby, Mike's gaze landed on the custody papers he'd tossed onto the table when he and Abby had gotten home. He'd left them facedown, but he knew he needed to pick them up and put them away. Abby didn't need to know what was going on . . . yet. Mike stood and stuffed the papers in a kitchen drawer.

The papers reminded Mike of Jane's plan. Mike's attention shifted back to Abby.

"See?" Abby whispered. "Bears *can* do that."

A horrifying thought leaped out of the miasma of confusion in Mike's head. How would Aunt Jane deal with Abby's invisible friends if she had custody? As soon as Mike asked himself the question, he knew the answer. Jane would have Abby put in some kind of institution. And once Abby was put away, Jane would find a way to take all the money in Abby's trust fund.

Mike let go of the soda can, wiped his fingers on his jeans, then pulled the business card closer to him. He punched Raglan's number into his phone.

Abby continued to watch her cartoon and discuss it with her invisible friend. Mike took a deep breath as he listened to the phone ring in his ear.

A click. Raglan's voice. In its raspy mode. "This is Raglan."

"Hi," Mike said. "Mr. Raglan? This is Mike Schmidt."

Raglan didn't speak. All Mike could hear was the faint sound of breathing coming through the phone line.

"Um, the guy who, uh, stomped out of your, ah, office yesterday?" Mike tried.

More silence. Mike counted in his head. One . . . two . . . three . . .

"Ah, yes," Raglan said. His voice had switched to smooth. Then the voice turned gruff. "Mr. I-Can't-Work-Nights."

Mike pulled the phone from his ear and scowled at it. Man, he really did hate this guy.

Mike's gaze flitted to Abby. He gritted his teeth and returned the phone to its proper position.

"The job you told me about," Mike said between his clenched teeth. "Is it still available?"

"Yes, yes," Raglan said. "It's most definitely available. Why? Had a change of heart?"

No, Mike thought. His heart hadn't changed at all. But that didn't matter. He glanced at Abby again.

"How soon could I start?" Mike asked.

*   *   *

Mike's car sputtered as he turned onto the street that led through the most depressed part of town. He didn't blame the car for its hesitation. Mike didn't want to go down this street, either.

Potholed and swaddled—even though the sun was still grasping on to the last of the day, the long, straight road was bordered by testaments to business collapse. On both sides of the cracked and broken asphalt and the crumbling sidewalk that ran alongside it, an endless march of failed or failing enterprises hulked in the descending dusk. A boarded-up factory, a derelict gas station, a small strip mall with only three still-open, dimly lit businesses, a restaurant with only two cars in the parking lot and a half-dark neon sign, a couple of bars that would make a "seedy" bar look upscale—this whole area would depress even the most upbeat person. Since Mike hadn't been upbeat in years, he started at a deficit, and the area shoved him even further down into the dark hole of despair.

Keeping one hand on the steering wheel, Mike used the other

one to hold up the piece of paper he'd scribbled Raglan's directions on. The paper was the cover page of the custody papers.

Mike frowned at the directions and leaned forward to peer left and right through his windshield. "Where the hell is this place?" he asked.

Too bad he didn't have an invisible friend to answer him.

Instead of a helpful invisible friend, Mike had Raglan's voice—in singsong mode—in his head.

"So, here's the deal," Raglan's voice replayed in Mike's mind. The voice rose and fell and sounded muffled, as it had when Raglan had spoken over the phone. "This place, it's pretty out there. It was hugely popular with the kids back in the '80s, but it's been shut down for a long time now. Only reason they haven't given it the wrecking ball treatment is the owner's kind of . . . sentimental. Just can't bring himself to let it go."

There was something weird about the way Raglan said "sentimental," but Mike couldn't figure out what it was. Then or now.

Checking his notes again, Mike spotted the turn he'd been told to look for. He urged the car past another shuttered business—an ex-nail salon. No great loss. There were too many of those in town anyway.

The new street was narrower than the last one. And after just a couple hundred feet, it was no longer bordered by old businesses. Thick stands of tall trees pressed close to the road. It felt like Mike was heading into the countryside.

Before things got too rural, though, Mike saw a deserted parking lot. It was just as Raglan had described it. Mike turned on his signal—out of habit; no one was around. He pulled off the road, into the lot.

As his car crept forward, swirls of drying leaves skimmed across the cracked pavement illuminated by the car's headlights. A few paper cups, a discarded newspaper, and a wadded-up fast-food bag skittered past with the leaves.

Mike pulled his car farther into a lot designed to hold at least fifty or more cars. Judging from the faded-to-almost-invisible white paint demarking the parking spots, it hadn't held that many vehicles in a very long time. Mike pulled into what once would have been the prime parking spot, just a few feet from the night-shrouded entrance of a building that was so hidden in the dark, it was little more than a sprawling shadow. Surrounded by trees and far removed from other businesses, the building had no exterior lights. The old car's headlights did little to give Mike a complete picture of the place. All he saw was red double doors and a boarded-up window.

Mike turned off the engine. Typically, it chugged for a few seconds and then went quiet. Mike looked out his side window.

Even though only minutes had passed since Mike had reached this part of town, dusk had abruptly given way to the night, a night completely lacking in any sort of lighting. Mike was one hundred percent sure he was not in a safe place.

But there was no turning back now.

Looking left and right, Mike steeled himself. He picked up the backpack he'd loaded his overnight needs in. He got out of the car and slung the bag over his shoulder.

Making sure his car was locked—as if anyone would want to steal it—Mike took a few steps toward the barely visible building entrance. Once again, Mike heard Raglan's voice in his head. Back to the rasp. *"Anyway, there's been some trouble with break-ins over the years,"* Raglan said. *"Vagrants, drunks. Obviously, not ideal."*

"No kidding," Mike said aloud now.

He looked around, turning full circle. He seemed to be alone, but there were a lot of places to stay concealed. He gripped the flat strap of his backpack and thought about what he'd packed. He thought he'd remembered everything, but like a dolt, he hadn't thought of a flashlight.

Suddenly, Mike wanted to be inside the building. He felt way too exposed.

Hurrying forward, Mike headed toward the double doors. The doors were faded red, and judging from a few dents on their panels, they were made of metal. He quickly found the security pad next to the doors, just where Raglan had said it would be. The code was an easy one; Mike had it memorized. So, he quickly typed it in.

A loud click came from the door. The disengaged lock, Mike figured. He stepped to his left and grabbed a thick, vertical, black metal handle; he pulled open one of the heavy doors.

The door creaked. Of course it creaked.

Mike ignored the shiver that frisked down his spine. It felt like one of the dry leaves from the road had gotten inside his shirt and was tumbling end-over-end toward his tailbone. Mike stepped into the building.

Leaving the door open . . . just in case, Mike hesitated on the edge of deep gloom. He inhaled several odors that made him doubt whether he'd made the right decision. The air smelled stale . . . not a surprise for an old, mostly unoccupied place. But more than just musty air met Mike's nostrils. Beneath the—

A resounding *clang* nearly launched Mike straight up out of his black sneakers. He whirled.

Either the wind had shoved at the door or it was on a self-closing hinge. The door was shut.

As threatening as the deserted area outside had felt, the closed door was an even more powerful trigger of Mike's fight-or-flight response. His heart rate doubled. He had a powerful urge to throw himself at the door and run for his life.

Which was silly. "Get a grip," he told himself.

Mike's words seemed to caper away from him before coming back. The faint echo rotated him around. He ignored the disconcerting smell of the place and studied his surroundings.

Barely lit beneath fluorescent light panels that had old, dim bulbs and dirty frosted glass coverings, the expanse in front of Mike was a large—maybe thirty feet around—lobby. The right and left sides of the lobby were lined with low, red-vinyl-covered benches. The opening of what looked like a long hallway extended off to the right. The other side of the lobby, opposite Mike, was a large archway. A little light shone through it, but not enough for Mike to see what was beyond it.

Although the lobby's lighting was down-in-the-fathoms dingy, Mike could see enough to be struck by the lobby's almost circus-y décor. The walls above the benches were striped red and white, and the floor beneath Mike's feet was covered with black-and-white-checked linoleum. The linoleum was cracked, and whole sections of it were peeling away from the floor. Hanging on the striped walls, rows of large old-fashioned posters behind glass advertised FREDDY FAZBEAR'S PIZZERIA.

Mike took a step forward. His shoe caught on a curl of linoleum, and it crackled.

Once again, Mike heard Raglan's voice in his head. *"The security system's dated, but it's fully operational. Floodlights on the exterior. Cameras inside and out. Fair warning: The power can be a bit . . . screwy. If you have any issues, you'll find the system breaker in the main office. Just give it a flip."*

As soon as Raglan's voice faded from Mike's brain, the

already-weak overhead lights flickered. Mike looked up at them. "Oh, no you don't."

He'd better find the office, he thought. Quickly.

Mike crossed the lobby and looked down the hallway. The six-foot-wide corridor was long, and it wasn't any better lit than the lobby. At the far end of the hallway, fifty feet away from Mike, a bright red EXIT sign glowed. Mike used it as his North Star as he stepped forward into what felt like a creepy, dark tunnel.

Raglan's voice spoke up in Mike's head again. Mike made a face. He really didn't like having the rasp/singsong on automatic play in his mind.

"Now," Mike heard Raglan say in his memory, *"the rest of the building is on a different breaker, which was probably installed back when Reagan was still in office."*

Mike mentally hit mute on Raglan as he carefully continued forward. Mike kept his gaze sweeping left and right as he went.

Mike's footsteps made a *swish-tap* sound as he walked over more of the old black-and-white linoleum. Mike could hear his breathing, too. He was still on edge.

The hallway's walls were painted in the same red-and-white stripes Mike had seen in the lobby. They also were lined with large, framed posters. These posters, however, weren't pizzeria advertisements. They were more art than marketing. Some of the posters had images of pizzas and playing children. The rest of the posters featured portraits of odd-looking cartoon animals. One of the images was of a brown bear wearing a bow tie and a top hat. The bear looked friendly enough. But Mike took pause when he continued on and spotted a bright yellow chick wearing a bib and holding a googly-eyed cupcake, a bluish-purple bunny gripping an electric guitar, and a fox wearing an eye patch and sporting a lethal-looking hook at the end of one arm. The toothy grins on those critters didn't look as benign. Mike found the fox especially to be disconcerting. The fox's one uncovered eye seemed to sparkle with good cheer, but the way the fox brandished the hook suggested that the amiability was a façade.

Mike kept going. Above him, another bank of fluorescent lights dimmed a little.

Raglan's voice returned to Mike's mind. *"My advice to you: Don't mess with anything. Unless, you know, you've got a burning desire to die in an electrical fire. No pun intended."*

Ha ha, Mike thought as he looked up at the feeble light.

Mike took another step, and he stiffened when he heard a loud crunch. He looked down and relaxed. Just broken glass from one of the poster frames. Mike looked up at the one to his right. It featured all four of the cartoon animals. All but the fox stood on a stage behind old-fashioned microphones. The fox was off to the left, on his own purple-curtained stage. Something about the separation felt threatening to Mike.

He quickly went past the poster. He looked ahead and spotted the doorway he was aiming for.

Raglan's voice kicked in again. *"You'll find the office at the end of the main hall. Last door on the right."*

Mike reached the door. Like the main door to the building, it was red metal, scarred, and dented. Very dented. It looked like someone, or something, had tried to bash the door in. The frosted glass window in the upper part of the door, however, was intact. Strange.

Mike frowned at the dents, but he reached for the black knob. It turned readily, and Mike eased the door open. Once again, he was tense, poised to flee.

Geez, he thought. *Why am I so freakin' jumpy?*

When Mike stepped into the office, nothing attacked him. Nothing reassured him, though, either.

The office, dimly lit only by a red, round blaze coming from a colored bulb above a large breaker box with a prominent red handle, was small and confining. Probably because of the single red bulb, the room made Mike think of the command rooms in submarines. The sensation of being submerged was heightened not just by the room's darkness but also by its rank air. The last time Mike had smelled something like the air in this room, he'd been in a boxing gym with a friend. The smells there had been a combination of sweat and blood.

Mike's nose twitched as he looked around. He might as well get used to the smell and familiarize himself with the space. He was going to be spending a lot of time in it.

The office was pretty sparse. It contained a long, narrow, black metal desk, which sat in front of a matching credenza. A small black fan and a landline phone next to an answering machine sat on it. The desk held an old TV sitting on top of an equally old VCR, a desktop computer, and several CCTV monitors, stacked on a rack at the back edge of the desk. Two gray metal filing cabinets were pushed against the wall opposite the desk. One of the filing cabinets was missing a couple drawers. The other was badly banged up along the front, as if it had been knocked over. Mike's gaze dropped to the floor. He saw long scratch marks that seemed to match the length of the filing cabinet. The marks didn't make him any happier than the office's smell did.

Mike pulled his gaze from the scratch marks. He looked up at the unlit fluorescent lights above him. He noticed the bank of lights was next to an intercom speaker.

Mike looked toward the breaker box again. Next to the breaker box, a large gray metal locker stood alone, looking like it had run away from its friends in a high school hallway. Mike raised an eyebrow. Was he supposed to keep his stuff in that?

"Mostly you'll just be hanging out in the office," Raglan's voice played out in Mike's head again. *"The job's pretty easy. Just keep an eye on the monitors . . . and don't let anyone in. Piece of cake, right?"*

The very second that Mike's inner-Raglan-voice stopped, the feeble light in the office and in the hallway went out completely. All the electricity cut out. The only remaining illumination came from the red emergency bulb.

"Uh, uh," Mike said. "Nope."

He immediately strode toward the bulb and grabbed the lever on the breaker box. As he shoved the lever upward, Raglan's voice started up again. *"See you on the flip side,"* Raglan had said.

CHAPTER 7

Mike stood next to the chair behind the desk and stared at the CCTV monitors. His gaze was locked on the middle one, which provided an exterior view of the building Mike was in.

Apparently, flipping the breaker lever had done more than get the interior lights back on. It had also tripped whatever switch controlled the outside lights.

Staring at the lights on the monitor now, Mike wasn't sure whether seeing the exterior lit up would have encouraged him or discouraged him from coming inside. The garish signage was supposed to be welcoming, he was sure, but it had the opposite effect on Mike. Maybe that was because the lights, although on, were constantly flickering, alternately casting a harsh glare and uninviting shadows out from the sprawling building.

Resembling a slumped, sleeping giant in the warring glare and shadows, the building clearly had seen better days. Roof sagging, paint peeling, gutters dangling, the building's windows were boarded over. Even so, the CCTV monitor revealed a lit-up, faded red sign that read FREDDY FAZBEAR'S PIZZERIA. In the blossom of a sputtering spotlight, a cutout of the famed dude himself, the big brown bear Mike had seen on the hallway posters, looked out over the empty parking lot. The bear's full-toothed grin was probably supposed to shout, "Come on in!" Again, it had the opposite effect on Mike.

Sighing, Mike looked at the VCR. Raglan had told Mike to look for a tape in the desk's top drawer. Mike reached out and pulled that drawer open. Sure enough, a VCR tape sat next to a few pens. Mike grabbed the tape before he sat in the desk's rolling gray-vinyl office chair. Then he shoved the tape into the old VCR. He hit the power button on the TV.

A *click*, a *whir*, and a *thunk*, and a few wavy tracking lines crackled onto the TV screen. Staticky old-timey cartoon music played, and the tracking lines gave way to a graphic version of Freddy Fazbear and the pizzeria's logo.

Mike raised an eyebrow at the tinny music but he leaned back in the chair and put his attention on the TV screen as the logo dissolved into a title: "Freddy Fazbear's Pizzeria— Security Brief." The cartoon music faded and loud '80s rock music began.

Mike watched the tape's title break into a gazillion pixels as the title was replaced by a large restaurant dining room filled with happy families eating, talking, and laughing. A dozen or so little kids played or danced in the aisles between the tables.

A merry-faced woman with curly strawberry blonde hair beamed at the camera. Her jolliness would have put Santa to shame. Mike found himself leaning back farther, as if he could escape the woman's merriment.

The woman had pretty blue eyes and pouty, red-painted lips

that she stretched into a big smile as she sang out, "Welcome to Freddy Fazbear's Pizzeria, a magical place for kids and grown-ups alike, a place where fantasy and fun come to life!"

The woman flung out her arms, and for a second, Mike thought she was going to twirl with glee. But she didn't. Instead, she said, "If you're watching this video, it means you've been selected as Freddy's newest security guard. Congratulations! We're going to have so much fun together!"

Mike raised an eyebrow. "We are?" he asked the TV screen. He shook his head as he kept watching.

On the TV, the dining room scene and the woman flip-flopped away, and then the woman reappeared in front of a packed, brightly lit arcade. The arcade, lined with full-sized games—pinball machines, Skee-Ball machines, as well as a bunch of games Mike didn't recognize—featured a huge network of plastic towers and tunnels. These crisscrossed over a giant plastic-ball pit. Even without all the blissed out little kids playing, it was clear the place was any child's dream playground.

The woman began speaking again. "The genius who created Fazbear Entertainment opened Freddy Fazbear's Pizzeria to indulge in his two greatest passions: Family-Friendly Fun and Cutting-Edge Animatronic Technology!"

On the screen, the arcade swirled into a black hole, and another room burst into view. Mike didn't think this room looked like nearly as much fun. Stuffed full of metal shelves and work tables, the room on the screen now was filled with what looked like robotic parts. In the center of the room, a reclining metal chair was occupied by an unmoving animatronic. It was tough to tell what the animatronic was meant to be. Mike could only see some blond fur at the edges of an expanse of metal endoskeleton and a tangle of wires. A white-coated man Mike guessed was a technician was probing at the wires with a tool that looked like a cross between a pair of pliers and a pair of snipping shears. The tool was almost evil-looking—sharp and hard.

The woman reappeared on the screen. Still looking relentlessly happy, she trilled, "State-of-the-art robotic engineering enables our characters to interact with guests in truly lifelike fashion, while cleverly concealed, rechargeable lithium cells give the characters limited range to roam free." The woman rose up on her tiptoes. "Safety first!"

The screen suddenly went dark, and then the woman reappeared. Now she stood in front of an expanse of velvety red stage curtains.

"This should be good," Mike muttered.

The woman on the screen said in hyped-up tones, "Let's introduce you to the stars of the show! Hit it, guys!" The woman made a sweeping gesture with her left arm.

The woman on the screen disappeared, and the TV was filled with the image of a hand striking a palm-sized red plastic button. The label above the button read SHOWTIME!

The curtains once again filled the TV screen. The woman was no longer in front of them, and the curtains were starting to part. An inch. Two. Three. Four. The hems of the curtains fluttered as they moved, and then . . .

The image on the screen froze and then dissolved into a blur of tracking lines. Mike leaned forward and whacked the side of the small TV. He didn't think it would do any good, but . . .

The TV emitted the sound of distorted laughter, and the woman suddenly reappeared on the screen. She now stood in front of the pleated, pulled-back curtain. She was looking to her right, apparently toward whatever was on the now-exposed stage. "Adorable, aren't they?" the woman asked, using a cutesy voice. "These cuddly critters, and the proprietary technology that brings them to life, are now your sacred duty to protect. Keep them safe. And help ensure that Freddy Fazbear's Pizzeria is here to delight, dazzle, and entertain for years to come!"

The screen went black. Mike stared at it. "Seriously?" he asked aloud.

The desk chair let out a squeal as Mike leaned forward and pulled the tape from the VCR. He stuck it back in the desk drawer and then shifted his attention to the CCTV monitors. There were nine of them. Each one was streaming footage of various rooms in the restaurant or some angle of the restaurant's exterior or its surroundings. All of the images were black and white, and they were blurry . . . low resolution. The obscure, monochromatic scenes reminded Mike of setting shots in old horror movies. Even though the areas appeared to be empty, they clearly hinted at trouble lurking off-screen. They were supremely creepy.

Mike lifted his gaze and looked around the room again. His attention landed on the lone locker. Randomly, his mind was suddenly filled with the image of seeing one of the boys in his school—Bobby, a poor skinny kid who was teased relentlessly—being stuffed into his locker. The little hairs on the back of Mike's arms bristled as he looked at the slats at the top of the locker. What exactly was in the thing?

Mike tried to dismiss the question, but he knew he wouldn't be able to settle until he satisfied himself that the locker was empty . . . or that it was at least filled with something benign and inanimate.

Leaving his backpack on the desk next to the TV, Mike got up and walked over to the locker. Hesitating only a second, he reached out and yanked on the locker's unsecured lock. The locker door swung open and slapped back against the wall with a clang as Mike looked into the locker.

His gaze met the bug-eyes of a rosy-cheeked, grinning little boy.

Mike yelped and immediately slammed the locker door shut again. He backed away from the locker and stared at it. His heart felt like it was detonating in his chest.

What the hell was that?

Mike's brain provided him with a replay of what he'd seen. He'd seen a boy. Shiny skin. Too-colorful face. Too much white in the eyes. And most important . . . the boy was very, very puny. Conclusion: it wasn't a real boy.

Mike rolled his eyes at his own skittishness. He breathed in and out evenly, and then he stepped forward. This time, Mike pulled the locker door open slowly.

Sitting on the locker's top shelf, the boy gazed at Mike placidly. Not a boy. A doll.

The doll wore a pin-striped, propellor-topped cap and held a satiny red balloon. The doll was too short to have been mistaken for a real child. Unless you'd gotten yourself worked into a jump-at-your-own-shadow state of high anxiety.

"I really need to calm down," Mike said.

The boy doll didn't agree, but it didn't disagree, either. The boy's grin, however, did make Mike feel like the doll was laughing at him.

Mike looked at the doll's bulging eyes. Little worms of unease crawled up Mike's neck.

He quickly reached out and turned the doll's head so its face was aimed toward the back of the locker. "There, Balloon Boy," Mike said. "Laugh at that."

Mike dropped his gaze from the doll and inspected the rest of the locker, wanting to be sure it didn't hold any more creeptastic toys. Thankfully, it didn't. There were only two other things in the locker. One was . . . great! . . . a flashlight, one of the big black ones that could be used as a weapon if necessary. (Mike really hoped it wouldn't be necessary.) The second thing in the locker was a Freddy Fazbear–branded red security vest. Mike studied the vest for a second, then he shrugged.

"Why not?" Mike tugged the vest from its wire hanger.

Mike grabbed the flashlight, gave Balloon Boy one last glance (to be honest, he wanted to make sure it was still turned toward the back of the locker), and shut the locker door. Stepping over to the desk, he set the flashlight where he'd be able to grab it quickly if the power went out again. Then he slipped on the vest. He might as well look the part.

*　*　*

Armed now with the hefty flashlight and a determination not to be so on edge, Mike decided he'd be more comfortable if he explored his surroundings a bit. The office itself didn't feel like much of a safe haven, and so Mike wanted to know what else the building held. He decided to start with the main dining room he'd seen in the video.

Mike left the office and headed back down the main hall. Bypassing all the closed doors (not because he was afraid of what was behind them . . . nope, not afraid at all), Mike retraced his steps back to the lobby. As he went, he shone his flashlight every which way. He didn't see much that he hadn't noticed before, except he did see that the hallway ceiling had intercom speakers like the one in the office. He figured they were probably all over the restaurant.

When Mike reached the lobby, he turned toward the archway. Then he strode through it and looked around.

Although the building's power was full-on, the cavernous dining area—it had to be at least a hundred feet square—was still filled with puddles of black and gray and the palest of dirty yellow. Mike looked up, and he saw that the yellow came from moonlight shining through a bank of dirty skylights.

Mike looked around and he saw a light switch to the left of the archway. He took a step toward it, but then he remembered Raglan's warnings about the electrical system. He didn't want to risk plunging the entire building into pitch darkness again. So, he flicked on his flashlight.

As soon as Mike aimed his flashlight at the expanse in front of him, he kind of wished he hadn't turned it on. The scene was bleak.

Maybe if Mike hadn't watched the video, he wouldn't have been as put off by the vacant, filthy, desolate room. Mike's mind, however, was still filled with the bright, happy scenes from the video. He'd expected to find a colorful room filled with tables. Instead, he was looking at a wasteland. Only a few tables remained, and these were covered with dust or filthy, torn tablecloths. A few toppled stacks of chairs were scattered around the room. The black-and-white floor was littered with debris—party hats, paper plates, napkins, empty cups.

Kicking one of the cups, Mike walked toward the two stages on the opposite side of the room. One of the stages was covered with an older version of the red curtain he'd seen in the video. The velvet on the curtain now was matted, and the red was faded. Over a smaller stage to the left, a purple curtain with gold stars sagged. Mike recognized it from the poster in the hallway. He sincerely hoped the fox from the poster wasn't lurking behind the curtain.

To counter the sudden melancholy the neglected and forgotten dining room had created, Mike whistled . . . loudly. The sound rang through the room, swirling out away from him and then returning. It reminded him of the way his words had echoed back to him in the lobby. Weird.

Mike shook his head, reminding himself that he'd decided not to be spooked. He whistled again, even louder. He started to take a step forward.

A loud clatter jerked Mike into full-startle. He sucked in a gasp and snapped his flashlight beam toward the sound.

His flashlight's rays were aimed at the curtains that covered the stage. What was back there? Was someone else here?

"Hello?" Mike called out.

As soon as he threw out the word, he regretted it. How many times had he laughed at a character in a movie when they called out "Hello?" If someone was here, it probably wasn't someone up to any good. And now, Mike had announced his presence and his exact location. Brilliant.

Mike kept his flashlight aimed at the curtains. They didn't move.

Staying very, very still, Mike listened. He heard nothing. Not even his own breathing.

Mike realized he'd stopped breathing. He started again.

Shining his light in a full circle, Mike decided there were way too many potential hiding spots in the room . . . not the least of which was behind the closed curtains. The flashlight . . . and the wimpy moonlight . . . didn't give him even close to an acceptable view of the area around him.

Mike turned and strode to the light switch. Using it was worth the risk.

Mike reached the switch quickly. He flipped it upward.

Nothing happened.

Mike flicked the switch up and down several times. *Click, click, click.* No light.

"Perfect," Mike said.

The word toyed with him the same way his whistle had. Mike decided to keep his mouth closed from now on.

For a second, Mike thought about retreating back to the office. But if someone was in here, wasn't it his job to find them?

I'm not getting paid enough for this, Mike thought. Even so, he stepped away from the light switch. Taking a deep breath, he advanced farther into the room.

Feeling vulnerable out in the middle of the room, Mike decided to hug the right wall. That wall, he noticed, was covered with children's drawings. Maybe a hundred or more stick-figure drawings, not unlike many of Abby's masterpieces, plastered the dining room's wall like wallpaper. Yellowed and curling, the drawings fluttered as Mike passed them.

Although Mike's flashlight beam illuminated the drawings, he gave them only cursory attention. His focus was on the main stage. That was where the sound had come from.

Past the drawings, Mike reached a short flight of stairs that led up to the stage. Near the steps, a hand-sized red button was on the wall. It was the button from the video. The SHOWTIME letters above it were faded, barely legible. If Mike hadn't known what it said, he might not have been able to piece the word together.

Mike aimed his flashlight at the button. He shook his head. No way in hell was he going to press that thing.

Mike passed by the button. He climbed the steps up to the stage.

Making sure to walk far enough in front of the curtains that he was beyond arm's reach of anything that might want to come out from behind them, Mike stepped softly over the dusty wood stage floor until he reached the middle of the stage where the two sides of the curtains met. He shone his light at the half-inch gap between them.

Straightening his posture, as if a shoulders-back, soldier-like stance would prepare him for whatever he was about to face, Mike reached out and took the edge of the curtain in his left hand. The velvet was crusty beneath his fingertips.

Mike pulled the curtain farther back. Leading with his flashlight, he poked his head behind the curtain.

When Mike's flashlight beam landed on the first grinning, bigtoothed mouth, the beam immediately jerked away. That took the light to another massive grin. And another.

Stunned and awed by the size of the tooth-filled mouths he was seeing, Mike steadied his light and aimed it so it illuminated as wide a view as possible. As soon as he took in the whole scene, his awe morphed into dread.

Mike immediately stepped back. Still clutching the curtain in his left hand, not because he wanted to but because his fingers had spastically clamped on the velvet material, he retreated. The curtain came with him, pulling up and away from the stage floor and opening a wider gap. Mike swept his flashlight left and right, and then he quickly shot the light away from what he was seeing.

Finally dropping the curtain, Mike turned. He didn't bother to head for the stage stairs. He just leaped off the stage and started hotfooting it through the dining room.

As Mike ran, his brain provided him with a recap of what he'd just seen: the huge white eyes that hovered above all the leering grins that had sent him scampering away like a bunny rabbit pursued by a hawk.

The eyes. Bunny rabbit.

Had Mike really seen what he'd thought he'd seen?

A chill cascaded through Mike's body like a freezing waterfall. He ran faster.

Mike tried to tell himself that his brain was playing tricks on him. He hadn't seen what he thought he'd seen.

But he knew he was lying to himself.

Just as Mike had dropped the curtain, one set of white eyes, the set that belonged to the big blue bunny, had shifted. It had watched Mike's retreat.

CHAPTER 8

Sticking to his trusty nighttime routine was more than a little challenging for Mike, given the circumstances. A multitude of obstacles stood between Mike and the normal flow of his bedtime ritual.

First, of course, there was the fact that he was at work. He hadn't been hired to sleep. But to heck with that. Who was going to know if he slept instead of watching the creepy monitors?

Second, there were the contents of the building Mike was in. As much as he tried to convince himself that he hadn't seen the bluish-purple bunny move its eyes to watch him, he knew he had. If the bunny could watch him, what else could it do? What else could the other animatronics do? Mike had assumed they were powered down . . . but were they?

Third, Mike wasn't tired. He was too freaked out to be tired. But then . . . that's what the pills were for.

Mike pondered these and other issues for an hour or so after he returned to the office. He also watched the office door, which he'd locked. When nothing had come to get him during that hour, Mike had decided to stick to his well-established bedtime habits. But first, he dragged one of the filing cabinets—the battered one—over to the door. Looking again at the scratches on the floor, he wondered if he wasn't the first one to use the cabinet as a barricade. If so, what did the scratches mean? He didn't let himself think about it.

Returning to the desk, Mike looked at the chair. Not ideal for sleeping, but if he put his head on the desk, he could make it work.

Mike opened his backpack and started pulling out what he needed. Pills . . . check. Bottle of water . . . check. Cassette player . . . check. *Dream Theory* . . . check. Alarm clock . . . Mike looked down at his watch. He'd decided to use his watch as his alarm clock instead of bringing his clock from home. He set his watch alarm now.

Mike laid the paperback book next to the cassette player. Then he took his pill.

Looking at the door one last time, Mike shifted his gaze to the wall clock opposite the desk. The hour hand was halfway between midnight and one a.m.

Mike looked at all the monitors in turn. Parking lot, lobby, hallways, kitchen, arcade, dining room, storage rooms, back of the restaurant, front of the restaurant. All empty. All quiet.

Mike put his head down on his folded arms. He closed his eyes.

Besides his bed, of course, there was one piece of Mike's nightly arsenal that he hadn't brought with him—the poster. But even so, when he closed his eyes, he immediately saw the swaying pine trees. He heard the breeze, too.

Drifting into unconsciousness, Mike twitched and frowned. Was that a breeze he was hearing? It didn't sound quite right. It sounded more like static than a breeze, as if he was hearing the scratchy modulation of feedback coming through a speaker, maybe an intercom.

This thought almost derailed Mike's descent into dreamland, but the pull of the pine trees' undulation was too strong. Mike ignored the crackling that marred the soothing sound of the breeze. He let the pine trees drop him into the scene that was so familiar to him.

The scene, however, didn't flow smoothly in Mike's mind tonight. It came in snatches.

Gyrating tree branches.

Orange toy airplane flying through the air.

A spray of ketchup.

"How about some burger with that ketchup, hon?" Mike's dad asks.

Thump.

Fizz.

Mike's mom's voice calls out, "Keep an eye on your brother."

Frisbee whizzing.

Car engine revving.

Twelve-year-old Mike shouts, "Garret!"

Branches slapping Mike's face.

Black car zooming away.

Garret's pale face in the car's back window.

Mike opens his mouth to scream. And for once, the scream makes it out of his mouth.

"Garret!"

Mike watches the black car disappear around a bend. Then . . .

Mike hears children laughing. The sound comes from behind him.

Confused, Mike turns.

Five children stand in the middle of the now-empty road. One of them wears a paper top hat. One has a paper bib tied around his neck. One wears paper rabbit ears on her head. One holds a paper hook.

The fifth child, a blond boy with icy-blue eyes, stands out in front of the other children. He has no paper props.

Mike stares at the blond boy. "Who are you?" he asks. "How did you get here?"

The boy says nothing.

In the periphery of Mike's vision, he sees the other children playing. For a moment, they seem strangely abstract, oversimplified. They're almost two-dimensional, like paper dolls instead of real children.

As soon as Mike turns and looks at the children full-on, though, the children are perfectly real. Mike shifts his gaze back to the blond boy. As his focus transitions, he gets the same cardboard-cutout impression of the kids.

Quickly reorienting to look at the kids straight-on, the flattened affect disappears again. Mike frowns, baffled.

As bewildered as he feels, however, Mike has a little fire of exhilaration flickering in his belly. Whatever's happening is new, different than anything he's seen before.

Mike steps toward the blond boy as he gestures back over his shoulder to where the car disappeared. "Did you see that car?" Mike asks. "Did you see what happened?"

The blond boy studies Mike as if Mike is an ant invading a picnic.

Mike tries again. "Did you see who took my brother?"

The blond boy smiles. Beyond him, the other children are back in 2-D, like they've stepped off the page of a book.

Mike looks directly at the children. They're real again.

Once, twice, three times, Mike adjusts his gaze. Focusing. Unfocusing. Focusing. Unfocusing. Focusing. Unfocusing. The children turn into flattened images and then swell back into 3-D.

Finally, the children abruptly scatter. All five of the kids run. They go in five different directions.

Mike calls out, "Wait!" He looks from one fleeing child to the next, trying to decide which one to follow.

Mike finally chooses the blond boy, who is just starting to disappear into the woods. Mike takes off at a full sprint.

Pine branches thwack at Mike's face as he strains to keep the boy in his sights. He can see flashes of blond hair through the branches. If he can just stay with the boy until they're out of the trees . . .

Thunk! *Mike's foot hits a rock. He loses his balance and pitches forward, his body flying toward the ground.*

Mike opened his eyes and discovered he was pitching forward out of his chair. His body flew toward the floor. His head cracked against the hard linoleum.

Moaning, Mike put a hand to his forehead. He winced when his fingers pressed against a lump near his temple.

"Ow!" Mike pulled his hand back from the tender area. He pushed off the floor and managed to get to his knees. Just as he started to get his bearings, a shrieky *beep* started stabbing at the pain in his head.

Mike scrambled to his feet and clumsily poked at his watch, managing to shut off the alarm. He looked at the digital numbers. It was six a.m.

Dropping back into the office chair, Mike slowly leaned forward and hit rewind on his cassette. He picked up his paperback book and fluttered its pages absently.

What had happened to his dream? Who were those kids?

Mike rubbed the sleep from his eyes. He flinched when he once again encountered the bump on his forehead.

Mike dropped his hands and looked around the office. It was as he'd left it before he'd gone to sleep. But something about it . . .

Mike had never had a dream like that before. It couldn't be a coincidence that it happened when he was in this room.

He thought about the dream. The kids. The top hat. The bib. The bunny ears. The hook.

Had he just so weirded himself out that his fears had penetrated his dream? Or was something more going on?

Mike's stomach was contracted with fear and confusion. But it also fluttered. It fluttered with excitement. Was he on the verge of a breakthrough?

* * *

The rising sun's beams followed Mike through the door as he stepped into his house. The beams stretched out ahead of Mike and landed on Max, who was prone on her stomach on the sofa. The TV was, predictably, on QVC.

Mike, his body feeling like it was buzzing, dropped his backpack and a white bakery bag on the kitchen table. He'd been so spun up by what had happened in his dream that he'd splurged and gotten donuts from the bakery at the grocery store. Chocolate-iced. Their sweet scent now combined with a lingering smell of microwaved egg rolls. Mike didn't like egg rolls, but the fried smell was far better than any smells he'd encountered at the pizzeria.

The pizzeria. Mike had thought the job there was going to be nothing but a pain in the butt. Who knew it would have such an effect on his dreams? Mike hadn't felt so buoyed in . . . well, he wasn't sure he'd ever felt this way, at least not in thirteen years.

Max let out a soft snore. Mike stepped over to the TV and turned it off. Then he touched Max's shoulder, barely. Just a brush against the dark purple fabric of her blouse.

She raised her head with a snort, wiped drool from her mouth, and yawned. When she spotted Mike, she quickly sat up and finger-combed her long hair. Then she wiped sleep from her eyes.

Max's cheeks looked flushed. He hoped she wasn't coming down with something. She was the best . . . make that the most affordable . . . sitter he'd found for Abby.

"How'd it go?" Max asked.

Mike thought again about his dream. He lifted one shoulder. "It was . . . interesting. Not the best job in the world. But I need it, like as a reference. For the judge who might try and take . . ." He waved a hand. "Never mind."

Max nodded, then quickly looked away from Mike. Weird. He'd never seen her act so . . . skittish.

"You want a donut?" Mike asked.

"No thanks." Max's response was flat. Weird again.

Max wasn't exactly Miss Bubbly, but she was usually good for some sarcasm or sass. And she always looked him in the eye. Why was she avoiding his gaze?

Mike frowned. "I do intend to pay you, you know. At some point." He picked up the donut bag. "You sure you don't want a donut? Advance against your pay?" He tried a grin.

Max shook her head. She didn't smile. "It's okay," she said. "I know where you live."

Mike chuckled. Max didn't.

Max gathered up her stuff. Mike thought her posture was off, a little hunched. Maybe she was sick.

"You feel okay?" Mike asked.

Max startled. Her flush deepened. "Huh? Yeah, sure. I'm fine."

She wasn't fine. Something was off. Mike thought about pushing to see what was up, but he had his own stuff to think about.

"See you tonight?" Mike asked.

Max gave him a half-nod. She looked at Mike and started to open her mouth. Then she closed it.

For several long seconds, Mike and Max looked at each other. Out of the blue, and for the first time, Mike thought, *Max is a pretty girl*. Mike had always had too much going on to think about Max as pretty. She was just his babysitter. And now she looked like a babysitter who had something she wanted to say. Was she going to quit? Mike held his breath and waited.

Finally Max spoke. "She's a really good kid, you know," she said.

Huh? That was not what Mike had expected. At all. *What did Max mean by that?*

Mike didn't get a chance to ask. Max was already out the door.

*　*　*

Abby's room was bright with early-morning sunlight. She could feel it warming her closed eyelids. But she wasn't ready to open her eyes yet. Abby hugged Dolph close and burrowed deeper under the covers. She wanted to spend just a few more minutes with her friends.

Abby could be with her friends when her eyes were open, too. But sometimes it was easier to hang out with them when she was sleeping, or when she was just going into or coming out of sleep.

Abby heard Mike open her door and walk over to her bed. Not

ready to talk to her brother, Abby pretended she was asleep.

Abby listened to Mike walk to her bed. She concentrated on keeping her breathing slow and even.

The mattress dipped as Mike lowered himself to the edge of her bed. What was he doing? Abby couldn't remember the last time Mike had sat at the edge of her bed while she was sleeping (or pretending to sleep).

Tempted to open her eyes and find out what was going on, Abby decided to wait it out. She kept breathing slowly.

When Mike reached out and brushed a lock of Abby's hair from her cheek, she was sure she jerked a little. But maybe she didn't, because Mike didn't seem to notice. He smoothed her hair and stayed where he was.

Okay. That was enough. This was too weird.

Abby opened her eyes.

"Hey, Abs," Mike said.

"Hey."

Abby looked at her brother. Something was different about him. He didn't look as tense as usual. He almost looked . . . happy? No, not quite. But something.

Mike stood. "I need to grab a shower. Then we have to get you to school."

Abby nodded. Mike ruffled Abby's hair. That was strange, too.

He gave her a quick grin and left her room.

* * *

Slouched in the corner of a cracked, gray-vinyl booth that smelled like lemon cleaner, Maxine put her shoulder against the adjacent window. The window glass felt cool through the mud-brown top she'd put on just for this meeting at Sparky's Diner. The top felt appropriate: it looked dirty, and this meeting made Maxine *feel* dirty.

Usually, Maxine loved the aromas of a diner—that distinctive mix of bacon-and-eggs and waffles-and-pancakes breakfast foods and burgers-and-fries lunch fare. She was probably one of the few people in the world who loved the smell of fry oil. Today, however, the food smells were making her feel queasy. Or, no. It was why she was here that was making her feel queasy.

Ignoring the conversational buzz and glasses-and-dishes clinks and other clatter around her, Maxine stared out the window and watched a swelling black cloud rush toward the sad, faded octagonal building. The cloud's shape was eerily skull-like—complete with what looked like vacant eyeholes and a hungry maw. The cloud had already consumed the bright sun that had dominated the morning, and now it looked like it wanted to gobble up the old, run-down greasy spoon.

A sharp elbow jabbed into Maxine's rib. She turned and frowned at her brother. "Space," she said. She didn't have to say more. Jeff understood her shorthand. He scooted a few inches away from her.

Even though Jeff was ten years older, the two of them were close. When Maxine was little, both of their parents had worked two jobs. Jeff had been more than a brother to Maxine—he'd been something closer to a surrogate dad, even if he was a screwup at it. At ten, Jeff hadn't known squat about taking care of a baby. In the weeks after Maxine's mom's maternity leave had ended, Jeff had done his best. Even so, he'd lost his sister more than once, nearly drowned her, dropped her, scalded her, and fed her more candy than nutritious food. It was a wonder Maxine had survived.

"Sorry," Jeff said in a tone that made it clear he wasn't. He picked up a paper-covered straw and tore off the end of the wrapper. Pulling the paper back just a half inch, he put the straw to his lips and blew, shooting the paper wrapper at Maxine's face. It hit her in the nose.

Maxine sighed and glared at Jeff. "Age?"

Jeff snorted out a laugh. He elbowed Maxine again, this time on purpose.

Maxine sighed once more and shook her head. Movement from the other side of the table caught her attention. She looked across the scarred pine-wood table at the lump sitting on the opposite side of the booth. The man's name was Doug. *Just Doug*, he'd said when he'd introduced himself. Doug was supposedly a lawyer. What kind of lawyer only went by his first name? A scuzz-lawyer, that's what kind. She noticed Doug was staring at her breasts as he slurped at a cup of coffee, to which she'd watched him add four creams and six packets of sugar just a few minutes before.

She immediately lowered her gaze and crossed her arms over her chest. *Total sleazeball*, Maxine thought.

What was she *doing* here?

Maxine glanced at Jeff. He was sucking his soda noisily. She could feel his knee bouncing under the table. She knew he felt as awkward as she did, but probably for different reasons.

Maxine loved her brother, and she thought he had a lot going for him. Having gotten more of their mother's looks than their father's, Jeff's hair was sandy brown, and his features were small and balanced. His features, however, didn't fit his size. At a good-sized six foot two, Jeff's body was too large for his small face. Even so, Maxine thought he was cute. He was kind, too—he had a big heart. Jeff, however, was the king of bad choices. He'd already done time twice, for relatively minor stuff—car theft, breaking and entering. He couldn't seem to hold on to a job. She really shouldn't have let him talk her into this . . . or anything for that matter.

Maxine already felt terrible about what she'd done. She didn't want to do anything worse. No, she shouldn't be here.

Outside, rain started tapping on the window. Maxine nudged Jeff. "Move," she said. She needed to get out here.

Before Jeff could even twitch, a clamorous crash cut through the normal diner hubbub. Maxine's head jerked to her left as she instinctively sought the source of the sound. Jeff and Doug looked in that direction, too. Doug had to swivel his thick neck to look over his shoulder.

Sparky's eating area was arranged in a C-shape around the kitchen, which took up about a third of the building's octagon. A squared-off counter cradled the cook's domain—from which came a constant din of sizzling, banging, and shouting—and booths lined the outer wall of the building. The door was at the end of the bottom leg of the C.

The racket that had cancelled out everything else in the diner was an explosion of broken dishes that apparently had fallen from a busboy's very full tray. The "boy" (actually a sad-looking thirty-something guy going prematurely bald), was mumbling something Maxine couldn't hear as he dropped to his knees to clean up the mess. Standing over him was a petite woman with an ash-blonde (no doubt from a bottle) pixie cut. Jane. Mike's aunt.

Probably in defiance of the storm kicking up outside the diner, Jane wore a pale pink pantsuit with matching high heels. She looked prim and proper. But Maxine knew she wasn't.

Hands on hips, Jane deliberately stomped on the broken glass beneath her feet. She narrowly avoided the bus boy's fingers. Max had a feeling the miss was an accident.

"No, *you* watch where *you're* going," Jane screeched. She kicked a shard of broken glass at the busboy's shoe.

The busboy glared at Jane as she flounced away from him. Jane headed directly toward the booth Maxine really didn't want to be in. She couldn't escape, though. Now that Jane was here, it was too late.

Nearly everyone in the place had frozen when they'd heard the dish explosion, and now most of the diners were returning to their food. Many pairs of eyes tracked Jane's progress, though. Her diva-like dramatics were designed to put her in the limelight. She made a point to huff theatrically as she moved on. Her high heels made emphatic little tapping sounds on the diner's scuffed burgundy linoleum.

Jane reached their booth and slid in next to Doug. When she didn't have enough space, she shot Doug a look and he appeared to attempt to let some air out of the balloon of his body. He squished himself against the window.

"Before anyone says anything," Jane said as she settled herself, "I have somewhere I have to be, so let's make this quick."

A tall, lanky, auburn-haired teen wearing a Sparky's uniform shirt and a white half-apron tied around his waist—Maxine knew his name was Ness; he was Sparky's son—approached the table. "Hey there," Ness said. "Welcome to Sparky's." Ness lifted a hand toward Maxine and gave her a little smile. She returned the smile.

"Can I start you folks off with some appetiz—"

"We're not eating," Jane said.

"Well, that's no fun," Ness said. He leaned toward Jane and gave her a wink. "You know what they say . . . lunch is the most important meal of the day."

"I thought that was breakfast," Jeff said. He frowned as if thinking hard on the subject.

Maxine mentally shook her head. Her brother was a sweetie, but he wasn't all that bright.

"Some people say that," Ness said. "But it's just a theory." He grinned.

Jane narrowed her eyes and looked at Ness like he was a gnat. "Are you getting paid by the word," Jane asked, "or can we have a minute?"

Ness's grin drooped. So did the rest of his face. He shrugged and walked away from the booth.

Jane curled her lip at Ness's retreating back. Her lips were painted in a color that matched her pantsuit. It wasn't a good look.

Jane shifted her attention to her booth companions. "Now, where were we?" she asked.

No one answered her.

Jane skewered Maxine with her best Cruella de Vil look. "Oh right," Jane said. "You were about to tell me what a miserable failure you are."

Before Maxine could open her mouth to tell Jane just what to do with herself, Jeff leaned over the table. He jabbed a finger in Jane's direction.

"Hey, screw you, lady," Jeff said.

Maxine felt a surge of love for her brother. He was sweet and kind, but he always turned into a bulldog when anyone tried to mess with Maxine.

"My sister went over every inch of that dump a hundred times," Jeff said. "If there was something to find, she would've found it." He slapped a hand on the table. "Now pay up."

Jane raised an eyebrow at Jeff. "I'm sorry?"

"You said two hundred," Jeff said.

Maxine, feeling unusually meek—probably because of the guilt that had been strangling her ever since she'd agreed to do what Jane wanted done—spoke up softly. "We had a deal," she told Jane.

Jane tilted her head to one side and slid her gaze up and down Maxine's torso. Maxine had to keep herself from looking down to be sure she didn't have a stain or something.

"Yes," Jane said, finally. "The deal was that you'd find me hard proof of criminal endangerment. Something actionable. Instead, all I've heard from you is about what a nice kid my niece is and how my nephew sleeps a lot."

"He really does, though," Maxine said.

Jane banged a fist on the table. Jeff's soda glass jittered, and Doug's coffee sloshed. His discarded little creamer cups and sugar packets hopped across the table like startled frogs.

"*Sleeping is not a crime!*" Jane shouted.

Heads at the diner's counter and at nearby booths swiveled to stare at Jane. She clearly didn't notice . . . or care.

Jeff ignored Jane. His gaze was on Doug. Maxine looked at the lawyer. He was red in the face, and his eyes looked like they were trying to explode out of his head.

"Hey, dude," Jeff said to Doug. "You okay?"

Doug moved his mouth around as if he was trying to work up spit. "I just realized," Doug said. He worked his mouth again, then cleared his throat. "I probably shouldn't be hearing any of this. I probably shouldn't even be here at all." He looked around wildly, as if seeking rescue. He began scooting toward Jane, as if he could hip-scoot her out of the booth and flee.

Jane raised a hand toward Doug. "Stay!" she commanded.

Doug stayed. Maxine felt like he should get a treat or something.

Jane looked from Maxine to Jeff. No one spoke. Maxine just wanted the whole thing to be over. She didn't even care if she got the money Jane had promised. She never should have agreed to search for dirt on Mike. Sure, Maxine needed the cash. She always needed cash. And yes, she was annoyed with Mike because he never bothered to look at her, really look at her. But . . .

"Well, I guess we're done here," Jane said. "Unless either of you have any bright ideas . . . which I do realize is unlikely."

Jeff piped up. "Why don't we just kill him?"

Maxine shot her brother a look. Was he serious? She couldn't tell. Jeff was kind, yes, but he had a comic-book view of life. There were "his" people . . . and everyone else. Mike was part of everyone else. In Jeff's view, Mike might have been disposable.

Doug tried to shove Jane out of his way with his big, soft shoulder. He half-attempted to stand in the booth. Jane immediately grabbed his tie, yanked him down, and used the flat of her hand to shove him back into place. He didn't resist her; he retreated toward the window.

Jane looked at Jeff with an expression somewhat similar to approval. "Tempting," Jane said. "But, no."

Not thinking before opening her mouth, Maxine whispered, "His job."

Jane turned toward Maxine and leaned forward. "Speak up, honey." The word *honey* was triple-wrapped in sarcasm.

Hating herself but apparently unable to stop herself, Maxine raised her voice and continued, "Well, Mike was saying how he really needs his new job. You know, so he can look good on paper. Like, for the judge?"

Jane snorted. "My nephew, the altruist. That's all very fascinating, *dear*, but I'm not hearing a plan."

Maxine glanced at Jeff. He returned her gaze, and he grinned. He looked back toward Jane.

"We toss the place," Jeff said.

Jane raised her eyebrows, clearly surprised that Jeff had said something semi-interesting. "Go on," she said.

Jeff shoved aside his soda glass and put both hands palms-down on the table. "Mike's a security guard, right? His job is to make sure no one gets in. So . . ." he looked from Jane to Maxine and back to Jane, ". . . we get in! Mess the place up good, help ourselves to whatever we find along the way." Jeff lifted a finger and pointed at Jane. "Your nephew gets canned. Judge gives you the kid." He hesitated, then leaned back and crossed his arms. "And you give us two thousand dollars."

Jane pulled in her chin and gave Jeff an "as if" look. "It's two hundred," she said.

Jeff shook his head. "Two hundred was for going through his underwear drawer. We're talking about breaking and entering. Destroying private property. Theft. That's like . . . five years, minimum.

"Probably more like ten," Doug inserted.

Jane shot Doug a death glare. Then she tapped pink-painted nails on the booth's tabletop. The skin at the outer edges of her eyes pulled in.

"One thousand," Jane said.

Jeff looked at Maxine. She leaned away from him, attempting to fuse with the window . . . or perhaps pass right through it. She couldn't believe she was having anything to do with any of this. Still, she gave Jeff a miniscule nod.

Jeff looked at Jane. "Okay," he said.

Jane stood. Adjusting the hem of her pantsuit jacket, she

bent forward across the booth's table. She leaned in close, just inches from Jeff's face. Maxine got a whiff of Jane's perfume—it was sharp and cutting, like it was a fusion of pepper and grapefruit.

In low, menacing tones, Jane spoke. "Do it soon. And don't mess it up." Jane twisted her lips. "I mean, do mess it up." She pointed at the table. "But don't just mess *this* up."

Jane stalked off. Doug hefted himself off the booth bench. Maxine watched Doug trail in Jane's wake.

Maxine looked at her brother. Clearly confused, Jeff was looking at the spot on the table that Jane had pointed to.

Maxine, fed up with everything, slapped Jeff's finger. He frowned at her, still baffled. She gave him her best "moron" look and sighed.

CHAPTER 9

Thunder rattled Mike's bedroom walls. He heard heavy raindrops *rat-a-tat* at the windowpane behind his blackout curtains. The brilliant sunlight that had ushered in the day had thrown in the towel when heavy storm clouds had descended on the town just before lunch. Since then, the day had been dark and dreary. Mike's mood had similarly changed.

The surge of optimism Mike had felt at the start of the day had diminished as the day had gone on. He wanted it back. And he had a plan to reclaim it.

Planting his feet wide on his bouncy mattress, one foot close to the edge, Mike reached up to try to untape his Nebraska poster from the ceiling over his bed. He managed to slide his fingers under one edge of the thick paper.

"What're you doing?"

Abby's voice came right on the heels of another clap of thunder. The combination of the boom and her unexpected appearance startled Mike. He jerked, and his foot slipped off the edge of the bed. Mike went tumbling. His fingers caught a big chunk of the poster, and he took the chunk with him to the floor.

Having managed to land head and shoulders first, Mike shifted to his rump and rubbed his head. He looked toward his doorway.

Abby stood just a foot inside Mike's room. Dressed in her usual overalls—today's were bright blue—she wore Mike's Freddy Fazbear security vest.

Even though Mike was annoyed by the interruption and his torn poster, he had to admit that Abby looked pretty adorable in the vest. Like she was playing dress-up . . . something he'd never seen her do before.

Mike massaged his throbbing shoulder. "Did you want something?" he asked Abby.

Abby looked up at the ceiling, and Mike's gaze followed hers. The part of the poster he hadn't just ripped free dangled down toward the bed. The remaining bit read PINING FOR FUN?

Mike sighed. He pointed at Abby. "All right. Come on. Take that off. I need to get to work."

Abby nodded. "I know. I'm coming with you."

Mike grunted and stood. He pressed a hand to his temple . . . another headache was coming on. It hadn't just been his collision with the floor; his mood had been spiraling downward all day. And now, even though he had a plan to retrieve the hope he'd felt earlier, he dreaded having to go back to the spooky restaurant. He wasn't up for Abby's games.

"Abby, please," Mike said. He held out a hand. "Just give me the vest."

Abby didn't move, so Mike walked over to her and reached for the vest. Abby stepped back.

"No!" Abby shouted.

Mike really wanted to scream at her. He hated when she got like this.

Summoning what little patience he had available to him—which wasn't much—Mike knelt in front of Abby. He took a second to make sure that when he spoke, he wouldn't explode. Then he said, in what he hoped was a calm but firm tone, "Give me. The vest. Now."

Abby made a face. Then she mimicked him. "I'm. Coming. With you."

Mike heard the front door bang open. Even from down the hall, the sound of Max's footsteps was clear. The *tap-tap* was joined by a fluttery noise. Given the thrumming of the rain on the roof overhead, Mike guessed that Max was shaking out her umbrella.

"Hello?" Max called out.

Abby turned toward the hallway. Mike lunged for her.

*　*　*

When Maxine heard Abby shriek, she rushed toward the hallway. Looking down the length of the narrow, empty space, Maxine started forward. Was Abby really in trouble or was she having one of her . . . ?

Abby screamed again. As she did, Mike, holding a wildly flailing Abby in his arms, stepped into view.

So that question was answered. Maxine wiped rain off her face—the umbrella hadn't been much help in the windy storm—as she watched Mike carry his sister to her room.

Mike set Abby down, and as she spun away from him, he grabbed the vest she was wearing and pulled it off. He quickly slammed Abby's door and locked it.

Abby continued to caterwaul from within her bedroom. Most

of her noise was just general wailing, but mixed in were some impressive beyond-her-age swear words and a few scathing opinions of her brother. Maxine agreed with a few of them.

Panting, Mike looked down the hall and met Maxine's gaze. "Hey, Max," he said.

She lifted a hand, signaling for him to stop.

Mike pointed at Abby's closed door. He acted like he couldn't hear any of the insults and yowling reaching through the flimsy wood barrier. "She's all yours," Mike said.

Max raised an eyebrow and quirked her lips. "Great."

* * *

When Mike got to work, he didn't waste his time freaking himself out by looking around the pizzeria. The lobby and hallway looked the same as they had the day before. He assumed everything else was status quo, too, and if it wasn't, he didn't want to know about it.

As soon as Mike entered the office and closed—and locked—the door behind him (he didn't bother with moving the filing cabinet because he felt silly for doing it the night before), he shed his wet jacket and took his backpack to the desk. Then he made his preparations.

Setup didn't take long. Within ten minutes, Mike was planting himself in the office desk chair. Once there, Mike swept his gaze over all the monitors. All the power was on (as on as it could get), and he had a clear view of everything on the monitors, inside and out.

A thunder crack assaulted the pizzeria. The building groaned, as if in protest.

Mike's attention landed on the main exterior camera. He watched a river of rainwater flow out of the parking lot into the street.

Satisfied that all was well with the pizzeria, Mike took his pill, turned on his cassette, and touched his paperback, as if it was a talisman. Then he leaned forward and looked at the Nebraska poster, which he'd managed to repair (shoddily) and tape to the wall opposite the desk. Mike turned up the volume on the cassette player so it could trump the sound of the thunderstorm.

Chirping birds. Rustling tree branches. A gurgling stream. Mike softened his gaze and allowed the pine trees—bisected diagonally by his ineptly repaired tear—to sway. As the pine needles shimmied, Mike's eyes lost their focus. His lids fluttered, then they dropped.

The tear marring the pine trees was gone. They moved seamlessly in the wind, one flowing wave of gauzy green.

Mike relaxed into the soothing sounds of the breeze, but he stiffened when thunder muscled its way into the breeze's swishing rhythm. The sun filtering through the trees began to flicker. Or was that the lights in the office?

Part of Mike's consciousness was still aware of where he was in his waking state. But it was hanging on tenuously.

Mike, determined to fall into the reality of the pine forest, blurred all the sounds he was hearing. He wove the thunder into creaking tree branches, and when he heard a crackling *hiss* and *pop*, he braided that staticky sound into the *crackle* of the bristling pine needles.

The sun, for one second, bathed Mike's face in warmth and then disappeared again, letting cool shade slip over him. In and out. The light blinked. The confusion of sounds continued, and Mike frowned.

What was that lower sound . . . off in the distance? Was that music?

Mike's awareness succumbed to the fog of sleep. He found himself in a series of quick-take impressions.

An orange toy plane flies through the air.

Ketchup spurts.

Tires spin on gravel.

Mike runs.

Shoving aside branches that slap at his face, Mike pounds through the forest. His movements are familiar, practiced. But something's strange about them.

Bursting out of the trees, Mike looks down the road just in time to see the black car disappear. Why does the black car look different?

Childish laughter bubbles behind Mike. He turns.

As Mike rotates around, his gaze drops. He jerks in surprise as he realizes he's looking down at his adult body.

This is different.

But the children aren't.

Mike looks at the five children. They're just as they were the last time that he saw them.

Mike watches the children but he doesn't approach them. They watch him in return.

What now?

Understanding clearly that he's in his dream but that it is diverging from its norm, Mike hesitates. Then he speaks.

"Please," Mike says to the children. "Don't run. I just . . . I just want to know what you saw."

The blond boy narrows his cold blue eyes at Mike. His upper lip lifts into a semi-sneer.

"I'm begging you," Mike says. "Who took my brother?"

The blond boy's expression doesn't change. The other children ignore Mike.

Mike runs a hand through his hair, frustrated. Why won't the kids tell him anything?

He takes a step forward. He raises his voice. "Who took Garret?!"

Mike's shout spooks the children. They bolt.

"No!" Mike yells.

Facing the same situation that he was in before, Mike makes an instant decision this time. He chases the boy with the paper hook.

Now that Mike is adult-sized, he can easily outrun the small child. The boy has reddish hair, and Mike keeps his gaze locked on that hair as he runs. Even racing over the forest's uneven ground, Mike quickly closes the distance.

Almost upon the boy, Mike reaches for the kid's shoulder. The boy spins around.

Suddenly, Mike sees a flash of silver. The paper hook is scything through the air.

Something sharp stings at Mike's arm. He staggers back, stunned.

Mike looks down at his arm. His shirtsleeve gapes open; the material is slashed apart. A narrow ribbon of red appears on Mike's skin.

Shocked, Mike looks back at the red-haired boy. The boy, whose freckled face has a pert little nose and soft cheeks, looks up at Mike with staggeringly fearsome green eyes. The boy opens his mouth and unleashes . . . a distorted mechanical shriek.

Mike recoils.

He opened his eyes.

Mike goggled at the overhead lights. They were flashing on and off with dizzying quickness.

Looking away from the lights, Mike slapped his palms over his ears because the lights were only half of the assault on his senses. Screeching feedback was blaring from the intercom on the ceiling over the desk.

Mike shifted his focus to the CCTV monitors. He gaped at them.

The monitors had gone haywire. Some of the screens were pulsing random flashes of colored lights. Some were streaming indecipherable lines of binary code, which were entwined around twisted, distorted images.

Abruptly, a frenetic '80s rock song blasted from the overhead speakers. Mike jolted at the sound, nearly falling from his chair. Throwing out an arm to steady himself, Mike knocked his pill bottle to the floor. The cap wasn't on tight; the little white pills scattered over the black-and-white linoleum.

Mike's gaze shot from the pills up to the intercom. He grabbed his head with both hands. "Stop!" Mike yelled . . . even though he knew hysterics weren't going to help.

But he couldn't help himself. His senses were saturated. He was totally overwhelmed.

Standing, Mike spun one way and then the other. What should he do?

On the verge of totally losing it, Mike got help from his memory banks. His brain provided him an inner Raglan replay: *"Fair warning,"* Raglan's voice said in Mike's head. *"The power can be a bit . . . screwy. If you have any issues, you'll find the system breaker in the main office. Just give it a flip."*

Mike stood. Starting to turn toward the circuit box, Mike did a double take. His gaze flitted toward the window in the office door.

The frosted glass looked perfectly normal. Mike could see well enough through the glass to reassure himself that nothing was out there.

But had it been? Mike could have sworn he'd just gotten a

glimpse of one eye watching him through the glass. One eye and one eye patch. Could . . . ?

Mike shook his head. No way. He'd imagined it . . . probably because of his dream.

The rock music crescendoed. The lights started going on and off even faster.

That's enough.

Giving the frosted window one more glance—nothing was there—Mike sprinted to the circuit breaker. He grabbed the lever and shoved it downward.

Everything went black. And the building was filled with blessed silence. Even the thunder had stopped.

The red emergency bulb above the circuit box clicked on. Mike leaned back against the wall and tried to get a grip on himself. His breath was coming in ragged gasps. His pulse was so fast that it felt like a Formula One race was being run in his veins. His ears were ringing from the raucous auditory assault.

Mike stood in the near darkness for a few seconds. Then his skin prickled. The darkness was unfriendly, suffocating.

Mike put his hand back on the lever. He shoved it upward.

A comforting *ka-chunk* relit the office. Mike looked at the bank of fluorescent bulbs. They were dim, but they were steady.

Stepping over to the desk, Mike looked at the monitors. They were back to normal.

Mike exhaled loudly. His pulse began to steady itself, and . . .

An insistent buzzer revved up Mike's pulse again. The buzz came once. Twice. Three times.

Mike leaned over and scanned the monitors. He frowned.

Centered in front of the entrance camera, a uniformed police officer stood in the steady rain, finger on the building's doorbell.

The thunder might have abated, but the storm was still dumping torrents of water on the pizzeria.

Mike peered at the wavy CCTV feed. Between the poor resolution, the rain, and the officer's hooded poncho, Mike couldn't make out the officer's face. All he could see was pale fuzziness within the hood . . . even when the officer looked up at the camera and waved.

Bracing himself for whatever was going to come next, Mike pulled open one of the pizzeria's heavy entrance doors. He peered out at the rain-parka-clad officer. Close up, in real life instead of on an old, hazy CCTV screen, the police officer's face was clear . . . and it belonged to a woman.

The female officer smiled at Mike. "About time!" she said in a pleasing, smooth voice. "I was starting to think you fell asleep on the job."

Mike, still disoriented by the commotion in the office and puzzled by why a cop was at the pizzeria's door, blinked at the woman like an idiot. He couldn't seem to get his brain to engage properly.

It didn't help that the unexpected cop at the door was a *very pretty* cop. Even though Mike couldn't see the woman's hair or body under the bulky rain gear, he could see enough of her big blue eyes, her high flushed cheeks, and her wide, upturned mouth to find her looks unsettling. Mike, having had little time or inclination to date, often got flustered when he was around a pretty woman. A pretty cop was even more muddling.

But he had to say something. Mike cleared his throat and managed, "Can I help you . . . officer?"

"Please." Pulling off her rain parka, the cop brushed a few strands of streaked blonde hair from her pale face. The hair was shiny and appeared to be long but was currently confined in some kind of twist. "My name's Vanessa," she said as she shook water off the parka.

Water sprayed Mike's pants. He couldn't have cared less.

Vanessa looked at Mike. "And you must be . . ."

Now that Mike could see Vanessa's sleek hair and the slender but curvy figure in her snug, dark blue police uniform, he was even more tongue-tied. All he was capable of was more idiotic blinking.

Vanessa smiled at Mike with what might have been pity. Or maybe she was being friendly. ". . . the new security guard," she concluded. She glanced down at Mike's arm. "You're bleeding, by the way."

That surprised Mike so much that he said, "What?"

Vanessa pointed. "Your arm."

Mike looked down at his arm, and his mouth dropped open. It fell open so hard and so wide that his jaw might have made it to the floor. Clearly remembering his dream, he couldn't believe what he was seeing.

The sleeve of Mike's black shirt was cut cleanly along the forearm. The sliced fabric was soaked in blood.

"That looks nasty," Vanessa said.

Mike suddenly felt woozy. "Um, yeah," he said. He wavered on his feet. Not from blood loss or anything. The cut was long, but it didn't look that deep. He was more dazed than badly injured.

While Mike made like a swaying pine tree, Vanessa took charge. She briskly stepped past Mike and started striding across the lobby. She moved as if she owned the place.

"Come on," Vanessa flung back over her shoulder. "I know where there's a first aid kit."

Mike's brows bunched. *She does?*

CHAPTER 10

"I love what you've done with the place," Vanessa said.

Fumbling with a roll of gauze, Mike glanced over at her. She stood on the other side of the office, examining his pieced-together poster.

"Why Nebraska?" she asked.

When Mike didn't answer, Vanessa looked back at him. She watched him struggle to wrap the gauze around his injured arm. "Need a hand with that?" she asked.

"I'm fine," Mike said.

"Really?"

Mike looked down at the mess he was making with the gauze that Vanessa had pulled from a kit that had been stashed in the bottom drawer of one of the filing cabinets. He was pretty sure a two-year-old could have done a better job at wrapping his wound. He sighed. Clearly, this was not something he could do on his own.

Flushing, Mike held out his arm toward Vanessa. She grinned and crossed to the desk. Perching on the edge of the desk near the VCR, she leaned over and removed the tangled mess Mike had made with the gauze.

Vanessa, Mike discovered, smelled very good. Was it her perfume? Her shampoo or lotion? Whatever it was, it was nice . . . a combination of something flowery, along with vanilla and apples.

Vanessa began wrapping his arm efficiently. Her movements were quick and precise. Mike hoped she couldn't hear his heartbeat. It quickened when her cool, soft fingers brushed against his skin.

While she worked, Vanessa started talking at a rapid-fire pace. "I'm a certified EMT, you know. I did that first before I decided I'd rather be a cop. I don't do rescue runs anymore, but if your heart ever gives out, I'm the one you want to call . . . assuming you can still speak . . . and hold a phone."

Vanessa spoke so quickly that her words ran together. Mike had trouble keeping up. Her hands flew over his arm, too. She was acting almost manic.

Nonplussed by pretty much everything about this unexpected cop, Mike was mostly perplexed by her familiarity with the pizzeria. So, he said, "You seem to know your way around."

Vanessa's fingers jittered against the bandage, which was almost complete. She spoke quickly again. "Freddy's on my beat. I like to stay well-informed." She looked up and gazed around. "I also loved this place when I was a kid."

Vanessa tugged on the gauze, tightening it. *Really* tightening it. Mike grunted.

"That should do it," Vanessa said. She patted his upper arm. Then she pushed off the desk and stood. She extended a hand. "Vanessa Shelly." She grinned. "Might as well finish our meet-cute."

Mike blinked at Vanessa.

She laughed. "Just kidding. But seriously." She shoved her hand forward forcefully. "Let's see if we can do this. Vanessa Shelly," she repeated.

Mike was a little reluctant to take her hand. She was such a powerhouse that he wouldn't have been surprised if he somehow lost his hand in the process of shaking hers.

Mike took Vanessa's hand. She shook it twice, vigorously, as he said, "Mike Schmidt."

"Pleasure to meet you, Mike," Vanessa said, squeezing his hand once before she let it go. She stepped back and looked up the intercom before returning her gaze to Mike's face.

Unnervingly speaking in a totally different tone of voice, Vanessa said, "So are you doing all right this evening, Mike?" Gone was the breakneck, light chatter. Her tone was measured and low. All cop.

Mike fidgeted as Vanessa's eyes narrowed. She seemed to be studying him with suspicion.

What the hell?

Not sure how to respond to the out-of-the-blue, hard-right turn, Mike could only say, "What?"

Vanessa's eyes narrowed even more. A muscle at her strong jawline twitched. "Are . . . you . . . all right?" she repeated, more slowly, as if speaking to a person with an IQ of ten. "As in, are you okay? Are you cool? Is everything . . . copacetic?"

Huh. Mike crossed his arms, ignoring the pain in his left forearm. "I know what *all right* means," he said.

Vanessa's demeanor flipped again. She smiled brightly and began speaking quickly once more. "Hey, that's great!" Still talking fast, she dropped the smile as she continued. "Did you also know that your eyes are bloodshot and your pupils are dilated and your heart rate is through the roof? All of this is aside from the gash on your arm, which . . . let's be honest . . . is pretty dang bizarre. And you've been acting shifty and suspicious since the moment you opened the door. Did you know that, too?"

Mike stared at Vanessa, open-mouthed. "It's . . . uh . . . ."

Vanessa put her hands on her utility belt. The leather creaked. "Yes?" she said with mock tolerance.

Mike sighed. What was the right way to go here? He couldn't tell her about his dream, obviously. But maybe he should be honest . . . to a point. "It's been a really, really weird night," he said.

Vanessa tapped her blunt, unpolished nails on her baton. She eyed Mike for a long, disconcerting moment.

Then someone invisible flipped a switch; Vanessa's cop-mode deactivated. She flashed a wide, warm smile at Mike and said, airily, "Sounds like Freddy's."

Mike was now totally mystified. What did she mean by that?

Mike's befuddlement must have shown on his face. Vanessa let out a short laugh and waved an arm to indicate the building around them. "This place . . . it gets to people."

Vanessa leaned toward Mike. "That's why you're going to quit." The light tone was gone again. She was cop-serious.

Mike felt like he was being spun on a merry-go-round. "What?"

Vanessa nodded twice. Her voice returned to cheerleader sprightly. "Oh, yeah. You security hires never last long here. It's like . . . a fact."

Mike had no idea what to make of that. The only thing he could think to say was "Maybe I'm different."

Vanessa studied Mike. Her eyes darkened, and her face went still. She looked like she'd fallen down a deep, dark rabbit hole of introspection.

Then the dark Vanessa-clouds cleared. The sun came back to her face. She beamed at Mike. "So, have you met them yet?"

"Met who?"

"Them," Vanessa said. "You know. Freddy, Bonnie, Chica . . . Foxy?"

Mike gaped at her. Vanessa smiled at his cluelessness. She turned toward the door, then looked back at Mike and motioned for him to follow her. "Come on," she said.

*　*　*

The dining room was dim but its lights were on. Strangely, when Vanessa had used the light switch near the archway, it had worked.

Even in better light, though, the dining room was still not one of Mike's favorite places. There was something haunting about the open space, the trash, the children's drawings . . . and the expanse of crusty, red stage curtain.

Vanessa didn't seem to be bothered by any of the things that made Mike's skin crawl. She strode confidently and purposefully toward the stage.

Mike trailed behind her, hanging back enough to soothe himself but not far enough to look like a total coward. Attempting to distract himself from his nerves, Mike called to her, "So, what are the other reasons?"

Vanessa glanced over her shoulder. "Huh?"

"You said I'd quit my job because this place will get to me, among other reasons," he reminded her. "What reasons?"

Vanessa stopped. They'd reached the stage, and she now stood in front of the main stage. Mike sidled away from it, ending up in front of the small purple-curtained stage.

Vanessa faced Mike. She put her hands on her hips. Something flashed in her eyes. Annoyance? Challenge?

"You tell me," she said. "Is this where you see yourself in ten years? How about in twenty years? Look down the line. What do you see? I mean, what do I know? Maybe the benefits are great. Pension? 401K?"

Mike felt like he got whiplash every time Vanessa spoke. Even though the pendulum pace of his interaction with her was giving him a headache, he laughed.

Vanessa smiled. "Didn't think so." She cocked her head. "Add to that the thing with those kids going missing . . ."

It felt like Vanessa had just kicked Mike in the solar plexus. He struggled to get his next breath. "What did you just say?" he asked.

Vanessa acted like she hadn't heard the question. Walking away from Mike, she strode to the wall and stood in front of the red SHOWTIME button.

"Prepare to have your mind blown," Vanessa said.

Vanessa hit the big red button. The instant she did, it felt like a dozen things happened at once.

The first thing to get Mike's attention was the swish of the purple curtains. They swung apart, and . . .

Mike yelped and scuttled backward.

The pirate-fox animatronic was lurching forward out of the darkness. It shot to the edge of the stage, just inches from where Mike had just been standing.

At the same time, the main curtains reeled open. The entire room was suddenly lit up with psychedelic color. Floodlights came on, shooting blinding streaks of colored light toward the stage.

Also simultaneously, a rousing '80s rock song began thumping from the overhead speakers. Mike recognized it immediately. It was the same song he'd heard in the office when all hell was breaking loose.

The deranged-looking fox that had nearly scared the pants off Mike started jerking around in a spasmodic dance. Mike was mesmerized by the convulsive motions. He especially couldn't take his eyes off the gleaming silver hook, which cut through the air over and over as the fox gyrated.

When the fox looked down at Mike . . . or at least it seemed like the fox looked at him . . . Mike finally moved. He stepped over to join Vanessa, who now stood center-on, at the base of the main stage. Mike looked up at the stage.

And there they were . . . the rest of the characters Mike had seen in the posters. The yellow chick with the cupcake. The blue bunny with the electric guitar. The brown bear with the bow tie and top hat.

Mike put all the names to the toothy-smiled faces. Foxy. Chica. Bonnie. Freddy. Rocking out.

His gaze locked on the bopping and twirling animatronics; Mike couldn't decide whether to be entertained, repulsed, or sympathetic.

The display was at once fascinating, disgusting, and sad. Maybe when they'd been in their heyday, bright and pristine in all their glory, the animatronics might have been fun to watch. Now, however, the faux-fur-covered robotic animals were filthy and mottled. The fur, which was rotting, was riddled with holes, and through those holes, the metal endoskeletons beneath were rusting. Wires poked out of gaps in the fur, and the animatronics' mechanisms made chunky, glitchy, whirring noises. The bunny's . . . Bonnie's . . . electric guitar was faded, battered, and bent.

"This is . . ." Mike tried.

"The best thing you've ever seen in your life?" Vanessa filled in.

Mike shook his head. "I was going to say 'deeply traumatic.'"

Vanessa shot a look at Mike. He shrugged.

Vanessa returned the shrug, and then she held out a hand. "Wanna dance?"

Mike stared at Vanessa's hand. Was she serious?

He wasn't going to find out. Because while he tried to work out the answer to her question, a burst of sparks exploded from Bonnie's guitar. At the same time, the music sputtered and screeched to a jarring stop. Red-hot and bursting with bright color, sparks spewed from the stage. As a few of the sizzling bites of heat hit the black-and-white-checked dining room floor, the floodlights went out. Then the swirling lights were gone. The curtains began to close.

Agog, Mike couldn't take his eyes off the suddenly rigid animatronics. His gaze went from one to the other, landing finally on Freddy.

The curtains were sweeping together in front of the bear. As they did, Freddy's gaze seemed to shift. It appeared as if the bear was staring directly at Mike.

The curtains finished closing. Mike shivered.

Surely the animatronic couldn't have been making direct eye contact with Mike. They weren't that sentient. Were they?

"Maybe next time," Vanessa said.

Mike pulled his gaze from the closed curtains. He looked at Vanessa. She was expressionless. He couldn't read her.

Vanessa headed toward the archway. Mike started to follow her, but he felt compelled to check the closed curtains again. They remained shut, but they swayed back and forth ever so slightly. Now that all the bright lights were out, the curtains were engulfed in shadows.

Mike felt goose bumps on his arms. He rubbed them. And the gesture brought back what Vanessa had said earlier.

Hurrying after Vanessa, who was still heading toward the lobby, Mike called out, "You said some kids went missing?"

Vanessa stopped. She turned and looked at Mike. She cocked her head as if she found Mike interesting . . . or maybe dense.

"Sure," she said. "Back in the '80s."

"What happened to them?" Mike asked.

Vanessa crossed her arms. "It was big news." She made a face that Mike couldn't interpret. "It's why the place shut down," she explained.

Mike felt like the floor under his feet was falling away. *What?*

Glancing at his face, Vanessa said, "Wow. You really didn't do your homework, did you?" She looked him up and down as if in mock disapproval. Or maybe her disapproval was real. She shook her head. "And you're not even wearing your badge."

"Huh?" *Badge? What badge?*

Mike was pretty sure Vanessa had seen his face arranged in expressions of totally vapid ignorance more than pretty much anyone he'd ever met before. And that was saying a lot.

Raising an eyebrow at him, she motioned for him to follow her as she veered away from the arch and headed to the far side of the dining area. Skirting around an overturned table and a pile of chairs, Vanessa led him into the arcade. Their footsteps made little purring and *tsk*-ing sounds as their feet scuffed over the dusty floor and kicked aside debris. The dry smell of dust mushroomed up around them.

At the front edge of the arcade, a long, thick-with-dust glass counter enclosed a display of decrepit game prizes. Mounds of moldy, limp, faded plush animals lay pathetically next to clusters of cracked plastic toys and crusty Freddy's paraphernalia—Mike spotted hats and mugs and pendants and rings and figurines and posters.

When they reached the counter, Vanessa went behind it and slid open a cabinet door with a tap and a whoosh. She reached into the conglomeration of wasted prizes. Mike cringed as her fingers kicked up dusty green spores and tossed aside what looked like colorful dead baby animals. He wanted to tell her to stop what she was doing. It was too . . . disconcerting.

Before Mike could speak, Vanessa pulled her hand out of the display. "Got it!" she said triumphantly.

She held up a red plastic tub filled with play badges. Mike took a step closer and looked at them. The plastic emblems read FREDDY'S HONORARY SECURITY.

Vanessa plucked one of the badges from the tub and stepped over to Mike. Smoothing the vest that, in spite of everything that had happened tonight, he still wore, Vanessa pinned the badge to it.

Vanessa patted Mike's shoulder, then she stepped back. Her gaze lifted to his face and then dropped again. "There," she said in a tone that came across as oddly resigned. "Now you're official."

The words sounded tired, and her tone dropped at the end of the sentence. Vanessa seemed to be . . . almost sad. Why?

Mike opened his mouth to ask what was upsetting her, but before any words came out, the *beep, beep, beep* of his watch alarm cut through the moment. It acted like a thrown bucket of cold water, putting a harsh end to the night.

Vanessa looked at her own watch. Mike knew it would read six a.m. That's what his alarm was set for.

"Looks like our time is up," Vanessa said. She gave Mike a

weirdly somber smile. "Come on. Let's go get your stuff. I'll walk you out."

*   *   *

The storm had finally thrown in the towel. Flat, ashen clouds lay supine over the pizzeria, as if spent and depleted. Between a narrow gap in the clouds, a hint of the day's coming sun sidled over the tops of distant trees, casting surreal golden light over the wet black sheen of the pizzeria parking lot's broken asphalt.

Mike's car door was protesting its required movement with a clunking groan when an engine's drone and the *swish-hiss* of tires rolling through shallow rain puddles turned Mike around. Vanessa's black-and-white cruiser rolled to a stop behind him. She lowered her window.

"If you want," Vanessa called out, "I can check in from time to time. I know how lonely these nights can get."

Mike kept his face neutral, but inwardly he cringed. He liked Vanessa, even though her fickle personality made his head spin. The last thing he needed, though, was her dropping in unannounced. It would totally mess up his nighttime routine.

Mike realized Vanessa was watching him with a bemused quirk of the lips and a raised eyebrow. He spoke quickly. "I keep myself busy."

Vanessa left her gaze on him for several long, inscrutable seconds. Then she shrugged. "Some friendly advice?" She narrowed her eyes. "Don't let this place get to you. Just do your job, and you'll be . . . fine."

Vanessa's intense stare and the hesitation before the word *fine* landed on Mike like a physical blow . . . not a hard one, more like a warning tap. A shot across the bow. It felt like Vanessa's words were more threat than advice.

Ignoring the tightening in his gut, Mike said lightly, "Sounds good."

Vanessa gave Mike a friendly wave (there was that flip-flop again; Mike couldn't keep up). Then she raised her window. She looked straight ahead and drove out of the parking lot.

Mike watched the cruiser's taillights for a couple seconds before getting in his car. As he started to close the car door, which let out a loud grinding sound, he thought he caught a hint of movement by the pizzeria.

Mike leaned forward to look through his windshield. Unfortunately, he couldn't see much. Leaves and pine needles were stuck to the wet glass, and Mike's view of the restaurant was obscured. He hesitated as he considered whether he should get out of the car to go investigate.

As quickly as Mike thought about checking out what he thought he'd seen, he dismissed the idea. The building was locked up tight. He was tired. And his arm hurt.

Mike turned the ignition . . . four times. Finally, the car started. He cleared the windshield with the wipers, and he looked toward the slovenly building again. It was still. Mike shrugged. His mind must have been just winding him up again.

CHAPTER 11

Jeff watched the pathetic pile of rust lurch out of the parking lot. His heart rate, which had tripled when Mike had almost spotted him, settled back into its normal rhythm.

As the junk heap on wheels chugged off down the road, Jeff pressed back against the pizzeria's warped siding. Immediately, he yelped and stepped away. He'd forgotten the paint-peeling wood was so wet.

Shaking himself off, Jeff dug in his pocket and pulled out his old flip phone. He punched in a number.

One ring. *Click.*

After the click, all Jeff heard was silence. No, not silence. His sister's breathing came through the line, faint and uneven.

"Max?"

"Yeah." The word was soft but clipped off. Even with just the one word, Jeff knew Max was on edge.

"It's showtime," Jeff said. "Soon as he's back, get the guys and meet me here. I think I found a way in."

Max said nothing. Jeff pressed the phone closer to his ear. He couldn't even hear her breathing now. "Max?"

Finally, Max repeated. "Yeah." The tone was even edgier. The one word poked at Jeff's ear like a thorn.

"Time to get paid," Jeff said.

Max sighed in his ear, then hung up.

* * *

Maxine dropped her phone on the sofa and put her face in her hands. How had she gotten herself into this?

"I'm not a bad person," Maxine muttered, muffled, into her palms.

Her conscience laughed at her, and accused scathingly, *Then why'd you agree to spy on Mike?*

Maxine shook her head. Then she felt the anger and hurt rise up, the feelings that had goaded her into betraying Mike.

He deserved it, she'd told herself when she'd acquiesced to Jane's request to search Mike's house. Sure, Mike was never rude to her; he always said hello and good-bye and thank you. It wasn't like Mike ignored her; he did interact with her. But he never really saw her. If he did, he'd realize how she felt about him.

Jane had caught Maxine on a bad day, the day Maxine had put on extra makeup and worn a new shirt in the hopes of catching Mike's eye, the day that Mike had looked right through her, as usual. That was why she'd agreed to do something that was so not who she was.

Yeah, but then you're the one who suggested messing up his job, her conscience prodded her.

Not exactly, she argued back. *All I said was . . .*

Maxine's conscience snorted at her, and Maxine dropped her

hands. She looked around the shabby little house and shook her head. Mike didn't deserve what she and her brother and the others were about to do. But how could she stop it now?

I'm scum, Maxine told herself.

*   *   *

Jeff grinned when his crowbar easily snapped the old padlock. The rusted hunk of metal dropped to the concrete with a *thunk*, and Jeff reached out to grab the equally rusty vertical handle of the rolling steel door.

The sun shone directly on the back of the pizzeria, and as its heat hit the still-wet platform of the pizzeria's loading dock, steam wafted upward. The slithery mist made Jeff think of graveyard scenes in horror movies. He shivered and immediately shook off the sensation, annoyed with himself.

Putting on a swagger of confidence he was starting to lose, Jeff turned and faced the men leaning against his old green pickup truck. Hank, heavyset with long, graying sandy-brown hair and a scruffy goatee to match, was lounging against the truck's chrome grill, his thick forearms crossed over a large belly. Hank's down-turned pale blue eyes studied Jeff like he couldn't decide whether to laugh at Jeff . . . or kill him. Jeff had always been a little afraid of Hank . . . even more so today. Hank had an old wooden baseball bat resting on his beefy shoulder, and the way he twirled the bat was more than a little off-putting.

Jeff shifted his gaze to Carl, Hank's son. Even though Jeff had known Carl for several years—they'd done time together, both as juvies and adults—Jeff had to admit Carl intimidated him, too.

Dark-haired, Carl's eyes had the same downward tilt as his dad's, but Carl's eyes were spaced wider apart, and they were brown, like his mother's. Something about the way Carl's eyes squinted at the world, and the way his thin lips were usually pressed into a snarky smile, made Jeff perpetually nervous around Carl. Like Hank, Carl had a goatee, but his was much sparser than his dad's. That, Jeff thought, made Carl seem even more dangerous. Right now, for instance, Carl was toying with the six-cell flashlight he had tucked into his belt as he threw menacing glances at Max's German Shepherd, Bonesy. Jeff thought that if Carl had been carrying a gun, he'd probably have shot the dog.

Jeff would never shoot a dog, especially Max's dog. But the dog was being a pain. He was barking his head off like he was announcing a coming apocalypse.

Bonesy was in the pickup's cab, and Max was standing by the driver's side door. Her face was pale, and her lips were pressed tightly together.

Hank saw the direction of his son's gaze and turned to look at the spun-up dog. Bonesy was really going for it. Froth was building up at his jowls as he barked and growled.

"Dog's gonna be a problem," Hank said in his deep, scratchy voice.

Carl kept eyeing Bonesy. "Yup," Carl said. His voice was higher-pitched than his dad's, but it had a coarse tone.

Hank spun the bat again and then lazily glanced around at the nearby trees and the vacant expanse of asphalt behind the pizzeria. "That's a whole lot of noise," he said.

"Sure is," Carl agreed.

Hank pushed off the truck's grill and stepped to the open driver's-side window. He looked at Max. "Told you not to bring that dog," he said. His tone was more than a little threatening, but it didn't seem to faze Max.

Max lifted her chin and glared at Hank. Jeff knew that Max wasn't afraid of Hank or Carl. She'd known them, and Hank's wife, Darlene, since Max was a little kid . . . because they were neighbors. She thought of Hank and Darlene as an aunt and uncle, she'd told Jeff. She tried not to think about Carl at all. She put up with him; she didn't like him.

Hank shifted the bat. Carl stepped up next to his dad. He gave Max what Jeff thought was awfully close to a creepy leer.

Jeff needed to get things under control. Stepping away from the now-open loading dock door, Jeff took three long strides to reach the pickup. He pointed at Bonesy and shouted at Max, "Shut him up. Now!" He lifted his crowbar. "Or I will," he said as severely as he could.

Max lifted an eyebrow at her brother, but she reached into the pickup and put her hand on Bonesy's shoulder. She leaned through the window and began speaking soothingly to the dog. Jeff couldn't make out her words.

Whatever Max said worked. Bonesy's barks subsided into a deep rumble at the back of his throat.

Jeff quickly turned to Hank and Carl. Reaching into the bed of the truck, Jeff grabbed a large army-green canvas duffel bag. "C'mon," he said as if he was the boss.

Jeff wasn't sure he was the boss of anything. Yeah, this had been his idea, and he'd been the one to ask Hank and Carl for help, but now that they were getting ready to head inside, Jeff was feeling like he wasn't as in charge as he wanted to be.

Jeff motioned for the other men to follow him as he headed

back to the open loading dock door. As he went, he saw Max getting into the pickup's cab.

* * *

Maxine watched her brother lead Hank and his idiot son into the old pizzeria. "Or I will," she whispered, mimicking Jeff's voice.

Maxine knew Jeff would never hurt Bonesy or any other animal—he was just posturing for Hank and Carl. Still, the words had stung.

Maxine wrapped an arm around Bonesy's neck. She stroked his black-and-butterscotch fur in long, smooth motions.

"There you go, boy," Maxine said. "It's all right. Shhhh."

Bonesy's grumbling rumble subsided into a high-pitched whine. He began to pant heavily, and his whole body trembled. He turned and gave Maxine several agitated licks before looking back toward the pizzeria. When the dog's gaze settled on the old building, his trembling intensified, and his whines turned into whimpers.

Picking up on her dog's obvious fear, Maxine's mouth went dry. Her stomach was as tight as a drum, and it felt like her intestines were clutching in rhythm to her heart's driving beat. She peered through the pickup's windshield and looked at the obscured area beyond the loading dock door. She pulled Bonesy closer.

* * *

Jeff had thought that getting past the loading dock door was going to be the "open sesame" he needed to access the rest of the pizzeria.

However, the loading dock, he discovered, was separated from the rest of the restaurant by a locked metal door.

Not wanting to fail at what had been his idea, Jeff ran at the door and gave it a strong kick. The kick came more from desperation than confidence, but . . . to Jeff's surprise . . . it worked.

The lock cracked, and the door snapped off its hinges. Flying backward, the door landed with a reverberating *wham*.

Jeff exhaled in relief and looked at Hank and Carl nonchalantly, as if he'd totally known he had the strength to knock down the door. Moving forward with a "Yeah, I'm the man" strut, Jeff stepped through the doorway and found himself in a shadowy kitchen lit by only a couple of dim fluorescent bulbs. The faint light only sort of revealed the kitchen's expanse, but it did a fine job of spotlighting the hundreds of cobwebs networked through the dusty space.

Hank and Carl looked around, both starting to heft their weapons of choice. Jeff spoke up. "Let's go check out what we have to work with before we start," he suggested.

Neither Hank nor Carl argued with Jeff, so he led them out of the kitchen. Stepping into a long, dark hallway, Jeff shook off the heebie-jeebies that had started on the loading dock.

For the next ten minutes, Jeff and his henchmen meandered through the empty restaurant. "This is going to be a gas," Carl said, as they did a quick, eager tour of the place.

After one circuit through the pizzeria, they returned to the huge wreck of a dining room. Standing just inside the archway that separated the dining room from the deserted lobby, the men exchanged grins.

"Okay," Jeff said. "Let's be quick . . . but thorough. Maximum damage. Minimum time."

Hank and Carl exchanged a glance. Then they nodded.

"Anything that looks valuable," Jeff said, "grab it. We'll settle up when we're done. Good?"

Hank and Carl nodded again in unison. One lift and one drop of their goateed chins.

Jeff, suddenly feeling more excitement than fear, let out a whoop. He brandished his crowbar like a berserker about to head into battle. This might have been inspired by the Vikings movie he'd seen the night before, but whatever. He was fired up and ready to go.

"Let's get to it!" Jeff shouted.

The three men exchanged fist bumps, then charged into action. Jeff and Carl ran into the dining room; Hank turned and strode into the lobby.

After a couple steps, Jeff's and Carl's paths diverged. Carl marched straight across the dining room, aiming at the curtain-covered stage. Jeff veered left, heading to the arcade.

Angling toward the games area at a full run, Jeff was raising and getting ready to swing his crowbar as he got to the glass cabinetry of the prize counter.

Jeff yelled, "Yeehaw!"

His berserker energy exploded into a frenzy as he brought down the crowbar on the dingy expanse of glass. A satisfying crack and crash preceded a rain-like tinkling of glass that showered down onto the black-and-white floor. Jeff grinned and raised his crowbar again.

Striking the glass over and over, Jeff quickly obliterated the prize cabinet. He pulverized the glass into sparkling fragments that twinkled in the rays of sparse light that illuminated the arcade.

Tromping over the nearly vaporized glass, grinding his heel against any large shards he saw, Jeff tore into the arcade and began thrashing every game console he encountered. Pinball machine glass disintegrated the same way the prize counter did. Plastic bumpers and flippers cracked. Wood cabinets splintered. The other arcade games succumbed in similar ways as Jeff's crowbar chewed through them.

Jeff's brain had gone into hibernation as he gave in to the fury of striking and pounding on the machines. Exhilarating beyond belief, the demolition charged Jeff up and gave him the strength to swing the crowbar over and over and over. Sweat poured off his face, and his breath came in jerky heaves, but he didn't care. He was having the time of his life.

*   *   *

Hank was boogying to music only he could hear. The drumbeat of a jazz-rock song was thumping in his head, and he was matching his moves to its rhythm. Lunging left and right, cross-stepping, spinning, and hip-wiggling, Hank was dancing his way past all the glass-framed posters in the front hallway. As he went, Hank was shattering the fragile expanses, hopping fluidly out of the way as jagged fragments flew toward him. In spite of his size, Hank thought he was pretty darn graceful in his ability to avoid the flying shards.

Hank danced his way down the hall and back, crushing glass and battering frames. He was having a blast.

Back in the lobby, Hank took care of the posters there, too. Then, full-on in his groove and not wanting to stop the boogie mode that had overtaken him, Hank started on the walls, wielding his bat as nimbly as one of those baton twirlers who pranced around in front of marching bands. His trusty bat punched gaping holes in the lobby's drywall. Clouds of dust exploded out from the walls; Hank figured he was probably turning white, but he didn't care. He was having too much fun.

* * *

Carl hopped onto the stage and grinned at the closed curtains. Having been told about Freddy's Pizzeria, Carl knew what was probably behind the curtains. He couldn't wait to start his annihilation. Twirling his flashlight like he was spinning a parade rifle in a drill line, Carl affected a cocky saunter as he stepped toward the gap in the curtains.

Lifting the large flashlight with his left hand, poised to strike, Carl stuck his head between the curtains. Smirking, he called out, "Honey, I'm home!"

Carl gazed into the darkened expanse. His brash grin faded. Frowning, his flashlight wavered. He used his right hand to pull back the curtains so more of the dining room's weak light could brighten the backstage area. He looked left and right.

"Huh," Carl said.

The old crusty Freddy's characters he'd expected to find waiting to be beaten into smithereens weren't there. The backstage was empty.

Carl stepped forward and let the curtains close behind him. He felt like he was walking into the choking smoke of a dense fire. He could see little more than the faintest shapes around him, and the air felt thick and weird. It kind of smelled like . . .

well, kind of like the smell that had come from under his family's house when the rats he'd poisoned had died and started decomposing.

Carl looked around, half-heartedly seeking something to destroy. He thought there might be costumes he could shred or props he could wreck.

But Carl didn't try very hard to find something to bash with his flashlight. He was losing interest in the backstage area.

Yeah, sure. That was it. The problem wasn't that Carl was starting to feel spooked.

Carl was feeling very strange. Even though his life (as an uninterested underling to his mechanic dad during the day and a rabid sports fan after hours) left little room for intuition, his gut was telling him that something was wrong here. Something felt . . . off.

Carl quickly scurried back through the curtains. He jumped off the stage.

Surveying the empty dining room, Carl listened to the sounds of cracking and crashing and clattering coming from the arcade and the front hallway. The sounds settled him. Even better, they gave him back his pluck. His smirk returned, and he turned to face the stage.

Laughing at himself for letting the backstage get to him, Carl was tempted to thumb his nose at the stage curtains, which were still swaying slightly from his movement through them. Then he got a better idea.

Carl's parents had never instilled in him the idea that he was anything other than a disappointment who wouldn't amount to much. As a result, Carl had been walking around for years with a frustrated ball of "I hate you" in his stomach. It wasn't like he hid his disdain for the world; he flung around plenty of grousing and sarcasm. But Carl had never fully expressed the depths of his scorn. Now he was going to.

Tucking his flashlight in his belt, Carl started whistling as he unzipped his fly. "Place smells like a sewer," Carl muttered. "So . . ."

Carl planted his feet at the base of the stage. "Fire in the hole," he said.

* * *

Jeff cackled in giddy elation as he looked down at a fount of quarters erupting into the air. Tinging and trilling and chirring, the coins scattered over the black and white squares on the floor. When they hit the dirty checkerboard, the coins spun and rolled and hopped.

"That's what I'm talking about," Jeff said.

He looked down at the coins and started to bend over to gather them, but then his gaze landed on the next machine's locked coin box. *One more*, he thought.

He stepped to the next machine and used his crowbar to pry open the vault. It gave way as easily as the last one had, and another waterfall of change gushed out over the floor.

This time, Jeff couldn't help himself. He dropped to his knees, and he grabbed a handful of glittering bounty. "Yes!" he shouted as he raised his fist and savored the feel of the coins' rough, round edges.

Yeah, they were just quarters, not gold doubloons, but Jeff still felt like an adventurer unearthing treasure. The last time he'd been this jubilant was when he'd hit a modest jackpot with the quarter slots at a casino in Vegas. Then his haul hadn't been all that great, but the sound of the dings and hoots and cascading coins had given him a rush. He felt that same rush now.

Jumping to his feet, Jeff shot toward the next machine in line. He raised his crowbar.

*   *   *

After expressing his opinion of Freddy's—and the world in general—Carl had moved on to the kitchen. There, he found plenty of things to beat up on.

Carl hooted as mountains of red plates and saucers shot forward out of the stainless-steel shelving unit he'd just knocked over. The dinnerware exploded out over the floor, and Carl hopped up and down on the broken pieces, his heavy boots grinding into the crockery's sand-like bits.

"Yeah!" Carl shouted.

He turned toward the expanse of stainless-steel cabinets on the opposite wall. Anticipating more ruinous fun, Carl threw open one of the cabinet doors.

The shelves behind the door were empty. Carl let out an involuntary sigh, his bubble burst.

Shrugging, Carl slammed the cabinet door. "Whatever," Carl muttered. He moved on to the next cabinet.

Flinging its door open, fully prepared to dump more fragile porcelain . . . or whatever it was . . . Carl's shoulders slumped when he once again found empty shelves.

Angered, Carl tried the next door. And the next.

Empty. Empty.

Carl tried one more.

The last cabinet wasn't empty.

A small, painted-plastic-and-metal cupcake sat on the cabinet's bottom shelf. Bright pink, with googly eyes and two big white teeth, the cupcake, sporting one upright candle, was centered on a small, white plate.

Carl frowned. "What the . . . ?"

*　*　*

Hank ambled into the dining room, whistling along with the music in his head. Ever since he'd started pounding on the drywall, Hank had been hearing the frenetic notes of the "Toreador" song from *Carmen*. Hank loved that music. It always made him feel like a winner when he heard it, and it had become sort of his personal theme song.

Hank twirled his bat as he rambled past a collapsed stack of bent and dirty chairs. His whistling got louder, and he directed the music with his free hand.

The urge to dance returned as Hank looked for something else to destroy. A clatter came from the arcade, and he looked that way, tempted to join Jeff. Hank, however, didn't want to step on the kid's toes. Jeff tried to act tough, but Hank knew the guy was a closet pussycat. Hank also knew Jeff was afraid of him. Hank thought that was a hoot, and he played into it as much as possible. But today, he'd decided to let Jeff feel like he was the leader. Nah, Hank could find something else to play with.

Maybe the kitchen, Hank thought. He started meandering in that direction, using his bat to destroy as much furniture as he could along the way.

* * *

The kitchen, although not by any means bright, was lit up enough that Carl hadn't needed his flashlight to see. The cupcake nestled in a misshapen patch of darkness under the shelf above it, however, required more illumination. What was that thing?

Carl lifted his flashlight and aimed its beam at the bulging white eyes nestled in hot pink. The ants-crawling-on-the-skin feeling he'd gotten backstage returned. The cupcake was just plain . . . *wrong*. The way its gaze appeared to be locked on Carl made him want to . . .

The cupcake blinked.

Carl yelped.

Before he could decide what to do about the animated mini-cake, a resounding *clang* came from behind him. Carl spun around.

Not sure what to expect when he turned, but totally pent-up and ready for . . . well, anything . . . Carl was relieved when he saw no movement except the back-and-forth motion of two large copper pots hanging from a stainless-steel rack above the heavy-duty restaurant range. Carl rolled his eyes at his overreaction and reversed direction to return his attention to the weird little cupcake.

He once again aimed his flashlight at the—

The cupcake was gone.

Carl sucked in his breath as he stared at the uneven light jittering out in front of his flashlight. His gaze backed up to his hand. It was shaking.

Well, hell yeah, it was shaking. *Where did the cupcake go?*

His eyes as wide open as he could get them, Carl slowly rotated, clutching his flashlight as he swept the area around him with its beam. The wobbly ray of light cut through the kitchen's splotchy grayness, and landed on . . .

Carl's eyes nearly popped out of his head.

He'd found the cupcake.

And that wasn't all.

The pink cupcake, and its plate, were now being held in a massive yellow-furred hand.

Carl's flashlight beam waggled as it rose upward from the cupcake. When the light encountered the moth-holed, dingy-yellow face of a massive chick with a huge mouth full of bared teeth, Carl only had a second to feel a surge of shock before the psychotic-looking bird lunged at him.

CHAPTER 12

Just a couple steps from the service door that separated the kitchen from the back hallway, Hank was readying his bat when he heard a shriek that stopped him in his tracks. The shriek was so loud it felt like it radiated right through Hank's skin and drilled into his veins, congealing the blood that was trying to flow through them.

The sound very clearly came from the other side of the door Hank was approaching. His whole body was quivering in response to the chilling sound. The shriek had been so piercing that it hadn't sounded human.

But if the shriek was human, it had to have come from . . . his son.

Hank stepped forward and cautiously peered through the round window set in the service door. Tense, ready to react . . . and hanging back a couple feet from the door . . . Hank looked through the dirty glass.

Because the kitchen's lights were so lame, Hank couldn't see much of anything through the glass. He had to get closer.

The "Toreador" song having come to a screeching stop . . . and

the tinkling sounds in the arcade having ended a few minutes before . . . Hank shook off the sudden grim silence that
pressed in around him. He put his face up to the door's glass.

The silence gave way to another crescendo of noise. This
time, screams intertwined with heavy gasps and a clamorous
chaos of *taps* and *clangs* and *thunks*.

Hank's gaze looked toward the sounds and he saw . . .

Hank let out a mewl of surprise and horror. His breath—
caught half-in and half-out—threatened to choke him.

Hank gawped at the prone body of his son.

Starting at Carl's flopping feet and moving up to his
writhing body, Hank's gaze landed on something that just . . .
couldn't . . . be . . . possible. But it was.

A small, bright pink cupcake with a toothy mouth was
chewing its way through Carl's face . . . or what was left of it.

"Carl," Hank breathed.

The truth was, Carl no longer had a face. The cupcake
was burrowed halfway into Carl's head. The bone structure of
Carl's face was obliterated.

And the cupcake was still going.

Too stunned to even begin to process what he was seeing,
Hank yanked his gaze upward. It tracked along strips of
fuzzy yellow and orange material clinging to exposed metal.
It ran over the bulge of more fuzzy yellow, past a dirty bib
with the words LET'S EAT, and it landed on an open orange
beak revealing two rows of vicious-looking teeth. Above
the teeth and the beak, irradiant white eyes were staring
directly back at Hank.

Hank screamed.

*   *   *

Once he'd emptied all the coin vaults of their booty, Jeff had filled his duffel bag with his loot and slung it over his shoulder. Straining, happily, Jeff had headed toward the front of the restaurant.

Jeff had seen Hank heading toward the back hallway. He didn't know where Carl was, and at that moment, he hadn't cared. He was in search of more spoils.

Doing a quick exploration of the front hallway, poking his head briefly behind each of the closed doors, Jeff had found the security office at the end of the hall. When he'd spotted the old security camera equipment, he knew he could do some real damage in that room.

Jeff had smiled wildly as he stepped into the unlit room—its only light came from the security monitors. Eager to lay waste to the equipment, Jeff hadn't bothered swiping at the light switch. He'd dropped his duffel bag on the floor; it had landed with a satisfying rush of *clinks* and a few tinkles as a handful of coins escaped from the canvas carrier.

Jeff had started toward the desk that held the monitors. He'd raised his crowbar in preparation for some more body-buzzing vandalism.

Stepping behind the desk, Jeff had taken aim at the monitors . . .

And that was when he heard the screams.

It started with a screech that didn't even sound like it had come from a person's mouth. A stretch of silence. And then another set of screams. More silence. Then one long, drawn out scream.

Instead of laying waste to them with his crowbar, Jeff looked at the monitors. His gaze whipped from one to the next.

The last, long scream had been deep and uneven. Jeff was sure it had come from Hank.

"Hank?" Jeff leaned forward and looked at the monitors. He scanned all the interior views.

There!

On the dining room camera feed, Hank could be seen sprinting through the wide-open space. He was running flat-out, as if being chased by a whole hoard of ghouls.

Rapt, Jeff watched until Hank disappeared from the dining room feed. Jeff's gaze shifted to the adjoining monitor, and sure enough . . . there was Hank pounding down the main hallway. He was coming toward the office.

But wait . . .

On the monitor, Hank stopped and looked back over his shoulder. His movements were spasmodic. He was clearly scared out of his mind.

As Jeff continued watching the monitor, Hank flung open one of the doors that lined the hall, one about midway down. Hank dashed through the door and disappeared from view.

Jeff frowned and looked at the other monitors. None of them provided a view of what was behind the door Hank had gone through. It was a supply closet; Jeff knew this from his cursory check of the area.

"What the hell are you doing?" Jeff asked a Hank who couldn't see or hear him.

* * *

When he'd broken out all the poster-frame glass, Hank hadn't thought to destroy the frosted glass set into all the doors. He wasn't sure why he hadn't, but now he was glad he had left the doors alone. Hank was hoping this one was going to prevent him from having his face eaten . . . or something worse.

Hank wasn't sure what kind of enclosure he was in. A closet? A room? The most weensy bit of light from the hallway seeped through the frosted glass in the door, and that light revealed little more than the doorframe and the doorknob. Everything else around Hank was so black that it was like the void of light had mass and substance. It felt like that mass was crowding in around Hank, attempting to wrap him in a less-than-friendly hug.

The sounds of Hank's wheezing breaths filled the darkness. He could smell the reek of his own sweat and the stink of his breath—it smelled like the stale coffee he'd swilled before coming to the pizzeria.

Outside the door, a shout reached down the hall. "Hank!"

It was Jeff's voice . . . and the guy didn't sound particularly scared. His voice was laced with more curiosity than fear.

Hank exhaled in relief. If Jeff was coming down the hall calling Hank's name, the big yellow bird thing couldn't have been nearby. Jeff wasn't the sharpest tool in the toolbox, but he wasn't stupid enough to be calling out like that if he was facing a threat.

"Jeff?" Hank shouted.

"Hank!" Jeff responded. "What're you doing?" His voice was a little faint. He was still a ways down the hall.

A force of two was better than a force of one. Together, they could get out of the building. Hank grabbed the doorknob. He tried to turn it.

It wouldn't budge.

Hank jiggled the knob . . . forcefully. It held fast.

He threw his considerable bulk against the door. It held up to his weight.

No longer thinking about Jeff . . . or anything else . . . Hank was now single-mindedly intent on getting out of the room he was stuck in. He tried battering the door with his body again, but that got him nothing but a sore shoulder.

Hank turned and looked into the outer space–like vacuum behind him. He quailed and turned back to the door. He began swiping at the wall with the flat of his hand.

"C'mon," Hank muttered. There had to be a light switch.

But there wasn't. Hank's groping hands found nothing but rough wall. Even when he stepped to the right and the left . . .

A telltale jingling came from above Hank's head. *Not a switch*, he thought. *A pullcord!*

Hank reached up and felt around. His hand encountered the end of a heavy string. He grasped it and pulled.

Nothing.

"C'mon you stupid . . ." Hank began as he yanked again.

This time, the cord did its job.

A single, bare lightbulb came on.

Hank blew out a pent-up breath. "Yeah," he said.

Now all he had to do was find something in the room that could break the door's knob or its glass. Hank turned . . .

. . . and looked right into a pair of glowing eyes.

These eyes didn't belong to the ugly, lethal-looking chick. But they didn't belong to anything cuddly, either.

Hank was looking up into another tooth-filled face. This face, topped by two bent rabbit ears, was missing most of its fur. Its bright white eyes were surrounded by a mass of metal and exposed wires. Hank screamed yet again.

*   *   *

Just a few feet from the closet Hank's calls had come from, Jeff, who was walking slowly—lugging the heavy duffel bag—froze when he heard Hank's scream. Jeff looked toward the door.

The first scream was followed by a second one. Then a third.

The sounds of whipping and crunching, which wrapped around the screams like devouring serpents, reached out from behind the door. The door rattled. Then . . . smack!

A silhouetted hand hit the door's frosted glass. Jeff's breathing caught in his throat when he watched the hand leave an opaque smear across the glass. The smear streaked downward above the hand, and the hand dropped from view.

Hank wasn't screaming anymore, Jeff realized.

When the hand disappeared from the glass, all Jeff could hear was a faint gurgle. Then silence.

Jeff's crowbar slipped from his hand. It hit the linoleum with a *clang* that rebounded down the hall and then seemed to boomerang back to Jeff.

His gaze still riveted on the door, Jeff adjusted the duffel bag strap that cut into his shoulder. It felt like the bag was getting heavier by the minute.

Jeff took a tentative step toward the closed door. "Hank?" he whispered.

Jeff wasn't sure why he said Hank's name. He didn't know what had happened to Hank, but he knew it wasn't good.

Still, maybe Hank was injured and needed help. Jeff shuffled forward another half-step, but he stopped when the door shimmied ever so slightly.

Jeff locked his gaze on the door. He looked back down the hallway toward the office. Should he retreat and lock himself in that room?

He looked on down the hall. Should he make a run for it? Head for the main doors?

Jeff's brain was chained by the blood-engorged veins that pulsed madly in tune with his heart's clacketing pace. He couldn't think.

The door began to open. Inch by excruciating inch, more and more mysterious murk was revealed.

"Hank?" Jeff asked.

Hank did not appear.

But something else did.

Jeff felt like the floor beneath him turned into the yawing deck of a boat caught in a hurricane when he saw what was stepping out into the hallway. Reality folded in on itself.

Jeff was looking at the oversized, dilapidated mass of a . . . robotic bunny? Jeff tried to process the torn and dirty fur, the exposed metal beneath it and the blue, bent ears.

And as Jeff looked at the bunny, it turned toward him. The bunny had blazing-white eyes set in the exposed metal of a ravaged face dominated by an impossibly wide mass of horrible teeth. Those eyes were looking . . . right . . . at . . . Jeff.

Jeff's brain, overcome as it was, managed to get a message to Jeff's feet. "Run!" his brain commanded.

Jeff spun around and shot like a rocket down the hall, back toward the office. The heavy duffel bag slammed against Jeff's hip over and over as he ran. The pounding hurt, and yet Jeff couldn't bring himself to drop the bag. He kept lugging it with him as he galloped down the hall.

He could hear the tinkling *clink* of coins hitting the floor behind him, but even that didn't discourage him from hanging on to the bag. He clutched it even as he rushed into the office and slammed the door behind him.

Jeff fumbled with the door lock, eventually clicking it into place. He stared at the door as he finally dropped the duffel bag. More coins spilled over the floor with a clatter. Jeff didn't care.

Looking wildly around him, Jeff spotted the landline phone on the shelf behind the desk. He dashed over to it and snatched up the receiver. He immediately started punching in 911 as he put the phone to his . . .

Jeff pulled the phone from his ear. He winced and stared at the receiver.

A nightmarish clamor of children's laughter was blasting from the phone. The laughter was high-pitched and frenzied.

Jeff dropped the receiver back into its cradle. He looked over at the door. It was still closed, and Jeff couldn't see anything through the glass.

He turned his attention to the CCTV monitors. His gaze immediately landing on the exterior feed that was focused on the back of the building, Jeff saw his truck still sitting next to the loading dock. Max remained in the cab with Bonesy.

For an instant, Jeff's heart rate slowed. That truck was safety. All he had to do was get to . . .

Movement on another monitor caught Jeff's attention. He looked at it.

Glaring directly back at Jeff—or rather, at the camera that fed this monitor—were the blue bunny and . . . a yellow chick with a sharp yellow beak. Although the chick's face was in better shape than the rabbit's, it didn't look any less threatening.

Both the chick and the bunny continued to study the camera. Jeff could feel them looking past the lens, down the wires, directly at him. He took a step back from the monitors.

At the same time, the chick on the monitor moved. Jeff stepped forward again, leaning in to see the monitor more clearly.

Jeff watched the chick bend over and crouch down. It was right in front of a vent cover low down on the wall.

Jeff felt his brows bunch as he tried to figure out what the chick was . . .

The chick wrenched the vent cover off the wall. Then she held a plate out in front of her.

Jeff blinked. He hadn't even noticed the plate . . . until a bright pink cupcake with buck teeth hopped off the plate and disappeared into the now-open vent.

"What in the . . . ?" Jeff began.

Metallic banging and clanging resounded through the building. It was muffled and distant, but it stretched out and reached, like fingers, into the office.

Jeff looked at the walls around him. The sound was coming from within them.

He returned his attention to the monitors, urging his brain to help him out. What was going . . . ?

Jeff looked at the walls again as the banging continued. And then he got it.

"No," Jeff said.

The banging began getting louder. The cupcake was moving fast.

Jeff stepped away from the desk and quickly scanned the room, his gaze going left and right, up and down. *Was there a . . . ?*

His gaze landed on a vent cover on the wall. Jeff stared at it as the banging's volume went up another couple notches.

Getting close, Jeff thought. He immediately dropped to his knees. He ducked under the credenza and looked at the vent cover. He had to find a way to block . . .

A noisy, clinking bang . . . Jeff spotted bright pink on the other side of the vent cover.

Instantaneously, Jeff braced himself against the slatted metal. It thrashed against his shoulder.

Jeff yelped and looked down between the slats. He could see a fury of bright pink through the dark gray openings. The office's fluorescent bulbs caught the white of gnashing, razor-sharp teeth snapping viciously at the slatted metal.

Jeff hiccupped several panicked breaths. Trying to brace his rubber-soled hiking boots against the dusty linoleum, Jeff attempted to press harder against the vent cover. The dust, however, created a surface as slick as ice, and Jeff's feet slipped away from him.

The teeth against the metal slats sounded like metal meeting a power saw—the high, tinny sound was drilling into Jeff's eardrums. Whimpering, he tried to replant his feet, but they once again slid across the floor.

The vent cover shuddered, and a corner of it popped loose from the wall. Jeff wailed. He squeezed his eyes shut and shifted his shoulder to press against the loose edge. Another clamorous slam and . . .

Silence.

His breathing still ragged, his pulse pounding, Jeff opened one eye and looked through the slats. He saw . . .

. . . nothing.

Jeff tilted his head and looked hard into the air shaft's gloom.

The chute behind the vent cover was empty.

Jeff exhaled loudly. He pulled his shoulder from the vent cover and brought a shaky hand to his face, wiping away the sweat that matted his hair to his skin and ran down his neck. Weakly, Jeff levered himself to his feet. He took another deep breath. As he started to exhale, he turned back toward the desk.

Jeff froze.

His breathing stopped mid-exhale.

The office door was open.

Feeling like his eyeballs were vibrating in his head, Jeff strained to look through the open doorway. At the same time, he tried to reason out *why* the door was open.

He had locked it. Hadn't he?

And even if he hadn't, who had opened it?

Jeff's gaze whipped around the office. He was the only one in it, but . . .

His attention snapped to the filing cabinets on the opposite wall and to the single upright locker next to a breaker box on the wall opposite the door. Could something small have gotten into . . . ?

That disturbing thought lit a fire under Jeff's feet. He hustled toward the open door.

Hesitating next to the doorjamb, equally afraid of what might be hiding in the office and what might be lurking outside of it, Jeff inched his head through the door opening. Once he had his head far enough out into the hall to see, he looked along the length of the hall in both directions. He saw nothing.

Jeff couldn't belief his luck. And he wasn't going to waste it. He immediately dashed out into the hallway and started toward the . . .

"Da dum dum dum diddly dum."

Jeff turned into a statue. *What was that?*

The voice, which seemed to be bouncing every which way at once, was a cross between a chant and a monotonous song. It was a teasing voice, but not a nice teasing. The tone was one a bully would use . . . taunting, torturing.

Jeff rethought his action plan. Maybe running through the hall wasn't such a great idea at the moment. He turned and started back toward the office.

As soon as Jeff took a step, though, the office door whipped shut with a resounding *wham*. Jeff recoiled but he recovered quickly. Rushing forward, Jeff grabbed the doorknob and tried to turn it.

The knob wouldn't move.

Jeff shook it. The knob didn't give at all. It was locked.

And worse, from down the hall toward the lobby, a tinkling, skittering sound was heading in Jeff's direction. A scrape and a clink. A cascade of clinks.

Jeff knew exactly what that sound was. He was hearing the coins that had leaked from his duffel bag when he was running. They were strewn through the hallway, and now, they were being moved by . . .

. . . footsteps.

Shuffle. Clink. Scrape. Clatter.

Something was moving the coins across the linoleum.

"Diddly dum dum diddly da . . ."

Each note of the jeering little ditty drilled into Jeff's body, like each tone was one of a billion nanobots boring in through his pores. Jeff's whole body began to tremble. He could even hear his teeth chattering.

Jeff whipped away from the office door. He took off down

the hall, away from the lobby, toward the red EXIT sign at the hallway's end.

In full gallop when he reached the emergency exit door, Jeff slammed into the crash bar . . . and bounced back. As he shifted his feet to keep his balance, he heard a rapid rush of footsteps whizzing toward him.

Jeff turned . . . just in time to see the flash of a pirate's hook arcing through the air, heading directly at his face. Jeff opened his mouth to scream . . .

. . . but the sound was cut off before it could begin.

CHAPTER 13

No matter how steadily Maxine stroked Bonesy's fur, the dog wouldn't settle. Maxine had cuddled close to the dog in the pickup cab, but still he hadn't stopped whining and whimpering since Jeff and the others had disappeared into the pizzeria. Bonesy's jowls were frothed with drool, and his whole body was quivering. It was making Maxine nervous, primarily because Bonesy's anxiety was contagious. And Maxine didn't need the dog's apprehension added to her own. She was plenty agitated already.

For maybe the twentieth, or fiftieth, time, Maxine pushed up the cuff of the long-sleeved black shirt she'd worn for this stupid, ill-conceived venture. She frowned at the digital numbers on her black sports watch.

Where the hell are they? Maxine asked herself.

Enough was enough. Maxine couldn't sit here waiting any longer. She couldn't imagine what was taking them so long. They were supposed to have made a quick mess, grabbed anything valuable, and come back out. That shouldn't have taken this much time.

Huffing, Maxine reached for the driver's-side door handle. She flung the door open.

Before Maxine could move a muscle to leave the pickup, Bonesy leaped across her. In a fraction of a second, the dog was out of the truck and bolting away.

"Bonesy, wait!" Maxine scrambled out of the truck and started after her dog.

"Bonesy!" she shouted again.

Bonesy didn't break stride. He crossed the broken asphalt in a flash of fur. Maxine ran, but before she'd made it even ten feet, Bonesy had disappeared into the trees at the edge of the pizzeria's lot.

Maxine stopped. Her heart was a jackhammer in her chest. Her mind immediately filled with images of Bonesy getting lost. Or stolen. Or hit by a car. Or mauled by a wild animal.

Maxine hugged herself.

Reluctantly, she turned back to the pickup. She couldn't outrun her dog. Her best bet was to go after him in the truck.

But she didn't have the keys. Her brother did.

Maxine had no choice. She had to go inside the building and get Jeff so they could go after Bonesy.

Maxine looked up at the open loading dock door. What lay beyond it looked like the yawning opening to a demon's lair.

"Not smart," Maxine muttered as she took a step forward.

Yeah, but she didn't have a better idea. So, she kept going.

Picking her way across the dirty, disintegrating concrete of the loading dock, Max went slowly, allowing her eyes time to adjust to the insufficient light. Once she had more night vision, she was able to spot a flattened door. That must have been the battering sound she'd heard right after Jeff and the others had disappeared from her sight.

Maxine crept forward. She reached the open doorway and leaned through it. She peered left and right and saw that she was on the threshold of the pizzeria's stainless-steel-filled industrial kitchen.

"Jeff?" Maxine called softly.

Nothing but silence answered her.

Maxine gingerly stepped into the kitchen. She looked around.

"Carl?" she tried.

This time, Maxine got a response. Of sorts.

The trill of a child's laughter came from behind Maxine. The sound felt like a light touch, a tickle between her shoulder blades.

Maxine twirled around.

Immediately, she saw the source of the laughter.

Standing in a muted golden luminance emanating from a door on the opposite side of the kitchen, a little sandy-haired boy stared at Maxine coolly. No smile. No expression at all. The child's expression was blank.

He must be lost, Maxine thought. *And traumatized.*

Maxine opened her mouth to say hello, but the boy turned and dashed away before she could even begin her greeting. He flashed through the open doorway and disappeared into the dapples of gray outside of the kitchen.

"Hey, wait!" Maxine shouted.

No longer thinking about her brother or Bonesy, Maxine strode forward, following the boy. A lost little kid trumped everything. She had to help him.

Exiting the kitchen, Maxine found herself in a long hallway that was as dark and uninviting as an abandoned tunnel in a coal mine. She looked left and right down the black-and-white-checkerboard-floored hall. It was empty.

"Hello?" Maxine called out.

The word danced down the hall, spun around, and came back. A pervasive hush chased it.

Max tried again, more loudly. "*Hello!*"

Once again, the word twirled away from her and came flying back. Once again, utter stillness followed it.

Maxine frowned, gazing down the hall again, both ways. Which direction should she go?

Maxine shrugged. She turned to her left.

"Cold!" The word came out in two syllables: "Co . . . old." It was a child's voice. From the pitch, it sounded like the same little boy who had giggled.

The sound came from the right end of the hallway. Maxine reversed her direction. She took a step forward.

"Warmer!" Same little boy's voice. Playful.

Maxine made a face. "You've got to be kidding me," she muttered.

The kid wasn't as traumatized as she'd thought he was. Maybe he wasn't even lost. Still, she should probably find him in case he was. And she still needed to find Jeff, too.

Maxine took a half-step forward. Her head swiveled left and right. All of her nerve endings were on alert.

For the next few minutes, Maxine pushed deeper into the bowels of the tomblike building. Pausing to listen at closed doors (but lacking the courage to open them), Maxine followed the hallway until it went around a corner.

"Warmer," the boy said again.

His voice sounded both close and far away at the same time. Maxine still couldn't figure out where the kid was. It almost seemed like he was in the walls, moving along with her. But that was impossible.

Maxine looked down the stretch of corridor in front of her. And for the first time since she'd left the kitchen, she saw movement.

A set of double doors at the far end of the hall was swinging, as if someone had just pushed through them. Maxine eyed the wagging doors.

Had the boy gone that way?

Or was it someone else?

Maxine opened her mouth to call her brother's name, but some instinct closed her mouth again. Wrapping her arms around herself to ward off the chill that made it feel like her skin was inching its way along her bones, Maxine walked slowly toward the doors.

Each of her steps ticked a shy cadence on the cracked linoleum. *Tap, tap, tap.* Maxine, fighting the overpowering urge to run in the opposite direction, forced herself forward. She felt oddly disconnected from herself, as if she wasn't so much moving as she was *being moved.* It felt like she was being compelled through a black hole by some magnetic force.

And then she was pushing through the double doors herself. Halfway through them, she paused.

Pencil-like lines of golden light, three of them, inched toward Maxine. She looked ahead at them, and she realized she was seeing sunlight coming through dirty, narrow windows. The light was odd, almost sepia-toned.

Maxine took another step and let go of the doors. A *shush-shush* and a tickle of air current told her the doors were falling closed behind her.

"Hello?" Maxine called. "Are you in here?"

When she got no answer . . . again . . . Maxine checked her surroundings. As soon as she did, her crawling skin picked up its pace. So did her heart rate.

What is this place?

Maxine rotated to take in the metal shelving and stainless-steel worktables. Her gaze scanned piles of tools and what looked like robotic parts. Metal legs and arms and torsos and eyeless heads were . . .

Maxine's gaze stopped scanning and locked in. It had gotten stuck on something Maxine hadn't noticed at first. Beyond the worktables, a reclining metal chair with straps sat empty. Above the chair and spaced throughout the room, metal pendant lights hung low, dripping only the barest hint of illumination.

That's not good, Maxine thought.

Maxine so wanted to run. Why wasn't she running?

Against her own will, Maxine took another two steps into the room. She intended to look around to see if she could spot the little boy, but her gaze remained riveted on the chair.

Even when Maxine felt a shiver of warning skittering down her spine, the sensation of being watched strong and urgent, she kept her gaze fixed on the chair. For all she knew, a monster was behind her, but she couldn't seem to turn to find out.

"Psst." It was the little boy again. Close . . . and loud.

Maxine yelped and finally spun around.

She scrutinized the area behind her, but she couldn't see the kid. Where was he?

Maxine was getting really, really tired of this game. It was beyond creepy in here.

The robot parts Maxine had first seen in the room were bad enough, but now her gaze had landed on a more complete robot. An animatronic. A big one. Maxine had to tilt her head back to inspect the full height of it.

The jitters that were still prodding Maxine to run kicked up a notch, but Maxine stayed where she was. She studied the massive thing guardedly.

What Maxine was looking at appeared to be a decommissioned version of one of the animal characters that had been part of the pizzeria's heyday. In fact, Maxine thought, as she looked at the motley, broken-down bear more closely, this might have been Freddy himself.

Although the stiff, ragged-looking robotic bear had all its parts intact (unlike whatever critters had lost the pieces lying around the room), it had seen better days. Its brown fur, matted, grungy, and smelling disgustingly of decay, had large chunks missing, as if something had eaten its way through the plush covering from the inside. The missing pieces of fur revealed ropey twines of wires and sharp lengths of aging metal. The bear face was the most intact part of the robot's structure. It's impossibly wide mouth was stuffed full of what looked like very sharp white teeth, and its round, white eyes were in pristine condition.

"In here!" It was the little boy again. His voice was muffled, and it was coming from . . .

Maxine gave herself a mental shake. *That can't be right*, she thought.

But replaying the boy's words in her head, Maxine realized she had heard what she'd thought she'd heard. The boy's voice was coming from inside the ratty bear.

"How in the heck did you get in there?" Maxine asked. Her question was hushed, disbelieving.

Steeling herself, Maxine took a step forward. She kept an eye unwaveringly on the bear as she stepped forward yet again. Hesitating an instant, she finally leaned in and put her ear against the grimy bear's chest.

Maxine immediately heard a childish giggle. She jumped back and gawked at the bear's belly.

The kid was inside the bear. How did it . . . ?

It didn't matter. Maxine had to get the kid out of the thing. Giggling or not, the boy was little, and Maxine couldn't just leave him inside a mountain of gross fur and metal.

But how was she going to get the boy out?

Maxine walked around the bear. Gingerly, she poked and pushed at various parts of its anatomy. *There must be a switch or something*, she thought.

Nothing that Maxine messed with on the bear did anything, except the jaw. When Maxine reached up and put her hand against the side of the bear's head, the jaw moved. Encouraged, Maxine shifted her hand and levered the jaw downward. The bear's mouth yawned apart, revealing an opening that got bigger. And bigger. And bigger.

Maxine goggled at the huge, gaping hole that now made up the lower half of the bear's face. She frowned at the aperture. Was it big enough for a child to get through?

Probably.

But from where Maxine stood, well below the bear's open mouth, she couldn't see down inside the bear.

Maxine looked around the room. She needed something to stand on.

Maxine spotted a folding chair tucked against the end of one of the long shelves. She trotted over and grabbed it.

Bringing the dirty, gray metal chair back to the animatronic, Maxine positioned it in front of the bear's legs. She stepped up onto the chair's seat.

The chair let out a snapping *ping*, and it wobbled. But it held. Maxine shifted her feet and leaned toward the gaping mouth.

It was amazing how a human being could powerfully want to

do one thing and yet do the exact opposite. Every fiber of Maxine's being was yelling, "*No!*" as she put her face toward the bear's parted teeth.

As soon as Maxine got close enough to the mouth, she tilted her head to look down inside the cavern of the bear's torso. She gasped when a small hand rose up, reaching toward her face.

"There you . . ." Maxine began.

But then her words, and her face, were snatched downward.

The little hand had seized her by the mouth, small fingers curled around her lower teeth and lip. It yanked, and Maxine, squealing, was heaved downward through a metal-filled tunnel wrapped in wires.

Maxine was on the skinny side, but she wasn't skinny enough to fit comfortably through the confines of an animatronic trachea. Metal scoring at her skin, Maxine screamed as her feet came off the chair.

Vaguely aware of the sound of the chair clattering to the floor, Maxine scissored her feet and pressed her hands against the bear's crusty shoulders. She pushed against the hard surface and kicked frantically.

Maxine felt her foot graze against something, and she heard a *ting*. She'd hit one of the pendant lights.

Trying to twist one way and then the other to get free, Maxine saw the pendant's light rays careen frenziedly back and forth.

Still being lowered inexorably into a seemingly bottomless, lightless well, Maxine kept fighting, even as her skin was ravaged by serrated metal. She craned her neck, looking up toward freedom. On the ceiling, she caught a glimpse of a shadow play. Her churning legs and flapping arms created a tangle of light and dark entanglements that looked like the battle between a knight and a tail-whipping dragon. Watching her struggle this way almost made it seem impersonal, like Maxine was outside of it, not caught within it.

Another powerful tug came from inside the bear, and Maxine had to admit that this was happening to her, and it was *very* personal. Maxine slipped even farther into the darkness, and then . . .

A shocking, searing, jagged pressure sliced through Maxine's waist, and she screamed. Through her screams, she heard a wet *thud*.

Maxine's brain had only seconds left, but in those seconds, Maxine knew she'd just heard the sound of her lower body hitting the floor. The bear had bitten her in half.

* * *

Mike sat at his kitchen table. He wasn't doing much of anything, just sitting there. Well, actually, he was doing something. He held the plastic-and-tin fake security badge, and he was turning it over and over in his hand . . . staring at it, as if it were a crystal ball that could give him answers to his endless questions.

Most of Mike's questions were related to the odd happenings in his dreams. Those questions were so complex that he knew he had no hope of answering them.

Another set of questions were related to Vanessa. What an odd woman. But odd in a good way. Mike was powerfully drawn to her . . . and at the same time, she made him profoundly nervous. No way his brain could think him out of that tangle, either.

Of course, there were the usual questions about how Mike was going to clean up the trainwreck that was his life. But those questions were old and boring. And they, too, had no answers.

So, Mike settled on the most immediate puzzle. How could he make up with Abby? His sister was seriously angry with him for locking her in her room the night before. As a result, she was even more distant than usual.

Mike wished he could explain to Abby that everything he did was part of his attempt to take care of her. His overriding goal was to protect her, keep her safe. But Abby didn't want to hear anything Mike had to say.

A few feet from Mike, high-pitched chatter and canned laughter came from the TV. Abby sat on the sofa, but she didn't seem to be paying attention to the cartoon on the screen. She was, as usual, bent over her drawing pad. She scribbled constantly, a furrow between her brows, her tongue clamped between her teeth and protruding from her lips.

Mike sighed and stood. He walked over to the couch and sat down next to Abby.

"What are you working on?" Mike asked.

Abby stopped drawing. She got up and flounced into the kitchen, sitting down in the very chair that Mike had just vacated. Mike sighed.

"So, what's the plan here?" Mike asked Abby's back.

She was wearing banana-yellow overalls today. The crisscross of the overall's back straps seemed to glare at Mike. "You're never going to speak to me again?" he pushed.

Abby said nothing. She centered her drawing pad in front of her on the table. She arranged a dozen or so drawing pens next to it, then she bent over her drawing again.

Seems like it, Mike thought.

Mike fingered the badge once more. He held it up, out in front of him. "I guess you don't want this, then," he said.

Abby looked up.

Mike smiled. *Gotcha*, he thought.

Mike tossed the badge to Abby. She lifted a hand and caught it.

"Pretty cool, right?" Mike asked.

Abby held the badge and glanced at it with apparent disinterest. Mike knew her well enough, however, to recognize fake nonchalance when he saw it. Maybe he'd cracked her armor.

But no. Abby threw the badge back at Mike. He barely snatched it from the air before it hit him in the nose.

Abby picked up a pencil and returned to drawing. Mike looked up at the ceiling and exhaled loudly.

"Forget it," he said.

Mike stood. Striding back into the kitchen, he grabbed the knob of the junk drawer near the sink. He went to pull it open. It jammed. He jiggled it, biting back a curse.

Finally, he got the drawer open, and he dropped the toy badge in with the other junk. He rammed the drawer back into place.

Turning toward his sister, Mike said, to the back of her head, "I'm trying my best, Abby. I really am."

Abby remained mute.

Okay, so it's like that, Mike thought.

Mike headed toward the hallway. At first, Abby didn't move, but then, out of the corner of Mike's eye, he saw her lift her head . . . just a little.

Mike pretended he didn't see Abby's gaze flit his way. He also pretended that he didn't see her expression, which looked every bit as remorseful as he felt himself.

Maybe she'll come around soon, Mike told himself as he headed to his bedroom.

There was nothing he could do if she didn't. And certainly, there was nothing more he could do right now.

On to other mysteries.

Mike entered his bedroom. Leaving the door open so he could listen for Abby . . . in case she decided to call to him . . . or get in some kind of trouble, Mike opened his closet and plucked his laptop from the single shelf above his pitifully sparse collection of clothes. Heck, make that his sparse collection of his belongings, period.

Mike had no furniture in his room, other than a bed and a nightstand, not just because he couldn't afford anything more. He also had no need for other pieces of furniture. He had nothing to put on or in dressers or bureaus or desks. Besides his clothes and shoes, his laptop, and a few tools, all his closet held was a box of old photographs and a plastic container of wooden blocks. The blocks had been Mike's favorite toy when he was a kid—he'd always loved building things. In spite of everything, he couldn't bring himself to throw the blocks out.

Taking his laptop to his bed, and feeling supremely sorry for himself, Mike fluffed his pillow and settled himself back against the headboard. He opened his laptop. After logging in, he clicked on his browser icon, and he started typing in a search box.

Mike began with "Freddy Fazbear." He hit ENTER and looked at the screen.

Mike's search brought up not much more than a bunch of stock images of Freddy and his weirdo cohorts. Mike got up-close looks at the bunny, the chick, and the fox, as well as a few other critters he didn't know about. But he didn't find anything interesting.

He backed out of the search. Then he tried again, typing, "Freddy Fazbear missing children."

"Now we're talking," Mike said as a slew of news headlines

popped up on his screen. Mike scanned them, and he picked, SAD NIGHT AT FREDDY'S.

Clicking on the header, Mike skimmed the article. Unfortunately, it didn't tell him much more than Vanessa had.

But wait. There was an embedded video.

Mike clicked on the video and hit the PLAY icon. Watching the white circle spinning in the middle of his screen, Mike tapped his fingers on the side of his laptop as he waited for the video to load.

Finally, the image of a blonde, pert-nosed female reporter filled Mike's screen. The woman's drop-shouldered top and leggings, as well as the curly wildness of her big hair, screamed '80s. *Mid-'80s*, Mike thought.

The woman had a painted-on face typical for the time. She had large eyes and a wide mouth, and at the moment both eyes and mouth were arranged in a theatrical expression of tragic regret.

The woman was precisely positioned in front of a bright, shiny version of Freddy Fazbear's Pizzeria. It was the Freddy's Mike was "guarding," but it was a blast-from-the-past variant of the place. The paint was fresh. The lighting was bright. And there were people milling around it—lots of people.

And police cars. Several uniformed officers were corralling onlookers. Men in suits, obviously detectives, were strutting about importantly.

The puffy-haired woman wasn't the only reporter on scene, either. A bunch of news vans were parked just beyond a ribbon of yellow crime scene tape, which fluttered in a steady breeze. A few other men and women with microphones posed in front of cameramen who had heavy '80s-era video cameras weighing down their shoulders.

The blonde reporter began speaking. "Tragedy struck tonight," she began predictably, "at a local pizzeria. Freddy's Pizzeria has become renowned for family fun, a great place for kids. But tonight, it was anything but that. Instead, it was the heartbreaking setting of abduction and terror. Five children, who were attending a birthday event at the pizzeria, suddenly and mysteriously vanished into thin air."

Mike was immediately caught up in the scene. He leaned closer to his screen.

CHAPTER 14

Abby tried to concentrate on her drawing, but she was distracted. Her gaze kept drifting up from her pad. Her attention was drawn to the drawer . . . the drawer that held the Freddy's badge.

Abby turned and looked down the hall, toward her brother's room. His door was open, and she could hear a woman's voice, faint . . . just a murmur. Abby couldn't make out the woman's words. It sounded like Mike was on his computer.

Abby turned toward the drawer. Abandoning her artwork, she stood. She stepped over to the drawer and looked down at it.

Okay, so maybe the badge was pretty cool. Just because her stupid brother had tried to give it to her to make up for being mean the night before didn't mean the badge wasn't worth having.

Abby grabbed the drawer handle and pulled. The drawer didn't open. She tried again, but the drawer was jammed.

That wasn't something new. Most of the kitchen drawers got stuck regularly. Usually if you just jiggled them . . .

Abby tried that. She pulled again. Nope. The drawer was shut tight.

Abby turned and braced herself against the side of the counter. She thought that might give her something to push off of so she could pull with more oomph. She grabbed the handle and tried again.

* * *

The news reporter on Mike's laptop screen was stepping into a lobby that was both the same and totally different than the one Mike knew. The floor was the friendly old black-and-white checkerboard. The walls were red-and-white-striped. Freddy's posters. Red vinyl benches.

Beyond these touchstones, however, the lobby was very different. For one thing, it was bright, lit up with brilliant white light. And it was crowded.

The blonde reporter stepped in front of a cluster of uniformed . . .

Crash!

At first, caught up in the video, Mike thought the sound had come from his screen. He quickly realized, though, that the racket wasn't recorded. It was real.

"What the hell was that?" he asked out loud.

Immediately an answer put him in motion. *Abby*, he thought.

Mike quickly set aside his laptop. He jumped up and ran out of his room.

It took Mike only seconds to trot down the hallway. In those seconds, his mind suggested a number of possible catastrophes. He ignored the images and burst into the kitchen. There, he stopped and looked at the floor.

The first thing Mike saw on the floor was the upside-down junk drawer. It lay at an angle against a battered old flashlight. Around the drawer, an explosion of miscellaneous items—old pens, tacks, scraps of paper, a half-empty spool of thread, a pair of scissors, a couple old business cards, several take-out menus, a purple-haired troll, and the fake Freddy's security badge—was scattered across the kitchen's faded green linoleum.

Abby was standing over the mess. Mike opened his mouth to yell at her about being careful, but when he saw the look on her face —and what she held in her hands—his words dissolved in his head. Oh, man, Mike thought.

Missing its cover page, the thick, stapled packet of paper that Abby clutched was the custody proposal Jane had given Mike. Clearly, given the crumpled, devasted expression on Abby's face, she'd read the custody summons' header. He'd never seen her look so hurt.

Why didn't I stash that in my bedroom? Mike asked himself. *Stupid!*

"I made a mess," Abby said. "Sorry."

"It's okay," Mike said. The mess was beside the point. How was he supposed to handle this?

"I'm not mad," Mike said. He held out a hand. "Can I have that?"

Abby hesitated, then she held out the packet of paper. Mike took the papers, wanting very badly to beat himself over the head with them.

"Look," Mike said, "they're just papers. They don't mean anything."

Abby wrinkled her nose. She wasn't falling for that. "Then why do you have them?" she asked.

"It's complicated," Mike said.

Abby gave him a "Oh, come on," look.

Mike tried again. "Your Aunt Jane . . ."

"I hate her," Abby erupted. She stomped a foot and crunched one of the old pens lying next to the crashed drawer. "She smells like cigarettes." Abby made a "something stinks" face. "And she's *mean*," she added.

In spite of the seriousness of the situation, Mike couldn't help himself. He cracked a smile.

Abby stomped her foot again. This time, her heel narrowly missed the poor troll.

"Stop smiling!" Abby commanded. "It's *not* funny!"

Mike kept smiling. "I know," he said. "It's just nice that there's something we can finally agree on."

He was trying to lighten the mood. But Abby wasn't having it.

"You're gonna give me away?" Abby asked. Her voice was small, forlorn.

How do I answer that? Mike asked himself. How could he explain the complexities of the situation to a ten-year-old?

Three sharp raps on his front door saved Mike from dealing with the issue. Attempting to hide his relief, Mike turned and strode toward the door. He pulled it back . . . and his mouth gaped even farther open than the door.

"Vanessa?" Mike wouldn't have been more surprised if he'd found the news reporter with the '80s hair on his front porch.

An avalanche of questions rushed through Mike's head. What was Vanessa doing here? How did she even know where he lived? Was this official business? Was he in some kind of trouble?

Mike looked past Vanessa, who was in full uniform, and eyed her black-and-white cruiser, which was parked in the street beyond his rolling heap. His poor car looked like it was trying to sink down into the gravel drive, humiliated by the comparison of its junkyard appearance next to the cruiser's sleek, shiny paint and chrome.

"Hey, Mike," Vanessa said lightly. It was the friendly Vanessa speaking. She didn't sound official at all.

Mike couldn't get his tongue to work.

Vanessa didn't seem to mind. She looked past Mike's shoulder, and her eyes widened in obvious surprise. "And hello . . . ?"

Mike glanced back and watched his sister tiptoe forward. He returned his attention to Vanessa and pulled the door farther open. "Come in?" he asked.

Vanessa hesitated but then stepped through the doorway. She didn't come all the way in, though. She stood in the doorway, blocking it, so he couldn't close the door. He shrugged. It was warm outside.

Mike felt Abby come up behind him. He looked down and watched her lean out around him to eye Vanessa.

Mike engaged his tongue. "Vanessa," he said, "this is Abby. Abby, Vanessa."

"Hello, Abby," Vanessa said, smiling.

Mike thought the smile looked a little strained.

"Mike didn't tell me he had a daughter," Vanessa said.

Abby made a stink-face. "Gross."

"She's my sister," Mike explained.

Vanessa's smile relaxed into something more genuine. "Ah. Well, he didn't tell me he had a sister, either." Vanessa pointed at Abby. "Love your overalls," she said. She gave Abby a thumbs-up.

"Are you here to arrest Mike?" Abby asked.

Vanessa put her hands on her utility belt. She pulled her brows together into a stern frown. "Why?" she asked. "What did he do?"

Abby stepped out from behind Mike. She sighed dramatically and threw out her hands. "Where do I start?"

Mike watched Vanessa pull her lips together to suppress a smile.

"Hey, Abby," Mike said to his sister, "why don't you go play in your room? I'm going to talk to Vanessa, and then we can clean up that mess in the kitchen."

Abby looked from Mike to Vanessa and back again to Mike. Shrugging, she said, "Okay."

Mike felt like he'd been beamed into another universe. Abby was going to cooperate?

Abby rocked up onto her tiptoes and gave Vanessa a polite smile. "Nice to meet you." She turned and skipped down the hall.

"You too," Vanessa called.

Vanessa and Mike both watched Abby go. When she disappeared into her room, they looked at each other. Then they both spoke at once.

"What are you doing here?" Mike asked.

"Somebody broke into Freddy's," Vanessa said.

Say what? Mike thought. Vanessa's question won.

"Seriously?" Mike said. "What happened?"

Vanessa shook her head in disgust. Mike noticed that the sunlight made streaks in her hair that flashed like light streamers.

"From the look of the place," Vanessa said, "World War III."

Mike couldn't process that. He was distracted by the light show in Vanessa's up-twisted hair.

"We got a call," Vanessa said. "Apparently, someone drove by and saw that the front door was open."

Starting at the word *Apparently*, Vanessa's voice took on a different tone. Gone was the light and friendly. Her words became clipped and severe.

Mike glanced up at Vanessa's face. Her lips looked like they weren't even capable of smiling. They were carved of stone and threatened to crack as she went on, "It doesn't look like anything was taken. But whoever was there sure had their fun."

She was back in full-on cop mode, Mike realized. Her eyes were narrowed and she was inspecting him like he was a criminal suspect. He was half-tempted to ask if he needed a lawyer.

Mike's shoulders stiffened. He clenched his teeth and ground out, "Well, those cameras are everywhere. They must have recorded something."

"They did." Vanessa crossed her arms. "They captured eight hours and forty-two minutes of . . . static." She lifted a brow and looked at Mike questioningly.

No doubt about it. Mike was a suspect. She was interrogating him!

Mike had been joking around with himself when he'd thought about asking for a lawyer, but now he realized this wasn't a joking matter. Even so, it was laughable. And annoying. Mike was tired of being accused of being a screwup.

"Right," Mike snapped. "Okay. Just so we're clear . . . you're suggesting I had something to do with it?"

Vanessa fingered her baton.

Give me a break, Mike thought.

"Are you saying you didn't?" Vanessa asked.

Mike lost his temper. "Of course I didn't!" he shouted.

Vanessa pulled her chin in and raised both eyebrows. She lifted the hand that wasn't caressing her police baton. She held out the hand, palm up. Mike looked down . . . and saw his prescription pill bottle. It was empty.

"Recognize this?" Vanessa asked.

An engine revved in the street. Mike glanced past Vanessa and saw his neighbor's shiny-new red SUV rolling past. Great. The news of his arrest would be passed all through the neighborhood. No doubt Jane would get wind of it. Hell, she probably already knew.

Mike, who had been working up a head of steam that had heated up his cheeks, felt the blood drain away. He was sure he was probably look-at-me-I'm-guilty pale.

He swallowed and tried to work up enough saliva to speak. When he finally did, he stuttered out his response. "It . . . it . . . it's not what you think," he said, sounding like it was exactly what she thought.

Vanessa gave him a disbelieving look. He couldn't blame her for it.

Mike tried again. "They're sleeping pills," he said. "I take them to sleep." He knew that wasn't exactly a stellar proclamation of righteous innocence. A night guard who took sleeping pills on the job wasn't a pillar of virtue.

"I know what they are, Mike," Vanessa said. "It's written right on the bottle." She didn't say, "*Duh*," but her tone got the sentiment across.

Mike couldn't come up with anything to say. He was busted, and he knew it. His shoulders slumped, and he hung his head.

But then, he felt a stirring of annoyance in his belly. Okay, so he'd been sleeping. But nothing had happened while he slept. The place had been fine when he'd left it. How was the break-in his fault?

That thought gave Mike words. "It wasn't my fault," he said.

Vanessa snorted. "News flash. If you're too whacked out to remember to lock the dang door when you leave your shift . . . accident or not . . . you're liable. It's called criminal negligence."

"You were there, too," Mike said.

Vanessa bristled. "I left the building before you did. And it's your job to lock up."

Mike frowned. "But I was sure I did." He winced at the whine in his tone.

Vanessa sighed. Her face softened, just a little. Maybe the whine had made her feel sorry for him.

The cop side of Vanessa retreated a bit. Her hand dropped away from her baton. Her lips were no longer granite-like. She even reached out and put a hand lightly on Mike's forearm. Maybe she was on his side after all.

When Vanessa spoke, her voice was gentle. "Mike, what the hell were you thinking? You're a security guard. Literally, your entire job description is 'Do not go to sleep.'"

Mike looked at the warped wood floor in front of his door. He really needed to take better care of this place. But when? And with what money?

Mike was distracting himself. He sighed and looked up at Vanessa. "You wouldn't understand," he said.

Vanessa pulled back her hand. "So, help me understand," she said. "Explain it. Because the second I file a report, the whole thing will be out of my hands."

Mike glanced down the hall toward Abby's room. He looked back at Vanessa. How should he handle this? Could he trust Vanessa with his story?

Vanessa watched Mike steadily as he vacillated. He probably didn't have much more time before . . .

"Hey," Mike said, deciding. "You want to walk with me?"

Vanessa looked startled. Then she frowned and looked down the hall. "Your sister?"

Mike pointed out through his front door. Vanessa turned and looked toward the large concrete V that stretched away from Mike's house, from the opposite of the street. It was a stormwater runoff.

"We'll only go that far," Mike said. "I'll be able to see the house from there."

Vanessa hesitated. Then she nodded. "Sure."

Mike followed Vanessa out of his house. He closed and locked the door, then he led her down his driveway and across the street. Crossing a strip of gravel, he offered Vanessa a hand, and he helped her up a grassy embankment that ran along the narrow concrete storm drain. The trough was filled with a brown, sludgy stream of water. *Not exactly Venice*, Mike thought.

"Sometimes I sit over here," Mike said, gesturing at the green slope. "Game?" he asked.

Vanessa looked at the scruffy grass. In spite of the recent rain, the tufts of green weren't wet; the sun had dried them out.

"Sure." Vanessa lowered herself to the ground, adjusting her utility belt with a snappy creak.

They sat together in silence for a couple of minutes. The sun settled on the back of their shoulders. Mike thought it felt like a warm blanket.

The water in the storm drain trickled past. In spite of its constant motion, it had a stagnant-pond odor. Maybe not the best spot for a heart-to-heart talk, Mike thought. But then, what did he know about heart-to-heart talks? It wasn't like he'd had a lot of them.

Mike cleared his throat. He might as well go for it.

"I used to have a brother," Mike said. "His name was Garret."

Mike glanced at Vanessa. She was just a couple feet from him, close enough for him to enjoy that vanilla/apple/flowers scent he'd noticed before. She sat with her knees drawn up, her arms wrapped around her legs. She was at an angle, half-facing the "view," and half-facing Mike. Her gaze was steady and focused only on Mike. He squirmed a little, but he kept going.

"When I was twelve," Mike said, "a little older than Abby is now, Garret got taken. Kidnapped."

Vanessa made a little sympathetic sound in the back of her throat, but she didn't speak. She just waited.

"I was there when it happened," Mike went on. "I saw the car drive away. But the driver—the license plate—I couldn't tell the police anything useful. So, they never found the guy who did it." The guilt and helplessness Mike had felt then, and had carried with him ever since, slapped him like an actual blow to the face. He rubbed his jaw and managed to say, his voice breaking, "They never found my brother."

Vanessa still didn't say anything. Mike forced himself to go on.

"So, there's, uh, this theory." He hesitated, trying to figure out how to explain it. "It's psychology, I guess. Maybe neurology. Whatever. It's a theory that we never forget things. Even when we think we've forgotten, we haven't."

Vanessa frowned, obviously not tracking. Mike needed to do a better job of explaining things.

"Basically," Mike said, "the theory says that all of the events we've experienced, everything we've seen . . . all of it, even down to the tiniest detail . . . are stored somewhere in our brain. In our . . . what do you call them? . . . Our neuropathways. Like, the brain's highways. The stuff might seem as if it's lost, but it's not. It's just buried. No memory is actually *gone*. Memories are always retrievable. You just have to know where to look."

Vanessa nodded. She seemed to be getting it. "You're talking about witnessing something. We deal with that all the time in law enforcement. Trauma buries stuff."

"Exactly," Mike said.

Vanessa nodded again. "So, your brother. You think you saw the person who took him?"

Mike shifted to face Vanessa. "I know I did!" he said. "And I know the creep is in here." Mike tapped his head. "Buried somewhere."

Vanessa nodded again, this time more emphatically.

Mike hurried on, wanting to get it all out while she was still following along. "So, every night," he said, "I make sure I dream. I dream that dream, the one where I relive the kidnapping. Over and over. I go back through it, and I search for details. I look for anything that I might have missed at the time. Or anything I might have seen but stuffed away because I couldn't deal with it."

Mike paused. He studied Vanessa's face. It was impossible to read.

"I've tried explaining this to a couple of people," Mike said. "And this is the point where they told me I was crazy."

Mike waited, and because he was still watching Vanessa's face, he saw the instant it transitioned. He'd seen this alteration before. It was unmistakable. The narrowing of the eyes, the stiffening of her mouth. The slight spasm of the muscles along her jawline. The woman sitting next to Mike was no longer the warm and supportive friend she'd felt like when he'd started talking. She was back in cop mode.

No, Mike thought. It wasn't cop mode. It was something else.

Mike watched, mesmerized, as Vanessa's irises deepened noticeably in hue. They went from their usual soft, almost grayish-blue to a deeper indigo. The color shift was so pronounced that it almost looked computer-generated. It was also enormously disquieting. Mike felt like he was watching a human turn into . . .

"I know what crazy looks like, Mike," Vanessa said. Her voice was comfortingly human. Hard, but human. "What you're saying . . . that isn't it." She shook her head, and her gaze drifted past Mike's face. Her eyes widened, and her lower lip trembled, as if she was seeing . . . what?

"Not even close to crazy," Vanessa said.

From a nearby gnarly oak tree, which stretched its branches over the slowly moving storm water, a crow cawed. It flapped its wings and took off, dipping low in front of Mike and Vanessa and then soaring away.

And just like that, Vanessa was relaxed again. She reached into her pocket and pulled out Mike's pills. "So, these?"

Mike looked at the pills lying on Vanessa's palm. He shrugged. "It's not easy finding your way back to the same place every night. It's taken years of practice, and I still need help. The pills," he gestured at them, "they help. So do other things. Familiar sounds, familiar sights."

Vanessa smiled and nodded. "'Pining for fun . . .'" she quoted his poster.

"'. . . visit Nebraska,'" Mike finished. He looked down, suddenly embarrassed.

His embarrassment turned into surprise when Vanessa reached over and took his hand. Mike was so stunned that he almost snatched his hand back, a reflexive movement. He was glad he didn't, though. Vanessa's hand was warm and soft. It felt . . . heartening. And very welcome.

"I'm sorry," Vanessa said.

Pressure welled up behind Mike's eyes. He felt them begin to moisten. Clearing his throat, he turned and looked down at the concrete trough, as if he was gazing at a gorgeous river instead of a mucky storm drainage system. And speaking of storms, Mike was battling one that was stirring up from within him, swirling like a forming hurricane over calm water. Years of regret and grief were blowing up inside of him, threatening to hit landfall and wreak havoc. Mike blinked away the tears that wanted to spill down his cheeks.

And then, just like that, the emotion was quelled. The storm blew through. Or maybe Mike was just in the eye of it. Whichever. All he knew was that he now felt clear . . . determined.

Mike turned to face Vanessa again. When he spoke, his voice was strong. "I can't change what happened to Garret," he said. "He's gone. That's on me. But the guy who took him . . . he's still out there. I know he is."

Vanessa let go of Mike's hand. "And if you find him? Then what?" She cocked her head. "Just a reminder . . . you're still talking to an officer of the law."

Her words sounded like a challenge, but Mike caught the hint of a twinkle in her eye. He smiled. "Well, then, officer of the law, you can kick his door down and throw him in prison. Obviously."

"Of course," Vanessa said. "But . . ." She shook her head. "Not to burst your bubble, but I'm pretty sure 'I saw him in a dream' won't hold up in court."

Vanessa and Mike grinned at each other, and Mike felt something zing inside of him. It was a palpable "wow" feeling that was much more intense than his casual appreciation of her beauty. And the zing felt like it was going both ways. The look Vanessa was giving Mike was one he hadn't ever seen before . . . not directed at him anyway. Her reciprocation of his feelings was so strong that he felt himself leaning toward her.

Vanessa's cheeks flushed. She looked away from Mike.

"Your sister seems cool," Vanessa said. "Is it just the two of you?"

And the moment was over. *Okay.*

Mike nodded. "Yeah. Our parents are gone." He hesitated. How much should he share?

Vanessa had returned her gaze to Mike. Her eyes had settled back into their usual soft blue.

Encouraged, Mike kept going. "Mom kind of went bonkers after Garret was taken. She was . . . gone. I mean, not gone-gone, but . . . they called it catatonic depression. She wouldn't speak. Barely moved. For a long time. When she came out of that, she just sort of went through the motions. This continued on for even longer. She acted like a mom, but she wasn't the mom she used to be."

When Mike paused, Vanessa didn't move. Her direct gaze pulled the rest of the miserable story out of him.

"Then she got pregnant," Mike went on, "and suddenly, I had my mom back. She was cheerful, energetic. She joked and laughed. The whole time she was expecting, she was like that. I didn't know then . . . I found out after . . . she thought she was going to have a boy. In her mind, which was still broken even though she was acting normal, the baby would be another Garret."

Vanessa nodded, but her lips were twisted. In sympathy?

"But the baby was Abby," Mike continued. "And instead of being happy about her baby girl, Mom lost it. Worse than the first time. She just kind of . . . wasted away. We—our family—limped along like that for another three years or so. Then, on my eighteenth birthday, Dad took off."

Vanessa sucked in her breath. "No," she whispered.

"Yeah," Mike said. "I was already a screwed-up mess. Hard to be a regular teen when you're dragging around a semitruck full of guilt. And even when Dad was there, he didn't do much parenting. Mom was AWOL, spent most of the time in bed. I took care of Abby pretty much from the time she was born. But once Dad was gone, it was all on me, even figuring out how to support her. Then Mom died. And that was it for me. No college. No nothing." Mike pressed his lips together, once again holding back tears.

Vanessa put a hand on Mike's thigh. The warmth flipped his focus from bad memories to the good ones.

"You know," Mike said, "when Garret and I were kids, my mom and dad . . . they were like those perfect parents you see on old TV shows. Lots of fun. Gave me tons of attention. Family dinner every night." Mike bit his lip and lifted one shoulder in a half-shrug. "We even used to hold hands around the table and say grace."

Vanessa squeezed Mike's thigh lightly. "That actually sounds really nice," she said. Her words sounded genuine . . . and maybe a bit melancholy.

Mike sighed. "I always thought it was silly . . . until it was over."

Vanessa looked down at the eddying sludge in the culvert below them. For a full minute, she said nothing. Mike, talked out, sat silently.

"The way it was with your parents before," Vanessa finally said, "it sounds like you were happy."

Mike nodded.

"And you and Abby . . . you still have each other," Vanessa went on. "From where I sit, I'd say you're pretty lucky. College or not."

Vanessa lightly bumped his knee with hers. Mike took that

to mean she wasn't judging him for his bitterness. Mike smiled at her.

Vanessa returned the smile, and she gazed at him steadily. Vanessa's attentiveness drained the remaining tension from Mike's body. He felt more relaxed than he had in a long time.

But then, once again, the blue in Vanessa's eyes got darker, and her focus, although still on Mike, blurred. He felt like she had drifted off in her mind. He sensed a startlingly strong disconnect. Something had cut the link that was forming between them. That something, Mike thought, hinted at a secret, something hidden in Vanessa's past. Would she share it with him?

The police radio clipped to the shoulder of Vanessa's uniform spat static. Vanessa tensed and glanced down at it.

"Did you always want to be a cop?" Mike blurted. He wanted to jump-start the personal connection with her again.

Vanessa lifted her gaze to Mike's face. "Yes," she said.

Mike waited to see if she'd elaborate, but she didn't. Still, the one word had said enough. Mike was sure it contained a novel-sized story. Vanessa had reasons for wanting to be a cop. She wasn't, however, going to share them with him now.

"I always wanted to be a builder," Mike offered. "A contractor. Maybe own a construction company." He blew out air. "Maybe in another life."

Vanessa didn't say anything. Mike felt awkward, like he was oversharing.

"I should go," Vanessa said. She brushed off her dark blue pants.

Mike stood and similarly swiped at his jeans. Fragrant blades of grass and a few leaves spiraled around his legs and settled at his feet.

Mike and Vanessa started walking back toward his house. Mike glanced at her. "What about your report?" he asked.

Vanessa lifted her hand. She still held Mike's pill bottle.

Mike tensed. But then Vanessa turned and tossed the pill bottle over her shoulder. It bounced down the concrete sides of the storm drain and landed in the dribble of gunky brown water. It began tumbling away from them in slow motion, spinning around and around.

"Promise me one thing," Vanessa said.

Mike looked at her. She was leaning toward him, her irises once again dark blue, her eyes squinted forcefully.

Mike almost physically recoiled from the power of her gaze. "What?" he asked.

"No more sleeping," Vanessa said. "When you're at Freddy's, you stay alert."

Mike nodded, but he was glad he didn't have Pinocchio's nose. He was lying; he wasn't sure it was a promise he could keep.

CHAPTER 15

A couple hours after Vanessa left, Mike stood in his kitchen and watched the sky outside his window turn orange. For the fifth time, he redialed Max's number. When he put the phone to his ear, he heard the same thing he'd already heard four times. "Hey, it's Maxine," Max's voice said. "Leave a message. Or don't."

Mike sighed and dropped his phone. He glanced over at Abby. Already in her flannel pj's—pink with bright red stars all over—Abby was sitting on the sofa. She had Dolph tucked under one arm, and her drawing pad was on her lap. Of course she was drawing. The TV was on in the background, and of course she didn't seem to be paying any attention to it.

Mike looked back outside again. The sky was still orange, and the orange color was getting deeper. He looked at his watch. He was running out of time.

"Where are you?" Mike asked out loud as he dialed Max's number for the sixth time. Mike listened to Max's message once again. He heaved another, louder sigh. He looked over at Abby. She lifted her head and met his gaze.

* * *

Rubber crunching over loose rocks and broken gravel, engine lugging, Mike's old car coughed to a stop against the curb in front of Freddy's. Mike looked through his windshield at the old building.

This is a very bad idea, he thought.

When the sun had gone down, a thin fog had rolled down out of the hills at the edge of town. The moon, slightly larger tonight than the night before, still managed to deliver its shine, but that shine was smeared by the dense, moist air.

The hazy moonlight on the pizzeria made the building look otherworldly. Mike's imagination turned the building into a big hand, just wanting to reach out and grab the car.

Mike turned and looked at his sister, who sat primly upright in the back seat. Still in her pj's, and still clutching Dolph, Abby was ensconced next to a large backpack, which Mike had stuffed with blankets—for a hidey-tent—and a sleeping bag. Abby was looking eagerly at Freddy's. You would have thought they were outside an amusement park.

"This isn't a vacation, Abs," Mike said. "You're not here to have fun."

Abby kept her gaze on the pizzeria. "Okay," she said.

Mike deepened his voice, attempting to sound stern. "I will work," he said. "You will sleep. And under no circumstances are you to leave my office."

Abby kept staring at Freddy's.

Mike leaned over the seat and waved a hand in front of his sister's face. "I need you to look at me and tell me you understand."

Abby didn't shift her gaze. "I understand," she said.

Mike raised his voice. "Abby!"

Finally, Abby looked at him. "I un-der-stand." She managed to burden the word with two tons of attitude.

*   *   *

The heavy metal door clanged shut, as usual, after Mike ushered his sister inside the restaurant. As the bone-rattling clank stopped reverberating, Mike stared at the lobby in dismay.

"What happened?" Abby asked.

Mike's gaze hopped from the broken glass to the ragged holes in the drywall. He took in the benches' torn vinyl. He frowned at a stream of quarters that seemed to lead down the hallway.

Mike adjusted the strap of the large backpack he had slung over his left shoulder. He looked down at his sister. "Give me your hand."

Surprisingly, she did so without hesitation. Mike began guiding her forward. He did his best to weave around the worst of the glass shards, but navigating Abby through the destruction was unnerving. He felt like he was leading his sister to her execution.

"It smells funny in here," Abby said as Mike deliberately put his body between hers and the archway to the dining room.

One glance through the arch told Mike that the damage in that room was even worse than what he was seeing in the lobby. Not that the hallway was much better.

Like the lobby, the hallway floor was carpeted in glass. And the trail of coins continued.

Abby was right about the smell. Freddy's had never smelled

great, but now its odors were even worse. The smell was pungent and made Mike's nostrils burn.

Continuing to step carefully, Mike got Abby down the length of the hall. He ushered her into the office. Once there, he let go of Abby's hand and shut the door. Abby stepped forward and looked around, her eyes bright and curious.

The office, strangely, appeared to be untouched by the vandals. All the electronic equipment was as it should be. *Huh*, Mike thought.

Dismissing the mystery of why vandals hadn't destroyed the CCTV monitors, Mike turned his attention to getting Abby settled. He slipped the backpack off his shoulder.

"Help me make your hidey-tent," Mike said to Abby.

Abby, who had been inching toward the desk—and the monitors—turned back toward Mike. She nodded.

For the next few minutes, Mike and Abby worked together to form a hidey-tent from the blankets, using the filing cabinets as tent posts. They unrolled her sleeping bag, and Abby crawled inside of it. Once there, she snuggled into a ball on her side, Dolph firmly pressed against her chest.

Mike, crouching on his heels in front of the makeshift tent flaps, was happy to see that Abby's lids were drooping. "Do you want me to turn off the lights?" he asked.

Abby shook her head. Her lids fluttered even lower.

"Goodnight," Mike said.

Abby didn't respond. Her eyes had closed.

Mike backed through the overlapping blankets. He started to let them fall together, but he paused when Abby spoke.

"It's like we're camping," Abby said. Her voice was nearly whisper-soft, groggy.

Mike opened his mouth to respond, but he saw his sister's mouth drop open slightly. Her breathing slowed.

Mike smiled and closed up the hidey-tent. He exhaled softly, the concern that he was making a mistake bringing Abby to Freddy's abating now that she was tucked in.

It's going to be okay, he thought.

Mike straightened and crossed over to the desk. He checked the CCTV monitors, scanning all of the interior feeds. *Wow*, he thought. Someone really did do a number on the place.

Mike frowned. He was sure he'd locked up the night of the storm. But he still felt guilty about what had happened.

He glanced at the hidey-tent. Peewee, childish snoring sounds were coming from within the overlapped blankets.

Mike looked back at the monitors. He sighed. Vandalism cleanup wasn't in his job description, but he couldn't leave the place this way.

He listened to Abby's snoring for a few more seconds. Then he left the office, closing the door behind him.

Looking at the closed door for a moment, Mike hesitated. She was safe in there, wasn't she?

He shook off his willies. Sure, she was.

Mike took a step forward . . . and cringed at the crunching glass beneath his feet. Step one, he decided, had to be sweeping up all the glass.

Resolved, Mike strode down the hall. He ignored the crackling and tinkling sounds that his feet made as they shattered more glass and kicked errant quarters.

Halfway down the hall, Mike stopped in front of the frosted-glass-fronted door of the supply closet. Opening the door, he reached in and up. He put his hand on the pull string that hung from the closet's single bulb. Then he hesitated. The closet wasn't covered by CCTV, and given the chaotic shambles in the rest of the pizzeria, he wasn't sure what he was going to find in here.

Mike yanked on the pull string.

The bulb came on, and Mike gazed at . . .

. . . a perfectly ordinary collection of janitorial equipment. Maybe it was a little jostled, but otherwise, all seemed to be . . .

. . . wait. *What was that?*

Glancing at the open door, Mike noticed a few drops of red on the frosted glass. And a faint smear. *Was that blood?*

Mike shrugged. Maybe one of the vandals cut themselves.

Mike stepped forward and turned to his left. Instantly, he jumped back.

"Oh, good grief," he said.

What had startled him was the stupid Balloon Boy. Mike made a face at the grinning, little, bug-eyed doll.

"How'd you get in here?" Mike asked the doll.

Vandals with a sense of humor, he thought.

Mike turned the boy's face toward the wall. Ignoring the little *pit-a-pat* of his nerve endings—why did the stupid doll get to him?—Mike grabbed a push broom. He quickly turned around, tugged on the light cord, and left the supply closet. He shut the door firmly behind him.

For the next couple hours, Mike put his nose to the grindstone. Having been a janitor several times, Mike could handle a push broom like a pro. So, the work, though not the most fun in the world, wasn't difficult.

Starting in the hallway, Mike swept everything that littered the floor into a pile that he pushed against one side wall of the dining room. The pile included all the glass from the hall and the lobby and all the coins that were strewn around. He was tempted to go through the pile and pull out the coins—it would be kind of like panning for gold—but he decided to deal with that later.

Mike consolidated all of the dining room furniture, making another pile of broken chairs and tables. In the arcade area, he couldn't really do much with the destroyed game cabinets. All he could really do was more sweeping. The glass that littered the floor there joined the other glass in the dining room pile.

When he was sweeping in front of the stage, Mike encountered a yellow puddle and a strong ammonia order. "Gross," Mike said.

Pushing his broom ahead of him, Mike headed to the kitchen. When he passed through the service doors into the vast stainless-steel domain, he sighed. This was going to be another big job. But Mike tackled it.

Righting shelving units, returning pots and pans—dented but still usable—to their places, and sweeping up more broken shards—these were thicker pieces of dinnerware, Mike got the kitchen back in semi-order. Then he returned to the task that had originally brought him in here. He filled a couple buckets with warm, soapy water.

Mike took the buckets to the stage, returned to the supply closet to get a mop, and then headed back to the stage again. He spent the next several minutes thoroughly cleaning the area at the base of center stage. He even cleaned past that area, wanting to be sure he didn't miss a single speck of what one vandal had left behind.

Once Mike was done with that cleanup, he left the buckets where they were. He'd take care of them later. He was running out of steam, and he still had a lot to do.

Returning to the supply closet, Mike found a dustpan and a box of heavy-duty garbage bags. He then tackled the task of turning his pile of glass and debris into four tidy bags of vandal detritus. And he filtered out the coins. Not sure what to do with the pile of quarters, Mike put them in another bag. He took the overstuffed bags back to the loading dock, where he discovered how the vandals had gotten in. He found a broken padlock lying on the floor (a new one had already been installed on the outer door), and he saw that the back door to the kitchen was broken down. The break-in hadn't been Mike's fault at all.

Finally, *finally*, Mike retreated to the archway with the bag of coins and his mop and broom. He stopped there to survey his handiwork . . . and he wasn't fully unsatisfied with it. The room looked . . . better than it had. And it was the best he could do at the moment.

Mike took the mop and broom back to the supply closet. He stowed the bag of coins there, too. Then, his shoulders and back yelling at him for all the physical labor he'd put them through, Mike returned to the office.

Mike opened the office door slowly, and he stepped softly as he entered. He looked toward the hidey-tent, and he was happy to hear Abby still quietly snoring away. He glanced up at the clock above the tent. It was almost four a.m.

Mike looked at the desk chair. Briefly, he thought about the promise he'd made to Vanessa. But the chair beckoned, and he was wiped out.

Mike gave in to his need for rest and the compulsion of his routine. He set up his cassette player, rested his gaze on his taped-together poster, and in seconds, his eyes were closing and the pine trees were swaying in his mind. No pills needed.

CHAPTER 16

Abby wasn't sure what woke her up. But something did.

Sitting up, Abby rubbed her eyes and yawned. She listened, expecting to hear Mike moving around. When she didn't, she parted the overlapped blankets of the makeshift hidey-tent. She grinned.

Mike was totally zonked out in the office chair. His head lolled backward, his mouth hanging open.

Tucking Dolph under her arm, Abby stood. She tiptoed toward the desk. "Mike?" she whispered.

Abby stepped forward and poked Mike lightly on the bicep. He snorted, but he didn't wake up.

She grinned again, wider this time. Cool.

Abby quickly ducked back inside her hidey-tent. Setting down Dolph, she dug inside her sleeping bag to get the overalls she'd stashed there.

Mike had thought she'd spend the night in her pj's, but she'd hoped she'd get the chance she had now, and she was prepared for it. Abby quickly changed into a pale pink tee and pulled darker pink overalls over it. She stuffed her pj's into the sleeping bag, and she tucked Dolph into the bag, too. Then she stood.

"I'll be right back," Abby told her dead-to-the-world brother.

Abby stepped over to the office door. She eased it open, and she slipped out into the hallway.

*　　*　　*

At the fringes of his consciousness, Mike thought he heard the soft click of a door closing. Or was that a clipped-off chirp of one of the birds he could hear in the trees?

A single bird chirped from a branch undulating in the breeze. The branch creaked, and its leaves rustled.

*　　*　　*

Abby stepped through the archway and surveyed the huge empty room that stretched out before her. No, not empty. Abby spotted a big pile of sad-looking tables and chairs. The shape of the pile reminded Abby of a sleeping bear. She hoped the table-and-chair bear was happy.

Abby's gaze moved past the table-and-chair bear. On the other side of the room, wide stage curtains were closed over a long stage. She smiled and headed that way.

Climbing up the short flight of stairs to the stage, Abby headed toward the middle of the curtains. When she got there, a *thud* sounded from behind the curtains. Then a *clickety-clack*.

"Hello?" Abby called out. She parted the curtains and looked behind them.

The stage was like the inside of a hidey-tent in the middle of the night. Abby couldn't see a thing.

"I know you're back here," Abby said. "You might as well come out."

A burst of children's laughter crackled from the stage speakers. *How fun*, Abby thought, looking up at the speakers above her head. She giggled. "Clever," she said, smiling.

As if in response to Abby's comment, the *grr* of grinding metal and several thumping footsteps started coming Abby's way. Abby's smile wavered a little, but she was sure—well, pretty sure—everything was okay.

The footsteps belonged to something *really big*. Maybe it wasn't what Abby thought it was.

Abby took a step back, but she kept hold of the curtain. She strained to see into the backstage area.

A lurching surge of movement. More footsteps—they made the stage shake under Abby's feet—were coming toward Abby.

And then . . .

. . . Abby tilted her head back and gazed up . . . way, way up . . . into the big white eyes of a bear. It was a much more real-looking bear than the table-and-chair bear.

*　*　*

Mike, feeling no need to run because there's no point, walks out of the thicket of trees at the edge of the road. The black car roars away, but Mike doesn't even glance at it. He's more interested in the blond boy, who is sitting by himself in the middle of the dirt and gravel road, his back to Mike.

Mike moves toward the boy. "I know who you are," he says.

The boy ignores him.

"All of you," Mike goes on. "You're those kids. The ones who disappeared."

Mike stops a few feet in front of the boy, who is using a stick to draw something in the dirt.

"A long time ago," Mike says, "I had a brother who disappeared, too."

The stick stops moving. The boy's head lifts . . . just a little.

"I don't know how it's possible that you can be here like this," Mike says. "Inside my dream. But I have to believe that you're here to help."

The boy doesn't respond.

"Please," Mike says, bending toward the boy. "Help me remember the man who took my brother. Help me so he never hurts another kid again. I can't do it by myself. I've tried. But it's buried too deep."

The boy drops his stick. He stands and faces Mike.

In flat tones, the boy speaks. "If we show you, what will you give us?" he asks.

Mike doesn't hesitate. "Anything," he says. "Anything you want."

The little boy rubs his upturned nose with a dirty hand, leaving a smudge of dirt on the tip of it. His pale brows furrow together as he twists his lips, clearly thinking hard.

Mike waits, and then . . .

. . . the boy vanishes!

Mike dashes forward and stands where the boy just stood. He's frustrated, but he's also invigorated. Things are unfolding differently. The boy talked directly to him. He's making progress!

Mike glances down at the dirt. He leans in to look at what the boy drew.

The drawing is a stick figure, but its shape is unmistakable. The boy drew a rabbit.

Mike opened his eyes and rotated his stiff neck. He rubbed the sore muscles and looked around the dim, quiet office. Remembering that he wasn't here alone, Mike looked over at the hidey-tent.

He erupted to his feet. The office chair skidded backward and slammed into the credenza.

The tent was wide open. The sleeping bag inside of it was empty.

Mike immediately charged toward the closed office door. Before he got halfway to it, a high-pitched scream stopped him in his tracks.

Mike's heart went from zero to infinity in a nanosecond. He spun around and rushed to the CCTV monitors. Scanning them quickly, his eyes nearly shot out of his head and ping-ponged around the room.

"Abby!" Mike gasped. He took off, pell-mell, toward the dining room.

How could I be so stupid? Mike asked himself as he barreled down the hall. It was Garret all over again.

"Abby!" Mike shouted as he burst through the archway and charged into the dining room.

Mike's intestines felt like they were reaching up inside of him to strangle his lungs as he blasted through the room. He kept his gaze, his horrified gaze, on the massive jumble of animatronics that were writhing in front of the main stage.

Abby's screams were coming from within that snarl of metal and rotting fur. What were those things *doing* to her?!

"Stop!" Mike screamed. "Stop it! Let her go!"

Racing past the pile of furniture, Mike grabbed a broken chair. It was the only weapon available to him.

As Mike raised the chair over his head, poised to strike, one of the metal-and-fur mounds wrapped around Abby broke free of the melee. It was Freddy.

The gargantuan bear charged straight toward Mike. Mike's breathing choked in his throat. He wanted to turn and run. But he couldn't. He had to save his sister.

Mike tightened his grip on his makeshift weapon. He braced his feet on the linoleum floor.

Freddy came closer. And closer. And closer and . . .

. . . he stopped a few inches from Mike.

Mike held his breath.

Gears grinding, eyes flashing in obvious anger, the animatronic bear leaned down and put his face right in front of Mike's. The bear's scratched and dirty black nose nearly touched Mike's nose.

Mike closed his eyes and screwed up his face. He started to swing the chair, even though he knew it wasn't going to help him at all.

"Mike!" Abby called out. "You're here!"

Mike opened his eyes and watched in disbelief as his sister, who was just fine, skipped toward him and the bear. She let out a carefree laugh . . . and she gave the robotic creature a big . . . hug.

Mike gaped at his sister.

"They wouldn't stop tickling me, Mike," Abby said. "I thought I was gonna die!"

Seriously? Tickling? Mike lowered his arm. The chair hit the floor with a clatter.

What in the heck was going on? Mike struggled to compute the situation, to put it into some comprehensible box. But he couldn't do it.

"Freddy," Abby said. "This is my brother, Mike. He works here."

Freddy raised his head away from Mike's face, just a little.

Mike didn't move a muscle. His intestines eased up on his lungs, infinitesimally.

The animatronic's eyes were still bright, but the candescence didn't give off the same signal. The rage Mike had felt, viscerally, coming from the bear, was giving way to what seemed to be cautious curiosity.

Freddy straightened, but he kept studying Mike. He scanned Mike from head to toe. Mike hoped he passed muster.

"Abby," Mike said quietly, as if he stood in front of a wild animal. Actually, a wild animal might have been an improvement on his situation. "Are you okay?"

Abby grabbed Mike's hand. She giggled.

"What's going on?" Mike asked, just as softly.

Abby looked up at Mike with more happiness than he'd ever seen in her eyes. "Come on," she said, "I want you to meet the others!"

The others?

Feeling like he had little choice, Mike let Abby pull him forward. Too dazed to resist, Mike realized Abby was dragging him over to where the rest of the animatronic pile had separated itself into different characters. The chick, the bunny, and the fox. The fox with the sharp metal hook. *Great*, Mike thought.

Mike was still ultra-wary, but the other three animatronics seemed to find Mike as interesting as Freddy did. They eyed him with what truly looked like eager curiosity. Mike found himself intrigued by how aging monstrosities of metal and fur could look so . . . childlike.

"Mike," Abby said, "this is Chica, Bonnie, and Foxy." She turned to the animatronics. "Everyone, this is Mike!"

One by one, and more than a bit shyly, the animatronics lifted ragged paws and waved at Mike. Acting from social conditioning,

Mike started to lift his hand for a return wave. He immediately realized what he was doing, and he lowered his arm.

In spite of the animatronics' apparent friendliness, Mike's self-preservation system backed him up a step. When it did, Mike nearly bumped into Freddy, who was lumbering back to rejoin the others.

Mike looked from the furry robots to his sister. "This . . . is a joke, right?" He asked his sister.

Mike frowned at the animatronics. Every one of them had broken parts, exposed and unconnected wiring, and clearly crushed gears. How were these things moving around?

Sure, the animatronics were jerky and cumbersome. But they were functional. How was that possible?

Mike looked around. "Someone else is here, right?" he said. He raised his voice. "Someone's controlling them?"

"Someone" didn't step forward to take credit.

Was it Vanessa? Mike wondered. Who else did he know who might be able to do this?

Annoyed, Mike shouted, "Very funny! You got us. Congratulations!"

Mike glowered as he spun in a circle. He saw nothing but the empty room, empty that is, except for him and Abby and the moving animatronics.

"You hear me?" Mike bellowed. "The joke's over! You can come out now!"

The room threw Mike's words back at him. Otherwise . . . silence.

Mike tried again. "Hello!"

That, too, after seeming to bounce off the dining room ceiling, returned to Mike. He ground his teeth and looked at the animatronics.

"There's no way," Mike muttered. "It's *not* possible."

Mike felt Abby take his hand. He looked down.

For once, Mike felt their roles reversing. Mike was the kid—a very dumbstruck kid—and Abby was the knowing adult.

"It's okay, Mike," Abby said. Her voice was low and even, as if she was talking to a scared kitten.

Mike frowned at Abby. Then he looked from one animatronic to the next.

Since his intestines had settled back where they belonged, and his lungs were giving him more air, Mike really looked at the creatures in front of him. Top hat. Bib. Bunny ears. Pirate's hook. These were . . . the kids from his dream.

The truth hit Mike like a battering ram between the eyes.

Whatever was happening with the animatronics was supernatural.

Mike's voice cracked when he uttered, in low, low tones, "You're them."

Beep! Beep! Beep!

At first, Mike thought the sound was coming from inside his brain, a sort of *Ding! Ding! Ding!* of realization. Then he came to his senses.

He looked at his watch. His alarm was going off. He silenced it.

Abby frowned at Mike's watch. "Do we have to go home now?" she asked.

Mike looked at the animatronics. "I think that's probably a good idea," he said.

Abby nodded, her smile gone. She was clearly let down, but she didn't argue.

Mike started to pull Abby toward the lobby. She freed her hand from his grasp. "Hang on," she said.

Abby pulled her drawing pad from the pocket of her bright pink overalls, and she dropped to a cross-legged position on the floor. She began scribbling away with one of her colored pencils.

"Abby," Mike said.

"One sec," she said. "I'm almost done."

It was more than one second, but it wasn't more than twenty or so. Abby popped to her feet and tore off the paper she'd been drawing on. Skipping over to the blue bunny, she handed it to him.

The bunny, Bonnie, took the paper from Abby delicately, as if it was the most precious thing in the world. He held up the paper so the other animatronics could see it. Mike took a step to his left so he could see it, too.

Mike's chest tightened with an emotion he couldn't quite quantify. Was he touched? Worried? Freaked out?

Abby had drawn a red heart on the paper.

"I had a lot of fun tonight," Abby told the animatronics. "Thank you for playing with me."

Before Mike could stop her, Abby rushed forward. She threw herself at the animatronics, and they all folded their arms around her.

Every muscle in Mike's body went taut, like a bow drawn back, ready to fire. Immediately, he relaxed, though, when he realized the intimidating robots were just giving Abby a good-bye hug.

Mike was tempted to pinch himself to see if he was in a dream, not his usual dream, but a dream nonetheless. The scene was as nonsensical as a dream, but Mike knew it wasn't one. He really was watching a bunch of mottled, old, jumbo-sized robot animals hugging his little sister. The spectacle was both tender . . . and terrifying.

CHAPTER 17

Mike carried his limp sister through her bedroom doorway. She'd fallen into a deep sleep in the car, and she'd snored most of the way home. He'd thought she might wake up when he lifted her out of the car, but she was totally out of it.

I guess playing with animatronics is exhausting, Mike thought as he gently placed Abby in her bed.

Mike was trying to keep his mood light, but he wasn't really feeling it. The truth was that he was thoroughly frazzled by the night's events.

Mike pulled Abby's bright red blanket up to her shoulders. He watched her chest rise and fall slowly for a few seconds. Then he turned and started toward her door.

As Mike passed Abby's desk, his gaze landed on a pile of drawings. He hesitated, and then he stepped over to pick them up.

Mike usually didn't pay a lot of attention to what Abby drew. Yes, he'd seen the drawings she's done that included him, but he hadn't looked at anything she'd drawn lately. Given what had happened at Freddy's, Mike had a sudden feeling that he should see what his sister had been up to.

Expecting to see Abby versions of the animatronics at Freddy's, Mike flipped through the drawings. And he nearly dropped them. He couldn't believe what he was seeing.

Abby's drawing had improved a lot over the last year. She was no Picasso, but what she drew was usually recognizable.

The drawings Mike held in his hand were *clearly* recognizable. He knew exactly what he was looking at.

Mike held in his hand a whole series of drawings of Abby playing *with the children from his dream*. And one of them . . .

Mike pulled the fourth drawing from the pile. Frowning at it, he placed the others back on Abby's desk. He folded up the drawing he'd taken and put it in his pocket.

*　*　*

By the time dinner rolled around, Mike felt like a limp noodle. After he'd put Abby to bed, he'd tried to sleep himself. Visions of Abby's drawings, however, kept Mike awake. He was only able to get a few snatches of dreamless sleep. He'd finally given up and tried to jump-start his body with his usual regime of push-ups. The exercise had woken him up enough to be functional, but he'd still dragged all day.

All day, Mike tried on and off to get a hold of Max. Why had she flaked out on him? Sure, he hadn't paid her, but it wasn't like her to just ignore him.

Somehow, Mike made it through the day. He even put together a meal—grilled cheese sandwiches and canned tomato soup. And now, shockingly, Abby was eating it.

Watching Abby plow through her sandwich, Mike leaned back

in his seat and spun his spoon around and around on the kitchen table. Pleased with his sister's appetite, Mike inhaled the tang of the soup and the cheddar cheese he'd put in the sandwiches. And he tried to relax. But the thoughts in his brain were too much of a thicket. A thicket with thorns.

Abby finished the sandwich and raised her soup bowl with both hands. She slurped down the soup and put down the bowl. She let out a loud burp.

Giving Mike a sideways glance, she giggled and said, "'Scuse me."

Mike put his elbows on the table. "Abby, we need to talk."

Clearly noticing Mike's serious tone, Abby frowned. "I said 'scuse me.'"

Mike waved a hand. "Not about that." He leaned forward. "You know what happened last night isn't . . . normal . . . right?"

Abby wiped the soup moustache from her face. "I'm not stupid, Mike."

"No, you're not."

Mike chewed on the inside of his cheek. *How to word this . . .*

"So, the machines," Mike began.

"My friends," Abby corrected.

"Sorry. Your friends." Mike collected himself. "Uh, are they . . . ?"

"Ghosts?"

Okay, Mike thought. *That was easier than I'd expected.* "Yeah," he said.

Abby tilted her head and gave Mike a "Way to catch on, Captain Obvious" look. "Of course," she said. "How else could they make the robots move?'"

Mike nodded. "So, they're kids, then. Like you?"

Abby nodded and then shook her head. "They're younger," she clarified.

"And they've explained to you how they got to be the way they are now?" Mike asked.

Abby dropped her gaze to her empty soup bowl. Her shoulders hunched inward. "They don't like to talk about it."

Abby lifted her head. She pushed her bowl toward Mike. "Can I have more soup?"

Almost glad for the distraction, Mike took the bowl and jumped up. "Sure."

Mike stepped to the stove. A half-empty pot of soup sat on one of the burners. He knew the soup was cold, so he turned the burner on. He thought he was doing a very good job of acting like he was having a perfectly ordinary conversation with his ten-year-old sister. *Doesn't everyone talk about ghosts at the dinner table?*

Mike's patient, calm demeanor wasn't as genuine as Abby probably thought it was. Inside, his adrenal glands were in overdrive. Mike had an agenda, but he thought he had to get at it in a roundabout way.

Mike picked up a wooden spoon and stirred the soup as it started to steam a little. "You know we used to have a brother, right?" he asked Abby without turning around. "Garret. I know I don't talk about him."

"Neither did Mom and Dad," Abby said.

Mike blinked. He was surprised Abby remembered. She never spoke about their parents; she'd only been three when their mom had died and their dad had left.

"It was hard for them," Mike said. "Hard for me, too."

Mike turned away from the stove and dug into his pocket. He pulled out the folded-up drawing he'd tucked away earlier that day.

Mike handed the folded drawing to Abby. "Can you explain this to me?"

Abby spread open the drawing on the table. She looked down at it. Mike didn't need to look at it again. He knew it was the drawing of a black car with a blurry-faced child—a child clutching an orange toy airplane—in the back window.

Abby looked at Mike, her face tight. She pressed her lips together and blinked several times. A classic "you caught me" look.

"Do you know what that is?" Mike retook his seat and pointed at the drawing.

Abby didn't speak. She studied the table.

"I'm not mad at you, Abs," Mike said. "I just want to know."

Another few seconds passed. Then Abby said, "It's when Garret got taken."

Mike leaned forward. Little fireworks of excitement were sizzling through his whole body. "Who told you about this, Abby?"

More silence.

"Was it a little boy with blond hair?" Mike pushed.

Abby nodded. "I don't know his name."

"But he's one of your friends?" Mike asked.

"Yes."

"And when did you meet them?"

Before Abby could answer, a spitting fizzle came from the stove. Mike looked over to see the soup boiling over. He leaped up and shifted the pot to a cold burner. He turned off the stove.

Mike turned back to Abby. She had picked up her napkin and was tearing it into little pieces, clearly upset.

Mike crouched down next to her. He put a hand on the drawing.

"Abby," he said in the gentlest voice he could muster, "this is very important. Did the blond boy ever say anything about the man who was driving the black car?" Mike tapped the car in the drawing. "Please think hard."

Abby shook her head. "No. No, he didn't."

Abby looked up and frowned at Mike. He knew he hadn't hidden his disappointment.

"But . . ." Abby began.

"Yes?"

"Can I ask him?" Abby asked.

Mike let out a long pent-up breath. This was where he'd been heading all along. He smiled. "I'd really appreciate it if you would."

*   *   *

Vanessa looked at her watch as she let Freddy's front door clang shut beyond her. It wouldn't be long before Mike got here.

Vanessa glanced around the empty lobby. The walls still had gaping holes, and all the poster frames were bare of glass, but the floor had been swept up. *Mike was busy last night*, she thought.

Vanessa's boots thudded on the floor as she strode forward, heading through the archway into the dining room. She looked around and nodded in satisfaction. He'd cleaned up in here, too.

She glanced across the room and cocked her head. He'd left the stage curtains open. *Strange.*

She eyed the animatronics. They were poised in show-ready positions, frozen on the stage as if in mid-performance.

Okay, Vanessa thought.

Vanessa turned away from the stage, walking slowly toward the dining room's right wall. Her gaze locked on the children's drawings that covered the wall. Actually, her gaze locked on just one of the drawings. It was the one she always had to revisit—the one that called to her like a siren song.

Vanessa stepped up in front of the central drawing on the wall. She stared at the image of the yellow rabbit and the five smiling children. She felt the blood drain from her face, as it always did when she looked at this drawing. She shivered.

*　　*　　*

Mike's car rattled up next to a black-and-white police cruiser parked in the spot he'd been using, near the pizzeria's front door. He stared at the police car and then looked at the pizzeria. He frowned.

What's she doing here? he wondered.

"That cop lady is here," Abby said. "Vanessa."

Mike nodded but didn't respond. He was still wondering *why* Vanessa was here.

"My friends talk about her sometimes," Abby said.

Surprised, Mike turned around and looked at Abby. "What do they say?"

Abby shrugged. "That she's nice."

Mike looked back at Vanessa's cruiser. He liked Vanessa, but he wasn't so sure he liked that she was here now.

Mike returned his attention to Abby. "If I told you to wait in the car, would you?" he asked.

Abby rolled her eyes. "Probably not."

At least she's honest, he thought. He sighed and opened his car door, but before he could throw a leg out of the car, Abby had flung her door open, bounded out of the car, and was racing for Freddy's entrance.

"Abby, wait!"

The night sky was a quilt of black and gray so tightly tucked in that the moon couldn't peek out at all. The building's lights were out, so a legion of walking dead—or angry robots—could have been lurking, and Mike couldn't have seen them.

Mike hustled to grab Abby's things and his own backpack. He locked up the car and rushed after his sister.

"You can't do that," Mike huffed when he caught up to her. "It's not safe."

Abby was hopping from one foot to the other in front of the locked door. She threw Mike a look that made him feel like a fuddy-duddy. He gave in and unlocked the door.

As soon as the door was open, Abby brushed past Mike and ran through the lobby. She scampered toward the archway. "I'm back!" she called as she breezed into the dining room.

The front door of Freddy's clanked shut. Mike, still not happy with Abby cavorting with giant robots . . . or ghosts . . . dropped his backpack and Abby's things, and trotted after his sister.

"Abby, wait up!"

Mike reached the archway just in time to watch Abby wave at Vanessa, who stood near the wall of children's drawings. "Hey, Vanessa!" Abby sang out.

Vanessa, Mike noted, didn't look the least bit surprised to see Abby. Vanessa waved at his sister's back as she darted toward the stage, where the animatronics were clustered as stiff as statues.

Mike, torn between his need to talk to Vanessa and his imperative to keep Abby safe, hesitated in the middle of the dining room. He was, therefore, close enough to see Vanessa's reaction when the animatronics stopped being statues and became galumphing furry robots making awkward attempts to play like children.

Abby scrambled up onto the stage to greet her "friends" as Vanessa ambled over to stand next to Mike. Vanessa said nothing, and neither did he. They both just watched Abby and the animatronics in silence.

Giggling, Abby poked Chica in the middle of her bib and shouted, "Tag! You're it!" Chica opened her beak in a big grin and gracelessly doddered off behind the half-open stage curtains. Abby and the others watched for a few seconds, then started chasing the chick.

It's like watching a bunch of Frankenstein's monsters at play, Mike thought.

Vanessa elbowed Mike lightly. "Hey, Mike."

Mike kept his gaze on the animatronic antics on the stage. "Vanessa," he responded.

They both continued looking straight ahead. Mike kept his face blank, primarily because he hadn't decided which of his battling emotions was going to win.

"I guess you figured it out," Vanessa said.

Mike finally turned toward her. He shot her a "ya think?" look.

Vanessa was giving him a half-smile, but her gaze was empty. He couldn't tell what she was feeling any more than he could figure out his own emotions.

"You mean, did I figure out that there are ghost children possessing giant robot animals?" Mike asked. "Yeah, thanks so much for the heads-up on that."

"Technically," Vanessa said, "they're animatronics. Not robots."

A squeal of laughter turned them both back toward the stage. Apparently, the tag game was over. Bonnie was giving Abby a piggyback ride.

Mike really wanted to get Abby away from the giant robot rabbit; every protector instinct in his body was screaming, "No!" But Abby was clearly thrilled.

He turned back to Vanessa. "What are you doing here?"

Vanessa pursed her lips. "I did say I'd check on you." She nodded toward Abby. "So, what's *she* doing here, Mike?"

"Can't reach my babysitter."

Vanessa's half-smile had disappeared. She'd replaced it with her cop stare, which was dialed up to an eleven.

"Hey, you guys!" Abby called. "We need help!"

CHAPTER 18

So, Mike, what are your plans for the evening? Mike thought. *Well, I'm going to build a fort with my sister, four fuzzy animatronics, and a cop.*

Mike shook his head at the absurdity of . . . everything . . . as he stood with the animatronics and Vanessa. They were clustered in a circle on the stage, and they were all looking down at Abby, who was scribbling on her drawing pad. Under the heading *fort*, she was sketching a rudimentary structure.

"It needs to be big," Abby said as her pencil skimmed over the paper, "so we can all fit inside."

Mike couldn't take it anymore. "Wait," he said. "Hold on. I know this is very exciting and new, Abs, but I think we need to set some ground rules. Okay? I mean, these things," he gestured at the behemoths who stood with him, "are big and are probably danger-ous, so . . ." He turned toward Vanessa, who stood next to Bonnie. "What do you think?"

"Some of the tables over there are probably still strong enough to use for the fort," Vanessa said.

Abby turned to look at the pile of furniture Mike had left at one side of the dining room. She smiled. "Everyone, follow me!"

Abby jumped up and leaped off the stage. As she ran toward the table-and-chair pile, Mike met Vanessa's gaze. She grinned at him and shrugged.

The animatronics were already stomping across the stage to follow Abby. *Why not?* Mike thought as he and Vanessa trailed after them.

For the next several minutes, Abby went from being Abby the little girl to Abby the construction foreman. Waving her hands and pointing her finger and standing with her fists on her hips while she waited for her orders to be fulfilled, Abby set the animatronics, and Mike and Vanessa, to work untangling the pile of broken and battered furniture.

The animatronics were uncommonly strong. Mike wasn't sure if that strength was robotic or ghostly, and he didn't want to think about it. Therefore, it didn't take much time for them to extract several tables and chairs that were, though beaten up by the vandals, structurally sound.

Once these materials were gathered, Abby directed Mike and Vanessa and the robots in the assembly of a wacky-looking, four-sided structure. The arrangement of tables and chairs would not have passed any building code on the planet, but it was unexpectedly fun to build.

Mike surprised himself when he began laughing along with Abby and Vanessa as they worked with the animatronics. He even contributed his own ideas to the structure, tapping into his old enjoyment of building things. He came up with a way to interweave the chairs that helped everything be more stable.

Of course, the big robots didn't speak, but they were capable of acting goofy without words. Freddy, for instance, staggered around with a chair balanced on his nose, and Foxy pretended to use a table as a pirate boat. The Fox animatronic's pantomime of riding ocean waves was so convincing that Mike found himself calling out, "Avast, ye landlubbers!" This earned him a big smile from Vanessa and an eruption of giggles from his sister. Mike couldn't honestly remember the last time he'd had such a good time.

When they'd managed to stack the tables three-high and get them linked together with chairs well enough to be relatively stable, Abby stepped back and assessed her minions' work. "It needs to be higher," she decreed.

Mike, Vanessa, and the animatronics exchanged looks. Mike knew he was getting used to the big metal beasts when he easily read skepticism in their expressions.

When no one moved, Abby said, "Come on, guys! More tables!"

"You heard the boss," Mike said to the animatronics. He tried to ignore the flutter of fear in his belly when they all turned and flashed their big teeth his way.

Without the use of a crane, Mike didn't know how they'd stack more tables on the already tall structure, but he figured he'd humor Abby. Once they'd gathered the tables, she'd see it was a futile endeavor, and she'd give up.

Or so he thought.

Mike, however, had underestimated the animatronics, both their devotion to Abby and their teamwork. A few minutes later, he was watching in awe as Bonnie and Freddy, each gripping two legs of a table, rode on Chica's and Foxy's shoulders. Thus elevated, they managed to lift the table to the top of the stack. If they could get it to balance in place, it would extend the now-much-taller fort almost to the dining room ceiling.

Mike took Abby's hand and drew her back away from the fort as they watched Bonnie and Freddy set the table in place. Vanessa joined Mike and Abby, and all three of them looked on, breath collectively held, as Bonnie and Freddy let go of the table.

The table-and-chair skyscraper wobbled like a giant, unsteady tower. Mike was sure it was going to come tumbling down. But it didn't.

Abby broke free of Mike's grasp. She threw two triumphant fists above her head. "Yes!" she shouted.

"I'll be . . ." Mike said. Who knew his sister had architectural talent? She might have a career ahead of her.

Abby skipped toward the animatronics. "You did it!" she trilled.

Freddy and Bonnie, still on Chica's and Foxy's shoulders, gave each other a high five. Chica, getting in the spirit, threw out her arms in celebration.

Oops, Mike thought.

He saw the cascade effect in his mind before it unfolded. Chica's movement threw off the equilibrium that was holding Bonnie and Freddy aloft. Both bunny and bear lost their balance. Chica stumbled one way, and Foxy reeled the other. And then there was an animatronic blur as all four metal and fur critters tumbled to the dining room floor.

They hit the linoleum with a *whomp* that would have been bone-cracking if they hadn't been made of metal. The entire dining room rattled and rolled like it was caught up in an earthquake. Mike and Vanessa had to widen their stances to stay upright, and Mike managed to grab Abby before the ripple effect of the concussion knocked her off her feet.

As soon as the tremors stopped, Abby shouted, "Guys!" She dashed over to the upended animatronics.

Vanessa was close on Abby's heels. Mike, concerned (irrationally) about the animatronics, hurried after Vanessa, even though he had no idea what he could do for robots if they were "hurt."

Abby reached the heap of fur and exposed metal. "Are you okay?" she asked.

A few seconds of squirming robotic limbs and more thuds on the floor. Then four fuzzy thumbs shot up through the convulsing bundle.

Mike couldn't help himself. He burst out laughing. Vanessa and Abby quickly joined him.

After that, Mike pretty much forgot that the animatronics were animatronics, so much so that when they all crawled inside of their completed fort, Mike had no problem lying on his back next to Foxy. He did prefer, however, the warmth of Vanessa, who was pressed up against his other side.

Mike thought the completed fort was incredibly, well, fort-like once it was done. After the animatronics had righted themselves, everyone had worked together to fill in the gaps in their edifice with more chairs. The result was a structure that had remarkable symmetry—an equal number of chairs tucked between the legs of each table—and even a semblance of style. Mike thought the combination of chrome tables and plastic chairs created a pretty cool modernistic design.

And as soon as he had that thought, he snorted inwardly. What was happening to him? He'd just built a fort with possessed animatronics and now he was getting all artsy-fartsy.

"I like it in here," Vanessa said.

"Me too," Abby said.

The animatronics were, of course, silent, but four robotic thumbs reached into the air again. The repeated gesture made Mike smile.

"But I think," Abby went on, "that it's going rain soon." She sat up. "And my friends can't get wet because they're made of electricity."

"Sounds like we need a roof," Vanessa said before Mike could pooh-pooh his sister's critique of what they'd built.

Vanessa's knuckles grazed Mikes. He liked the feel of her skin against his.

"Mike," Vanessa said, "why don't we see what we can find?"

* * *

Mike trailed Vanessa down the back hallway. Dusty, musty, and even darker than the front hallway, this part of Freddy's wasn't his favorite.

"What are we looking for, exactly?" Mike asked.

"Tablecloths. They used to keep them back here"—Vanessa gestured down the hall—"for big events."

Mike shot a look at Vanessa. She had an awful lot of knowledge about this place. It was one thing, he thought, to know the building's layout and its history, but she knew about tablecloths and where they're kept? What was up with that?

Mike eyed Vanessa's back as she stepped out ahead of him and opened a closed door. She disappeared through the doorway.

"Remind me of how you know stuff like that?" Mike called after her.

Silence came from behind the door. Mike frowned. The

mystery of Vanessa was starting to really bug him. He clamped his teeth together and went after her.

Right, Mike thought, remembering his tour of the building as he stepped into an even mustier space. This was the main storage room. Cluttered with stacks of collapsing boxes and decorated with cobwebs, the storage room was stuffed with several rows of floor-to-ceiling metal shelves. The shelves, and everything else in the room, appeared to have escaped the vandals' attention. All was the same as it had been the last time he'd been in here.

Midway along the outermost row of dust-laden shelving, a smaller door gaped open. It was the entrance to the boiler room

From the scraping and tapping within that room, Mike could tell Vanessa was in there. He stepped forward and looked through the door. Sure enough, Vanessa was off to one side of the boiler, rummaging in a semi-crushed cardboard box on the top of a leaning stack of similar boxes.

Mike wrinkled his nose. The boiler room smelled like rotten eggs. He knew the smell came from sulfur gas, which emanated from the growth of bacteria encouraged by the warm, moist enclosed spaces in the boiler. He hated that smell.

Mike backed away from the boiler and left Vanessa to her table-cloth hunt. He moved farther into the storage room. Just to amuse himself, he started scanning the shelves. He hadn't looked around much when he'd been in here before.

Mike reached the end of one row, which contained nothing but empty shelves or shelves stacked with pizza pans. He started to turn to go up the next row, which held a tangle of kitchen utensils and janitorial supplies, but then his gaze landed on . . .

Mike's steps faltered. He stopped and stared.

Sitting on the ground, leaning against the gray cement blocks of the storage room's back wall, a small—about three feet tall—clearly decommissioned animatronic sat with its . . . her . . . legs stretched out in front of her.

With rosy cheeks like those of the Balloon Boy doll that Mike disliked intensely, the animatronic, which was actually more doll-like than robot-like, had red pigtails and a frilly skirted dress. Beneath the sweetly smiling doll face, the animatronic's chest was hinged open. The metal cavity was bordered by a gruesome cage of severe-looking steel ribs. The contrast of the girly face and the shiny metal spoke-like protrusions was . . . sinister.

"What are you?" Mike asked. Intrigued in spite of himself, Mike dropped to his heels and started extending a hand toward the lethal-looking tip of one of the ribs.

"I wouldn't do that if I were you."

Vanessa's voice so startled Mike that he fell back onto his butt. He looked up.

She gestured at the metal ribs. "They're called springlocks. A lot of the older animatronic models have them."

Vanessa's irises did the light-blue-to-dark-blue thing. Mike saw the familiar muscle twitch at her jawline.

She took a step back and foraged through the junk on the shelves. She pulled out a broom.

"The springlocks are designed to keep the animatronic parts locked in place so a person can safely wear the suit." Vanessa stepped forward in a flash and jabbed the handle of the broom into the animatronic's chest cavity.

A loud series of mechanical snaps clapped out a swift, almost hip-hop-sounding rhythm. The ribs sprang closed. The broom's wood handle cracked in half.

"They're unstable," Vanessa said unnecessarily.

Mike knew his mouth was hanging open. He inched away from the animatronic and then looked up at Vanessa.

"People *wore* these?" Mike returned his gaze to the metal springlocks. "You'd have to be suicidal to—"

"Like I said. Unstable."

Mike looked back toward Vanessa. Her eyes had turned an even deeper blue, navy blue now. Almost black. Her chin was lifted, and her eyes were slit nearly closed.

Who is this woman? Mike asked himself. He was almost afraid to move, afraid that she would—

A muffled burst of rock music reached into the storage room. Mike's head whipped in that direction. *What now?*

"It's just the show music," Vanessa said. "The animatronics are probably putting on a performance for Abby."

Vanessa's voice was flat. She wasn't smiling.

Mike stood and brushed himself off. "Yeah," he said, "and Abby is probably dancing with them." His tone was light, and he smiled. He wanted to shift the mood, which was desolate. He could almost feel waves of despondency radiating from Vanessa.

"Anything else you want to let me in on?" Mike asked. "Killer clowns? Fire-breathing dragons?"

Vanessa's expression didn't change.

"I'm just curious," Mike went on, "since you somehow seem to know everything else about this place."

Vanessa turned away.

That angered Mike. He took a step toward her and raised his voice. "What if Abby had come in here?" he shouted. "What if she'd found that thing?" He pointed at the animatronic, even though Vanessa wasn't looking at him.

Vanessa spun back toward Mike. Now her expression had

changed. Her eyes were almost spitting sparks. "*You* brought her, Mike! Not me!"

Mike had no response for that.

The coals of Vanessa's eyes cooled . . . just a little. "What I still can't wrap my head around is why. Honestly. Why'd you bring her?"

Mike thought about lying, but maybe he and Vanessa should stop that crap. "I think the kids know who took my brother," he said.

Vanessa's brows rose nearly to her hairline. Her anger was gone.

Mike rushed to explain. "I think . . . that they're connected somehow. It's hard to explain, but when I'm here, I feel closer to Garret. My dreams are more . . . vivid. Almost like I can—"

"Change what happened?" Vanessa filled in.

How does she know? Mike asked himself.

"Have you asked them about this?" Vanessa persisted.

"One of them. He seems to speak for the others."

"Blond-haired boy?"

He nodded. "I don't think he likes me very much. But he likes Abby."

"And you figure if he won't tell you, he'll tell her."

Mike shrugged.

Vanessa put her hands on her hips. She sneered at him. "How stupid can you be?"

Mike bristled at both her posture and her expression, but he said evenly, "I'm sorry?"

"Mike, you need to stop."

Mike's bristles turned into spikes. "Honestly," he threw at her, "I don't really see how it's any of your business."

Vanessa—as if transporting herself through the space between them—was in Mike's face. She grabbed his shirt collar. Her breath smelled sharp, even bitter.

When she spoke, she nearly growled. "I'm telling you to let. This. Go."

Mike couldn't have been any more taken aback if he'd been nose-to-muzzle with a snarling tiger. And maybe his reaction was plastered to his face, because Vanessa once again moved in a flash. This time, she whipped back, ending up three feet away from him.

Vanessa seemed to shrink into herself. Her face was bright red, and she dropped her gaze to the floor.

Mike didn't take pity on her shame. Instead, he blurted the question that wouldn't leave his head. "Who the hell *are* you?"

Vanessa pulled in her shoulders. She didn't look up. "Someone," she said in an almost little-girl voice, "who's trying to help you." She raised her gaze. "You idiot."

The last was said with a little more strength, but at least she didn't growl at him again. And apparently, she was done. She strode away. Mike heard a rustling of papers. Footsteps. A slammed door.

CHAPTER 19

When Mike burst into the dining room, close on Vanessa's heels, he found Abby doing exactly what he'd predicted she was doing. She was dancing . . . sort of.

Abby was up on the stage with the animatronics, and she was throwing her hips back and forth like an Elvis impersonator. Bonnie was copying her.

Vanessa's boot-clad feet thumped across the dining room floor. Mike looked her way. Her head down, her shoulders still bowed inward, Vanessa was going for the exit.

Mike ran after her. "Vanessa, wait!"

Mike caught up to Vanessa. He grabbed her arm and yanked on it, forcing her to face him. Vanessa's cheeks were stained with tears. As if his fingers were getting burned, he let go of her.

"Talk to me," Mike said quietly.

Vanessa wiped her face with the back of her hand. "I'm trying. You won't listen."

Mike grabbed his head to hold in the *"Arrrgghh!"* that wanted to come out of his mouth. He took a deep breath, then dropped his hands. "I need to know what happened that day. Don't you get it? Finding the guy who took Garret is the only thing that matters."

Vanessa shook her head. She opened her mouth. Closed it. Took a breath. Exhaled. She looked to her right, toward the children's drawings. She frowned.

Mike thought Vanessa looked like someone who badly wanted to confess something. But what?

Vanessa's throat convulsed. She bit her lip. Then she managed, "You don't understand."

"Then explain it to me!"

Vanessa's gaze locked on Mike's. She set her jaw and took a deep breath. He was sure she was finally going to open up and . . .

Vanessa seemed to flip a switch . Every muscle in her body tensed. Her eyes, focused past Mike, shot wide.

"What . . . ?" Mike began.

Vanessa took a halting step toward the stage.

Mike started to turn.

Vanessa yelled, "No!"

Mike completed his turn.

On the stage, Abby was laughing euphorically. Bonnie was holding his guitar out to Abby, inviting her to try playing it. Abby eagerly accepted it. She flung the strap over her shoulder and positioned the guitar across her chest and belly.

Mike frowned. An inner "red alert" alarm was going off. But why?

"Abby, don't!" Vanessa screamed.

Vanessa was well past Mike now, sprinting toward the stage. Instinctively, Mike followed her.

As he took his first step, Mike's memory banks put an urgent rerun on his inner screen: *Red hot and bursting with bright color, sparks spewed from Bonnie's guitar.*

"*Abby!*" Mike shouted. He held out a hand like he could make like a magician and stop what was about to happen.

Mike wasn't a magician.

All he could do was watch as everything unfolded in snatches, like Mike was seeing a series of still photographs: A grinning Abby strumming a hand over the guitar fret. The grin disappearing. Abby's eyes drawn together in confusion. A burst of blinding white light. Abby disappearing in the incandescence.

*　　*　　*

All Abby could see was the brightest of whites. It was light, blinding her.

All Abby could hear was a high-pitched ringing. Like an alarm, only louder. It hurt her ears.

Abby rubbed her eyes. She pressed her hands to her ears.

And then the white light was gone. But it left teensy little stars in her eyes. Abby blinked.

Mike's face and Vanessa's and the faces of all Abby's friends were inches from Abby's. All the faces above Abby looked weird . . . distorted . . . and really scared.

Abby shook her head like a dog, trying to stop the ringing in her ears. She blinked again.

"What happened?" she asked Mike.

Before Mike could answer, Vanessa leaned in and hugged Abby . . . tight.

Vanessa let Abby go and leaned back. Abby saw Vanessa's gaze flick to Mike. Mike was still staring at Abby. He looked guilty. Like he'd done something really bad.

He still didn't answer Abby's question. But Vanessa did. "It was an accident, sweetheart," she said. "Just a silly accident."

* * *

Crickets chirped madly in the trees that surrounded Freddy's parking lot. Mike couldn't see either the trees or the crickets. The pizzeria's exterior lights were out, and the moon had left the night sky. So had the stars. The sky looked like one broad dome of soot so thick that Mike was finding it hard to remember what daytime felt like.

Mike and Vanessa stood next to her cruiser. They both looked toward the back seat of his car, where Abby was curled up, hugging Dolph.

"Thank you," Mike said to Vanessa.

Mike was leaving the pizzeria mid-shift. Vanessa was going to cover for him.

Vanessa shook off the gratitude. "Just go home, Mike. Take care of your sister."

Mike nodded, but he didn't move. He pulled his gaze from Abby and he put it on Vanessa. "What is it you're so afraid of?" he asked.

Vanessa shot him a look he couldn't read.

"In the storage room," he pressed. "I saw your eyes. You were terrified."

Vanessa's face instantly did the rock-hard thing again. The caring Vanessa was gone. Enigmatic Vanessa, grim Vanessa, brooding Vanessa . . . they were all back. She—they—stomped a foot.

"Do whatever you want with your life," Vanessa flung at Mike. "But if you ever bring Abby back here? I'll shoot you."

Vanessa squinted her eyes and leaned toward Mike. He didn't need her to pull a gun to convince him she might actually be serious.

Vanessa stormed back into Freddy's. Mike waited until the slam of the heavy metal door quieted the crickets for an instant. As the crickets chirped back into gear, Mike got in his car.

"She looked really mad," Abby said from the back seat.

"She's fine."

"Why does everyone always look at you that way?"

Mike turned the key in the ignition. The engine sputtered.

"Everything is fine," Mike said.

*   *   *

Everything was not fine.

Mike sat at his kitchen table and watched the first hint of dawn begin sneaking in through his window. From the intensity of the early light, Mike concluded that the clouds that had hid the moon during the night had moved off. Mike wished his own personal clouds would move on, but they appeared to be stuck over his head with superglue. Not even Mike's soul-flogging push-ups had managed to clear his stormy skies.

The sounds of Abby's snores, a little louder than usual, reached him from her room.

He couldn't believe he was about to do what he was about to do. But what choice did he have? Vanessa was right. He couldn't take Abby back to Freddy's.

Sighing, and feeling like he was going to throw up, Mike lifted his phone. He punched in a number.

As soon as he heard the click on the other end of the line, Mike spoke. He had to while he still had the stomach for it.

"Hey, it's Mike," he said. "I need your help."

As soon as he said them, he immediately regretted his words.

Two hours later, Mike still hated the choice he'd made. But he was trying to make the best of it.

The sun was full-out now. It intruded into the kitchen and tried to convince Mike he was doing the right thing.

Checking the pancakes on the griddle, Mike started some bacon in a cast-iron skillet. The sweet and savory smells came together and attempted to join with the sun's "all is well" message.

Mike wasn't buying it. Deliberately keeping his back to the kitchen table, because he couldn't look at what he'd done, he kept cooking anyway. He finished everything and stuck it in the oven to keep warm. Then he took a deep breath and went to wake up Abby.

* * *

Abby opened her eyes and saw her brother sitting at the edge of her bed. Yawning, she grinned at him. Then she noticed what her nose was telling her.

"Is that bacon?!" she asked.

Cool. They didn't usually have bacon. And Abby loved bacon.

"Why don't you get dressed and come to the kitchen when you're ready," Mike said. "There's something we need to talk about."

Abby frowned. *Uh-oh.* Was he bribing her with bacon?

She shrugged. *So what?* It was bacon.

Mike left the room, and Abby jumped out of bed. Popping into the bathroom, she did all the usual morning stuff, then she went back in her room and dressed in her maroon corduroy overalls . . . with a gold shirt . . . because she was sure it was going to be a gold-star day. Then she skipped down the hall to get her bacon.

"I'm ready for—"

Abby stopped mid-skip when she saw who was sitting at the kitchen table. The bacon was a bribe. Not a big enough one.

"There's my favorite little girl," Abby's Aunt Jane said.

Abby tried to make her aunt . . . with her stupid short hair and her dumb old pale blue pantsuit . . . disappear with laser eyes. Abby wrinkled her nose, choking on her aunt's stupid grapefruit-y perfume.

"Abby, come sit down," Mike said.

Abby turned the laser eyes on Mike. But she couldn't hold the laser. Her hate turned to hurt. "What did you do?" she asked her brother.

Abby could tell Mike knew she was upset. But he was pretending he didn't.

"Come sit down," he said again. "We can talk."

Abby shook her head. No way. She started retreating from the kitchen, backing down the hall.

"I know what you're thinking," Mike said. "I promise you, you're wrong. Please, Abby. Let's just talk."

Abby looked at her aunt, then she returned her gaze to Mike. His face looked like he was trying to eat a pot of brussels sprouts. No, his face looked like he couldn't stand to be him.

"I hate you," Abby said to him.

Abby turned and ran back to her room. As she went in and slammed the door, she heard her aunt say, "I think that went well."

Putting her back to her door, Abby closed her eyes and clutched her hair in both hands. She let out a cross between a howl and a roar. Tears took over her eyes and forced them open. She couldn't stop the tears from pouring down her cheeks, but she rubbed them away as fast as they flowed.

Abby's gaze landed on her desk . . . and her drawings. She stomped toward her desk and threw herself in her chair.

Jerking open a desk drawer, Abby dug around in it and found the biggest, blackest marker she had. Then she reached for the stack of her most recent drawings. Fisting the marker, Abby started to black out every image of her brother that she could find.

*   *   *

Mike couldn't look at his aunt as he grabbed his keys and pulled on his coat.

"She reminds me of you," Jane said. "Always with the temper."

Mike shot a look at Jane, figuring she was trying to pick a fight. He was surprised when he found her looking at him with a softer-than-normal expression. If Mike hadn't known better, he might have believed she was looking at him with fondness. Nah.

"When she calms down," Mike said, "tell her I'm sorry. And I'll be back soon."

"When is soon, exactly. You've been a little fuzzy with the details."

There was the snarky Aunt Jane Mike knew . . . and didn't love.

"Soon," Mike said.

Aunt Jane shooed Mike away. "Go, then."

Mike turned toward the door.

"But Mike," Jane said to his back, "there's a larger conversation that still needs to happen here. When you get back, you and I are going to talk." She picked up a piece of bacon and nibbled on it.

The image of a vulture chewing on carrion flashed through Mike's mind. He practically ran from his house.

*　*　*

Clutching the white bag that the pharmacist had put Mike's refilled prescription in, Mike stalked toward Freddy's entrance doors. The elderly druggist's judgmental advice—*"You know what works for me? A warm glass of milk with chamomile and honey."*—replayed in Mike's head as he went.

Right back at you, Mike thought now.

A crow let out a long cackle. Mike looked up into the trees around Freddy's. He couldn't find the crow, but his gaze landed on the wood cutout of Freddy Fazbear's head. The bear's grin seemed to be jeering at Mike.

"Stuff it," Mike said. He let himself inside the pizzeria and went directly to the office.

There, Mike wasted no time. He plopped in the desk chair, set up his cassette player, and dry-swallowed three of the white pills from the bottle he'd pulled from the white bag. He locked his gaze on the poster opposite the desk.

Maybe because he was so determined, or maybe because he hadn't slept well in days, the effect of Mike's routine was immediate. His vision blurred as he listened to the sound of the wind and the trees coming from the cassette. His lids fluttered closed.

Sunlight is warm on Mike's shoulders as he walks forward. The breeze picks up a lock of his hair. It tickles his cheek.

Mike hears laughter, and he looks toward it. Stunned, he stares at his family, all gathered by the picnic table.

Mike's mom is setting the table for lunch. His dad is standing next to her; he's spinning an overjoyed Garret around like a spiraling airplane. Garret's laughter fills the campsite.

"All right," Mike's mom says, "enough games, you two!"

Mike's mouth hangs open as he watches his dad swoop toward the picnic table with Garret.

"Emergency landing!" Mike's dad shouts.

His dad makes a whooshing sound as he sweeps Garret's spread-eagled body over the table. Mike's dad plunks the boy onto the table with a flourish. Then Mike's dad looks toward Mike.

"Hey, buddy," Mike's dad calls out.

"Don't just stand there," his mom says to Mike, "come and dig in."

Mike's parents settle on the table's benches. Garret climbs off the tabletop and joins them. Then the boy turns and gives Mike the biggest, most adorable happy-kid smile Mike has ever seen. Mike's eyes are awash in tears.

His mom looks his way. "Sweetie, what's wrong?"

Mike wipes his eyes. He clears his throat. "This isn't . . ."

He stumbles back from the picnic table. "This . . . isn't the way it happened." He shakes his head. "This isn't real."

Mike's parents, and Garret, exchange confused glances.

"But it could be." The voice is coming from behind Mike. It's a child's voice.

Mike turns to find the blond boy, and the other four children, standing behind him. He shakes his head again, this time more vehemently. He bites his lip. His hands are clenched into fists.

"What is this?" Mike asks the blond boy. "This isn't what I asked for."

The blond boy cocks his head. "No," he says, "but it's what you want."

More head-shaking from Mike. He's trying to erase the entire scene by rejecting it.

"I want to find—" Mike begins.

"You're lying!" the blond boy interrupts.

Mike looks at the ground.

"You want to save Garret," the boy says. "That's really why you're here."

Mike tries another head-shake, but it's a feeble one.

"You want to change what happened," the boy says. "You want to go back."

Mike throws up a hand as if to shield himself from the boy's words. "That's not possible," he says. "He's gone. They all are."

"Really?" The boy points past Mike.

Even though he doesn't want to, Mike turns around and looks at his family. They're staring back at him with concern and compassion . . . and hope.

Garret scrambles off the wooden bench and dashes toward Mike, who drops to his knees. He's eye-to-eye with his little brother.

"You can have this dream every night," the blond boy says. "You can be together, like before." The boy's voice drops to a near-whisper. "You can change what happened."

Mike's head-shakes have turned into a tentative nod. His tears have escaped his eyes; they're rivulets sluicing down his cheeks.

Mike looks at the blond boy. "How . . . ?"

"You said we could have anything we wanted," the blond boy says. "It's only fair." He steps up close to Mike and leans in.

Mike expects to feel the boy's warmth, but a puff of chilly air touches Mike's ear as the boy says in a gentle whisper, "We want Abby."

Mike wipes at his tears, his face twisted. He's struggling to grasp . . .

Mike's eyes widen. He gets it now.

"Abby," he whispers.

Garret clutches Mike's hand. "They love her, Mike," Garret says. "And she loves them."

Mike looks at Garret. Mucous runs from Mike's nostrils, joining his tears. He sniffs.

"It's for the best, buddy," Mike's dad calls from the picnic table. "It really is."

Mike looks over at his dad, who smiles reassuringly. Even as wracked as he is, Mike can't help but return the smile.

Mike's mom chimes in. "You've seen her with them. You've seen how happy she is."

Mike looks over at his mom. She's tearing up, too.

"Doesn't she deserve a real family?" his mom asks as she gets up and comes over to kneel next to Mike. She uses her thumb to wipe tears from his cheeks.

Mike's tentative nod is becoming more assured.

"It's time to let her go, sweetie," his mom says. "You were never the right person to take care of her."

Now Mike's nod is emphatic. He's not just nodding because he wants to believe her. He does believe her. He agrees with what he's hearing.

Mike looks from his mom to his dad to Garret. His conviction solidifies.

"Okay," Mike says. He nods one last time. "Yes."

The blond boy lifts one side of his mouth in a small, satisfied smile.

Mike looks again at his brother. His gaze lands on the flop of hair that is obscuring Garret's eyes. Mike reaches out to brush the lock of hair back. His hand stops mid-motion.

The sun's spotlight suddenly glares in Mike's eyes, and he feels its heat. It catapults him out of the campsite and into a memory.

Mike's vision turns inward. He sees his sleeping sister in his mind. He knows he's sitting on the side of her bed. He sees his hand reach out and brush a lock of her hair from her face. He's in a memory, he realizes.

But then the memory becomes something else. It becomes more of a vision, something Mike wants to experience instead of something he experienced in the past.

In Mike's mind, Abby's eyes open. She's groggy, but she smiles at him. "You're home," she says.

In his mind, Mike smiles at his sister. "I'm home," he says.

The picture in Mike's mind disintegrates. He's back at the campsite.

The sun disappears behind a cloud. In the instant shade, Mike stares at Garret. Mike realizes his hand is still touching the lock of Garret's hair. Mike pulls his hand back.

With that motion, it seems like a veil drops away. Garret's face is startlingly pale. Too pale. And his eyes are wrong. The adorable . . . Garret-ness . . . is gone from Garret's eyes. Mike's brother's eyes have turned to deep wells of hollowness.

Mike staggers to his feet. "Wait! This isn't—"

He looks at his parents. They too are pale now. They too have bottomless eyes.

Mike returns to head-shaking. "This is wrong," he says. "I'm sorry, but I don't want this. You hear me? I don't want it!"

Mike spins to confront the blond boy, but the boy . . . and the other children . . . are gone. Mike scans the campsite and can't find them. He turns back to his —

His family is gone, too. Everyone has vanished.

Mike is completely alone.

Mike hears the tree branches swish. The wind picks up. A creak of branches. Through the sounds of the wind and the trees, a chorus of whispers starts to build in volume.

The content of the whispers is indistinct at first. It's just a susurration, a white noise. But then the whispers begin to separate into something clear.

"Abby!" the whispers say.

Mike turns in a circle. It's the children, he realizes. Their voices are taunting him. He turns and he turns, trying to find the kids.

"Listen to me!" Mike shouts. "You stay away from her!"

The whispers are louder now. "Abby. Abby. Abby."

Mike screams, "Stay away from my sister!"

The whispers stop, replaced by a giggle. Then a rush of footsteps.

Mike whirls toward the sound. All he sees is a blur of motion. And then a paper hook arcs toward him. A bolt of heat scores into his chest. Gasping, Mike throws up a hand toward his chest. Before he can get it there, he sees another blur. This time, it's the top hat. The boy wearing it rakes claws across Mike's back.

Mike cries out and flounders in a circle. He doesn't see anything but trees.

A flurry of motion out of Mike's range of vision precedes another lava flow of pain. This one courses through his left calf.

Mike's legs go out from under him. He tries to curl into a ball, but the scourging pain stops him. The strikes land too fast for him to defend himself. His clothes are being shredded.

Mike falls back, lying prone in the dirt. Above him, the wind picks up. He hears a whir, low and soft.

Mike looks up into the trees. His vision is hazy.

The tone of the whirring changes. It no longer sounds like wind. It sounds . . . mechanical.

Mike's lids flutter. He's giving into the pain, but when the grinding, metal-on-metal sound gets even louder, his eyes bug open.

CHAPTER 20

The mechanical thrum was deafening now, almost as loud as helicopter rotors . . . *vrum, vrum, vrum.* The sound demanded Mike return to full consciousness.

Mike tried to get his eyes to zero in on whatever was causing the head-splitting sound. His eyes weren't fully cooperating, but they were giving him glimpses.

Mike struggled to process what he was seeing. His head was pounding because the visual snatches were coming at him like they were being hit with a strobe light.

Mike saw . . .

. . . a robotic arm suspended above his head.

. . . a bear mask, peeled open, held by the arm.

. . . honed bits of metal inside the mask, like miniature but lethal knives in constant motion.

Mike's brain brought his sight completely back online, and Mike put it all together. He was lying on his back . . . on a hard metal surface—a reclining chair?—and he was looking at the inside of a robotic mask full of sharp, continually moving metal. The mask was coming toward his face.

Mike yelped and tried to get up. That's when he realized that he was bound to the chair. Steel bands were clamped around his wrists. A heavy leather strap was cinched tight around his chest.

The metal juggernaut started to descend toward Mike's face. He did the only thing he could do. He brought every muscle he had into play and sent them all into motion. He squirmed and twisted and wriggled. He kicked his legs, and he jolted his body up and down and side to side.

Mike knew, of course, that his efforts were going to fail. He wasn't strong enough to break . . .

Above the relentless metal chirring, Mike heard a *crack*, a distinctive, pinging crack. He knew that sound. A bolt had given way.

Mike felt his arm fall away from him as one of the chair's armrests detached. His gaze still on the plunging mask, Mike jerked on his arm without much hope.

To Mike's astonishment, the metal clamp disengaged from Mike's wrist. He had an arm free!

But that wasn't enough. The mask was closer now. It was moving slowly, but unalterably, lower and lower.

Sharp metal. Soft face. Not a good combination.

Frantic, Mike sent his fingers in search of something . . . anything . . . on the side of the chair that could help him get free. He ran his fingers over an expanse of metal, thrust them between sharp gaps. And then . . .

Mike's fingers stopped on something flat and round, some kind of control button. Mike strained to see his hand, and he saw a quarter-sized green light. He didn't hesitate. He pushed the green button and . . .

Eureka! The other wrist band uncoupled.

The mask was now just inches from Mike's nose. It was so close that the burring of the rotating and constantly cycling metal was blowing his hair.

Feverish with the crucial need to move, Mike fumbled with the leather chest strap. Maybe because he got lucky or maybe because necessity is the mother of getting the hell out of Dodge, Mike managed to click the strap apart and slide off the chair. His escape couldn't have come any later. The blitzing metal grazed the side of his forehead as he turned downward.

Mike dropped to the floor. Metal-on-metal screeches told him the mask, aka buzz saw, was grinding into the chair. Fireflies of hot sparks seared the little hairs on Mike's arms as he rolled away from the chair.

All of Mike's muscles demanded a break. He flopped into a glob of exhaustion.

The continuing spray of sparks . . . and his understanding of his foe's strength . . . got Mike back into motion. He tried to stand.

Fiery pain in Mike's calf sent him careening off-balance. He toppled backward into jabbing metal and sticky, crusty, faux fur. Mike scuttled away from what was grabbing at him. His gaze shot around him wildly. He saw a litter of faded, matted-fur-covered animatronic characters.

It's just costumes, Mike told himself.

Again, he tried to stand. This time, ready for the pain, he made it. But as he wavered on his feet, he heard a peculiarly familiar *hop-hop* beat of snaps. Looking down, he watched the costume's clamshell open.

Mike squawked and blundered backward. His hand whipped to his nose and mouth as the sick stench of rotting corpses hit him.

No longer thinking about running because his brain was now overwhelmed by what he was seeing—and smelling—Mike's stomach threatened to heave as he gazed at the mutilated remains of three men . . . and Max.

Mike gagged as he looked at poor Max's body. It was severed in two. No, not severed. It looked like something had bit her in half at the waist. Her upper body lay back against one of the two men, and her lower body was draped across her stomach. Mike, his hand over his mouth, quickly shifted his gaze to her face. Her eyes and mouth were open wide in a rictus of pure terror.

"Oh, Max," Mike whispered.

Mike jerked his eyes away from her. When he did, he saw that the faces of one of the men had been similarly chewed, all the way into the man's brain.

Mike quickly moved his gaze to the other two men. One was older, and one younger. Mike sucked in his breath. He recognized the younger man; it was Jeff, Max's brother. Jeff and the older guy looked like they'd been run through a meat slicer. But no, the cuts weren't straight. They were curved, like the wounds you'd get from a pirate's hook.

This last thought finally galvanized Mike. He turned away from the putrefying cadavers, and he limped past the still-sparking mask and chair. He staggered toward the door.

At the room's threshold, Mike paused. All the way up and down the main hallway, the lights were surging on and off, on and off. The rhythm wasn't even, though. It was chaotic, as if the lights were being manipulated by someone too enraged to stay in control.

Mike squinted to see through the disorienting flashes of light and dark. It was hard to know for sure, but the hallway appeared to be empty.

Mike reeled into the hall. His feet fumbling as if he'd never properly learned to walk, Mike zigged and zagged his way toward the lobby. If he could get there, he could get out of the building. Out of the building meant salvation.

Mike tried to pick up the pace. His feet shuffled faster.

Just a few feet from the lobby now.

From behind Mike, a crash boomed after him. A roar joined the crash. They partnered in their pursuit.

Mike didn't bother to look back. He called on every ounce of strength he had, and he stepped on the gas. Managing to break into a jerky gallop, he spilled into the lobby. He threw himself toward the double doors.

But when Mike hit the doors, they wouldn't open. They were locked.

A new sound joined the crashing and roaring. No, not a sound. A voice. A singing voice.

"Dum dum diddly da . . ."

The lights were now going totally bonkers. They were winking in and out so fast that it was impossible for Mike to see what was coming toward him.

But something was. Something big. Something fast.

Mike summoned the last bit of his perseverance. He pounded on the heavy metal doors.

Sensing rather than seeing that his time had run out, Mike looked to his left. He screamed and fell into a total eclipse of any light he'd ever seen or hoped to see.

* * *

Abby, curled up in her bed, hugged Dolph tighter than she ever had, and it still wasn't tight enough. Outside Abby's window, the sun was a deep red ball hovering just above the hills in the distance.

Soon it would slip out of sight. Abby thought the ball looked like a big drop of blood, like the sky was hurt and needed a bandage.

Of course, Abby knew the sky wasn't hurt. *She* was hurt. But she wasn't hurt in a way that a bandage could help. A bandage couldn't fix the stuffed-up nose and stinging eyes that hours of crying had left her with. And it couldn't fix the fact that the happiness she'd been feeling ever since she'd been united with her friends at Freddy's had been ripped away. Abby's happy was gone. That was why she kept hugging Dolph tighter and tighter and tighter. Hanging on to something familiar, something Abby loved . . . and who loved her . . . was the only thing that could stop her tears. Maybe. She hoped. It hadn't worked yet.

A knock on the door caused Abby to smush Dolph even more. Abby put her face in Dolph's gray-blue fur.

"Abby, sweetheart?" her Aunt Jane called through the door.

Abby let go of Dolph with one arm, and she pulled a blanket up over herself and the dolphin. Even through the blanket and the door she could hear the TV in the living room. She'd heard it for hours. The stupid fake laughter coming from the TV told Abby that her Aunt Jane was watching old-timey sitcoms.

"You can't stay in there forever, kiddo," Aunt Jane called.

"Leave me alone!" Abby shouted. She sniffed again.

Jane's exasperated sigh came clearly through the door. "Suit yourself," she said.

Abby could tell that her aunt was annoyed. But who cared? She listened in satisfaction as the *tap-tap-tap* of the dumb high heels her aunt always wore retreated from her door.

* * *

Jane gave Abby's closed door a long, searing look. *Spoiled brat.*

The obnoxious little twit wouldn't be acting like that much longer, Jane thought as she strode back into her nephew's ratty, pathetic living room. Ha! Living room. How could anyone possibly live in such squalor? Jane sure couldn't.

But she could tolerate it. For now.

Jane had to keep her eye on the end goal. That was why she was here pretending to help. Oh, she was helping all right, helping *herself.*

Once Abby was in Jane's custody, Jane would be one step closer to getting control of the big, fat trust fund that should never have been Abby's in the first place. Why Jane's father had left his money to his granddaughter instead of his daughter was beyond Jane. She understood why he hadn't left it to Jane's brother. For one thing, he'd disappeared off the face of the earth after he left his family. For another, he was an idiot. He never should have married such a weak woman.

Curling her lip at the couch's sagging cushions, Jane plopped onto one of them, wriggling to try to create a comfortable position. She reached for the TV remote and made yet another attempt to find something decent to watch on the ridiculously old television. Landing on yet another sitcom, Jane heard an odd whirring sound.

Crappy TV. Must be feedback, she thought. She turned up the volume so she could hear what was being said instead of hearing the static.

Jane smoothed the creases of her pants. *I'm going to have to get this pantsuit dry-cleaned*, she thought. Who knew what kind of parasites were living in the grungy sofa cushions?

A funny line on the TV pulled a laugh from Jane. She shook her head at the antics on the screen and—Jane stopped mid-head-shake.

What was that? She'd caught a glimpse of movement in the kitchen.

Was Mike finally home?

Jane turned and opened her mouth, preparing the scolding her nephew deserved for expecting her to cool her jets in . . .

Jane dropped the remote.

Half in shadow and half in the bloodred smear of the dusk light coming through the kitchen window, a giant bear stood next to Mike's fridge. It was just a few feet from Jane, and it was staring at her with radiant white eyes.

Jane closed her eyes. *I'm hallucinating*, she thought. Just a little time in the dregs of Mike's life and she was already losing her . . .

Jane opened her eyes again.

No way.

The bear was still there. And it was taking a step toward her.

* * *

Still under her blanket, still hugging Dolph, and crying even harder now, Abby went rigid when a big thud shook the house so hard that Abby's bed joggled beneath her. Abby shoved back the blanket and sat up.

"What was that?" she whispered to Dolph.

Dolph had no answer, but he was there for support when Abby got out of bed and hurried to her door. Laying her ear against the painted wood, she listened.

She heard nothing, except the TV.

Since Abby had burrowed under the covers, the red ball in the sky had disappeared. Now just a red sheen outlined the top of the hills Abby could see in the distance through her window. Night would be here very soon.

"Aunt Jane?" Abby called. Abby didn't really want Aunt Jane, but she didn't feel right about ignoring the big bang.

The only response Abby got was more of that fakey-fake laughter from the TV. Abby frowned. She looked back toward her bed. Maybe she should just get back in bed.

Abby listened at the door again. No, she had to know what had made that big sound.

Abby reached for the doorknob, but then she hesitated. She backtracked to her desk so she could grab her drawing pad and some pencils. Abby always felt better when she had a pad and pencils in the pocket of her overalls, so she stuffed both into place.

A bit more confident, Abby returned to her door and opened it. She peeked out into the hallway. Then, hesitantly, she walked down the hall toward the kitchen. It was empty. So, Abby looked toward the living room, where—

"Freddy?" Abby's happy came back to her.

The animatronic bear separated itself from a blobby shadow near the end of the sofa. As soon as it did, Abby could see she wasn't looking at Freddy. The bear looked like Freddy in every way, except for one obvious difference. His fur wasn't brown; it was golden. The gold was almost the color of the shirt Abby was still wearing with the maroon overalls she'd put on that morning.

A Golden Freddy!

"Wow!" Abby said. She no longer cared about the miserable hours she'd just gone through. Her eyes stopped stinging. She could breathe through her nose again.

"Who are—?" Abby stopped mid-question when a little boy with tousled blond hair, the same color as the big robotic bear's fur, magically came out of the robot.

"Not Freddy," the blond boy said.

Abby stared in awe at the little boy. He looked just like an ordinary boy, but not exactly. The boy was kind of sparkly, and Abby could see through him, just a wee bit. Abby thought the boy looked the way an angel might look.

Abby gave the fairy-tale-like boy a big smile. "You came for me?" she asked.

The boy nodded. "Everyone's waiting. It's time to go play."

Abby squealed and clapped her hands. The blond boy gave her a smile and then dissolved into a shimmer that went back into Golden Freddy. The big bear gestured at Abby to follow him as he took a giant step toward the front door of the house.

Abby looked down at Dolph. She didn't want to risk losing him while she was playing with the others, so she set the dolphin on the kitchen table. As she did, her gaze caught a glimpse of light blue in the living room.

Abby turned. On the floor, jutting out from behind the end of the sofa, the hem of Aunt Jane's pants was visible. Her aunt's feet, still in her high heels, stuck out of the pants. The heels seemed to be lying in the pool of something. Ketchup, maybe? How had her aunt spilled ketchup behind the sofa?

"Silly Jane," Golden Freddy said. The animatronic spoke in the little boy's voice. "She fell asleep."

Abby started to ask herself why her aunt would sleep on the floor, in spilled ketchup, but then she shrugged. She didn't care what her aunt did. She turned and followed Golden Freddy out the front door, closing it behind her.

Golden Freddy trudged stiffly off the little porch. Abby paused as she listened to his heavy footsteps.

All the sun's red was gone. It was full-on night now. A third of the moon was hovering over the concrete-sided stream across the street, and the moon's light made the bear's fur seem like it was about to catch fire. It looked really cool.

Abby gazed up and down the street. "How do we get to Freddy's?" she asked Golden Freddy.

Golden Freddy cocked his head. One of his big white eyes blinked shut and then opened again in a slow-motion wink. His teeth flashed in the moonlight as he gave Abby a wide smile. The smile was more creepy jack-o'-lantern than warm and friendly, but Golden Freddy couldn't help that. Abby knew that the animatronics couldn't move and make expressions like normal kids. That was okay.

* * *

Abby had never ridden in a taxi before, so she felt a fizz of excitement when she opened the shiny yellow back door and got into it. Taking a seat, she grinned at the fun, old country music playing on the radio. She looked at the back of the driver's head.

All Abby could see around the driver's headrest was curly brown hair sticking out from under a dirty baseball cap that looked like it had been worn for thousands and thousands of days. The hair, and the cap, were bopping to the twangy music. Abby shifted her gaze to the rearview mirror, and she saw crinkled green eyes looking back at her. The driver turned his head, and she noticed a toothpick sticking out between lips stretched into a friendly smile. The driver faced front again and asked, "Where to, little lady?"

As Abby opened her mouth to answer the question, the other backseat door opened. The taxi settled low, really low, as Golden Freddy squeezed himself in through the door and managed to sit next to Abby.

"What the hell?!" The driver spun around in his seat, jerking so much that he hit his head on the roof of the taxi. He spit out his toothpick and let out a shriek.

Abby smiled, but she didn't blame the driver for his reaction. She knew adults didn't understand.

The driver's mouth hung open as he stared at Golden Freddy. Golden Freddy gave the driver one of his big grins.

The driver turned around farther to look at Abby. She smiled at him sweetly.

The driver shook his head, then faced the front of the taxi again. "Not cool, man," he said. "Not cool."

Abby disagreed. She thought riding in a taxi with Golden Freddy was very cool.

Muttering something Abby couldn't make out, the driver took in a loud breath. Then he put the car in gear.

"We want to go to the old Freddy's Pizzeria, please," Abby said.

The driver eyed Abby in his rearview mirror. He shook his head. "Why do I always get the weirdos?" he asked.

CHAPTER 21

Mike opened his eyes, and the first thing he saw was an orb of bright, bright light above his head. The light was too bright to be in Freddy's. Or was it?

The next thing Mike noticed was that he was lying on metal. *Metal!* Not that chair again!

Mike put his hands on the cold, flat surface and tried to push himself off of it. That was when he noticed the third thing: His whole body hurt. Why did . . . ?

He levered up enough to look down at himself. He frowned at what he saw.

Mike wasn't in the chair at Freddy's. He was lying on a stainless-steel table. His shirt was gone, and his chest was wrapped in a swath of heavy bandages. Beyond his chest, Mike could see that his pants leg had been cut away from his left lower leg. The leg was wrapped up in bandages, too.

He gritted his teeth and sat up. He swung his legs off the metal table.

"Careful," a woman's voice said.

No, not just a woman. Vanessa.

Mike tracked the direction of the voice, and he found Vanessa, uniformed, sitting in a folding metal chair about six feet from him. The chair was tucked in the corner of a room filled with white metal and glass-fronted cabinets. Definitely not Freddy's. The room's walls were painted stark white, and the floor was a gleaming royal blue. Everything Mike saw looked fresh and sanitary.

"I got the bleeding to stop, but you'll probably need stitches," Vanessa said.

Mike looked at his bandages again. "Where are we?"

"Police supply outpost and aid station. I brought you here from Freddy's. You were . . . badly hurt."

A memory of the descending open mask flashed through Mike's head. "They tried to kill me."

Mike looked at Vanessa. She dropped her head, and her eyes got tucked into a pleat of darkness cast by the cabinet next to her.

"But I'm guessing you already knew that," Mike said.

Vanessa said nothing.

Mike leaned forward. "Max. Her brother. And the other men. Did you know about them, too?"

Vanessa lifted her head, and her eyes came out of the shadow. She looked at Mike, and he saw that her eyes were filled with tears.

"You did know," Mike said. He'd really hoped that she didn't.

"It's complicated," Vanessa said.

"Complicated?! You mean more complicated than a bunch of possessed robots murdering innocent people?"

"Those people trashed Freddy's!" Vanessa shouted. "They weren't innocent!"

"Well, Abby is," Mike said.

As Vanessa buried her face in her hands, Mike didn't bother to say that even vandals didn't deserve to have their faces gnawed off, or their bodies chewed in half.

Why, Max? Mike thought. Why had she been part of that? He shook his head. It didn't matter. Abby was the only thing that mattered.

"You watched her play with those things," Mike said to Vanessa's bowed head. His voice rose. "You knew what they were capable of, and you didn't say anything."

Mike shoved himself off the table. He took a weak step forward. He scanned the room. "Where are my things? I need to go. Now!"

Vanessa dropped her hands. When she looked up at Mike, her face was striped by glistening tear tracks. "Mike—"

"Abby's in danger!" Mike spotted his shirt lying on a stainless-steel counter under a row of cabinets on the far side of the room. The shirt was bloody, and it was torn, but it was a shirt. He limped toward it.

"Mike!"

He stopped and turned toward Vanessa.

Vanessa put up her hands. "Slow down. Take a breath." She switched to her stern cop voice, and her face flipped from contrite to authoritarian. "Tell me what happened."

Mike suddenly couldn't move. The memory of his dream—of everything he'd done—came rushing back at him. It was his turn to drop his head. If only he could take it all back.

It took superhuman effort to open his mouth and confess what he'd done. As he did, he couldn't face Vanessa. He talked to the floor. "In my dream," Mike began. He took a breath and tried again. "They wanted Abby, and I . . . gave her to them." He pressed his palm against the side of his head. "It was a terrible mistake, and when I tried to fix it . . . ." He pounded the heel of his hand against his temple.

Mike looked at Vanessa. "What do they want with my sister?"

Several long seconds passed. Mike thought Vanessa wasn't going to answer. And when she did, he wished she hadn't.

"They want to make her like them," Vanessa said.

* * *

The pretty yellow taxi drove away. Abby waved to the driver, but he didn't wave back. He didn't even look at her.

Abby shrugged. She gazed up at Golden Freddy, her friend.

Golden Freddy held out his big furry hand. Abby grinned and took it.

They swung their hands together as they walked toward the entrance to Freddy's. Golden Freddy's heavy steps *crackle-thumped* over the crumbly concrete sidewalk.

Abby felt like she might burst. She was so excited.

Golden Freddy pushed the metal door open. He let go of Abby's hand and motioned for her to go through in front of her. *Such a gentleman.* Abby skipped into the pizzeria's lobby. Behind her, the heavy door clanked shut.

Abby turned back toward Golden Freddy and—

He was gone!

Abby frowned. She turned in a full circle. "Where'd you go?"

Abby looked at the door. Had he left? No, she'd have heard his footsteps.

She turned toward the archway. She'd have heard his footsteps no matter which way he'd gone.

Abby shrugged. She'd seen some of Golden Freddy's magic. He must have used that to disappear.

Maybe he was with the others. Abby started across the lobby, heading toward the dining room. She couldn't wait to see Freddy, *original* Freddy, and the others.

The *scuff-tap* of Abby's footsteps seemed to bounce off the dining room walls as she walked into the room. She looked toward the stages. The curtains were drawn back but the stages were empty.

Abby frowned and looked around. "Hello?"

Most of the dining room was so dim that Abby could barely see it. Instead of the usual half-on-half-off fluorescent bulbs that lit the room, just one single floodlight came from the stage. It stretched out like a fat, yellow, ghostly finger, which pointed across the room at the wall of children's drawings.

"Freddy?" Abby called. "Chica? Anyone?"

Abby's calls circled around the room and returned to her. No one answered them.

Looking at the light finger, Abby gazed toward the end of it. Why was it pointing at the drawings?

Curious, Abby walked over to the wall. She looked up.

Abby had noticed the drawings before. It was impossible to miss them. The curled, brittle papers covered nearly one whole wall of the dining room. And the air currents in the room were always tickling the drawings, which made them crackle.

Abby had never really *looked* at the drawings before, though. Now she did.

Drawn by kids younger than Abby, the pictures were mostly of stick figures, but it was possible to tell what the figures were supposed to be. Abby could see, in the images, kids playing. Families eating. The animatronics performing.

The pale circle of light at the end of the yellow ghost-finger was centered in the middle of the drawings. And in the center of the circle, one drawing stood out.

Abby stepped over to it. The drawing was of a yellow rabbit, which was holding hands with five smiling children. Even though they were clumsily drawn, Abby recognized the children. They were her friends.

*   *   *

After she'd dropped her bomb, Vanessa had left her chair and started pacing back and forth by the cabinets. Mike, still stunned, could only watch her in silence.

Vanessa stopped pacing. Standing with her back to Mike, she began to talk. Cop Vanessa was gone again. This was the gentler side of Vanessa, and she spoke so softly that he had to strain to hear her.

"In the '80s," she began, "when those children went missing, the police searched Freddy's from top to bottom. Every square inch was accounted for. But they never found them."

Something about Vanessa's voice or her words turned Mike's shame on its head. Anger swelled up from his bandaged chest. He clamped his teeth together and clenched his fists.

"The man who took them," Vanessa went on, "he's . . . a very bad man. A cruel man."

Mike watched Vanessa reach into the pocket of her uniform pants. She took out a folded piece of paper.

"He's also a very clever man," she said. "He knew the parents would scream bloody murder and the police would come look- ing. And he knew there was one place that the police would never think to check. Because . . . why would they?" Vanessa turned around to face Mike. "Why would anyone?"

Mike's legs almost went out from under him as his mind replayed the gut-wrenching moment when he'd watched the animatronics open up in the torture chamber of the Parts and Service room. His memory flashed on Max's cleaved-in-half body . . . *inside the animatronic.*

As if she was seeing what Mike was envisioning in his head, Vanessa said, "It's not just the children's ghosts inside those robots."

Mike's stomach heaved. He kept his mouth shut.

"It's their bodies," Vanessa said.

* * *

The yellow light finger disappeared. That made it seem like a dark shade had come down over the drawings.

The shade came down over everything. For an instant.

Then four new light fingers extended down from the ceiling. They pointed at an angle, toward the two stages.

Abby turned around, looking toward the stages. She clapped her hands. There were her friends! Freddy and Bonnie and Chica stood at their microphones on the main stage. Foxy was set up on his smaller stage. They were all ready to put on a show!

* * *

Vanessa took a few steps toward Mike. The folded paper was

compressed in her closed hand, held to her chest. The hand was visibly trembling.

"You have to understand," Vanessa said. "The kids don't want to hurt anybody. It's him. He influences them . . . somehow."

"Who?"

"It wasn't their fault!" Vanessa's tone was pleading now. "They were scared, and alone, and they didn't know any better." Vanessa held out her empty hand. "You have to believe me."

Why did Mike think that Vanessa wasn't talking just about the kids at Freddy's?

He knew why. The urgency in Vanessa's tone was too intense. It sounded like she wasn't just trying to justify the behavior of some ghost kids. Her tone was too personal for that. It sounded like she was begging for absolution.

Mike stepped forward and put his hands on Vanessa's shoulders. He could feel them quaking in his grasp.

She's scared out of her mind, Mike thought.

* * *

Abby frowned at her friends. Why weren't they moving?

The animatronics were frozen in place. They looked like sculptures.

Abby's gaze shifted from one lit-up friend to the next. She took a step forward. "Guys?"

They still didn't move.

* * *

The Vanessa switch clicked again. The almost childlike "please forgive me" crimp between her brows disappeared. Her jaw took on the hardness Mike had seen so many times before.

Vanessa shrugged out from under Mike's hands. She stepped back, and when she spoke again, her voice had an edge. "I tried to warn you."

Mike gave Vanessa a "you've got to be kidding" look.

She nodded once, emphatically. "In my way, I really did try. You were just too dense, too . . . single-minded." She shrugged. "It's too late now. He knows you're looking for him."

The resolve wavered. Little-girl Vanessa reappeared, hunching Vanessa's shoulders. "He'll be coming," she said in a hushed tone.

"Who *is* he?" Mike asked.

Vanessa pressed her lips together.

"Vanessa, please," Mike implored her. "You have to tell me."

Vanessa held out the folded paper she held in a vice grip. "He's my father," she said.

Mike took the paper. His hands beginning to shake, he unfolded it.

The paper was an old, folded and refolded and refolded photograph.

Mike gasped. "No," he whispered.

He stared so hard at the photograph that his eyes started to hurt. And the photograph began to blur.

But it didn't matter. He'd seen it. He'd never unsee it.

In the photo, a little girl with streaked blonde hair stood in front of a bright and shiny Freddy Fazbear's Pizzeria. A screaming yellow GRAND OPENING! banner fluttered from the eaves of the building. Beneath the banner, all four animatronics

FIVE NIGHTS AT FREDDY'S

were crouched down on one knee, surrounding the little girl like they were all one big, happy family. The girl grinned from ear to ear. And in her hand, she held . . . Garret's orange toy airplane.

He dropped the photo. He took a step back as if the photo was a fire bomb that would incinerate him.

Mike lifted his gaze to Vanessa. He had to clear his throat twice before he could get his vocal cords to work. When he could finally speak, his words sounded like they were rattling over a gravel road. "You . . . knew."

Vanessa held out a hand. "Mike . . ."

"My brother. This whole time. You knew."

Vanessa shook her head. "Not about Garret. No. At least . . . not when I met you."

"But the others?"

Vanessa looked down. "I'm sorry, Mike. I'm so, so—"

The photo hadn't turned into a firestorm. But Mike's emotions did. All the shame, the confusion, the shock . . . they all fused together. They *exploded* into a ball of pure rage.

Mike lunged forward and grabbed Vanessa by her uniform collar. "Tell me how to stop them," he growled. "Tell me how to save my sister!"

If ever Mike expected to see the cop side of Vanessa, it was now. But she didn't react with power. She shrank inward like a victim. Her eyes were so wide that they almost filled her face.

* * *

266

Abby took a stutter-step back when the stage speakers crackled. An assault of whiny feedback forced her to cover her ears.

The multicolored performance lights sprang on, sweeping over the stage like whipping ribbons. Red ribbons. Blue ribbons. Yellow ribbons. Orange ribbons. Purple ribbons. Light ribbons went every which way.

And finally, the animatronics came to life. They exploded to life.

They all launched into the rock song that they were most famous for. Abby, relieved, clapped her hands and started dancing.

CHAPTER 22

In the driver's seat of Vanessa's police cruiser, Mike curled his fingers around the car's thick, leather steering wheel and stomped on the accelerator as he rounded a curve and hit a straightaway on the back road that led from the aid station to Freddy's. The V8 engine rumbled, and Mike felt the cruiser's power swell around him. He inhaled deeply, gathering his courage.

The interior of the car smelled like Vanessa. If Mike closed his eyes, which he wasn't going to do going this fast, he could have convinced himself he was sitting in a field of flowers, under an apple tree, eating a vanilla cookie. If only.

The night was pitch-black, and the only light on the road was created by the searchlight beams of the cruiser's headlights. Surrounded by all the LED-lit equipment inside the car, Mike felt like he was in the cockpit of a spaceship, flying through the farthest reaches of the galaxy.

It was too bad that all the bells and whistles that crowded the cruiser's dashboard and middle console were of no use to Mike. Too bad they weren't phasers or photon torpedoes . . . or something. Unfortunately, the two-way radio, laptop, radar gun, electronic ticketing console, video camera, in-vehicle router, and automatic license plate reader were not going to help Mike save his sister.

"Electricity," Vanessa's voice said in Mike's head.

With one eye on the spears of light drilling through the black tunnel of country road and forest and one eye in his memory, Mike relived his preparations for returning to Freddy's

He'd been getting ready to leave the aid station. Bloody and shredded shirt back on, Mike clicked Vanessa's utility belt in place around his waist. The leather band was heavy because all of its compartments and sleeves were stuffed full, except for the gun holster, because Vanessa wouldn't let Mike have her gun. Mike settled the belt as comfortably as he could on his hip as Vanessa opened one of the tall supply cabinets and leaned into it.

"Electricity is the key." Vanessa's voice was muffled because her head was in the cabinet.

Vanessa's head came out of the cabinet. She turned, holding up what looked like a long black-and-silver barbecue fork with a lightsaber-like handle. Vanessa pushed a button on the handle, and a blue sizzle of electricity sparked between the two prongs on the end of the "fork."

"We use these cattle prods for animal control." She walked toward Mike and pointed at his waist. "And you've got two taser guns on the utility belt. They won't do permanent damage, but they'll mess with the animatronics' circuitry . . . hopefully buy you some time."

The cruiser's heavy-duty tires hit a pothole deep enough to jounce the vehicle. Mike shut off his mind's replay. He glanced at the cattle prod, which lay in the passenger's seat. Would it really help? Given everything Vanessa had hid from Mike, could he trust her advice?

Mike put his attention fully back on the road, and when he did, he spotted a faint red aura low in the distance. Neon red. Plus some yellow and white.

Freddy's exterior lights were on. The bleary phosphorescence that reached out into the surrounding blackout looked to Mike like a dire omen. It pretty much screamed, "Abandon hope all ye who enter here."

*   *   *

Cattle prod hanging from a loop on the utility belt, Mike gripped the tire iron he got from the cruiser's trunk after he'd parked the car at the back edge of the pizzeria's disintegrating asphalt. He was skulking along the side of the grizzled old building, which struck him as a hostile enemy waiting for him, in stealth mode, eager for the coming battle. Bending low, Mike ran his hand along the rough, warped wood siding.

"You should avoid the main entrance," the memory of Vanessa guided him in his head. *"Look for an outlet vent on the east side of the building. It was sealed up years ago, but if you can get it open, that's the best way to get inside without being detected."*

Mike's palm transitioned from splintery boards to what felt like rusty metal. Bingo.

Step one, find the vent opening. Done.

Mike fumbled with the utility belt. He found the penlight's compartment, and he pulled it out. Aiming the light, briefly, at the metal he'd found, he saw that three two-by-fours had been nailed over the vent. Even in the on-and-off blip of penlight he shone on the boards, he could see that the lumber was gray with age. Shouldn't be a problem to remove.

Mike groped around on the utility belt and found the sleeve that held a folding knife. Flipping it open, he used the end of it to work the nails loose from the boards. The back-and-forth motion made a wheezy *scritch*, but it wasn't too loud. In just a few minutes, Mike had pried the boards away from the vent. After that, his knife made quick work of loosening the cover from the siding.

Step two, remove vent opening. Done.

Mike dropped to the ground and peered into the confined murk of the vent shaft. The penlight revealed a dusty mass of cobwebs just inside the opening.

Mike sighed and swiped away the webs. He eased into the meager space and snaked himself forward. As he slithered, his mind took him back to the aid station. He replayed his last few moments with Vanessa.

When Vanessa had handed Mike the keys to her cruiser, their fingers had brushed together briefly. The effect of the touch lingered far after Vanessa drew her hand back.

Troubled by the puzzle of his feelings for this woman who flipped so mercurially from friend to foe, Mike had lifted his gaze to her face. He'd found her looking directly back at him.

Of all the emotions Vanessa had triggered in Mike, the prominent one now was betrayal. Mike felt double-crossed, stabbed in the back. The throbbing pain of his wounds highlighted that sensation. Could she see the bitterness in his eyes?

Mike didn't know, but he could easily read her feelings. Vanessa's face was contorted with humiliation and regret.

For an instant, Mike had felt sorry for Vanessa. But then he thought about Garret.

"How many?" Mike asked. He clipped the words and swung them at her like he was hitting her with her own baton.

Vanessa flinched and looked away. She avoided the question. "You need to hurry."

Mike dropped his voice into an aggressive snarl. "How many, Vanessa? How many has your father killed?"

Vanessa's gaze flitted up to Mike's face and then away again. "I don't know. Honestly, I don't."

"Is Garret . . ." Mike couldn't finish the question. He swallowed and tried again. "Is my brother one of them? In the machines?"

Vanessa looked squarely at Mike and shook her head. "No. Garret was before Freddy's."

Mike felt the flames of his fury settle, by inches. It was small comfort, but at least his brother wasn't a ghost trapped in a robot.

Mike collected himself. Garret was gone. But he could save Abby. He had to get moving.

"Come with me," he said to Vanessa.

Vanessa shook her head vehemently. "No."

Mike leaned in toward her. "You owe them. And you owe me."

Vanessa's head shook even more emphatically, so much so that her hair twist came undone, and her hair fell down her back. "I can't, Mike," she said. "I can't." Obviously seeing that her refusal was rekindling the fire of his anger, she rushed on. "I really can't. If he's there . . . I won't be of any use to you. Believe me."

Mike did. He looked into her eyes, so soft blue right now that it seemed like some of her . . . essence? Life force? . . . was leeching from her. He saw it all clearly now—the reason for the way she acted, for the choices she'd made.

Vanessa had lived through even worse trauma than Mike had. She was beyond screwed up by her childhood. She was broken.

Mike's words came out thoughtlessly. "He really messed you up, didn't he?"

Vanessa turned away. She was visibly quavering.

"Please." Her voice was soft but insistent. "You have to hurry."

Mike fisted the cruiser's keys. He nodded.

As Mike turned away from Vanessa, he saw her sink to the floor. Her sobs followed him out of the aid station.

The replay in Mike's mind faded out as a rat scrambled past him. Mike's knee-jerk reaction to the rodent brought him to a dead stop, and he could've sworn he was hearing Vanessa's sobs murmuring through the vent shaft. The pitiful sounds wrapped around him just as heavily as the thick, sticky clumps of cobwebs that clung to his hair, clothes, and skin.

Mike wanted to cover his ears to block out the sound, but he knew it came from within him. And besides, he needed his hands and arms to continue his furtive army crawl.

Even over the memory of Vanessa's sobs, Mike could hear the sound of '80s music. He'd heard it faintly when he was just a few feet inside the building, and it got louder and louder as he progressed through the shaft. The driving rock beat muffled the imaginary sounds of Vanessa's pain, and they brought Mike fully into the present.

Mike inched his way around a turn in the shaft, and he saw a flare of painted light reaching toward him through the darkness. He was almost to the dining room.

Mike picked up his pace. This created more noise, but the booming music masked the tinny banging of his knees against the metal ductwork.

In just seconds, Mike, panting, reached the metal grate that covered the end of the vent shaft. Through the slanted slats, he could see— minimally—into the dining room, and the stage at the opposite end.

Mike turned his head so he could push his face up against the slats. He put his eye to one of the openings. He choked on one of his heaving breaths.

"Abby," Mike whispered urgently.

Abby was flushed and sweaty from dancing to the music. Her friends' act was amazing.

All the time they'd been performing, Abby's friends had seemed lost in the music. Now, though, Chica looked down at Abby and motioned for Abby to come up on the stage.

Yay! Abby thought. She hopped up onto the stage and ran to her friend.

Abby expected to be included in the performance, but instead, Chica took her hand and pulled her back away from the microphones. While the others continued to dance and sing, Chica led Abby to the back of the stage.

Abby was confused, but she didn't resist. Why should she? Chica was her friend.

Abby went along, wondering what Chica was up to, as Chica opened a door and stepped into a hall—a really small one that had almost no light. Chica started down the hall, pulling Abby along by her hand.

Although his view was obstructed, Mike could see through a door at the back of the stage. Chica was leading Abby into a narrow corridor.

Mike shoved at the metal grate. It didn't budge. Backtracking so he could throw more power behind his efforts, Mike pounded on the vent covering. It continued to hold.

Rabid in his need to get through the opening, Mike's hands groped Vanessa's utility belt. There had to be something he could use to loosen the vent cover.

* * *

Abby trusted Chica, but the cramped hallway made her think of a cave, a long cave, underground and cut off from light. It made her a little nervous.

Abby was about to ask Chica where they were going when Chica stopped and let go of Abby's hand. The chick stepped back, and Abby saw an open doorway.

"What's in there?" Abby asked.

Chica raised a hand and pointed a large, feathery finger into the room. Still a little nervous but game, Abby shrugged and walked forward. She found herself in a room filled with tools and parts of robots. It was kind of icky-looking. She didn't like seeing all the unconnected hands and arms and legs.

Chica nudged Abby and pointed again. Abby turned . . .

. . . and she immediately hugged herself. She really didn't like what she was looking at now . . . not even a little.

Sitting in the kind of light Abby had seen in haunted houses on TV, a big, red-haired doll with rosy cheeks lay in a metal chair.

Abby didn't like either the doll, which had staring eyes and a too-wide smile, or the chair, which was ugly and hard-looking.

Abby began backpedaling. She was no longer just a little nervous. She was feeling really bad, like something was very, very wrong. She thought it might be time to—

A sound, sort of like a purring cat, but not as friendly, began coming from the doll. Abby, stuck in place by growing fear, and the tiniest bit of curiosity, stared at the doll.

As Abby watched, the doll's torso began to open. The doll's insides looked like they were filled with sharp metal.

Abby's curiosity went away. Scared was the only thing left. She backed up another step.

"Chica," Abby began, "I don't like—"

Abby sucked in her breath when Chica lunged toward her. Before Abby could complete the breath—or make another sound—Chica had grabbed Abby by the waist and lifted Abby off the floor.

*　*　*

When Mike finally got the grate loose, with the help of a multi-tool from Vanessa's duty belt, one punch sent the vent cover flying. It clattered to the floor, but the noise was barely noticeable because the rock music was now blaring even more loudly. Its volume was nearly at speaker-exploding decibels.

Mike crawled out of the vent onto the floor. There, he lay still, looking toward the stage. Had the animatronics seen him come out of the vent opening?

It didn't seem like it. Foxy was still dancing on his small stage, and Freddy and Bonnie were singing their lungs out, eyes closed, boogeying cloddishly.

Figuring that if he stayed low, he could fly under the radar, Mike began crawling toward the main stage. As he went, he kept an eye on the animatronics, but they were still oblivious. They were like dervishes, lost in their performances. They moved with an almost maniacal intensity.

When Mike reached the base of the stage, he raised his head. He needed to reach the doorway at the back of the stage, but Freddy and Bonnie blocked his way. How could he get past them?

As Mike hesitated, a distant, and very loud, *clang-clang-chink* prodded Mike out of pondering and into action. He leaped to his feet and whirled toward the sound . . . which was coming from down the hall, not from the back of the stage. What if Chica had led Abby farther into the building in a roundabout way?

Mike was no longer thinking about the animatronics. He was thinking about Abby. He had to find her.

Freddy's eyes opened. He stopped singing and dancing. He looked in Mike's direction.

Mike immediately ducked low and scrambled backward. After just a couple yards of retreat, his foot whacked against something, and he felt a splash of water soak his shoe and sock.

He turned. The buckets of soapy . . . and now dirty . . . water were still sitting at the base of the stage, right where Mike had left them.

Mike glanced up at the stage. Freddy was back to performing again. Good. The buckets had triggered the idea for a plan, one that just might work.

*　　*　　*

"Chica, no!" Abby screamed as Chica carried her toward the awful doll in the metal chair.

Chica had Abby by the torso, head in front of Chica and legs behind. Grunting, Abby squirmed and twisted, but Chica's grip was strong.

Chica flipped Abby over and began pushing her into the open doll. Abby, her heart going faster than it ever had, did everything she could do to stay away from the doll's scary metal parts.

Abby kicked her legs like she was swimming. She threw out her feet to drive her shoe into Chica's hips. She balled her hands into fists and pounded on Chica's arms.

Abby's hissy fit–like struggle slowed Chica down a little because the chick had to try to line Abby up with the doll, and she couldn't because Abby kept moving. However, Chica wasn't slowed down enough. Abby knew why. She was just a little girl and Chica was big and made of metal. Abby couldn't get free. She felt herself being pushed back onto the metal parts.

"Help!" she shrieked.

Abby really wanted her brother. She really, really did.

*　*　*

Mike had gotten himself into a crouch next to one of the buckets when he heard Abby's cry. The sound moved him—fast.

Grabbing the bucket, Mike dashed toward the stage. He was fully visible to the stage now, but Freddy and Bonnie were too engrossed in their performance to notice.

Mike pulled back the bucket and tossed its contents to the stage floor, right under Freddy's feet. Mike whirled and went for the second bucket. This one he threw toward Bonnie's feet.

As soon as the second bucket was empty, Mike tossed it aside. He pulled out one of the taser guns from Vanessa's utility belt, and he planted himself in front of the stage.

Mike fired the taser without hesitation. Instantly, the gun's wires shot metal probes up and out toward the pools of water beneath the animatronics' feet. An arc of blue electricity hit the water and coursed like a heat-seeking—or robot-seeking—missile into those feet. The electricity shot up through both animatronics. A pyrotechnic display of sparks fountained over the stage.

Freddy and Bonnie stopped singing and dancing. They went stiff. The stage lights flickered, then went out. Both animatronics became felled redwoods. They hit the stage like they'd been dropped from the top of a fifty-story building. *Wham!* The impact literally shook the building's foundation.

While the floor beneath him was still pulsating, Mike turned. He ran toward the sound of his sister's screams for help.

*　*　*

Abby was almost completely pressed into the doll now. Her neck and back and legs and arms all hurt from the hard, sharp metal poking into her skin. Panting and crying, Abby was becoming too weak to fight anymore. Her throat hurt from screaming and yelling. And now she was crying, and her nose was so stuffed up she was having trouble breathing.

Abby looked up at Chica. Abby had never been so hurt

and let down. Not even Mike had ever made her feel this bad before.

Abby sniffed. "Please, Chica. Let me go."

Chica didn't even look at Abby. The animatronic was reaching down. Abby started to gasp even more frantically for breath. She was sure Chica was about to close her into the doll.

But then, the haunted-house light was gobbled up by bright white light. Abby squinted and tried to see around Chica.

"Hey!" Mike's voice shouted.

"Mike!" Abby called out.

I knew he'd come, she thought.

Actually, Abby hadn't known Mike would come. But she'd hoped. And then her fear had made the hope go away. Now the hope was back.

* * *

Mike, having flipped on the main lights in the Parts and Service room, stood in its doorway, his taser gun at the ready. "Get the hell away from my sister!" he yelled at the nasty yellow chick who was trying to shove Abby into the redheaded animatronic.

Mike recognized the doll-like animatronic. It was the one he'd seen in the storage room. No way was he going to let Abby get closed up inside that killing machine!

Chica turned away from the metal chair. Letting go of Abby, the robotic chick came at Mike. Mike immediately triggered the taser gun.

The taser wires streamed through the air. The probes separated, and each of them drilled directly into one of Chica's eyes.

Chica dropped as fast and as hard as her compatriots had. She hit the floor in a full-prone position, legs and arms akimbo, and she began to convulse. Her eyes blinked frenetically.

The instant Chica let her go, Abby had shoved herself away from the little-girl animatronic. Now she jumped out of the chair and ran to Mike. She threw herself at him.

Mike caught his sister in his arms. He hugged her close as she sobbed against his neck.

"Are you okay? Mike asked. "Are you hurt?"

Mike felt Abby's head shake against his shoulder. "No," she said in a tiny voice. But she was crying. Her tears were hot on Mike's skin, trickling down into his shirt.

Abby pulled her head away from Mike. She stole a glance back at Chica. Mike looked that way, too.

Smoke was spiraling up from Chica's charred eye sockets. The chick was dead-still.

Abby sniffled loudly and said, through more sobs, "I don't know what's wrong with her. I don't know why she's acting like this."

Mike patted Abby's shoulder. "I know. I know. It'll be okay."

Keeping an eye on Chica, Mike set Abby on the floor, but he held on to her. When it was clear she was steady on her feet, he crouched down in front of her.

"Listen to me, Abs." Mike put his hands on Abby's shoulders.

Abby pulled her gaze from Chica and looked into Mike's eyes. He looked right back, and he leaned closer to her.

"I've been an idiot," Mike said. "About so many things. I need you to know that I'm sorry, okay? Everything I've been hung up on . . . none of it matters. You're the most important thing in my life. And I swear to you, I'm going to make sure you know that. I'm going to show you . . . every day . . . how much you matter. I'm going to do . . . everything . . . better."

Abby's brows furrowed briefly. Then she swiped at her tear-covered face and gave Mike the biggest smile he'd ever gotten from her.

Mike felt like his heart was blowing up like a massive hot air balloon. But what was filling him up wasn't hot air; it was love. He gave Abby a smile to match her own.

"I love you, too," Abby said. Then she glanced at Chica.

"We should probably go now," Abby added.

Mike looked at Chica, too. He gave Abby's shoulders a squeeze. "Right." He straightened.

Mike tucked away the taser gun. He'd used both of its cartridges. It wouldn't be a lot of help now. He pulled out the cattle prod and looked down at Abby.

"We have to assume the others are also . . . out of whack," he said.

Abby nodded.

Mike linked his free hand in hers. "Okay," he said. "Let's get out of here."

Mike aimed them out of the room. They started trotting back down the hallway.

For the first twenty feet of their flight, Mike thought they had a good chance of getting away. But then, he heard a wasp-like buzz pursuing them down the hall. Tensing, Mike quickly looked over his shoulder.

What the hell?

A small hot-pink ball was flying toward them, coming with the speed of an arrow shot from a high-powered compound bow. Mike saw a flash of white in the pink. He realized what he was seeing. *Chica's cupcake.*

And then the pink ball was attached to his injured calf. Mike bellowed in pain, and his leg went out from under him.

The momentum of his fall disconnected Mike from Abby. He hit the floor . . . a solid impact. His landing knocked the cattle prod from his grasp. It skittered across the linoleum.

"Mike!" Abby started to crouch over Mike.

"Run!" Mike shouted.

Abby looked down the hall. Her eyes were fraught with terror. She didn't move.

"Go!" Mike urged, whipping his leg back and forth to try and disconnect the cupcake. "Hide!"

Abby finally ran. Mike, now trying to whack at the cupcake with his fist, watched Abby dash across the dining room. *Go!* he thought when she made a beeline toward the arcade.

* * *

Abby, her chest heaving, raced past the small stage, heading toward the first row of game machines at the front edge of the arcade. She could hide behind the games, she thought.

But Abby was worried about her brother. Slowing her pace just a little, Abby started to turn to look back toward Mike.

That's when she felt it—the strong sense that someone was watching her. Abby whipped her head toward the small stage.

At first, Abby saw nothing. Then she noticed a hint of movement. She quickly looked toward it. And she saw the ghostlike form of a little blue-eyed boy coming out from behind the small stage's curtains.

As fast as the boy appeared, he was gone. But Abby spotted

something else. Two pinpricks of red light spit into view from the back of the stage. Abby's gaze was caught by more movement. The silver tip of Foxy's hook came into view.

Abby ran harder than she ever had in her life. She shot down the first row of game machines and disappeared—she hoped—into the back of the arcade.

CHAPTER 23

Although Mike could feel chomping teeth against the bandages on his leg, he was pretty sure that the cupcake was getting mostly a mouthful of gauze and padding. It hadn't yet managed to sink its teeth into the meat of his leg.

Mike flung his leg against the floor, using the hard surface to scrape the cupcake off him. The cupcake tumbled back. Mike immediately scrabbled toward the cattle prod.

When Mike was still a couple feet from the weapon, he stretched out his fingers. He was almost—

Mike screamed as a jagged jolt of pain shot up his leg. He looked back.

The cupcake had reattached, and this time it got a better grip. It had a healthy mouthful of Mike's calf, and it was starting to gnaw its way up Mike's leg like it was an ear of corn.

Mike flipped over and started using his right leg to kick the cupcake on his left leg. The cupcake hung on as Mike stomped at it. Once. Twice. Three times.

Finally, his heel managed to land square in the center of the cupcake's googly-eyed face. The blow wrenched the cupcake free of Mike's leg. Unfortunately, it took a good-sized chunk of Mike's calf with it when it tumbled away.

Mike was hit with a wave of nausea, but he ignored it. He also ignored the rush of liquid warmth pouring down his leg. He had to get the cattle prod.

Mike surged toward the prod, and he grabbed it. He fumbled to find the power switch.

A clatter followed by a waspy buzz let Mike know that the cupcake was once again in motion. The buzzing sound grew louder, and Mike knew the thing had launched itself toward the back of his head.

Mike spun from his stomach to his back. He brought up the cattle prod.

His timing was impeccable. When he pointed the cattle prod to the space above his head, the prod skewered the cupcake right through its bucktoothed mouth. A spark show similar to the one Mike had seen on the stage—but on a smaller scale—blew up right in front of his face. The sparks came from the cupcake's round white eyes.

Mike flicked the cattle prod, sending the cupcake flying. It hit the floor, rolled . . . and was still.

That was when Mike's mind provided him with a sick vision of what would have happened if he hadn't turned over. The cupcake would have landed on the back of Mike's head. It would have chewed through him, the same way it had gone through the skull of the man Mike had found in the Parts and Service room.

Mike shook off the unwelcome inner movie. He concentrated on getting to his feet.

*   *   *

Abby risked a peek around the bright red–and–gold side of a big arcade machine—Abby didn't know what game it was. She immediately shrank back into her hiding spot.

Foxy was standing at the front of the arcade, next to the smashed prize cabinet Abby had darted past less than a minute before. The animatronic, who used to be Abby's friend, was turning his head from side to side. His eyes, which were really, really bright, looked mad. He was trying to find Abby, and not for anything good.

Or maybe Abby was wrong. Maybe Foxy was still her friend. Maybe he wasn't mad at her. Maybe he was worried for her. She decided to take another itsy-bitsy look.

Abby braced herself against the side of the big game cabinet. She started to lean forward, and her hand slid.

Tinny music busted out. The machine's lights fired up. *Pings* and *dings* and *beeps* blipped over Abby.

Foxy's head whipped around. He shot his gaze toward the look-at-me machine.

Abby flattened herself against the cold metal side of the machine while it continued to scream, *"She's over here!"*

Abby's finger must have grazed a power button. *Dumb*, she thought. She should've been more careful. She shouldn't have tried to look again.

She squeezed her eyes shut as she heard the *stomp, stomp, stomp* of Foxy's approaching footsteps. Then she chastised herself for being such a stupid baby. She shot away from the noisy machine and hurtled toward the ball pit. Once there, she quickly and quietly lowered herself into the sea of many-colored plastic balls.

Right before she pulled her head under the surface, Abby snuck a look back toward where she'd been hiding. Foxy had reached the still-shrilling cabinet. He looked down at it and then looked around it.

Abby kept very still beneath the plastic balls. She held her breath as if she were underwater.

* * *

Mike, limping heavily, reached the center of the dining room. He checked the stage. Freddy and Bonnie were still prone on the stage floor.

Mike looked toward the small stage. It was empty. Where was Foxy?

"Abby?" Mike called softly.

He'd seen her go toward the arcade. He headed that way.

Mike was still several feet from the arcade when he heard a voice calling his name. A child's voice.

Mike turned. And he felt the blood drain from his face.

Standing in the archway that led to the lobby and main corridor was a little boy. A little boy with tousled black hair and bow-like lips.

"Garret," Mike whispered.

* * *

Abby had to start breathing again. She opened her mouth and took a gasp of air. And another. And another. Silent little breaths. The air didn't smell good at all. It smelled dirty and spoiled, like food that was too old. But Abby did her best to ignore the yucky stink. She held herself super-duper still.

From the clomping footsteps, Abby could tell Foxy was getting close. If they'd been playing the warmer-colder game, Foxy was getting warmer. A lot warmer.

More clomps. Foxy was hot, hot, hot.

Abby was sure that if Foxy looked down, he'd be staring right at where she lay, hidden by the pool of brightly colored balls. She didn't move even the teeniest, tiniest muscle.

*　　*　　*

Mike walked toward his little brother. Garret didn't move.

All Garret did was stand in the shrouded archway. He stared blankly at Mike.

"Garret?" Mike said again, louder this time.

"He's here, Mike," Garret said.

The boy took a step backward. Then a second step.

"Wait!" Mike called.

Mike hurried forward as fast as his leg would let him. He crossed the few feet between himself and Garret in little more than a couple seconds. But when Mike was almost to the archway, Garret melted away.

It was as if Garret became part of the gloaming under the archway. He was there and then he was . . .

. . . something else.

In Garret's place, someone in a rabbit costume appeared. Not just someone. A man. Mike could tell this from the rabbit's height and its stride . . . and its grandstanding swank.

The rabbit strode toward Mike. Mike put on the brakes and began backing up. He wanted to turn and run, but he couldn't take his eyes off the repellant rabbit.

The animatronics were ragged and dirty, but they looked pristine compared to this atrocious costume. This rabbit suit looked like it had gone through an apocalypse. Tattered ears drooped over cloudy eyes that were surrounded by smudges of black. The rabbit's yellow fur was mottled with stains, some of which looked disturbingly like blood. Its fur was torn away in jagged strips, revealing blackened splotches beneath.

But the worst part about the rabbit was that it was striding toward Mike with a filthy-toothed smile spreading between broken whiskers that appeared to be pointing toward Mike with very ill intent.

Mike immediately went for the second taser gun on Vanessa's utility belt. He aimed. He fired.

The charged metal prongs hit their mark. They landed right in the middle of the rabbit's chest.

But the rabbit was unfazed. It kept coming.

Mike attempted another shot, but he wasn't fast enough. The rabbit quickly closed the distance between them.

Without breaking stride, the yellow rabbit ripped the taser probes from his chest. He reached Mike and swatted the taser from Mike's hand.

The taser hit the floor with a *crunch* and a *clickety-clack*. From the corner of his eye, Mike saw it spin away.

Before Mike could regroup, the yellow rabbit gave him a driving shove. The rabbit's strength was almost superhuman.

Mike went flying backward. His body hit part of the fort that he and Abby had built with Vanessa and the animatronics, which felt like it had happened in another lifetime. When Mike landed, he was sure he heard a crack of bone. Or maybe it was just a ligament giving way. Whatever it was, it hurt.

And that was just the start. As Mike crashed toward the floor, the fort above him came tumbling down. A torrent of tables dropped toward Mike like big, four-legged dominos knocking into one another.

At the same time, as if by the sheer force of the rabbit's evilness, the room was plunged into near-darkness. And a fantastical laser-light show began.

*　*　*

Abby looked up through the semitransparent layer of colored balls. Long thick strips of light, like neon crayons, were cutting through the air over the pit.

Abby thought the lights were pretty, and she wished she could see them better. But she didn't move.

It was a good thing she didn't. Because there was something else up there, too. Abby could see the boxy shape of Foxy's head coming down toward her.

*　*　*

Groaning, Mike extricated himself from under the pile of tables. He could feel the continual warm gush of blood flowing down his leg. His calf had been bleeding since the cupcake had taken a bite of him, and he hadn't had time to do anything about it. Now the tables' impact had sped up the bleeding. Mike could feel a river of blood coursing down his leg and saturating his sock.

The liquid heat wasn't confined to Mike's leg, either. From the sticky wet sensations on his chest and back, he knew his other wounds had reopened, too.

Mike needed to move, but he couldn't seem to get himself in gear. All he could do was belly-squirm across the floor.

Stopping to catch his breath, Mike looked for the yellow rabbit. He had to squint to see. The constantly moving laser lights distorted everything in the room. Mike had to squint to try to separate phantom shapes from real ones.

Thankfully, he didn't see the rabbit. Not thankfully, though, Mike did see movement on the stage. Or he thought he did. He turned his head and inched forward to get a better look.

No! Mike thought when he saw that Freddy and Bonnie were back on their feet.

Mike tried to get to his own feet, but he couldn't. His blood loss was worse than he'd thought . . . because the floor felt like the deck of a ship at sea. Mike tried again to push off the floor. He began to raise his upper body, and then he . . .

. . . stopped.

He'd found the yellow rabbit. It was coming his way.

Because of the disorienting laser lights, the rabbit looked like it was winking in and out of existence as it approached. It was hard to focus on. That, however, didn't prevent Mike from noticing that the rabbit was pulling out—from where?—a huge butcher's knife.

Mike looked behind him. Freddy and Bonnie were still advancing toward the front of the stage. At the snaillike pace Mike was moving, it wouldn't take the animatronics long to reach him.

Mike turned front again. The rabbit was closer.

Mike looked left and right. A wall on one side. The tables on the other. He was cornered.

*　*　*

Abby was barely breathing . . . which was a good thing. Not only did it keep her quiet but it kept her from having to inhale the scuzzy scent of the old, dusty plastic balls. The cruddy, powdery surface of the balls made her—

Uh-oh.

Abby crinkled her nose and attempted to hold in the sneeze that tickled her nostrils. But she couldn't.

Because she was trying to muffle it, Abby's sneeze came out as a hiss. But it still came out. And it was still loud enough for . . .

Strong hands clamped onto Abby's shoulder. She felt herself being hoisted upward.

Abby immediately started kicking and screaming. She tried to twist herself free.

But Abby was held tight. She came up out of the ball pit, and she let out another sneeze. She turned to face—

"Vanessa?"

Abby stopped fighting, and Vanessa pulled Abby the rest of the way out of the pit. She helped Abby get her footing on the floor.

Abby brushed herself off as she gaped at Vanessa—and at Foxy. Vanessa was holding the cattle prod that Abby had last seen in Mike's hand. And Foxy was on his back, jerking around like he was having a fit.

Abby threw her arms around Vanessa's waist. Vanessa used her free hand to return the hug.

Abby pulled back. "I don't know what's happening to our friends," she said. "I don't know why they're trying to hurt us."

Vanessa knelt down in front of Abby. Vanessa's hair was loose, and it was tangled around her face. She looked wild. But when she spoke, her voice was calm. "Abby, sweetheart. They're not themselves right now."

Abby nodded. She felt like she was going to cry, but she didn't.

Vanessa took one of Abby's hands. "Listen, Abby. There's someone here who wants to hurt us very badly. I need to get you somewhere safe. And then I need to go help your brother."

"I can help, too."

Vanessa started to shake her head, but then her gaze went to Abby's chest. Abby frowned, looking down to see what Vanessa was looking at. She didn't see anything icky on her overalls. So, what was the problem?

Abby lifted her gaze to Vanessa's face. Vanessa's eyes were wide, and she had that look that people got when they had an idea.

"What?" Abby asked.

"The drawings," Vanessa said. Her voice was a half-whisper, like she was amazed by something. She looked into Abby's eyes. "It's the drawings!"

Vanessa tucked the cattle prod under her arm and grabbed Abby's shoulders. "You're right, Abby," she said. "You can help!"

Abby made a face. *Huh?*

Vanessa started talking really fast. "Your friends, they don't remember. He hurt them badly. He took their families, their love, their lives. But they don't remember."

"I don't understand."

Vanessa let go of Abby's shoulders. She reached out and pulled Abby's drawing pad from her overalls' chest pocket. "You know what happened to them," Vanessa said. "But they don't remember." Vanessa pulled out Abby's pencils and used them to tap on the pad. "So, tell them."

Abby looked from her pad and pencils to Vanessa's face. *What . . . ?*

Abby suddenly jumped back to a memory, a really recent one. She remembered seeing the spot-lit drawing, the one of the yellow rabbit and the five kids. As her mind showed her the drawing again, she saw each of the kids in close-up. She saw the big smiles drawn on their faces.

The memory fell away, and Abby looked at Vanessa. "The picture."

Vanessa nodded, smiling.

Abby reached out for her pad and pencils. "You're right! I have to help them to remember."

* * *

The yellow rabbit bore down on Mike, waving the butcher's knife in the air like it was a baton and the rabbit was a depraved orchestral conductor. Mike couldn't stand and run. He couldn't drag himself away at the speed of light. He couldn't sink into the floor or turn invisible. All he could do was look up at the rabbit and say, "Go to he—"

The rabbit kicked Mike in the face.

Mike's head recoiled, and the back of his skull hit the floor. The mother of all headaches kicked in instantaneously. Hot, thick, coppery liquid filled Mike's mouth. It started to run down his throat. He gagged and spit it out.

Mike tried to get his eyes to focus, but they didn't want to cooperate. They were somewhere out in a la-la land of meadows filled with butterflies.

That was okay. Mike wasn't going to cower like a wimp.

Summoning what strength he still had, Mike turned his head

to face the rabbit again. "I said," Mike said as clearly as he could, "Go . . . to . . ."

The rabbit kicked Mike again.

This time, Mike's resolve to be hard failed him. His head bounced off the floor again, and the meadows and butterflies turned into a confusion of laser lights and crooked teeth and evil eyes in an inky, churning vision of hell. Mike saw this mind-choking landscape through a vapor of gray. Even so, he was able to see the knife . . . raised above his chest.

As he fought to stay conscious—and began to lose the battle—Mike heard . . .

"That's enough!"

Was that Vanessa's voice? It didn't matter. Mike agreed. He'd had enough. He stopped fighting. He closed his eyes and let his consciousness take a break.

* * *

Tucked behind a battered pinball machine that was missing its glass, Abby sat cross-legged on the floor. She was hidden, but she could still see the dining room. She was bent over her drawing pad, her pencil scribbling as fast as she could make it move.

When Vanessa shouted, though, Abby looked up.

Abby had to press her lips together to stop a cry from coming out. Her brother was lying totally still on the floor. Blood was all around him.

A yellow rabbit, holding a knife, stood above Mike. Vanessa was maybe twenty feet behind the rabbit. And she held a gun, in both hands, the way Abby had seen on TV. On TV, though, cops' hands didn't shake the way Vanessa's hands were shaking.

The rabbit's knife stopped in midair, but the rabbit didn't turn around. Vanessa's hands shook even harder.

Abby wanted to watch what was happening over by her brother, but the only way she could help Mike was to keep drawing. So, she looked back down at her pad.

As she did, she thought she saw movement to her left. Abby glanced that way. Nothing.

Where was Foxy? Was he still down?

It didn't matter. Abby had to finish her drawing.

From the dining room came the sound of a low growl. From the rabbit, Abby thought. She caught her lower lip between her teeth and put her pencil to the page again.

"Drop the knife," Vanessa said.

Abby started splitting her attention between the drawing and what was going on with Vanessa and the rabbit. That wasn't a hard thing to do. Abby was used to watching TV while she drew. She knew Mike thought she didn't watch the TV, but she did.

Abby drew. And Abby watched as the rabbit, back still to Vanessa, began to remove the rabbit-costume head.

Vanessa's shaking got worse.

Abby could see now that the person inside the rabbit suit was a man with graying dark hair.

"A little old for temper tantrums . . ." the man said.

Then he turned. ". . . aren't we, Vanessa?" he said.

Abby's pencil faltered. She didn't like the look of the man at all. He had a thin face and a high forehead. He also had very narrow eyes. He looked . . . slimy.

"I'm not kidding, Dad," Vanessa said. "Drop it."

Dad? Abby thought. *Poor Vanessa.*

"It's over," Vanessa said.

"I don't think so, sweets," the man said. "You may have forgotten your loyalties, but I assure you, *they* have not." The man gestured toward Freddy and Bonnie, who were at the front edge of the stage. They were standing at attention.

"Go on" the man said to the animatronics. He pointed at Mike. "Rip him into little-bitty pieces."

Freddy and Bonnie started across the stage, heading to its short flight of stairs. They weren't walking quite right, but they were walking well enough to get to Mike much faster than Abby wanted them to.

The man in the rabbit suit looked at Vanessa. "Now, why don't you put that silly thing away and help Daddy clean up the mess you made." He took a step toward Vanessa. "We both know you won't actually use—"

The sound of the shot made Abby's pencil scoot across the page in a jagged line. The point of the pencil gouged the paper. Abby ignored both the line and the hole in the paper as she kept drawing. At the same time, she saw the man kind of jump backward. He looked down at his shoulder. Abby could see that Vanessa's bullet had put a hole in the rabbit suit . . . and the man.

The man didn't seem to be bothered by the bullet. But he was angry. Abby could tell.

The man snarled at Vanessa and put his rabbit head back on. Then he charged toward her.

Abby wasn't as startled by the next three times the gun fired. She knew she didn't have much time yet, so she forced herself to keep drawing, even as she watched Vanessa's shots go past the rabbit.

Vanessa was shaking too much to aim right, Abby thought. And that was why the man in the rabbit suit was able to reach Vanessa. He grabbed her by the throat.

"You had one job," the rabbit said. "Keep him in the dark . . . and kill him if he found out too much."

Vanessa spit in her dad's face. "That's two jobs," she said.

You tell him, Abby thought, still drawing.

"*Shut up!*" the yellow rabbit screamed. At the same time, he shoved a big, awful knife into Vanessa's stomach.

Abby felt her own stomach get really tight, and she felt like she was going to throw up. But she didn't. She kept drawing.

The rabbit dug his fingers tighter around Vanessa's throat and lifted her up. Vanessa's feet flopped in the air several inches above the floor.

Abby screwed up her face. Abby was so scared for Vanessa that Abby thought she could feel icky, furry rabbit fingers wrapped around her own neck. But she kept drawing.

Vanessa clawed at her dad's chokehold. She tore at her dad's hand, but he didn't let go. As she fought, Vanessa looked toward Mike.

Abby shot a glance at her brother, too. Her pencil made one last mark on the pad. Freddy and Bonnie had almost reached Mike. Time to go!

Abby got up and ran.

Vanessa was again staring into the evil rabbit's eyes. The rabbit, still choking Vanessa with one hand, was totally focused on her. He didn't see Abby at first. But Vanessa did, and she smiled.

Abby ran toward the wall of pictures. Her drawing flapped like birds' wings in her hand.

"No!" the man in the rabbit suit yelled.

Uh-oh. He'd seen Abby.

Abby flicked a look at the rabbit, but she didn't slow down—not even when the rabbit let go of Vanessa's neck and turned toward her.

"Stop!" Vanessa shouted.

Abby knew Vanessa wasn't talking to her, but Abby's steps faltered when she saw that Vanessa had dropped her hands. Vanessa was gripping the blade of the knife, which was sticking out of her stomach. The rabbit still had one of his hands on the other end of the knife.

The rabbit looked down. Grunting, he tried to tug the knife out of Vanessas' belly. But Vanessa wouldn't let go.

Abby could see that Vanessa was hurting bad. Vanessa's face was really white, and it was all twisted up. But she still managed to say, in a gasp, "I won't let you hurt her, too."

CHAPTER 24

As much as she hated what was happening to Vanessa and wanted to run at the rabbit and beat at him with her fists, Abby knew she couldn't help that way. The only thing she could do was what she was doing: she had to keep going toward the wall. So, she didn't let her pace slow, even as she watched Vanessa struggle with her dad.

Abby finally reached the wall. She quickly looked over her shoulder, just in time to see Vanessa press toward the rabbit. Vanessa wrapped her dad in a big, hard bear hug.

Oh no, Abby thought.

She understood that Vanessa was trying to save Abby, but by hugging the man like that, Vanessa had to have driven the knife much farther into her body.

Abby started to cry just as the yellow rabbit roared. She watched the rabbit beat at Vanessa's back, trying to get free. Vanessa, however, didn't let go.

Abby had to make Vanessa's sacrifice worth it. Turning to the wall of children's drawings, Abby quickly found the drawing of the yellow rabbit with the five kids. She reached for it.

Glancing back, Abby saw that Vanessa was looking directly at Abby. Vanessa's eyes looked weird, like they were lights that were having a hard time staying on. Even so, Vanessa held Abby's gaze.

And the rabbit continued to fight to get free.

Abby got her hand on the drawing of the rabbit and the five kids. She crumpled the paper in her grip, and she whipped her hand away from the wall.

When the drawing let go of the wall, it tore. The sound of the long, crackling *riiippp* was much louder than the normal sound of paper tearing.

As soon as the sound ended, Abby saw Vanessa's arms start to drop away from her dad. "I'm sorry, Daddy," she said. Her voice was so weak that Abby barely heard it.

"Get off me!" the man in the rabbit suit shrieked.

The rabbit flung Vanessa aside, and he turned to look toward Abby. He let out a booming sound that made Abby think of a really angry dog. That rage, Abby knew, was directed at her. And the rabbit was now coming toward her, too.

Slap-thud. Slap-thud. Slap-thud. The sound of the rabbit's footsteps filled the room. He was charging toward Abby.

Abby quickly turned and pressed her new drawing to the wall, in the space where the other drawing had been. But the other drawing had been stuck to the wall by tape, and the tape had come away with the drawing. Abby had no way to attach her drawing to the wall.

Abby looked at the wall, hoping to find a free piece of tape, but all the tape holding other drawings was old. She knew none of it would work.

The rabbit's footsteps were really close. Abby didn't turn to look, but she knew the rabbit was almost—

I know! Abby thought.

Abby kept holding the drawing in place with one palm, and with her other hand, she dug in her overalls' pocket. She pulled out one of her colored pencils and . . .

. . . swinging her arm in a wide arc through the air, Abby rammed the pencil point through the drawing, jamming the pencil into the wall.

Abby hadn't been sure it would work because the wall wasn't soft like a bulletin board, but when she let go of the pencil, the drawing stayed in place. And every light in the dining room went out.

Abby hardly dared to breathe, much less move, but she had to see what was happening. Abby turned away from the wall.

Even though the dining room lights were dark, the fluorescent lights in the lobby were still on. They were weak, so they couldn't toss brightness very far. But what bit reached the wall of pictures, and the rest of the room, was enough for Abby to see that no one was moving.

The yellow rabbit was just a couple feet from Abby, but he was stopped dead. So were Freddy and Bonnie, who were standing over Mike. Vanessa was on the floor, lying very, very still.

Abby wanted to run to Vanessa . . . and Mike. But she stayed where she was.

Freddy and Bonnie turned their heads. They looked toward the yellow rabbit. Then they started moving toward the rabbit, their steps slow and unsteady.

The yellow rabbit's awful eyes locked on Abby. "What have you done?" he growled.

Abby was still scared, but she put her shoulders back and said, "They can see you now."

Abby took a step to the side. Suddenly, one of the stage spotlights came on. It landed right on Abby's new drawing.

Abby looked at her work. Even as panicked as she'd been as she'd drawn, even as worried for her brother and Vanessa, even as grossed out as she was by the yellow rabbit, Abby had done possibly the best drawing she'd ever done in her life. Or it could have just felt that way.

Maybe the colors weren't perfect and maybe some of the things in the drawing were a little shaky-looking, but the message of the drawing was perfectly clear. Abby had drawn the yellow rabbit, holding a bloody knife, standing over the dead bodies of five little kids.

Abby glanced at the yellow rabbit. She couldn't see the man's face behind the costume rabbit head, but she could tell the man didn't like the drawing. The yellow rabbit's grimace looked even meaner than it had before.

The yellow rabbit took a step toward Abby. She shrank back toward the wall.

A whisper of movement. A thud.

Foxy stepped out of the shadows beyond the spotlight. He put himself between Abby and the yellow rabbit.

Abby's heart began to pound hard in her chest. But then Foxy turned toward the rabbit.

"Move," the rabbit said to Foxy.

Foxy didn't budge.

"*I said, move!*" the yellow rabbit shouted.

A loud click answered the rabbit's bellow. A second spotlight burst on. It caught the yellow rabbit in a circle of white light so powerful that Abby couldn't look directly at it. Neither could the yellow rabbit. He threw up a hand to shield his eyes.

The yellow rabbit turned away from the light, and when he did, Freddy, Bonnie, and Chica were there. *Almost by magic*, Abby thought. But not really. They'd been moving in the darkness when Abby and the rabbit had been distracted by the spotlights.

The yellow rabbit was no longer looking at Abby. He was staring at the animatronics. And the animatronics didn't seem to care about Abby either.

Now she could move.

Abby sidestepped along the wall. No one looked at her. That gave her courage.

Keeping her steps as light as possible, Abby hurried over to Mike. She dropped to her knees next to him.

"Mike," Abby whispered. "Mike, wake up!"

The little hairs of Mike's eyelashes rippled against his skin, but he didn't open his eyes. Abby leaned over and put a hand on his shoulder. She shook him really hard. "Mike!" she hissed loudly in his ear.

Mike opened his eyes. He blinked several times, and then he seemed to zero in on Abby's face. "Abby?"

Abby nodded but tensed when she heard a scrape and a *thump*. She turned away from Mike.

It was okay. She and Mike were okay.

The animatronics were closer to the yellow rabbit now. They completely surrounded him, creating a circle that was about two feet from him. And they were pressing in even closer.

"Look at you," the yellow rabbit said. His voice was filled with disgust. He sounded the same way bullies sounded. "Look at what nasty things you've become! Look at how small you are!"

The animatronics stopped moving. Abby bit her lip. They weren't going to listen to the yellow rabbit, were they?

The yellow rabbit took advantage of the animatronics' hesitation. "Wretched, rotten little beasts," he said, his voice even crueler than before. "Look how pathetic you are!" The rabbit looked at each animatronic in turn. "Look how worthless you are!"

The yellow rabbit locked in on Chica, who stood before him with her cupcake platter raised. Her cupcake was back in place on the platter, poised but still.

The yellow rabbit took a step toward Chica. He pointed at Chica and then pointed toward Mike and Abby. "Now get over there," he commanded, "And rip them apart . . . before I rip all of *you* apart."

Abby held her breath. *What would the animatronics do?*

Abby got her answer in an instant.

The cupcake sprang off its platter. It flew directly at the yellow rabbit's chest, and it sank its big white teeth into the holey fake fur that stretched over the rabbit's heart.

The yellow rabbit screamed. He batted at the cupcake, but it hung on. He started twisting around and jumping this way and that, as if he was on fire. He was jerking around so violently that his costume head came off.

Abby watched as the yellow rabbit head shot through the air. The head hit the wall of drawings and then bounced to the floor. It rolled over and over twice. Then it lay still. The rabbit ears drooped downward. The toothy mouth gaped open.

Abby returned her attention to the man in the rest of the rabbit suit. He had collapsed to the floor. Kneeling, he grabbed the cupcake in both hands. He worked the cupcake back and forth and back and forth. Finally, he ripped the cupcake away from his chest.

When the cupcake was plucked loose, it didn't open its mouth. It hung on. So, a big, wide section of sickly yellow rabbit fur went with it. The gap in the rabbit suit made it possible to see the inner workings of the costume.

Abby made a face and hugged herself when she saw what was under the fake fur. She'd seen something like it before. It made her insides get all knotted up.

The yellow rabbit costume had the same thing in it that the little redheaded girl animatronic had, the one Chica had tried to put Abby into. The suit was lined with row after row of super-sharp metal things. Now that Abby could see them more clearly than she had when she was fighting Chica, she decided the metal things looked like a bunch of crab claws. The claws were closed up tight, curled inward toward the sides of the suit. *But if the claws opened . . .*

As Abby stared at the metal things, she heard a snap, like a lock shooting back. One of the crab claws opened. Then another. And another.

Abby saw blood starting to run into the metal. Then the blood stained the edges of the surrounding rabbit fur.

Abby looked at the face of the man in the suit. His teeth were gritted. His eyes were wide.

Abby thought of Vanessa, who was still sprawled on the floor. Vanessa might even be dead.

The horrible man in the suit *deserved* what was happening to him. Abby stopped feeling sorry. She even liked it when she heard another snap and knew that the man was being hurt even worse.

* * *

It felt like a hundred mini-drills were attempting to burrow into Mike's head and into the rest of his body, too. He couldn't see quite right, and his body felt as floppy and useless as a fish snatched out of water.

Mike was starting to get his bearings, though. He knew where he was—in Freddy's dining room. He knew Abby was with him and she was, as far as he could tell, okay. He also knew that the man who had tried to kill him was getting his comeuppance.

Mike recognized the snapping sounds he was hearing. He knew what was happing to the man. He was being skewered from inside his costume. *Good.*

"What are those things in the suit?" Abby asked. "They're like the ones in the girl suit that Chica tried to put me in."

Mike felt like a donkey was kicking him in the chest. The idea of Abby . . .

"They're springlocks," Mike said.

The man in the rabbit suit . . . it was him—Steve Raglan, the career counselor who had hired Mike, and whose voice had been echoing in Mike's skull for so long . . . Mike didn't know it, but Raglan wasn't his real name. His real name was Afton, William Afton, and fate had somehow brought them together once again. Afton looked over at Mike and Abby. Even though the guy was clearly incapacitated, Mike reached for Abby, wanting to protect her.

Mike didn't have to worry, though. Afton was just putting on a show of defiance.

Afton's face was misshapen by pain, and his body was being jolted savagely by what was happening inside the rabbit suit. Still, through the continuing chain reaction of springlocks, Afton was able to scoot over the floor. He dragged himself forward until he reached for the costume's head.

More snaps.

Afton put the yellow rabbit head back on. His motion unsteady and weak, the yellow rabbit managed to right himself. He faced the animatronics, who stood shoulder-to-shoulder, watching the rabbit.

"I killed you once," Afton said, his voice strained but strong inside the rabbit head. "I can do it again."

The yellow rabbit took a step toward the animatronics.

Mike heard a series of sharp sounds like a chattering of metal teeth. *Clack! Clack! Clack!*

The remaining springlocks were disengaging. And even Afton, seemingly impervious to destruction, couldn't withstand that.

The yellow rabbit's body contorted, hunching inward. Afton howled like a tortured animal. His yowls winged through the building like a flurry of bats wheeling through a subterranean chamber.

As if channeling the rabbit's torment, the pizzeria began to agitate. The building felt like it was whipping back and forth on its footings.

At the same time, the spotlights began to switch on and off. The laser lights started up. They went out. They started up again. A muddled patchwork of rock song snippets intertwined with bursts of static coming from the intercom speakers. Sensation overload. Chaos.

The building was now rattling at its very core. The remains of Abby's fort were stuttering across the dining room floor. Overhead lights were swinging and . . .

. . . one bank of fluorescent lights came crashing down.

The lights' metal frame landed just a couple feet from Abby. Way too close for comfort.

Mike forced his body into gear. They had to move.

"Come on!" Mike shouted.

Rejecting his body's weakness, Mike levered himself up from the ground. He had to lean a little on Abby to get himself in motion, but once he took a step, he got some momentum going. He started forward, aiming toward the lobby in a limping run, keeping a tight grip on Abby's hand.

But Abby resisted his attempt to urge her forward. "Wait!" she cried. "We have to get Vanessa!"

"Vanessa? She's here?" Mike frowned and looked around. *Why was Vanessa here? She'd been adamant that—*

"She saved me!" Abby shouted. Now she was tugging on Mike. "Come on."

Mike let Abby lead him, not toward the lobby, but farther into the middle of the dining room. As soon as they'd taken a couple steps, Mike spotted Vanessa. His feet faltered, and his breathing hitched. Vanessa was prone on the floor, not moving. A pool of blood that was far too large to make Mike optimistic about her survival, extended in all directions around her. *She might already be gone*, Mike thought.

Hindered now by not just his injuries but a choking grief, Mike was barely able to make it the rest of the way to where Vanessa lay. But he got there. When he did, he painstakingly lowered himself to one knee, which he planted in the thick, sticky red spill that surrounded Vanessa.

As Mike put two fingers against Vanessa's neck—and to his relief, felt a faint pulse—he saw movement on the other side of the room. Even over the continued mishmash of music and static, he heard the *clod-clod-clod* of animatronic footsteps. His muscles tensed, and he lifted his gaze.

Mike had been sure the animatronics were coming for him and Abby. But they weren't. They clearly could not have cared less about Mike and his sister. They were otherwise occupied.

Mike watched as Foxy used his hook to drag the yellow rabbit along behind him. The other three animatronics followed Foxy and the rabbit into the back hallway.

"Mike!" Abby said. She shook his arm. "I don't think she's doing good."

Mike whipped his gaze back to Vanessa. Abby was right. Vanessa was alive, but barely.

"Come on," he said. "Help me."

Neither Mike nor Abby should have been strong enough to lift an unconscious woman. But they did it anyway. They managed to brace her between them as they both got back to their feet. Then each of them hooked one of Vanessa's limp arms around their necks. Holding tight to Vanessa's arms, they managed to start dragging her across the dining room.

Mike glanced toward the back hallway as they went, but he saw nothing but a pipeline of black. The animatronics and the yellow rabbit were no longer within view.

The discordant chords and snatches of lyrics that still spilled from the speakers were louder now. The lights were playing now-you-see-me-now-you-don't even faster than before.

The floor began to move under Mike's and Abby's feet. It felt like the building was beginning to sway.

Mike heard a tinny *zing* above his head, and he looked up. He saw the brackets holding two sets of spotlights to the ceiling rend loose. The spotlights came crashing down; they landed just a foot to Mike's right.

Without a word, Mike and Abby picked up the pace. They were both grunting with effort, both panting. Mike's face was hot, and he kept having to blink sweat from his eyes.

On the heels of the falling spotlights, whole banks of fluorescent lights began exploding. A glass monsoon poured over the room.

"Look down, Abby!" Mike yelled. He followed his own advice,

which kept glass from getting in his eyes. But he felt barb–sized shards poking at his scalp as the glass showered onto his head.

Just a few more steps, Mike told himself. He strained to keep hold of Vanessa's arm. Her skin was slick with blood. So were his hands.

Mike glanced at Abby, worried that she wouldn't have the strength to keep going. But Abby was a trooper. Her lips were set, and she was frowning ferociously.

One step. Two steps. Three steps.

They made it to the lobby just as a guttural, hellish moan curled up from what felt like the most hidden recesses of the building. The sound reached for them like a killer's hands.

Mike shot a look back over his shoulder. He nearly let go of Vanessa when he saw a wraithlike bulkhead of smoke closing in on the lobby.

The smoke was coming fast. Too fast. *It's going to overtake us*, Mike thought. It would—

Cha-chunk! Mike pulled his gaze from the smoke-monster and saw that Abby had released the front door handle. She was leaning into the door, pushing it outward.

Mike tried to move forward, and he tripped. His head hit the door, and he saw . . .

. . . black.

CHAPTER 25

Mike had never heard birds sing so loudly.

Shielding his eyes against a sun that was playing hide-and-seek in a cloud-filled sky, Mike looked up at the trees that encircled the clean white lines of the Child Development Center. The massive oaks and pines appeared as if they were standing guard over the building and its precious occupants. The birds Mike could hear were hopping from branch to branch in the trees.

Mike realized he'd never really paid a lot of attention to birds in his real life. He'd heard the ones in his dreams every night. But had he ever listened to their songs during the day? Not really. Well, he was going to start now.

I'm going to start doing a lot of things, he decided. But right now, he needed to pick up his sister.

It took Mike a few minutes to get into the building and make it down the long hall to the Activity Center. He was still limping. Mostly, the limp was caused by the healing gouge in his calf, but he had a couple hairline cracks in his bones, too—in his tibia and fibula. Not big enough for casts, his doctor had told him. They'd heal on their own.

The rest of Mike's injuries were healing, too. He'd needed a lot of stitches, and for a couple weeks, he'd looked like he'd had himself inked with splotches of black and blue and purple. But three weeks out, the bruises had mostly faded. His stitches were gone. He was on the mend.

The sound of laughter hurried Mike along. He looked ahead and saw Dr. Lillian standing in front of the Activity Center window. They exchanged a wave, and Mike was at her side a few seconds later.

Mike grinned at Dr. Lillian and looked through the window. Inside the colorful play space, a group of six kids were in the midst of a rowdy game of tag, and—to Mike's total joy—Abby was one of the kids. His sister, wearing her favorite red overalls, was bobbing and weaving to avoid getting caught. She had some mad moves. Running from animatronics and a serial killer rabbit had honed her escape skills. And thankfully, it didn't seem to have dampened her spirit at all. Just the opposite. Right now, as she did an impressive drop-and-roll that got her out of range of a little boy with a flattop buzz cut, Abby grinned bigger and wider than he'd ever seen.

Abby shot to her feet and leaped away from a little redheaded girl. She spotted her brother and gave him a brief wave. Then she was off again, sprinting to the far side of the room.

"It's really extraordinary," Dr. Lillian said, "the turn she's taken these past few weeks. She seems almost—"

"Happy?" Mike turned to look at Dr. Lillian.

The doctor tucked a lock of white hair behind her ear as she nodded. Then she glanced down at the leg he favored. "One of these days," she said, "you'll have to tell me what happened." She pointed at the leg. "And how you got that limp."

Mike smiled, but he didn't agree to spill the beans.

Mike and the doctor watched Abby in silence for a few seconds. Then Dr. Lillian asked casually, "And still no word from Jane?"

Mike shook his head. He'd been ready for this question, and he answered it just as casually as Dr. Lillian had asked it. "You know," he said, "I think my aunt has finally decided to move on."

I mean . . . she kind of did, Mike thought.

*   *   *

Mike flipped on his car's turn signal. The creaky *click-click* led into the sound of his squeaking brakes as he maneuvered the old jalopy around a corner.

A belch of exhaust wafted in through Mike's open window. He gave the dashboard in front of his steering wheel a pat. The car's idiosyncrasies had started to amuse him more than annoy him.

Mike looked over at Abby, who had her feet pressed against the glovebox. Her sketch pad was propped on her knees. She was drawing something Mike couldn't see.

"It's really not that hard," Mike said.

Abby said nothing.

"I asked you a very simple question," Mike pushed, "to which there's a very simple answer. Pizza or spaghetti?"

Abby held up her drawing pad. Mike flicked a look at it. She'd drawn a platter of pizza and spaghetti. "I told you. I want both," she said.

"Hmm," Mike said. "I guess we're at an impasse."

Abby gave Mike a pretend glare. Then she half-grinned and applied a colored pencil to her drawing. She made a sweeping motion with the pencil, and she raised the pad for him to see.

Mike glanced over at the pad. Abby had circled the spaghetti. Mike returned his attention to the road. "Done," he said.

Abby smiled. She flipped the page on her drawing pad.

"Mind if we make a stop first?" Mike asked.

"Nope," Abby said, concentrating on her new drawing.

*   *   *

Mike lowered himself into the high-backed, tan vinyl chair that was pulled up next to a safety-railed hospital bed. He breathed shallowly because he hated the soup of odors in the ICU—bleach and medicines and rubber and urine and hospital food. Why did all hospital food smell like overcooked green beans?

The ICU beds were all occupied, so the U-shaped cluster of glass-fronted enclosures was filled with sounds. Mike could hear the rhythmic pumping of ventilators, the beep of monitors, the scrape of equipment being moved, the *snuff-snuff* of soft-soled nursing shoes, and a continual murmur of voices, some soft and some loud.

Vanessa's critical-care cubicle was on the outside wall of the area. So, the sun—still cavorting with puffy white clouds—put a soft hand of warmth against Vanessa's cheek.

If only Vanessa could feel it. Or maybe she could. One of the nurses had told Mike that even when patients were in comas, they were sometimes aware of what was going on around them. *"You can talk to her,"* the ponytailed nurse had told Mike.

He leaned forward and looked at Vanessa's pale eyelids. Other than the top of her cheeks, this was all that he could see of Vanessa's face. The rest was obscured by the ventilator that was keeping her alive while her body recovered from its massive blood loss. Surgeons had repaired her wounds, but her own system had to do the rest.

"So, the big news is," Mike said, "I finally got a new job. Not as exciting as the last one, but I'm thinking that's probably a good thing." Mike chuckled briefly, but the sound of his amusement didn't fit with the other noises of the ICU.

Mike went silent. He was lying about the job. In truth, he was very excited about his apprentice-level position with a construction firm that was building a big complex at the edge of town. The foreman, who'd said he had a past of his own, didn't have a problem with taking a chance on Mike. He even told Mike that he could use company tools and scrap wood to work on his own projects off-hours. Mike thought he might make himself some bedroom furniture.

Maybe Mike would tell Vanessa about his new job another day. For now, he said, "Look, I know we have a lot to talk about. There are some big things I still need you to explain. But I've made peace with a lot of what happened, and I know that . . . certain decisions . . . you made, well, you weren't in control of them. And I know that when it mattered the most, you were there for me and Abby."

Mike thought about Abby's description of all that had happened to Vanessa when he'd been out of it. He immediately shut his mind down. He didn't need to linger on that ugliness.

"I don't think either one of us would be here today without you," Mike told Vanessa.

Mike reached out and took the limp, soft hand that lay on top of a thin, white hospital blanket. At that simple touch, a current of emotion rushed through him. So many feelings. Which was the most dominant? Sadness? Anger? Regret? Caring? Maybe something even more than that?

Mike couldn't dissect his own psyche. He was not used to nuances like these. He'd been running on such limited settings—grief and regret—for so many years that these new sensations were going to take some getting used to.

Mike squeezed Vanessa's hand. "Heal up, Vanessa." His voice cracked on her name. He cleared his throat. "Get strong. And then we'll talk."

Mike got up and left the room without glancing back. He tucked all his emotions away for a later time as he navigated the beige-walled hospital corridors to get back to the cheerier, yellow-walled lobby. There, he found Abby right where he'd left her, in a plush blue chair within eyeshot of the young, brunette receptionist who had agreed to keep one eye on Mike's sister while he was gone.

Abby was, predictably, drawing when Mike walked up to her. Mike gave the receptionist a wave of thanks as he looked down at Abby.

Abby tucked away her drawing pad and stood. "Did you tell her I said hi?" she asked.

"Yeah." Mike gave Abby a quick hug. "Let's go home."

* * *

Mike looked out the living room window as he took a seat next to Abby at the kitchen table. The sun, possibly tired from its day of games with the clouds, seemed to be going down faster than usual. It had put on its dusk pj's, and it now looked like an orange ball. The bottom of the ball had already dipped behind the hills.

Mike looked down at his plate. Another ball, a meatball, was sliding off the top of a mound of spaghetti. It rolled to the edge of the plate and stopped.

Mike looked at Abby. She was toying with her fork, turning the handle around and around on her folded napkin. Her gaze was focused on the disappearing sun.

"Everything okay?" Mike asked.

"I was just thinking about my friends."

"You mean Freddy and Chica and the others?"

She nodded. "They're all alone. And no one takes care of them anymore." Abby pulled her gaze from the setting sun and looked at Mike. "Can we visit them sometime?"

No way in hell, Mike thought.

His thought must have been clear on his face, because Abby looked down at her food. She sighed.

Mike thought about the promise he'd made to her at Freddy's. He was going to do better. He meant it.

So, if it meant that much to Abby . . .

Mike touched Abby's arm. When she looked up, he made sure his expression was neutral. "You never know what can happen," he said.

Abby smiled. She stopped twirling the fork.

Mike noticed that the glass next to her napkin was empty. "I forgot the milk," he said, jumping up.

Mike stepped to the fridge. He opened its door and grabbed a carton of milk. As he closed the door, his gaze landed on Abby's latest drawing, secured near the door handle by a smiley-face magnet.

The drawing was of Abby, Mike, Vanessa, and the four animatronics. They were all inside the table-fort at Freddy's.

Feeling his lips tip upward in the smallest of smiles, Mike turned away from the drawing. He returned to the table and poured Abby's milk.

The milk sloshing into the glass made a *glug*, *glug* sound that acted as a catalyst, snatching Mike from the present and plunking him back in his childhood. In his mind, he was watching milk fill a different glass, his own glass.

Mike looked up from the glass, and he saw his mom set down the milk carton and sit across from him. She smiled at him and lifted both arms to join hands with Garret and Mike's dad. At the same time, Garret and Mike's dad took Mike's hands. Joined, the family bowed their heads.

Mike blinked, and he was back in the present. Mike reached for Abby's hand, and she took it. Sharing a brief smile, they bowed their heads and closed their eyes. Abby spoke. "Thanks for this food . . . and everything else. Amen."

Short and sweet, Mike thought. He squeezed Abby's hand, but he didn't let go of it.

Fancifully, Mike wondered briefly what the tip-top of the setting sun—almost gone now—was seeing as it peeked in through their window. He imagined the scene from the sun's perspective.

Brother and sister. Holding hands. Heads bowed. Holding the moment . . . because it was a perfect one.

For this moment, Mike and Abby were happy.

ABOUT THE AUTHORS

SCOTT CAWTHON is the author of the bestselling video game series *Five Nights at Freddy's,* and while he is a game designer by trade, he is first and foremost a storyteller at heart. He is a graduate of the Art Institute of Houston and lives in Texas with his family.

SETH CUDDEBACK was born in Western Massachusetts. He currently resides in Los Angeles, where he works as a screenwriter. *Five Nights at Freddy's* is his first feature film.

EMMA TAMMI most recently directed *The Left Right Game* (a ten-part scripted podcast), starring Tessa Thompson, which was acquired by Amazon Studios for series adaptation, and is attached to executive produce and direct the pilot of *Devil in Ohio* for Netflix. Previously, she directed *The Wind,* which premiered at the Toronto International Film Festival, and was distributed by IFC Midnight in 2019. The film is currently certified fresh on Rotten Tomatoes and Emma was recently named one of 25 Female Filmmakers to Watch by IndieWire.

ANDREA RAINS WAGGENER is an author, novelist, ghostwriter, essayist, short story writer, screenwriter, copywriter, editor, poet, and a proud member of Kevin Anderson & Associates' team of writers. In a past she prefers not to remember much, she was a claims adjuster, JCPenney's catalog order-taker (before computers!), appellate court clerk, legal writing instructor, and lawyer. Writing in genres that vary from her chick-lit novel, *Alternate Beauty*, to her dog how-to book, *Dog Parenting*, to her self-help book, *Healthy, Wealthy, & Wise*, to ghostwritten memoirs, ghostwritten YA, horror, mystery, and mainstream fiction projects, Andrea still manages to find time to watch the rain and obsess over her dog and her knitting, art, and music projects. She lives with her husband and said dog on the Washington Coast, and if she isn't at home creating something, she can be found walking on the beach.

EPILOGUE

The blond boy moved through Freddy's like he was giving a tour . . . to nobody.

Caught in shadow-upon-shadow, the rooms hunkered within the protective walls of the old restaurant. The empty lobby, posters still bare of glass. The long hallway, with more glassless posters. The security office, its monitors lit up but no one watching them. The kitchen, all shiny and still. The Parts and Service room, a mess of robot parts . . . and empty metal chairs. And, of course, the dining room, where the animatronics stood rigid on the barely lit stage.

Everything was totally quiet.

The blond boy went on down the back hallway. All the doors along the hall were closed, except for one, at the very end.

The blond boy went through the door into a small—hardly more than closet-sized—room. He looked at where light from the hallway landed on the room's bare, dusty checkerboard floor . . . and beyond that to the yellow rabbit slumped in a corner. The rabbit was reclined against the mildewed cement block wall.

Not a rabbit. A man. A man in a horrible costume. A twitching man, slouched in a massive spread of blood. It was rust-colored, dried blood that was stuck to the floor. Maybe forever.

The boy watched the man from the doorway, taking satisfaction in the man's suffering. The boy wanted that suffering to go on as long as the stain on the floor. Maybe longer.

The boy backed out of the room. He closed the door, sealing the yellow rabbit into a black, black prison.

There's more *Five Nights at Freddy's* to explore . . .

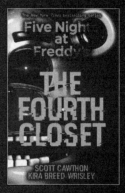

Five Nights at Freddy's

TALES FROM THE PIZZAPLEX

#5 THE BOBBIEDOTS
CONCLUSION

SCOTT CAWTHON   ANDREA WAGGENER

Five Nights at Freddy's

TALES FROM THE PIZZAPLEX

#6 NEXIE

SCOTT CAWTHON   KELLY PARRA
ANDREA WAGGENER

Five Nights at Freddy's

TALES FROM THE PIZZAPLEX

#7 TIGER ROCK

SCOTT CAWTHON   KELLY PARRA
ANDREA WAGGENER

Five Nights at Freddy's

TALES FROM THE PIZZAPLEX

#8 B7-2

SCOTT CAWTHON   ANDREA WAGGENER
KELLY PARRA

Five Nights at Freddy's

THE
SILVER
EYES

The Graphic Novel

SCOTT CAWTHON

Five Nights at Freddy's

The
Graphic
Novel

THE
TWISTED
ONES

SCOTT CAWTHON

Five Nights at Freddy's

The
Graphic
Novel

THE
FOURTH
CLOSET

SCOTT CAWTHON

Five Nights at Freddy's

FAZBEAR FRIGHTS
GRAPHIC NOVEL COLLECTION VOL. 1

SCOTT CAWTHON

Five Nights at Freddy's

FAZBEAR FRIGHTS
GRAPHIC NOVEL COLLECTION VOL. 2

SCOTT CAWTHON

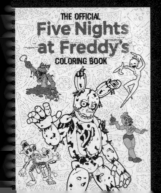
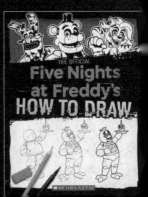